Southern

as a

Second Language

Lisa Patton

Thomas Dunne Books

St. Martin's Griffin / New York

*For Stuart,
in whom
I've found
my home*

This is a work of fiction. All of the characters, organizations, and events portrayed in this novel are either products of the author's imagination or are used fictitiously.

THOMAS DUNNE BOOKS.
An imprint of St. Martin's Press.

SOUTHERN AS A SECOND LANGUAGE. Copyright © 2013 by Lisa Patton. All rights reserved. Printed in the United States of America. For information, address St. Martin's Press, 175 Fifth Avenue, New York, N.Y. 10010.

www.thomasdunnebooks.com
www.stmartins.com

The Library of Congress has cataloged the hardcover edition as follows:

Patton, Lisa.
    Southern as a second language : A Novel / Lisa Patton. — First Edition.
        p. cm.
    ISBN 978-1-250-02065-9 (hardcover)
    ISBN 978-1-250-02273-8 (e-book)
    1. Women—Southern States—Fiction.   2. Female friendship—Fiction.
3. Restaurateurs—Fiction.   4. City and town life—Tennessee—Fiction.
5. Memphis (Tenn.)—Fiction.   6. Domestic fiction.   I. Title.
    PS3616.A927S68 2013
    813'.6—dc23

                                                                    2013023381

ISBN 978-1-250-02067-3 (trade paperback)

St. Martin's Griffin books may be purchased for educational, business, or promotional use. For information on bulk purchases, please contact Macmillan Corporate and Premium Sales Department at 1-800-221-7945, extension 5442, or write specialmarkets@macmillan.com.

First St. Martin's Griffin Edition: September 2014

10 9 8 7 6 5 4 3 2 1

Chapter One

Sometimes a little white lie is just the kindest thing. I mean, what in the world was I supposed to tell Riley, my agitating next-door neighbor, when he rang my doorbell one October morning and asked if he could work at my brand-new restaurant as Peter's sous chef? My mind raced in a thousand directions and my initial thought was to say, "That is so nice, Riley. I tell you what, though, I'll need to talk to Peter about this and get back with you." At the very least, it would have taken the onus off me. But just as I was about to open my mouth, my peripheral vision caught a glimpse of Kissie standing in the doorway leading from the dining room to the kitchen with hands firmly planted on her hips, mouth drawn tightly, and her head shaking from side to side. That was her not-so-subtle way of telling me that what I was about to do was a big fat no-no. She knew me all too well.

I knew she was right, but it's hard for me to be brutally honest with people, especially guys like Riley. I feel sorry for him, bless his heart. He's . . . well, he's pitiful really, and he can't help it. He speaks with a soft r, so when you first meet him you think his name is Wiley. Wiley Bwadshaw. Kissie, on the other hand, doesn't feel in the least bit sorry for him. She says he's just plain annoying and that his speech impediment has nothing to do with it. She says there's no reason to feel bad for him. "He gotta plenty money, a full head a hair, nice stature, and two strong legs to find honest work. There ain't no reason in the world to feel sorry for that man."

As he stood on my front stoop wearing a white apron and a chef's hat with RILEY embroidered in black, he tried selling himself. "Working as a Pampa'ed Chef Consultant qualifies me as a pewfect candidate for the sous chef position."

"I thought you gave up Pampered Chef for Amway," I told him, still not having invited him in. Kissie would rather spend an entire afternoon behind a shopping cart with a bad wheel than five minutes face-to-face with Riley.

"Actually, I did, but I've weconsidered my decision and I'm back in business. Anyway, these days," he went on, "PCCs have to do cooking shows as part of the job." Riley adjusted the tie around his waist and it was then that I noticed the lettering on the front of his apron: THE PAMPERED CHEF® DISCOVER THE CHEF IN YOU. "I've alweady hosted close to seven cooking demonstwations featuring the Pampa'ed Chef's best thirty-minute wecipes."

I stood silently in my doorway trying my best to be polite, bobbing my head with a kind note of approval. Quite honestly, at this point, my neck was beginning to hurt.

He went on. "That alone is another benefit, as I could make a huge diffewence in the efficiency of your westauwant opewation." An ear-to-ear smile spread across his face as he popped his index finger in my direction. "And here's the best part, you could stock your kitchen exclusively with all Pampa'ed Chef pwoducts, declaring the Peach Blossom Inn the first all-PC westauwant in Tennessee. Hey, you could even put a PC logo on the fwont door, as well as on all your menus, boasting that you are the first!" He further added that that one detail alone was sure to increase our foot traffic by at least 75 percent—given the Pampered Chef reputation and all. "It's a win–win!" Riley exclaimed as he snapped his fingers in the air and poked his head inside the entryway of my rental home, scanning his eyes from side to side. Riley's thirst for information could never be considered his strong suit.

Not only is Riley a Pampered Chef salesman ("consultant" is his word) but he "reps" Tupperware, Cutco, and of course, Amway, too. Kissie says that line of work is meant for women only and that he's flat-out embarrassing himself, but as he puts it, "It's a gweat way to meet the ladies." I can't help but feel sorry for him there, too, because he's in his late thirties, still a bachelor, and sports a military hairdo to boot. His cropped brown hair ripples in the back when he bends his head down, but he keeps a two-inch flattop growth on the top. When you go into his home, he'll show you around the house but you can't sit on the furniture. It's covered in plastic. So are the rugs. In fact, there's a see-through runner that extends all over the house. The one time I had to go over there to borrow an egg and made mention of the vast amount of Tupperware products in his kitchen, he swept his hand over the coated furniture in the den and said, "Well, how do you think I got all this? Nevah, my dear lady, unda'estimate the powa' of plastic."

So instead of putting off the inevitable and saying that I'd ask Peter about the sous chef position and get back with him, I took Kissie's body language into account, mustered all my courage, and said, "That's so nice of you to ask about that, Riley, but Peter already has a sous chef." It was technically a lie, I realize that, but I like to think of it as a harmless little fib meant to spare his feelings.

The news seemed to take him by surprise. "Oh. Well, hmmm. I didn't wealize you had alweady hired someone." The creases in Riley's forehead deepened as he considered his options.

I didn't say a word. "The less said the better," as Mama used to say, a quote she often borrowed from Jane Austen. *Emma,* I think it was.

"Never mind, then," he said, disappointment in his voice. "Well, good luck with your new hire."

"Thanks, Riley. Talk to you soon." I backed behind the door and waved as I slowly pushed it to.

With relief oozing from my pores, I bolted the lock and turned around in a rush, bumping noses with Kissie. "What'd you go and tell him that

for?" she asked in her indignant tone of voice, the one she's become famous for—at least in my mind. Her right hand alternated between pointing her finger in the air and resting on her large hip. "He gone find out the
truth as soon as you put an ad in the newspaper, *hm hm hm, hm hm hm.*
Lawd knows that man reads every word in it. Even the circulars." Kissie
chants little *hm*s when she's disgusted at something or someone. She also
does a variation of it when she's happy. This was not one of those.

I sighed loudly. Shifting my weight from one foot to the other, I
reached around and knotted my long, curly (ofttimes frizzy) red hair
into a bun, something I do whenever I'm nervous. Or whenever Kissie
is about to lecture me. I really and truly thought what I said was just
the kindest thing. "But this way I won't hurt his feelings."

"That may be, but in the long run, your fib gone get you in trouble.
And even if you get out of that tall tale, what you gone say about outfit-
ting your new restaurant with all Pampered Chef products?" Now both
hands were back on her hips. "He ain't gone stop there neither. He'll
want you to use Cutco, Tupperware, and Amway, too. Wait and see if
ol' Kissie ain't right. He's over there thinking he's hit the jackpot. You
better nip this in the bud while you still can." After enduring eight
months of maddening encounters with my meddlesome next-door neighbor, my other mother was flat done.

From the very first day I rented the house, Riley had had "his nose
in our business," as Kissie put it. She'd do almost anything to avoid
him, including drawing the curtains in the middle of the day to give
the impression no one was home. Incidentally, Kissie had been giving
me "the look" with her hands on her hips since the day I learned to
walk. And she was continuing the tradition with my two little girls.
Clearly a person's age had nothing to do with it. I was just short of
thirty-six, but to Kissie, age was irrelevant.

Twenty minutes later when two consecutive doorbell chimes interrupted our morning a second time, Roberta, my little two-year-old mutt
my girls and I found at the pound, hurled himself into a barking frenzy.
After sticking him in the kitchen so he wouldn't run off down the street
once I opened the door, two more chimes had followed in the space it

took me to make it to the foyer. This not only got Roberta going again, but Kissie—who was taking what she called "a breather" to watch Saturday-morning cartoons with my Sarah and Isabella—sprang out of her seat (she's nearly eighty-four) and beat me to the entrance hall. She knew exactly who was on the other side. "May I help you, Riley?" I heard her say while flinging the door open. Her voice could possibly pass for polite but there was not a bit of a happy-to-see-you lilt in it at all.

"Good morning, Kissie. May I talk to Leelee again?" Riley, on the other hand, was exuberant.

"All right. Leelee," she hollered behind her, with *no* enthusiasm, "Riley's back."

I strolled up and shyly peered over her shoulder. Panic about my fib had started to take root.

This time Riley wore one of his black sweatshirts with TUPPERWARE ROCKS embroidered in large red letters clear across the front. Until meeting Riley, I had no earthly idea that Tupperware clothing even existed. "Hi again." He waved at the two of us. "I just had a bwilliant idea." Riley's enthusiasm was made obvious by the way he rocked back and forth on his heels. "I was just looking awound my kitchen when the thought popped in my head that the Peach Blossom Inn will have all kinds of food-stowage needs. I could stock your kitchen with any kind of Tuppa'ware pwoduct you could possibly imagine. And Kissie, you could host the pawty!" He reached into his back pocket and handed her a rolled-up Tupperware catalog. "You won't believe the kinds of wewards you can earn. Why I've nearly outfitted my entire house."

Awkwardness hung heavy in the air. Hosting a Tupperware party would be the last thing eighty-three-and-a-half-year-old Kissie King would ever add to her bucket list. Just as I was pondering another little white lie to relieve us all of this misery, Riley piped up again. "And wait till you learn about the sharp world of Cutc—" The daggers in Kissie's eyes could have cut that poor thing's face in half. As for me, I just stood there expressionless, not knowing what to say. Riley backed down the steps and onto the walkway. "Uh, why don't you take your time and think about it; I'll get back with you later."

Kissie put her hand on the back of the door and shoved. "Sure, Riley," I said before it swung shut.

Even though I didn't want to, I met Kissie's glare straight on. I'd seen it a thousand times. Tight, pursed lips with eyebrows arched like upside-down crescent moons and coal black eyes staring right into mine. "Don't say a word," I told her. "I knew you were right the minute I heard the second doorbell chime." As she turned and ambled back to the den to join the girls, a peeved "hm hm hm" was the only sound she made.

Kissie is one of the loveliest people who ever lived. It's just that Riley crawls all over her. She puts it like this: "Sometimes that man sits on my last raw nerve." As irritated as he makes her, though, she doesn't stay that way long. In fact, she spends much more of her time laughing than glaring. If she finds something funny—anything at all—she'll tee-hee herself into a full-blown laughing attack quicker than anyone I know. Tears will stream from her eyes and pretty soon her entire face looks like she just stepped out of the shower. The sound of her laughter is the most contagious thing you've ever heard and it's virtually impossible not to join right in with her. When she's finished—with the laughing attack, that is—she'll end by saying, "oh me," or, "oooh-wee," however the mood strikes her.

Without question, she's the most wonderful person I've ever known, and that's been since the day I was born. My grandparents shared her with Mama and Daddy the minute I popped into the world. She was considered one of the best cateresses in Memphis when Granddaddy stumbled upon her at a cocktail party. He popped one of Kissie's cheese dreams in his mouth and knew he had to hire her. She cooked for them for ten years before I was born and all of a sudden she was both a chef and a nanny. Times were different then. Many families had a black lady working in the home. Some had a cook, a maid, and an ironing lady. Not many, but a few. Mama and Daddy had a maid who doubled as an ironing lady and a superb cook. And I had a black mama.

Sometimes I'm surprised she stayed with us. Mama had a tendency to be jealous of my affection for Kissie. As far as I'm concerned, the reason for that is as simple as two plus two. Kissie was the one taking care of me. Running my bath, cleaning my behind, and making sure my tummy was full; kissing my elbows and knees when I fell off my bike and bundling me up in the winter. Kissie worked in our home *at least* five days a week. Children bond to their caregivers whether they are blood or not, and that's exactly what happened with me. I fell in love with Kissie King like she was my own mother.

There was never a birthday party where Kissie didn't do most of the work or a dance recital when Kissie didn't help me get ready. Of course, Mama helped. I would be remiss if I didn't give her part of the credit. I know she tried. But something else in her life seemed to always claim the front seat.

My white eyelet dress with Juliet sleeves and an empire waist came from Goldsmith's, Memphis's hometown department store. The cutest thing I'd ever seen and just perfect for my first Junior Cotillion dance. Mama took me shopping and I couldn't wait to get back home to try it on for Kissie. Since I attended an all-girls school and Junior Cotillion was an all-girls organization, I had to invite my own date. All year my eyes had been set on Danny Weaver, a boy from the boys' school down the street. Sandy blond hair, a spray of freckles across his nose, big blue eyes—I had set my sights high. From the moment I spotted him at my first boy–girl party one year earlier, I pictured us a couple.

Calling him on the phone, God as my witness, took five years off my life. It was a Friday afternoon; I'll never forget it. I'd never called a boy before and as an eighth-grader with no brothers, I was scared to death to dial the number. His mother answered the phone and with Mary Jule, one of my three best friends, sitting right next to me, I said, "May I please speak to Danny?" That was just before the days of caller ID and I could have hung up right then and there if I wanted to but Mary Jule held my hand and urged me to "just get it over with." Once he said hello, Danny sat there on the other end of the line, barely saying anything until I finally blurted out the question. After an excruciating pause, he finally said yes but hurried off the phone. It's a wonder I survived.

The night of the formal, Kissie helped to straighten my hair and made sure my dress was pressed. Of course, Mama took all the pictures once Danny picked me up at the door, and that was an even more uncomfortable moment, since it was seven o'clock by the time he got there and, well, that's two hours past five. Without fail, no matter what day of the week it was, cocktail hour in our house commenced with the five o'clock whistle.

The evening could scarcely be described as romantic. Once we got to the dance, the girls clustered around the tables while the boys huddled around one another at the far end of the room, no doubt talking about basketball, football, or who knows what else. It could have been my curly-turned-straight red hair, for all I knew; it was and still is the bane of my existence. The parental chaperones urged us to dance but Danny and the rest of the boys just sat there like toads, never uttering a word. Four hours later Danny and I slithered into the backseat of his father's Lincoln Continental for the long ride home. Thank God for Mr. Weaver. At least he made conversation.

Mama was three sheets to the wind and slurring her words the minute we stepped inside the front door. To say I was embarrassed would be a lie. I was mortified. Daddy stepped in to say good-bye to Danny after Mama attempted an inebriated farewell, nearly tripping over her feet when she went to hug him. Danny looked at me, then the floor, back at me, over to Mama, and finally shook Daddy's hand before hurrying out to his father. I hid behind the front window and watched him bound into the front seat. The thought of their conversation sickened me as I ran up to my room. Hours passed before Kissie came into work the next morning and I could fall into her arms. She'd rock me back and forth while I cried but she never said a single unkind word about Mama—no matter what Mama did. All Kissie would say was: "She's your mama, baby. You need to love and respect her no matter what."

Scotch was Mama's cocktail. I can still picture the green bottle with the red top—Glenlivet 12 with the ivory-colored label. A bottle always sat atop our bar, right next to the small sink. Most of the other liquor bottles—Jack Daniel's, Tanqueray, Absolut, Bacardi, and several different liqueurs—were stacked on the shelves above the bar glasses, but the fifth of Glenlivet was always within reach, easy for Mama to grab. The sound of the silver tongs tinkering in the ice bucket (that Kissie had filled, incidentally) and the clinking of the ice cubes echoes in my mind even today. One, two, three, four, Mama dropped each one into her Waterford crystal highball glass as soon as the clock struck five. Mama would be finishing her second by the time Daddy got home, around six o'clock. She'd leave her chair in the living room and mix him a stiff one as soon as she heard his car engine enter the driveway. But only one. That's all Daddy ever wanted.

He never took the first sip until he kissed me hello. When I was little he'd make it a point to find me, throw me in the air, blowing funny raspberry kisses into my face and down my neck. By the time I turned into a teenager I was usually on the phone when he got home. Still he'd knock on my bedroom door and kiss me before Kissie served our dinner. I always knew my daddy loved me. Maybe it was because of the way he covered me when Mama had had two too many or the tears I saw in his eyes the day I graduated from college or the ones he wept on my wedding day. I suppose that's why I became a daddy's girl. Who could blame me?

It wouldn't have been a surprise to me if Mama died of liver damage had she lived to a ripe old age but instead Mama died of breast cancer when she was only forty-two. And I was only eighteen. It was a terrible time for a girl to lose her mother, only six weeks before leaving for Ole Miss. We were in that awkward phase; the one where mothers and daughters have a hard time getting along. No doubt the hangover from her alcoholism had already nauseated the essence of my soul, but even so I was devastated—heartsick when she died. Seventeen years later I'm finally dealing with it all. Thanks to Alice, another of my BFFs, I started seeing a therapist a few months ago.

Maybe Mama's beauty was her downfall. It was certainly her identity; that I know for sure. She was called beautiful from the day she was born and it became the main component of her self-worth. After graduating from Ole Miss she went back home to Greenville in the Mississippi Delta and spent the next year planning her wedding. She was born to be a wife and mother, all the while looking like a Miss Mississippi on the arm of my father, a dashing Southern gentleman from Memphis, Tennessee, named Henry Beckworth Williams, Jr.

Mama never worked. Not a single day. But she made up for it by volunteering at Le Bonheur Children's Hospital, our church, and the Junior League. She was a Master Gardener, and her roses were, as Celia, one of her best friends, often said, "The most gorgeous specimens in Memphis." Her Lucky Ladies and Velvets were often featured in her friends' floral arrangements and at her garden club meetings, as their fragrance could sweeten any size room.

I was her only child. When I asked her why, she said, in her heavy, r-rolling, Mississippi drawl, "I didn't want my fig'a marred any more than it already was. One day, when you're lookin' at your post-pregnancy body in the mirr'a, Leelee dear, you'll unda'stand what I mean." Despite all that, there is one thing I know for sure about Mama: I was her heart. She used to tell me so over and over again.

Once Mama died, Kissie became even more important. Someone had to step in. Daddy's mother had already passed away, and Mama's mother, my namesake, lived down in Mississippi, more than likely an alcoholic herself. Nobody ever admitted to being an alcoholic in those days. A "social drinker" was the term Mama used to describe herself, a phrase my grandmother used as well. "I only drink durin' cocktail hour," Mama liked to say, with a defensive tone. "I would nev'a take a drink durin' the day." I guess she had forgotten about her Budweisers on Saturdays during Ole Miss games or her "Bloodies" with Sunday brunch.

Thank goodness Daddy had the foresight to keep Kissie around. Looking back on it now, I can't imagine how my life would have turned out without her. If it weren't for her, I wouldn't have a clue how to cook, how to clean, or how to properly fold our laundry. But as wonderful and helpful as she is, that lady can put me in my place in half a second. I can always tell when I'm in trouble by that glare of hers.

The Memphis heat during August was hotter than "blowed coal," according to Daddy. As Alice and I readied ourselves for Jay Stockley's summer boy–girl party, Alice sat tailor-fashion on the floor in front of the full-length mirror in my bathroom and I sat on top of the counter with my feet in the sink. We painted enough baby blue eye shadow on our eyes to look more like cartoon characters than like fifteen-year-olds and wore enough Heaven Scent to warrant an arrest from the perfume patrol. When we were ready to leave for the party, we pranced out of my bedroom wearing short shorts and halter tops and headed down the long hall toward Kissie, who was waiting on us at the other end. She had the car keys in her hand—Mama and Daddy were out of town—and her eyes narrowed as we got closer. Her lips were pressed together, the glare on her face spreading from one side to the other. At first she didn't say anything but her head turned with each step we made around the den. Finally she said, "Where's your brassiere, Leelee?"

"Halters don't need bras," I told her.

"Hm," was her only response. But when my back was toward her, she yanked the sash of my paisley halter top, springing it loose with ease. "Kissie," I said, clutching my arms over my chest. (Incidentally, at that point, my tender breasts were A's. It would be the end of my junior year before my D's finally sprang to life.)

"Don't Kissie me," she retorted. "What you gone do when some junk-yard dog gets you in a lip lock and starts runnin' his hands all over your back? You think he ain't gone do what I just did? You need to get back in your room and change outta that thing you're callin' a shirt, young lady. Put on a blouse. Somethin' decent." Kissie pointed her finger down the hall. "You, too, Alice. What would your mama say? Y'all's shorts are bad enough. Might as well be wearin' underpants. You girls ain't gone go out under my watch looking like streetwalkers. Get on back there, you hear? Hm hm hm, hm hm hm, hm hm hm. I declare, you girls gone put me in Bolivar."

———

Bolivar is a place people from Memphis talk about ending up when they finally have a nervous breakdown. I've never seen it before but I've heard about it my whole life. It's actually the Western State Mental Health Institute in the town of Bolivar, Tennessee. People have just shortened it to "Bolivar." Mama talked about it and so did Daddy. In fact, everyone's parents did. When I was little I remember Mama calling mental hospitals insane asylums, and the very image of that scared the daylights out of me. I hear the town is as charming as any small Southern town could ever be, but I can't help but feel a little sorry for the citizens. I bet they are sick to death of people asking them all about the mental hospital when asked the simple question: Where are you from?

Daddy passed away of complications from diabetes ten years after Mama died. That was unquestionably *the* worst time of my life. I think something else dies when a girl loses her father, something inside the deepest caverns of her heart. It's her sense of security, that wellspring of protection and safety that only a daddy can provide. He's the one person she can count on to be there for her no matter what.

Chapter Two

I always assumed my husband would be there for me no matter what. Probably because of Daddy's unwavering commitment to Mama, despite her alcoholism, and the bottomless pit of affection and unconditional love he showed the two of us. It never once crossed my mind that Baker Satterfield and I wouldn't grow old together. I even pictured us side by side in hospital beds at the nursing home. Sadly, though, that was not to be the case.

Baker's dream, he revealed to me out of the blue exactly two years and three months ago this month, was to buy a quaint, rural Vermont inn and restaurant, of all things, raise our girls in a part of the world where door locks aren't needed, and live out the rest of our days watching the summer turn into a kaleidoscope of fall colors. He pictured us dashing through the snow in a one-horse open sleigh, spotting moose in our backyard, and the girls and I snow skiing to our hearts' content while he alternated his days off between snow skiing and fly-fishing the Battenkill, the official home of Orvis.

Nobody twisted my arm; I agreed to the move. After all, Baker Satterfield was my heart and had been since I first laid eyes on him in the ninth grade. I'd have done anything to make that man happy. Plus I loved an adventure every bit as much as he did. Moose had held a fascination for me my whole life, and the thought of spotting a real one in the wild was as thrilling to me as eyewitnessing an erupting volcano.

It took only a few months of Vermont life, though, to learn that my beloved moose are rarely—if ever—seen, and the snow Baker wanted to dash in is so deep, it piles up to the rooftops. Some days the temperature never climbs past twenty below zero, a fact I thought true only of Alaska, not the continental United States. And that summer he was talking about? It lasts a mere six weeks. I also learned that a no-see-um bug called a blackfly, indigenous to New England, is worse than a horsefly, with a bite that not only hurts like the devil but draws blood as well, and the only perennial that pops up in the spring, if you can even call it that, is mud. On top of all that, my helpless little senior Yorkie, Princess Grace Kelly, was forced to do her business *in*side instead of *out*side nine months out of the year. Who in the world could blame her?

But after following my husband all the way up there, I followed my heart back to Memphis only fourteen months later. My daughters and I crossed safely back onto Southern soil, but we left Baker behind. After living there five short months, my high school sweetheart left me for a rich, blond ski-resort owner sixteen years his senior. Seems he couldn't get enough of her newly lifted forehead, never mind her ultra perky, newly lifted breasts. She even had fake lips, I later learned from Roberta, my Vermont housekeeper, who heard it from Betty Sweeney in the Town Clerk's office, who heard it from George Clark, the gossipy gas station owner in Fairhope, one town over from where we lived in Willingham. He knew everyone's business and made it his business to spread it like quenchless fire. Between George Clark and the police scanner (home version), people in Willingham, Vermont, knew everything there was to know about everybody. Roberta and her husband, Moe, slept with a police scanner on in their bedroom every night of their married life. Roberta became both my source of gossip and a cherished friend—so much so that we named our *male* dog in honor of that bottled-redhead, a true Vermont firecracker.

No one could ever accuse me of not trying to make a go of the place. Even though I was heartbroken and tyrannized, I pulled up my snow bootstraps and ran that place all by myself. We bought the inn with my inheritance and to quote Kissie, I could not "run home and leave everything your daddy worked so hard to git." So I changed the name from the Vermont Haus Inn to the Peach Blossom Inn, hired a brand-new chef, and transformed it into a four-star cozy Southern getaway in the mountains of rural Vermont.

My decision to move back home was also forced by the former inn owner—and perpetual tyrant—Helga Schloygin, a German beast of a woman who not only introduced Baker to the nip-and-tuck cougar, but also stole back the Peach Blossom Inn from me after my departure. She tricked me into believing someone else was buying it, and by the time I signed the official closing documents, I had already made it safely back home to Southern soil.

Of course, I can't minimize the role the Vermont weather played in my decision to come home. Not only did I freeze *my* fanny off, but so did Gracie, all eight pounds of her. I have no doubt that her death was due to one too many subzero New England days. She's still buried way up there behind the inn, but the cross to her grave marker is now a memorial in a sacred spot in my Tennessee backyard.

Instead of moving into Memphis proper upon our return from Vermont, the girls and I found a rental home in Germantown, a suburb fifteen minutes from town and only six minutes from the new Peach Blossom Inn. The school system was superb, too, a necessity of utmost importance, and although I'd lived in the heart of Memphis my whole life, I was beginning to love the charm of Germantown. The most compelling part of its history—to me, anyway—is that way before the Emancipation Proclamation, a Scottish white spinster named Miss Frances Wright established a two-thousand-acre plantation called Nashoba as a utopian community intended to educate and emancipate slaves. It failed before Fannie, who had returned to Europe to recover from malaria, could make it back to Tennessee. But once she did, Fannie chartered a ship and delivered the remaining slaves of Nashoba to Haiti, where she emancipated them personally. Today that utopian community is part of Shelby Farms, a large urban park in Germantown. Germantown is my utopia, too, after finally escaping the wrath of Helga Schloygin, the ego of Baker Satterfield, and a Vermont winter lasting eight months, minimum.

Owning and operating another restaurant, after the Vermont fiasco, was the last thing I ever thought I'd want to do. But after working for a self-centered, vainglorious program director at a top Memphis radio station for the last six months, and realizing I truly was happy while running my own business, I took a grand leap of faith, believed in myself wholeheartedly, and dived off the high board back in again. I exhausted nearly every penny of my savings but I believed in myself in a way I never had before. The Peach Blossom Inn may have gotten its start in Vermont but it's as Southern as any fine eatery can be. At least it will be, three weeks from today when two hundred Memphians attend our grand opening party.

Virginia, another of my three best friends and my college roommate at Ole Miss, called not more than ten minutes after Riley left my front stoop. I was preparing to meet Peter, my drop-dead-darling head chef, so we could finalize our menu and send it on to the printer. "Hello," I said in a high-pitched, jovial tone, cradling the phone against my ear while I held a compact mirror in one hand, a mascara wand in the other, and dashed around my house to avoid another tardy arrival at the restaurant. Apparently my sunny disposition was too loud for the likes of my daughters, who were sitting on either side of Kissie with Roberta squeezed in between.

"Shhh, Mommy," Sarah said, staring straight at the TV. "We can't hear."

I knew I took a backseat to SpongeBob, but I would not tolerate rudeness from my seven-year-old. I placed my hand over the receiver. "Can you say that nicely, please, young lady?"

She turned her head in my direction and with genuine remorse said, "Please, Mommy, will you speak softly so we can hear."

"Much better," I said proudly, and moved into the kitchen, walking away from the TV.

"Have you made the guest list for the party yet?" Virginia wanted to know.

"I've jotted down most of the names, but I'm still thinking about it. Why?" By now I had taken a seat at the breakfast room table to finish applying my mascara.

"Beside the fact that you need to put those invitations in the mail *today*, I ran into Tootie Shotwell. Alice and I saw her when we were walking at the mall this morning. She was asking all about you and the Peach Blossom Inn and especially about your new chef from Vermont. She was fishing for an invitation," Virginia said, making "fishing" seem like *anything but* a gentle water sport.

"She can fish all she wants, but she will never land one. I don't want to invite her. You know that."

"I know you don't, but I'm thinking you should. You need to show off your gorgeous new restaurant, not to mention your gorgeous new chef."

You've got that right, I thought. *He's so gorgeous, I can hardly keep my paws off him.* "To the Big Brag? You know I don't care for her or her entourage. They always make me feel . . . oh, I don't know, *bad* about myself. If she's not belittling someone, then she's bragging about herself—it's just nauseating, Virginia. I'm trying to get people to like my restaurant, not get sick from it."

Virginia sighed. "Just trying to help you spread the word."

"She'll spread the word, all right. By gossiping about me, Peter, *you*. There's no telling what bad things she'll spread around." Agitated, I drummed my fingers on the table. I did not want to have to invite any gossipy women to my party. "Aren't we old enough to stop being friends with people we don't want to be friends with?" Catching sight of my watch, I jumped up from the table.

"I suppose, but I'm telling you it will be *worse* to leave her off the guest list."

"So in that case, I suppose I'll need to invite Sandy Greene, too?" I said, grabbing the mirror and mascara off the table. Sandy Greene was another local gossip. More important, Sandy's mother, Shirley, was Mama's nemesis, and even though Mama is long gone, that rivalry still exists to this day. Shirley's still around to maintain the feud, and shows no signs of leaving us anytime soon.

"Heck no. Why would you do that?"

"*Virginia,* it's the same thing. Sandy Greene is no different than Tootie Shotwell. They're both gossips and they both, for some reason, can't stand me." Eyeing a half dozen bacon strips atop a grease-stained paper towel next to the stove, I popped one in my mouth and hurried back to my bedroom.

"They are both jealous of you."

"Why? Look how much they have," I said, garbling my words. "Nice husbands, big houses, clothes out the wazoo."

"They've been jealous the moment you were voted president of Cotillion and became a cheerleader."

"Oh, for gosh sakes. That was in *high school.*" Eyeing my purse on the floor added to my frustration. I could hardly zip the top for all the junk inside.

"High school resentments can last a lifetime. Especially for people who live in the past." I could picture her in her favorite chair, twirling a piece of her hair into a knot with one hand.

"Like my charming ex-husband?" Baker was a University of Tennessee football semi-star, a second-string quarterback, and had been catching that pass since the day he made his first of three SEC touchdowns.

"*Exactly.*"

I threw the overstuffed purse over my shoulder and glanced inside my closet, just to make sure there wasn't something else I'd rather be wearing. Spying my brown boots, I kicked off the black mules I had on and plopped down to the floor. "I'll have to think about Tootie Shotwell but I'm not inviting Sandy Greene. Out of respect for Mama, for goodness' sakes."

"Okay, fine, but I'm telling you leaving off Tootie Shotwell will make it much worse. You're back in Memphis, and let's face it, we all run in the same circles."

I sighed loudly, yanking on the first boot. "I wish I had time to run this past Frances Folk. She'd tell me it's okay not to invite her. I just know it."

"Fiery," she said, using the nickname she gave me in seventh grade. "I'm usually in agreement with your therapist, but I'm standing my ground on this one."

"Okay, okay. I'll invite her," I said, pulling on my next boot and pausing for a brief check in the full-length mirror on the closet door. "But I have to run. I have an important meeting with Peter this morning at the restaurant, and I was supposed to be there an hour ago. I'm sure he's wondering where in the world I am."

"What's going on?"

"We're finalizing the menu. He's been working on it for the last two weeks. I can't wait to hear what he's come up with."

"Well, tell him hey. I'll stop by and see y'all in the next couple of days."

"Sounds great. Talk to you soon," I said, and hung up the phone.

I rushed back out to the den, circling around to Kissie and then to both my little girls, kissing each on the cheek. "Mind Kissie," I said. "And make your beds, please. I'll be home in a few hours."

"Yes, ma'am," Issie said, smiling as she crossed one of her little legs across the other, revealing the chipped pink polish on her tiny toes. My five-year-old is quite a girly-girl and has been asking for nail polish since she was first able to talk.

"Tell Peter I say *hello*," Kissie said, looking like a much younger woman. You would be hard-pressed to find a single wrinkle on her face. Looking back, I can scarcely remember a day when she's been sick, aside from the bursitis in her left knee and occasional bouts with her "sugar." Her doctor will give her a cortisone shot in that knee from time to time, and usually she'll lay off the sweets like a good girl, but I seriously can't remember her even catching the flu. Ironically, her only baby, a girl named Josephine, or Josie for short, died of pneumonia when she was only three years old. Kissie hardly talks about it, but there's a big picture of Josie hanging above the couch in her living room.

As I was leaving, Roberta leaped off the couch. I've made the mistake of taking him along from time to time; so when he knows I'm leaving, he jumps to my side. When I reached the door, he slid to a stop as I extended my foot in his direction. With a pitiful face, as far as doggy faces go, he cocked his head to the side and stood completely silent, as if saying: Surely you're not leaving me again. "No, Roberta," I said. "I'll take you next time, I promise." The vet told me that his grandfather was probably a full-bred Jack Russell terrier but he's mostly bichon—strong, fluffy, and adorable. If it weren't for him, my bed would be cold and empty, though I'm hoping one day soon that will change.

Chapter Three

My *Miracle on 34th Street* moment happened by accident. I was driving home from Virginia's last summer when I was forced to take a detour by a late-nineteenth-century Queen Anne Victorian. I caught a glimpse of the FOR SALE sign in the yard and screeched a U-ey not five feet past the house. The blue paint was cracked and peeling, hardly something to be proud of. Most people wouldn't have given the place a second glance. But something about it intrigued me. A large pecan tree with protruding roots shaded the thick carpet of zoysia, the only shade grass with a prayer in the South, and the thought of homemade pecan pies was all it took for me to turn on my blinker. After pulling up through the gravel driveway and ramming the gearshift into park, I ran up the boxwood-lined walkway and onto the wraparound front porch, peering in the front windows. The original front door still had its charming old turn-style bell. No one was living there, and after finding the back door unlocked I crept inside. The kitchen was frumpy, terribly outdated, but I am a visionary. Undaunted and curious, I pushed through the swinging door that led into the dining room and wandered through to the foyer, with its intricately carved grand staircase. Looking around at the twelve-foot ceilings and large rooms with fireplaces off to each side set my mind ablaze with possibilities.

As I was leaving on that hot July day, just three short months ago, I turned back around for one final look. Instead of cracked blue paint I saw a gleaming shade of peach with ivory trim and diners seated at candlelit tables on the wraparound porch. I knew then and there that it was my destiny. The warm glow of the old house reminded me that I still had what it took to succeed as a boutique restaurateur.

As one who loves a challenge, especially when adventure is attached, I transformed that old house into an elegant Painted Lady with a peaches-and-cream complexion. A yummy shade of peach now colors the clapboard siding. Ivory cream trims the gables and porch railings, with accents of coral on the gingerbread eaves and architectural details. The best part about it is that my radiant Peach Blossom Inn sign, the one that Helga Schloygin threw away in a trash pile, and I rescued at the last second as I was leaving Vermont, is now hanging from an ivory-colored wooden pole. Two peaches are in place of the *o*'s in the word "Blossom," and it dazzles from its spot near the road.

The biggest roadblock in my grand plan was finding care for my girls, since I'd be working nights. So at eighty-three years young, Kissie locked up her house and moved into mine. Every week I try to pay her but she won't take the money. "We're family, Leelee. I ain't gone take your money." She leaves me no choice but to sneak and fill up her car when she's not looking or pay her insurance or her property taxes. Daddy paid off her house when my grandmother died. It was in her will.

Another hurdle was finding the perfect chef. Lord have mercy, that's a long story, but Peter moved down from Vermont to fill the position. I had fallen in love with him when he stepped in as chef of the Vermont Peach Blossom Inn after Baker left us. I just didn't admit it to myself until the very day I was leaving and spent the next nine months pining for him. I had about given him up, too, thanks to much-needed therapy from Frances Folk, when he showed up in Memphis out of the blue and shocked the daylights out of me. My three crazy best friends get the credit for that. They went behind my back and set out on a GKA reconnaissance mission to find his address. Then they sent him the newspaper clipping from *The Commercial Appeal* with my ad for the chef's position circled in black Sharpie. It's a miracle I hadn't already hired someone. By the time he arrived, I had narrowed the list down to two strong candidates.

Incidentally, GKA is our acronym for the Gladys Kravitz Agency, named after the nosy neighbor from *Bewitched,* which was my mother's favorite TV show. She and all of her friends loved it, so I started watching the reruns with her. Pretty soon it became all of my friends' favorite TV show. Gladys became our inspiration, so way back in the seventh grade, we formed the GKA, born out of a need to find out information about Brooks Turley, the cutest boy in the class.

Alice, Virginia, Mary Jule, and I have been BFFs since kindergarten, when we all ended up in the same class at Miss Henderson's School for girls. With the exception of a few personality traits, the four of us are exactly alike, which is probably the reason we're so close. Alice can be a little bossy at times, Mary Jule is the sweet one, and Virginia is the comic. I'm, well, I guess I'm a mixture of the three, but what's most important is how well we get along. We rarely ever bicker, and if we do, it's usually over a bad decision the other is making. Like when I agreed to move to Vermont with Baker. Those three thought I had lost my mind. Obviously they were right. We've gotten in all kinds of trouble together over the years and I guess you could say we still are. Whether it's dumping all Baker's clothing on a ski lift in Vermont, spying on husbands at the golf course, or getting one another out of heaps of trouble, loyalty is our motto.

Thanks to those three, Peter moved permanently to Memphis just three weeks ago to work as the head chef of my new restaurant, and also to work his way back into my heart. After yearning for him so long, the very idea that I could park my car and walk up the back steps, push open the door, and see Peter in person stooped over the massive, eight-burner commercial stove while stirring his veal stock was surreal, not to mention delicious.

The aroma permeated the kitchen, and I smelled it the minute I stepped inside. Music blasted from a docking station that sat next to the coffeepot at the far end of the room, where Peter stood. The red bandanna that he wore around his forehead, sponging his perspiration, was knotted in the back, and his blond hair spilled out around it. If you looked closely, you could see the light brown hair on his forearms glistening from the dampness and his New York Yankees T-shirt clinging to his chest. Whenever he worked in the kitchen back in Vermont, the sides of his black chef pants were smudged with flour like handprints on a chalkboard. Today was no different.

With the volume turned up and his back to the door, Peter didn't hear me walk in. I crept up behind him and covered his eyes with my hands. "Guess who," I said, in the deepest non-Leelee voice I could muster.

A long pause passed before the edges of his mouth curled and he said, "Barry White."

"Nope," I said, low-toned and trying to suppress my giggle. "Guess again."

"Barry White's twin sister."

This time I had to laugh out loud.

Peter turned around and scooped me into his arms. "Good afternoon, boss, it's about time you got here." He glanced at the clock on the wall opposite the stove. "It's almost eleven."

I knew he was kidding but I played along. "You might as well learn this about me right now, Peter Owen. I never make a point to be anywhere before eleven. I don't even get out of bed before ten. Didn't you know that Sarah and Issie get themselves ready for school, cook their own breakfast, and hop on the school bus all by themselves? I've got the smartest, most considerate kids in the world."

His eyes brightened. "Is that so? No wonder you look so fresh-faced and beautiful this morning. You never miss out on a moment's beauty rest."

Beautiful. It felt lovely to hear that word spill out of Peter's mouth.

What woman doesn't want to be called beautiful? Strangely, though, as much as it brought me pleasure, a part of me felt uncomfortable, so I changed the subject. "You're already cooking? We don't open for three weeks."

"Of course I'm cooking. I thought I'd make several quarts of veal stock now and freeze it for later. I'll be glad I did."

I remembered this process from our restaurant in Vermont. I had watched Peter do it a hundred times. The whole process takes three days, a level of complexity that earned Peter his stellar reputation. Veal stock is the base for superior soups and sauces, beginning with ten pounds of veal marrowbones placed in a very large stockpot and filled to the top with cold water. Bring them to a simmer, never a boil. As soon as the simmer begins, rinse the bones under warm water to wash away any scum that may have accumulated. The first extraction, as Peter calls it, comes next, with the washed and blanched bones, twelve more quarts of cold water, two large onions, four leeks, one celery rib, one pound of quartered (but not peeled) carrots, three cloves crushed garlic, four sprigs each of fresh thyme and parsley, two bay leaves, two tablespoons tomato paste, two fresh quartered tomatoes, and ten peppercorns.

Some chefs roast the bones, but Peter always claimed that it's better to simmer them, as a cleaner, more sophisticated flavor would be produced in the stock. After reaching another simmer, once the ingredients have been added, he reduces the heat to medium low and cooks for four hours, skimming the top every twenty minutes or so. He then strains the stock into a large stainless steel bowl nestled in an ice bath in the sink, saves all the solid ingredients, and places the liquid in the fridge overnight.

The next day he cleans the stockpot again and puts all the solid ingredients back in for the "second extraction." He covers them with twelve more quarts of cold water and repeats the same process, allowing the pot to slowly come to a simmer for about an hour, repeating the skimming process for another four hours. After straining the mixture yet again, he nestles it in another ice bath and places it back in the fridge for another overnight.

Finally, when the third morning arrives, he removes any congealed fat from the top of the gelatinous stock. He combines both bowls together in a large stockpot and simmers one last time. He skims the pot often and cooks for *another* seven hours. This he calls "the reduction" because the stock reduces by half. He ends up with only a couple quarts of liquid in total but strains it all through a China hat three times, producing a very smooth stock.

That's his secret to delicious soups, demi-glace, béarnaise, sauce au poivre, even the duckling sauce à l'orange. Some of his recipes do call for chicken stock or others a fumet (fish stock). He prepares all three in similar fashion, with the obvious substitution of bones. Nearly every single day we were open in Vermont, one kind of stock or another simmered on top of that old stove. The aroma permeated the entire kitchen and wafted out into the restaurant. I'm convinced on cold nights it was the smell of Peter's stock that brought folks snooping to our front door. I was hoping for a repeat performance in Memphis.

On top of Peter's work station, I noticed a cutting board covered in flour with a big glob of dough resting on top. I gave it a glance and smiled. "So you're making bread, huh?"

"I'm *attempting* to make bread. Kissie dug into that head of hers the other day and described the process to me as best she could. But my last two attempts have been flops. I might as well have been working with a big pile of glue. Just what I thought. I'm not a baker."

"Let me assure you. You are certainly not a Baker," I said with a grin, adding, "Large pun intended, by the way."

A shy smile was his response, before lifting his arm from around my waist and lightly touching my nose.

"When Kissie offered to make rolls, she meant it," I assured him.

"I guess I'll take her up on it," he said with resolve, wrapping his arm back around me and pulling me in closer. "But I feel a little guilty. She's so busy helping you out with the girls."

"Kissie is not happy unless she's in the kitchen. She was up till midnight last night mopping the floors."

"Why?"

"She says you never know if somebody might show up in the middle of the night. She says you're always supposed to keep your kitchen spic 'n' span in case you have to cook a meal for a midnight traveler."

"I can't believe I've never asked you this before, but where did Kissie get her name? I'm assuming it's a nickname."

"It is," I said, reflecting back to my childhood. "Her real name's Kristine. When I was little I couldn't pronounce my r's, so I started calling her Kissie. Now everybody calls her Kissie. Even her own brother."

Peter's sweet smile intoxicated me from the moment I first met him a year and a half earlier. His arms felt heavenly wrapped around me, and I wanted to stay locked up like that for hours, forgetting work, forgetting everything and everyone else around us. I felt a sudden urgency to be kissed, and I squeezed him for an extra-long moment, hoping he'd take the hint. When I looked up, expecting a kiss, he was staring at me, his ultramarine eyes examining every inch of my face. *"What?"* I said coyly, not able to suppress the demure smile that appeared out of nowhere.

"Can't I look at you? Is that not okay?"

My face flushed at the thought of his so close to mine. Close enough to notice every flaw—every pore, every line, every scar. "I guess. I'm just, I don't know, a little shy I suppose."

"About me looking at you?"

"No. I mean—not really. Well, yes, sort of. Oh," I said, flustered, "let's change the subject. Let's talk about the party. Guess how many people are on my guest list."

"I'll give you my guess after you tell me why you haven't kissed me this morning."

"I was just about to ask *you* the same question." I dramatically closed my eyes and puckered up, waiting for him to dive in. When several moments passed and his lips hadn't even grazed mine, I opened my eyes and found him staring at me again. *"What?"* I shrieked.

He reared his head back with a burst of laughter. "I love to tease you. You are so much fun to mess with." Then he leaned in for a behind-closed-doors-only smooch. My hair, which started out in a ponytail, had become a mess of tangled curls from Peter ruffling his hands through it. At one point, he picked me up and sat me down atop the drying board on the large stainless steel sink. My legs were wrapped around his hips, pulling me closer into the aroma of our kiss, his subtle cologne and the odd but primal smell of veal stock. There's no telling how long we would have stayed like that if a voice wafting from the front of the restaurant hadn't interrupted us.

"Yoo-hoo," a female voice called from the dining room, growing closer.

We jerked away from one another. "Who in the world?" I whispered, gazing at Peter, but he shrugged his shoulders. Sliding off the sink in a hurry, I was attempting to smooth my hair and blouse when *Shirley Greene*, of all people, slithered into my kitchen without even ringing the doorbell, never mind an invitation. Out of all the persons whom I might be eager to see in this world, Shirley Greene would be dead last. I was serious when I said she was Mama's nemesis. She hated Mama with a passion that could only be described as venomous. I'll liken her to a brown recluse spider rather than a black widow; she lacked the allure. Plus Mama said she never knew when Shirley was lurking around the next dark corner, lying in wait to wound her at any given moment. She was jealous of every single thing Mama ever did. She delighted in her failures and swooned with jealousy at the very sight of her.

They were both from Greenville, in the Mississippi Delta, and from the limited details of what I was told, the feud began when they were little. Shirley had been invited to play at Mama's house and she stole Mama's gold locket, which was engraved with a cursive S for her first name, Sarah. Mama didn't even realize it was missing until the day Shirley Greene wore it to school. Naturally, Mama told the teacher, and once it was confirmed, Shirley had to apologize. That started a lifelong rivalry. In high school, Shirley Greene actually spread around a rumor that Mama was pregnant. It was a big fat lie, and Mama found out that it came from Shirley because a teacher confiscated the note she passed to fuel the gossip. Shirley was sent to the principal and made to give an apology to Mama and my grandparents, and then she got a three-day suspension from school. As luck, well, misfortune would have it, they both ended up at Ole Miss, but thankfully in separate sororities.

I suppose I can understand the jealousy; Mama was Miss everything. Miss Delta Queen *and* Miss University. I've never been able to live up to her legacy, at least where physical beauty is concerned. A thick-haired gorgeous blond with a turned-up nose and big blue eyes, my mother had elegant features in the classical sense. She could tan like a Norwegian and her body was a near perfect hourglass, even at forty-two. Daddy was the one with the curly red hair and albino skin. I can thank him for that.

Even after all Shirley did to Mama, a part of me felt sorry for her. It had nothing to do with her appearance, which was nice in my opinion, but everything to do with her spiteful disposition. Envy can work a number on somebody. It plants a baby seed of resentment, and before you know it it's grown into a grove of jealousy. Maybe there was more to the story, but Mama never shared it with me. But if there's one thing I've learned about a falling-out, there's usually three sides. My mother wasn't exactly a saint herself.

When Mama died, Shirley was the first to show up with a large silver tray full of Dinstuhl's famous chocolate-covered, cream-in-the-center strawberries and place it in a prominent spot on our dining room table. To make sure everyone knew they came from her, she brought a bountiful supply of paper cocktail napkins embossed with her initials and stacked them right next to the platter. "I'll pick up my tray in the next few days," I remember her telling me. "Just have Kissie polish it." As if Kissie had nothing better to do than polish Shirley Greene's silver. Kissie did it anyway. She said there was no point in giving that woman something extra to gossip about. Now, ever since Mama died, she acts like there was never a problem between them. Whenever I've expressed my disgust about that to Kissie, she always explains, "Baby, that's just the way it is around here. No point in trying to figure it out, 'cause you certainly cain't change it."

So here Shirley was in the commercial kitchen of my restaurant, eyeing me as if I were a street urchin. My pink cotton blouse was untucked and wrinkled, and I looked like I had just stepped out of a dirty clothes hamper. Conversely, she was dressed to the nines in a brand-new Talbots ensemble. To make matters worse, not only was my hair a muss but the black hair-tie that once held it in place was now screaming from its spot on the white tile floor, where Peter flung it during our rendezvous. On my way over to greet her, I stepped on the thing and slid it along under my right foot. Peter watched as I deftly kicked it under the coffee station, suppressing a smile and crossing his arms in front of him.

"Mrs. Greene. This sure is a surprise," I said, an understatement of large proportion. With unwarranted guilt smeared all over my face, I moved in closer and gave her a brief yet purely contrived side hug. She responded in kind, and I turned around to introduce her to Peter. "This is—"

Sweeping her hand through the air, she cut me off. "Why, Pete'a and I are old friends. We met earlier this mow'nin'." Her thick Mississippi drawl sounded just like Mama's.

"Nice to see you again, Shirley," he said.

With obvious dumbfoundment I managed to say, "You two have met?"

"Didn't he tell you?" She swiveled her gaze to Peter.

"We haven't gotten down to business yet," Peter replied with a wink, and turned to face me. "Shirley was here a little while ago."

Again she scanned my body from head to toe, and I thought I detected a slight smirk forming on her lips. "I hope I'm not *interrupting* anything."

"You're not interrupting. We were just discussing our grand opening party," Peter said. Knowing him, I could see he thought his comment disguised our tryst, but he had no idea of its potential for catastrophic damage. I whipped my head around and shot him a look of pure horror, deflating the poor thing's pride, to say the least. From the moment Peter Owen set his Sorel boots down on Southern soil, he has been utterly incapable of translating the language of Southern women—or any

Southerners, for that matter. He furrowed his brow and tilted his head, undoubtedly baffled by this contest of Dixie lip service.

"A grand opening party? Why, that sounds simply faaabulous. When is it?" she asked, pretending as though her plan were not falling right into place.

A long silence fell into the conversation. "Three weeks. Or so," I said, after letting the pause grow into embarrassment. Imagining her at my grand opening party was pure torture.

"I'll watch for my invitation in the mail." As Shirley moved around the kitchen fingering everything in sight, even the pots hanging above the cooking line, her heavy gold charm bracelet tinkered with each touch. "I was still in the neighba'hood and decided to stop in to see what all this ruckus is about." What I wanted to say was: *And why are you still in the neighborhood? It's a good thirty minutes from your neighborhood.* She must have anticipated my thoughts and offered this explanation. "I had some visitin' to do out in Collierville and I thought I'd drop back by on my way home. Everyone in town is talkin' about the new restaurant openin' up in Germantown and the handsome new chef." She looked at Peter over her shoulder. "Pete'a showed me around when I was here befo'a. It's mighty nice."

"Thanks," I said.

"I hadn't seen you since you returned from Vermont and Pete'a said he expected you midmow'nin." She took a step back and scanned me once more. "You look . . . great. You'd nev'a be able to tell you've been through all you've been through. How're you holdin' up?" she said, staring straight into my eyes.

I was seething and malicious thoughts were coursing through every inch of my body. I knew dang well she was gloating over my misfortune but I did not want her to think it had gotten the best of me.

"I'm great. Things are actually wonderful in my life." I smiled over at Peter.

"Un-huh. Where is Bake'a these days?"

"He's in Vermont," I told her. She knew full well Baker still lived in Vermont. My ex-mother-in-law and Shirley play bridge together.

"Does he see his girls much? I bet they'll spend their summ'as in Vermont. I hear it's glorious up they'a in the summ'a."

I was ready to throw up. None of this was her business. The real question was: what was she *really* doing here? I knew she loved to spy and gossip but I never thought she'd have the nerve to show up out of nowhere. I hadn't seen her in well over two years. As much as I hated to do it, but just to get her off the subject of Baker and my daughters, I said, "How's Sandy?" As irony would have it, Shirley's only daughter ended up in my class at school—all twelve years. And on top of that, she went to Ole Miss.

"*Sondra* is simply faaabulous. Just faaabulous. She and Bill are about to make me a proud grandmoth'a for the third time in January. It's a little boy. You'll have to come see the nurs'ry. After the first two children were girls, Bill gave her carte blanche to redo that room in snips and snails and puppy dog tails." She burst out laughing at herself. "Lord help us, he's finally got a namesake. William Curtis Fleming, Jun'ya. They're callin' him Will."

"One of my favorite names. I'm sure he will be adorable," I said, trying to keep the focus on *her* family.

"I'm sure you can relate to her joy. Not having a son yourself."

What a horrid thing to say, I thought, then smiled—but it was pure fake.

"Sondra has picked out the most gorgeous shade of Benjamin Moore blue you've ev'a seen, and she's ordered her fabrics from Brunswig's nursery line. There's talk *At Home Memphis and Mid South* will make it their cov'a photo."

Throwing up seemed more appropriate than ever. First off, she'd been Sandy as long as I'd known her. Now she was calling herself Sondra? Not Sandra—which is her real name, by the way—but *Son*dra. I was tempted to ask Shirley to spell *Son*dra, but I couldn't bring myself to do it. All I could think about was getting Shirley Greene the heck out of my restaurant.

The phone hadn't rung once, but that didn't mean I couldn't fake a cell phone call. I furtively reached into the back pocket of my jeans, pulled out my phone, and faked a vibration. Staring at the phone as if I recognized the number, which was actually a black screen, I laid the groundwork. "Excuse me. I have to take this. Hello," I said into the phone, walking out of the conversation circle but speaking loud enough for her to hear every word. "This is she. Oh, that's great. Today? Yes. We can be there shortly. We're in Germantown so it might take close to thirty minutes or so but we'll be there soon. Thank you so much." With an overexaggerated motion, I clicked the off button on my phone and thrust it back inside my pocket.

"I hate to do this, Mrs. Greene—"

"Oh, do call me Shirley. Don't you think you're old enough for that?"

Frankly, I was surprised she hadn't changed her name to Sheryl or Sheridan, something more sophisticated than Shirley. "Okay, Shirley, but Peter and I have some business downtown we have to take care of. We are going to have to leave right away." I didn't offer any of the details but had she pressed, I was going to say it had something to do with our liquor license. By the look on her face, I could tell she was dying to know, but I offered nothing. After scampering for my purse, I grabbed Peter by the arm. "Let's go."

He reared his head back. "Whoa. Hold on there, fireball. Can you give me a minute to change?" He looked down at his pants, still coated in flour. "Where are we going anyway?" There it was; no way out. I was going to have to use my premeditated fabrication.

"To get our liquor license." It was my third little white lie of the day, but the last two were absolutely mandatory. I had to get that woman out of my kitchen. "Hurry as fast as you can," I said sweetly to Peter, and he disappeared out of the kitchen. I could hear him skipping steps up the back staircase.

"Does Pete'a live here?" Mrs. Nosy wanted to know. Although my original plan was to move the girls and me into the upstairs of the old house, right along with Kissie, all that changed when Peter came to town. He needed a place to live, and it seemed only right that the chef move upstairs, at least temporarily. After all, I had a fine rental home in Germantown with another four months on the lease.

"Yes, he does. Excuse me, I'll need to lock the front door." I stepped out of the kitchen and took my time strolling to the front of the house. After locking up, I made a mental note never to leave it open again. It reminded me of living at the inn in Vermont when I had absolutely no privacy. People were in and out of my house all day long. And the worst part was, no one ever knocked.

Three long, alone-with-Shirley minutes later, Peter was back in the kitchen in a pair of jeans and a flannel shirt, looking more handsome than before. I could tell even Shirley thought he was handsome by the way she stared at his face. Probably his lips. She was probably staring at his cherry-colored, plump top lip. I knew I was. After following us through the back door, she headed out to the parking lot and I waved as she stepped into her permanently new red Cadillac Sedan de Ville. Before closing the door, she said, "Lookin' fo'ward to the pa'ty," and started her engine.

Peter and I jumped in my perpetually old blue BMW and I started the engine. "Ohhhh. That *woman*." I pulled out behind Shirley and followed her down Poplar Pike toward Germantown Road.

"Not your best friend, I take it."

"She's awful. Plain awful. I have no idea why she'd even want to stop by. The truth is, *she can't stand me!*" My voice reached a high-pitched crescendo as I slowed to a stop at the stop sign. "And she *really* hated Mama."

As we drove along, I contemplated which story to tell first. After catching the red light, I slowed to a stop right behind the red Caddy. Once the light changed, instead of heading west on Poplar Avenue toward downtown, right behind Shirley, I pulled into the Exxon station on the corner of Germantown Road. Pausing a moment in front of a pump until I was sure Shirley was out of sight, I headed on out the exit back in the direction of the Peach Blossom Inn.

"What are you doing?" Peter said, turning around and looking out the back window.

"I'm going back to the restaurant," I said as though there were not a thing unusual about it at all.

"Why?"

"To design our menu, silly. I thought that's what we were doing today."

"I thought we were headed downtown to pick up the liquor license."

"Did you really believe that?" I added a nervous laugh, still bothered by Shirley's appearance.

"Of course I did."

"Well, we aren't," I said with a bobble of my head. "But Shirley doesn't know that!"

Peter sat still for a moment cradling his chin in his right hand, a deep crease forming between his eyebrows. Finally he glanced in my direction. "I changed my clothes, we actually left the restaurant, got in your car, and drove down to the corner. For nothing?"

I nodded.

He cocked his head to the side, pressed his lips firmly together and blinked.

There were a few cars ahead of me at the first stop sign, so I turned toward him. "I thought you had that figured out."

"How did you think I had that figured out?"

"By that look I gave you."

"The look you gave me told me she wasn't your best friend, not that we were going to go through some big rigmarole just to get her out of the kitchen."

"I'm sorry, but I couldn't take her another second." I pressed the gas pedal and accelerated through the stop sign.

"Okay, why didn't you just ask her to leave? Or tell her we were busy." His voice had lost its usual tenderness.

In disbelief, I whipped my head in his direction. "Peter. You don't just ask someone like that to leave."

"You don't?" he asked with such sincerity.

"No. You don't."

"Why not?"

Thinking about it for a second, I couldn't come up with a good explanation. I'd never really thought about it before. Finally I said, "I don't know. I guess because . . . probably because you know deep inside that it'll make matters worse. You have to tread lightly around that woman. You know, gently navigate through the waters."

"What you're saying is, you can't be honest to her face."

Now I was the one just sitting there with an incredulous gaze.

"That's pretty crazy, Leelee. I'd have said, 'Thanks for stopping by but we have to get back to work.' Plain and simple."

"It's not simple. It's extremely complicated." My mind searched for a better explanation but I couldn't think of one, so I switched the subject. "I can't believe you told her about the party."

"She acted like she was a dear friend of your family when she stopped by the first time."

"Of course she did. However, she's anything but! She's a big, fat phony." My voice cracked as a lump formed in my throat, reliving our families' decades-long feud.

"Okay, I get it. But you were being one, too. By giving her a hug. Why did you do that?"

I kept my eyes on the road, knowing that if I looked at him, I might start to cry. "It wasn't a real hug, it was just a . . . well, it was a side hug and those don't count," I said, staring straight ahead.

"See? You're acting no different."

Pain pricked every nerve in my body. I had no recollection of him ever hurting my feelings intentionally. Somehow I knew he had a point but that's just the way it is in the South. I bit the inside of my cheek, tightening my face muscles so I wouldn't bawl. I saw him staring at me from the corner of my eye. He didn't seem at all ready to drop the subject. "Are we having our first fight?" I asked.

"Disagreement maybe, but I'd hardly call it a fight."

"Okay, *disagreement*. Same thing. And I can't believe it's over *Shirley Greene*. She's so not worth it." Tears stung my eyes and I swept away the first one with the back of my hand. "You're from the North. You've been brought up differently." I turned into our driveway, slowly pulling through the gravel till I reached the back parking lot.

"You're right. We say exactly what's on our minds."

"Good for you!" I said loudly. "That's great. I wish we could be more like that but we're not." I found an old napkin lodged between the seat and the middle console and dabbed the rest of my tears. I pushed the gearshift forward into park. We both got out of the car and walked into the back of the restaurant in silence. Once inside, Peter walked straight upstairs.

My mind spun as I tore off my coat, flinging it on top of the coffee station. Our first fight was worse than I could have imagined because I felt terribly misunderstood. How could I explain to him in five minutes an attitude of a culture that's taken hundreds of years to formulate? Southerners don't do that. We don't say exactly what's on our minds. We try to be polite and friendly and we don't like it when we're at odds with people. There was no doubt that Peter and I were now at odds, and Lord knows I didn't like anyone mad at me. I'd never really thought about it before, but Southerners, for the most part, hate confrontation. We'll say a little white lie as fast as a screaming roller coaster just to avoid conflict. It was, as far as I was concerned, the Southern person's curse.

I headed into the front dining room and pulled my cell phone out of my back pocket. I had to talk to Mary Jule. She'd agree with me in a minute and I needed someone on my side. She was the most understanding of all my best girlfriends and would have used the same evasion strategy I did with Shirley Greene. Five years ago, she hired Paul Brady's wife to do a faux marbling job to her fireplace. She came highly recommended but after six months, the job was still half-done, with paint cans strewn all over Mary Jule's dining room. She called Mary Brady and told her that they had decided to go in a different direction and not do the faux finish after all. That was not entirely true; Mary Jule had every intention of going with a faux finish. She was just going to hire someone else to finally get the job done. It may have possibly been better in the long run to tell her she was taking too long, but Mary Jule could never do that, and in order to keep the relationship intact, she sidestepped her way out of it with a kind little white lie. Today the couples are still amicable, all in the name of keeping the peace and not hurting anyone's feelings. No harm done. Granted, the Bradys have never been invited to a single thing at Mary Jule's home but at least they speak.

"Hello, Fiery," Mary Jule said after only one ring. All my friends called me by Virginia's nickname.

"That was quick. Did you have the phone in your hand?" I whispered.

"It was sitting right next to me. Why are you whispering?"

"Peter and I had our first fight."

"Uh-oh. What happened?"

"Shirley Greene *dropped by,* and in order to get her out of here I made up a story that we had to go downtown to get our liquor license."

"So?"

"We left the house and drove to the corner before I turned around and headed home. Apparently Peter wasn't too thrilled about it. I had no idea he'd get mad about something like that. He wanted to know why I didn't just ask her to leave in the first place."

Mary Jule made a loud exasperated sigh into the phone. "I'd like to have seen him do that."

"That's just it. He would have told Shirley we were busy and never left the kitchen."

"That's 'cause he's a Yankee. That's the way they are."

"I know but I guess I just thought—" I heard Peter's footsteps clambering down the back squeaky steps. "Here he comes. I guess I better get off and deal with it."

"Good luck," she said warily. Mary Jule and I always felt each other's pain.

After clicking the off button I shoved the phone back in my pocket and walked into the kitchen, catching a glimpse of him before he disappeared into the walk-in refrigerator. With the sun streaming in from the outside, I leaned against the windowsill and waited till he came out. The warmth on the back of my head felt nice, a welcome change from the chilly temperature outside. I was lost in thought until I heard the click as the walk-in door swung open. As he rounded the corner in front of the dishwasher, our eyes met. I feared he'd want to pick up where we left off but instead his solemn expression morphed into a smile.

"Your hair," he said as he strode toward me. "It's the color of sunset." Once he reached the place where I was standing, he tucked a few strands behind my ears. "Hold on a second." I watched as he made his way over to the coffee station and bent down on all fours. Seconds later, he arose holding the concealed hair-tie from earlier. Instead of handing it to me, he lifted the hair off my shoulders, gathering it tenderly behind my head and into a ponytail. "Turn around," he said twisting the black tie back in place. "There. All better." Patting my shoulders, he kissed the top of my head.

I swiveled back around and met his gaze. "Thanks. But are we all better?"

He sighed softly and waited a moment before speaking. "Of course we are. I'm sorry, Leelee. I don't know anything about the history of your relationship with that woman. I shouldn't have showed her around. It's just that she spoke like you were old family friends."

I rolled my eyes upon hearing mention of her. "Anything but." I paused. "I'm sorry, too."

"For what?"

"I don't know, the whole thing."

"Come here, sweetheart." He pulled me to him and cradled my face in his palms. "I understand that customs are different down here. I might not agree with them, but the last thing I want is to have a disagreement over someone who is not worth the time it takes to utter her name." A smile crept onto his face and he suddenly reared his head back in a roar of laughter.

"What's so funny now?"

"You calling our spat a fight."

I slouched in frustration. "I didn't mean a brawl. You say 'spat,' I say 'fight.' It's a tomahto, tomayto thing."

"Not exactly. But let's chalk it up to semantics, what do you say?"

"Fine."

"Like I said, the woman is not worth it." He slipped his arms around my waist.

"She's not worth a teaspoon of flour," I said, eyeing the cutting board covered in the stuff.

"Not hardly. And speaking of, I hate to point this out to you, but you've got flour on your tush. I saw it when we were walking out to the car."

"What?"

"Yeah. I think you have my handprints on either cheek."

I pulled away and contorted my torso in an attempt to look at my backside. "Shirley Greene saw this?"

"I wish she'd seen more than that—the ole biddy." He laughed as I frantically swept at my behind. "Here, let me help you." He dusted the back of my pants and then looked me straight in the eye. "I wouldn't hurt your feelings for anything in the world. You have to trust me on that."

I nodded lightly.

"That wasn't much of a yes. Do you trust me?" He'd been asking me to trust him since the day we met, and I had not yet had a reason to doubt him.

"Yes. I trust you."

"Good." He kissed me gingerly and I watched his eyes glance above my head where the clock hung on the wall. "It's twelve thirty already. Why don't I make us lunch and we'll sit down and discuss the menu."

"That sounds perfect," I said.

I was happy our "disagreement" was over, but somehow I knew that wouldn't be the last of our adjustments. I had a pretty good feeling other Rebel tendencies would ire my transplanted Yankee in the important months ahead.

Chapter Four

True to his word, Peter whipped up a gourmet lunch in minutes. Hickory-smoked bacon, mayo, melted mozzarella, tomatoes, and basil on thick slices of grilled ciabatta bread. He called it his Italian BLT. On the side he added a small vegetable salad of cherry tomatoes, roasted peppers, more basil, roasted corn, and sugar snap peas coated in white balsamic vinegar and olive oil. This was one of the menu items he had recently suggested should we ever open the restaurant for lunch, and I found myself eagerly giving it merit—if only by virtue of smell alone. We sat at one of the dining room tables in the front of the restaurant, enjoying our lunch and a few cherished minutes by ourselves. Once the Peach Blossom Inn was in full swing, those golden nuggets of privacy between Peter and me would be scant, a reality I had not forgotten after the Vermont venture.

I had dusted off a table in the front dining room while Peter was frying bacon, and when the food was assembled we carried our drinks and plates through the swinging door, settling into two seats right next to one another.

"Do we have everything you need to operate this joint?" I asked, taking the first sip of my Coke. Alice, Virginia, and Mary Jule had accompanied me last month, before he arrived, to Tunica, Mississippi, where I had purchased all our equipment from a restaurant going out of business.

"More or less."

"What's missing?"

"Besides a cooking tool or two, it's pretty much complete. You did a great job, boss." Peter started calling me "boss" right after I hired him to work at the Vermont Peach Blossom Inn. I didn't have a nickname for him yet, even though my girlfriends frequently referred to him as the Yankee Doodle Dixie—"his moniker," as Virginia teasingly called it.

"Well, thank you. I tried." I bit into my sandwich and as soon as the combination of flavors hit my tongue, I let out a small moan. "Mmmhhh, this is incredible." I peered over at him, astounded at the way he could make the simplest meal seem like the best thing I'd ever tasted. "Memphis will never be the same once your dinner menu is sampled. I can't wait to see what new palates have inspired you this time." Peter had transported his vast collection of cookbooks during the move South and he studied each one fondly, creating his own variations of the favored recipes.

"You inspire me." He cocked one eyebrow, grinning.

"Aww." I wrinkled my nose awkwardly, then changed the subject. "Are we keeping anything from our Vermont menu?"

Peter leaned back in his chair and raked his hands through his hair. "I've given this tons of thought, but actually, I've decided we should keep most everything." He looked at me, waiting for my reaction. Once I smiled he continued. "I've come up with several new recipes, but honestly, I keep coming back to, 'Why mess with a good thing?' No one in Memphis has tried anything off our Vermont menu." He moved forward in his seat. "Hang on a minute." After giving my ponytail a playful yank, Peter disappeared out of the dining room and hurried back in with a yellow legal pad. He sat back down and scooted his chair a little closer to mine. "Here's what I've got so far." He turned

over a few pages. "It's a slight variation from the way I prepared everything on our first menu. I want to appeal to your Southern tastes, too."

"French food at its Dixie finest. Who can argue with that?" Our elbows were touching, and just the feel of him titillated me. I fantasized
back to our drying board kiss—before Shirley Greene barged in and
ruined it.

"Nobody." He shook his head then grinned. "Let me see if I can make
your mouth water all over again," he said, seductively flicking his eyebrows. After straightening in his chair, he held the legal pad out front.
"For starters, I want to include a North Atlantic wild smoked salmon,
served in buckwheat crepes, with horseradish cream and golden caviar.
Like?"

"Love."

"Good. Naturally, we should keep the jumbo shrimp cocktail, with
both a traditional cocktail sauce and a new Creole rémoulade sauce." He
tilted his head to the side in an are-you-okay-with-that gesture. I nodded in approval. "But I'm not so sure about our Vermont house favorite.
What do you think? Will escargot go over well here in Memphis?"

"Are you kidding? We love exotic, gourmet imports in this city. *Especially* French influenced. Now that Justine's is closed, someone has
to serve escargot." Justine's was a famous Memphis landmark at one
time, specializing in French cuisine, out of business for years but still
considered Memphis's finest restaurant ever.

I watched him put a check mark beside escargot before looking
back at me. Keep the Crabmeat Henry?" Peter asked. In Vermont we
had borrowed that menu item directly from Justine's: lump fresh crabmeat lightly seasoned and topped with hollandaise, served over toast
points. We named ours after my daddy, as it was his personal favorite.

"But now that we're back in Memphis, it only seems right to call it
by its original name: Crabmeat Justine. We can name something else
after Daddy. He liked all French food."

"What about pâté? Did he like that?" Peter asked.

"Oh yeah."

"Then we'll call it Pâté de Henry." He scratched through the old name and replaced it with the new. "Sound good?"

"Sounds perfect. But we will not be feeding it to Roberta. I can promise you that." I was referring to the fact that Princess Grace Kelly enjoyed a rich diet of goose liver pâté once we moved to Vermont. That was thanks to my lovely French waiter and maître d', Pierre Lebel.

When Peter brought up Daddy, I thought about how proud he would be of me. First and foremost he'd be beside himself and relieved that I was back in Memphis, where our Southern heritage rooted down to the core of the earth. "Dah'lin," he would have said, "You nev'a belonged up there. I don't know how you stood it as long as you did." Mostly he would gloat over my tenacity and perseverance. Even though he was responsible for my becoming a daddy's girl, I think he'd revel in my independence. The way I see it, he was only doing what he'd been taught from many generations past.

"That's about it for the apps. Except, of course, the soups and salads, which I'll switch up nightly." Peter always told me that a great restaurant is judged by its soups, since they require innovation and finesse but were dependent on whichever foods were freshest at the daily market. His soups were spectacular: Creole corn chowder, roasted red pepper, butternut squash, even a Hungarian goulash. My personal favorite was Peter's she-crab. I could taste the sherry-flavored lump crabmeat just thinking about it.

"You're making me drool," I said. "What about the entrées?" In truth, I was drooling at him. I couldn't help myself.

"Actually, I have an idea for one more appetizer. And all I'm asking is for you to keep an open mind."

"It's not calf's liver bites, is it?" Peter had included calf's liver among our entrées in Vermont and I had put my foot down when we first started discussing our new menu for Tennessee.

"No. I told you I was going to leave that one off."

"Then what is it?"

He took a deep breath and paused. "Headcheese."

I jerked my head back in surprise.

"Hang on," he said, patting my hand, seemingly prepared for my response. "I've been reading a lot about it lately. It's making a comeback." There wasn't a hint of teasing in his voice.

"You are such a liar."

From the back of his legal pad, he pulled out a copy of an article he had obviously printed from the Internet and placed it in front of me. "Look, this is from a Louisiana restaurant. Apparently it's very popular in the Deep South."

I stared at him like he had lost his ever-loving mind. Headcheese was an appetizer on the Vermont Haus Inn menu, under Helga's regime, and I had had the very unpleasant experience of walking in on Rolf, Helga's brother and the former chef, as he was preparing it. A cow's head stared at me from Rolf's cutting board as he was about to douse it inside his large stockpot. As far as I was concerned, headcheese was *the* nastiest thing I could possibly imagine. Without realizing it, I found myself fiddling with my earlobe and scratching at the nape of my neck, staring off in the distance. The last thing I wanted to do was hurt his feelings or create another disagreement. I opened my mouth to speak but nothing came out.

"It's very European. In France they call it *fromage de tête*. I think we should start a trend here in Memphis."

Working up all my courage to put my foot down, I finally said, "I don't know, Peter. I'm not trying to be mean but . . . I think it's embarrassing." I involuntarily shrugged my shoulders and grimaced.

"Really?"

"Really."

After a few more seconds, the sides of Peter's mouth started to curl and he burst out laughing. He held his stomach and carried on until tears spilled over his eyelids. Usually I laugh when someone else is that hysterical, but I could only glare at him. "You are dead meat," I told him. "I hope you realize that." I went back to eating, staring straight ahead.

My comment made him laugh even harder. So hard, he could hardly breathe. In between gasps he lifted his chin in the air and roared, *"Mooooooo. Mooooooo,"* carrying on until he tumbled out of his chair. He laughed until he was out of breath and his watery face glistened with tears. I lunged at him on the floor but he used his hands as a barrier. I tried grabbing his bandanna, but he blocked his head so I tickled him under his arms until he blocked me. "Okay, you win," he managed to utter, breathless. "No headchee . . . se." As soon as he got the "cheese" part out, he turned over on his side and covering his face, mooing and laughing until he splayed flat out on his stomach and slapped the floor.

I returned to my seat and took a gulp of my Coke, determined to ignore him. "I'm getting you back when you least expect it, buster. You better watch out if you know what's good for you."

"Thanks for warning me," he said, crawling back onto his chair.

"Think nothing of it." He tried kissing me on his way up but I said, "Unh, unh unh, I'm not letting you off that easy."

He smiled and wiped his face before straightening his seat. "Okay, time to be serious." He turned the page on his legal pad and cleared his throat.

"Will we be serving entrées?" I asked with a straight face.

"Most definitely. Would you like to hear about them?"

"I would."

"We can't have a high-end French restaurant without a quality organic fillet with the usual béarnaise or sauce au poivre."

"I agree."

"Or calf's liver." When I started to object, he said, "Just kidding."

I rolled my eyes then took another bite of my sandwich.

"I'll use locally grown meat, herbs, and veggies whenever possible."

"That's nice, I love that idea."

He reached over to comb my chin with his fingers. "Next, veal scaloppini. We'll do either the marsala or the piccata. And we need something to represent my part of the country, so how does roast Long Island duckling sound? I'll change the sauces du jour to go along with it."

"Do you remember how much I love duck?"

He nodded.

"And your pasta. Your to-die-for pasta specialties."

He laughed as his cheeks blushed. "I've got that covered. It'll change nightly. And I know you want the shrimp dijonnaise on this menu." It was my personal favorite from Vermont. Jumbo shrimp sautéed with shallots and tarragon, flamed with cognac and finished with a white wine–grainy mustard cream sauce.

"Are you kidding? I'd almost kill somebody for it."

He laughed.

The thought of his scrumptious menu and how well it would go over sent a thrill through me as I anticipated the success of the new Peach Blossom Inn. "What about lamb? Are you keeping that?"

"Oh yeah. I'll roast baby lamb and serve it with roasted garlic and a port wine rosemary sauce." He kissed two fingers and swept his hand through the air.

I closed my eyes, remembering just how wonderful he was in front of the stove.

"And finally, we'll have two fish dishes. First—Dover sole prepared with a lemon butter sauce, white wine, and capers, just like the one I served in Vermont. And here's a new menu item. We'll offer a nice piece of halibut, when it's in season. I'll roll it in crushed pistachio nuts and serve it with a pistachio cream sauce."

I started to comment but he interrupted me.

"And of course, we'll serve the buttered pommes frites on the side with a vegetable of the day."

"You've outdone yourself, Chef Owen."

"I think you're the one who's outdone herself." He looked around the room, slightly shaking his head. "Look at this place. Have I told you how proud of you I am?"

"Not today."

"You've created another showplace."

"I can't take all the credit. I had some help." Mary Jule, Virginia, and Alice spent hours helping me with paint colors, fabrics, and the overall design. "So how are we gonna serve the food for the party?"

"We'll have mini-everything. That way people will know we can cater parties. Like I've told you, there's big business with catering these days: a great way to earn extra cash." Underneath the legal pad, Peter had stored one of the old menus from Vermont and as he handed it to me I saw a vibrancy in his eyes. It took me by surprise that he'd even kept a copy. It was printed on thick peach matte stock with dark gold lettering and I had added, YOUR HOSTS: LEELEE SATTERFIELD AND PETER OWEN at the top. Having his name on the Peach Blossom Inn menu was like seeing his name on a theater marquee. It meant everything to him. "I've been thinking about the menu design. I see no reason to change it, do you?"

"No need to mess with perfection," I said with a smile.

He lifted his water glass and clinked the side of mine. After taking another sip, he asked, "When you interviewed the other chef candidates, did anyone stand out as a possible sous chef?"

Riley's mug popped into my head and I had to blink twice to get rid of it, our doorstep conversation, only a few hours prior, still fresh on my mind. In truth, I had interviewed a woman straight out of culinary school in Florida, who was one of my lead candidates, but her gung-ho, over-the-top attitude was a turnoff. And an older gentleman with an abundance of local experience had once topped my list but that was right before Peter showed up. "There was this older guy," I said, "but I'm not so sure he'll agree to a *sous* chef position."

"You'd be surprised. Remember when you hired me in Vermont to be Rolf's sous chef? I told you I was taking the position because I wanted to be a head chef in the future. I welcomed the opportunity to work under a skilled French chef."

"That's a good point. I'm sure I've got his number around here some-where. Do you want it?"

"Maybe, I'll let you know."

"I suppose we could put an ad in the newspaper," I said cautiously. Just thinking about Riley reading that ad caused me to reach around and twist my hair.

He smiled. "I'll take care of it. You just worry about getting this place opening-night ready."

"How about the waitstaff and a dishwasher and a prep cook? We open in three weeks." The thought of all we still had left to do made me more anxious by the second.

"Relax," he said, caressing my hand before taking it in his. "It will all come together, trust me. I've got this under control."

I took a deep breath and decided to trust him. It was the first relief I'd had all day. "Virginia and them are dying to work here one night a week."

"That part's up to you, but as you know, we'll need a head waiter or waitress who gives this place character. Someone like Pierre."

Pierre was indeed a character. In Vermont, I was told he couldn't speak much English. I later learned that he spoke a little more than he let on. Although he had been working at the Vermont Haus Inn for twenty years before Baker and I took over, he turned out to be loyal to me. He was the one who saved me from Helga's wrath when Princess Grace marked her territory in the restaurant. After scooping it up with the white linen napkin he always wore draped over his wrist, he plopped it into his coat pocket, no worse for the wear. A part of me wanted to pick up the phone and call him again just to see if he'd consider finally leaving Helga and moving down South, but at sixty-something years old he was set in his ways and had dug his snow boots firmly into the Vermont terrain. It was only three hours from Montreal, and Pierre had French relatives living there with whom he spent all his holidays. Replacing him would be impossible, I knew that, but I couldn't help hoping we'd find a good substitution.

On Saturdays, Kissie made a habit of checking on her house. Her neighbors kept a watchful eye on things during the week but nevertheless she wanted to make sure everything was just the way she left it. As far as neighborhoods go, Kissie's isn't the safest in town. I offered to install an alarm system but Kissie said all the iron on the windows and doors was plenty enough to keep burglars away. "There ain't nobody gone get through this iron. You just keep your money, baby," she had said. Another reason Kissie liked to be home on Saturdays was to be close to her church on Sunday mornings. But on that Saturday night, she offered to stay so Peter and I could go out to dinner. She said, "Baby, y'all might as well take advantage of Saturday nights while you can. Ain't gone be many times where you and Peter can go out together on the weekend." Her words were a stiff reminder of what the restaurant business was really like, working long days and nights and spending precious time away from my girls.

After a nice evening, it was eleven o'clock when Peter took me home. We'd been to one of the most popular restaurants in downtown Memphis, Automatic Slim's, and the minute I opened the front door I could hear the familiar theme song of *The Tonight Show*. Kissie, the night owl, never missed it. Although she still carries a fifty-foot torch for Johnny Carson, she has grown to "appreciate" Jay Leno. As I walked inside, she was up scooting around the kitchen. She refers to it as "rambling" around the kitchen, wiping down the front of the refrigerator, mopping the floors, and of all things, wiping down the dry goods I had bought earlier at the grocery.

"Why are you doing that?" I asked her. I'd seen her do it a thousand times but never thought to ask why.

"Because someone's nasty hand been on every one of these cans. I don't put nothin' in my pantry *or yours* till I've wiped it down clean."

I sat down at the kitchen table and watched her for a moment. *What have I ever done to deserve you?* I thought. When she turned around, I stared at her lovingly while noticing the navy blue, elastic-waist stretch pants she wore almost every day. Kissie could stand to lose fifty pounds. The actual truth is she could stand to lose a lot more than that but she thinks she looks fantastic. "People don't look good when they're too thin," she's always telling me. "And that means you." No point in arguing with her. We've long since agreed to disagree. On that and another touchy subject: Now that she's living with me, Kissie's finally put away her white uniform. She'll drag it out every once in a while, but if I catch her, I insist it go back in the closet. I realize it's what she's used to but I remind her that we're family and on top of that it's terribly out-dated. When she worked for Mama and Daddy she was required to wear one. Whether she was cooking or ironing, running Mama's er-rands or driving my carpool in Mama's Cadillac car, Kissie always wore her uniform.

"I've got to talk to you about something," I said, sweeping away my recollections of the past.

"Go right ahead," she answered without turning around. She con-tinued on in the pantry but I knew she was listening.

"Even though things are okay now, I'm still a little bruised by some-thing that happened this morning. Peter and I had our first fight—well, he doesn't call it that, he says 'disagreement.'"

She whipped her head around. Any disharmony between Peter and me was cause for alarm. Not only did she think he was the best thing that had ever happened to me, I could tell she had a secret crush on him, too. "You don't mean it? What was it about?" Kissie stopped wip-ing cans, threw her rag in the sink, and moved toward the table, set-tling down in the chair next to me.

"Shirley Greene showed up at the restaurant this morning."

Kissie threw her arms up. "Lawd have mercy alive. What in the world did that nosy woman want?" I opened my mouth to explain but she in-terrupted before I'd said the first word. "She's got nothing but the Ser-pent's business on her brain." When she finally calmed down and folded her arms on the table, I noticed all the old burn scars. She never takes the time to wear long kitchen mitts.

I lifted one eyebrow. "*She said* she stopped in to see what all the ruckus about our new restaurant was about, but I know she has an ul-terior motive. I just can't figure out what it is."

"Her *ulterior motive* is to snoop around in your business. There ain't no reason in the world for her to stop by. She just cain't stand the fact that you're doing something successful. She don't want nothing else but to be nosy, hm hm hm."

"I don't know. Something tells me she's up to something. She stopped by once before when I wasn't there. Peter had no idea who she was. He mentioned the grand opening party to her before he knew our history."

"Oh Lawd." Kissie cradled her forehead in her palm.

"She told us she's waiting on her party invitation." I stood up and moved over to the fridge in search of a Coke. When I had one in my hand, I extended it to Kissie but she shook her head.

"Uh-oh. Did you get in a fight about that?" True to her Southern roots, Kissie referred to it as a fight, also.

"No," I said, grabbing the opener, and sat back down, popping the top. "When I told him how phony she was, he called me phony because I gave her a hug. Not a real hug, mind you, a side one."

Something about the way I said it must have tickled her because she burst out laughing, like it was the last time she'd ever do it. "Did you hug her for real, baby?" She slapped the table and bent over. "I bet she couldn't call that daughter of hers fast enough to fill her in on what you're doin'. Oh me." Kissie had been around so long, she knew not only every detail about every person in my family, but details about anyone who had ever been associated with us. On top of that, her memory, even at eighty-three, was far better than mine ever will be.

When I heard the merriment in her voice all the worry zapped away and I got tickled, too. "I almost forgot the best part, Kissie. Guess what?"

Kissie leaned in toward me, wide-eyed. "What?"

"Sandy changed her name."

"Did?"

"Uh-huh. Guess what to?"

"Well, her real name's Sandra. Is she going by that now?"

I shook my head. "*Son*dra."

Kissie splayed out on the table until tears streamed down her face. She held her stomach until she couldn't take it any more. "Uh-oh, baby, I'm fixin' to wet." After pushing herself back up, Kissie hightailed it to the bathroom.

Four minutes later she was back dabbing at her eyes with a Kleenex. "Oooh-wee," she said, with only a bit of giggle left in her voice. "I tell you what, some people never cease to amaze me." She lowered herself slowly back into the chair again.

When I started to make another comment about Sondra, she said, "Wait a minute now, let me tell you this 'fore it leaves my mind. I want you to understand somethin'. Peter is from the Nawth. Those folks say exactly what's on their mind. No mincing of words, no beatin' around the bush. They don't sugarcoat nothin'." She had her finger in the air and she shook it with every point she made. "They are not worried about how somethin' sounds or if somebody don't like what they're sayin'; they're more concerned with gittin' on with it and tellin' it like it is." By now, she was looking me dead in the eye. "Kind of like I tol' you about Riley this mornin'. If you just go on and tell the truth on the front end, it saves you a whole lot of worry on the back end. My people always tol' me honesty is the best policy."

I leaned in toward her, closing my eyes in frustration. "I wasn't trying to be dishonest. I . . . I just don't like confrontation. And I sure don't like to hurt anyone's feelings."

"I don't like it either, baby, but sometimes it cain't be helped."

"You grew up down here. Why isn't it hard for you?" Kissie was raised in the Mississippi Delta just like Mama. I didn't see why she was any different when it came to confrontation.

"Black folks ain't like white folks when it comes to sayin' what's on our minds."

"What do you mean?"

"We grew up fightin' for everything we got. We didn't have time to beat around no bush and worry about whether or not we were hurtin' somebody's feelings. Anyway, I don't worry about nothin'. Worry comes straight from the Devil. If you trust in the Lawd, you don't need to worry."

"Well, I wish I could be more like you but I think I'm just a born worrier."

"You need to ask the Lawd to help you with that then." Kissie has a tendency to spiritualize everything, not to mention putting me in my place even if it tortures me.

I peered over at her for another moment before a big yawn came out of nowhere and fatigue rippled through me. "I'll give that some thought."

Kissie caught my yawn. "Pray about it."

"I will."

She went around turning out the lights and I escaped down the hall to peek in on the girls. When I opened the bedroom door, I could hear their rhythmic breathing. When Issie inhaled, Sarah exhaled, and both had kicked off their covers. I slowly closed the door, turning around just in time to see Kissie heading into the bathroom. Her extra-large Lanz nightgown was slung over her shoulder. I reached out for her hand. "I love you so much, Kissie."

"I know you do, baby. And I sure love you."

"It worries me to think about something ever happening to you."

She took a step back. "Did you hear a thing I said about worry?"

I grinned, thinking about all the loving admonishments she'd given me over the years, but sometimes I couldn't resist teasing her. "Shoo, Devil, shoo!"

"You better git on in your room and get some sleep 'fore I shoo you."

After a tender hug, I told her goodnight, changed into my own nightgown, and climbed on top of my bed. Roberta jumped up and circled into a spot right next to me. While tossing the shams and throw pillows onto the carpet, I thought about Peter. Beautiful, honorable, irresistible Peter. In the last twenty-one days since he'd arrived I'd not had much sleep. Between spending time with him and then rehearsing every second of that time over and over before I drifted off, I'd hardly slept more than a few hours each night.

No different than the evening before, once my head was cradled inside my downy pillow and my body was cocooned under my quilts, I let my mind drift onto Peter's beautiful mouth, his succulent lips, and pretty soon we were tangled in a fanciful embrace, loving each other with burning, reckless caresses until slowly, ever so slowly, our bodies blended into one.

Chapter Five

I considered the old turn-style bell on the front door an asset when I bought the old Victorian, purely for its nostalgic value, a lively reminder of a time gone by. Although loud, one-quarter turn was a pleasant alarm. Anything past was downright irritating. If someone turned the bell around an entire 360 degrees, it was like being awoken in the middle of the night by the sound of a flushing toilet. Monday afternoon I was on the phone with a wine vendor when two of those extra-long, 360-degree turns rang. Surely not, I thought. It can't be.

But it certainly was.

From my position in the left dining room I could see his profile through the front window. Lord knows how long Riley would have kept turning that bell, so I hurried over to answer the door. Covering the receiver with one hand, I opened the door with the other. "I'm on a business call," I whispered, and motioned for him to step inside. "I'll be with you in a minute." A minute is never a minute in the South but Riley knew what I meant.

He held a briefcase in one hand, a black umbrella in the other, and wore his black Tupperware jacket with PROFESSIONAL TUPPERWARE

HUNTER inscribed on the back. An I SELL TUPPERWARE button was pinned to the front pocket. "This is for you," he whispered, and handed me the umbrella. I knew it came from Tupperware, too, by the purple lettering peeking out of the folds. I'd seen Riley use his whenever it rained.

I went back to my conversation with John from Athens Distributing while Riley showed himself around. "Wow, what a nice place," I heard him say, even though John rambled on in my ear. Riley moved slowly around the room with his head tilted back, admiring the tall ceilings and moldings. I watched him run his hand against the pocket door between the foyer and the dining room and check his fingers for dust. As he turned and shot me a thumbs-up, I thought back to the first day I met him. He had shown up at my front door with a bottle of Orange Glo for a housewarming present, and offered to dust my grandmother's sideboard. Kissie about took his head off. She would rather coat the whole thing in Vaseline than put Orange Glo on a piece of antique furniture. I shot the thumbs-up sign back all the while listening to John spout off about dishwashers, of all things, instead of wine. We'd become fast friends the first time he paid me a sales call and I found him easy to talk to. Rather than discussing wine, most of our conversations involved girl-talk. I was beginning to think it was his sales strategy.

Moments later Peter walked in from the kitchen and took a step back when he saw the lettering on the back of Riley's Tupperware jacket. He pointed toward him and mouthed, *"Who's that?"*

I covered the phone receiver and mouthed back, *"Riley, my next-door neighbor."* After a wink and an understanding nod from Peter, I relaxed into one of the dining room chairs as John talked. I even started to put my feet up and stretch my legs out on another chair when a hot streak of terror suddenly bolted through me. I had completely forgotten all about him applying for the sous chef position! And in light of the *disagreement* Peter and I had had about being honest, I couldn't possibly fess up about another little white lie, even if it was to spare Riley's feelings.

"You must be Peter," I heard Riley say once he had spotted him.

"That's me."

"Hi, I'm Wiley." As Peter walked over to shake Riley's hand, I stopped listening to a thing John said.

"Nice to meet you, Wiley."

"Actually, it's Wiley. With an *arrr*."

Peter drew in a short breath as if he suddenly remembered. "I think Leelee may have told me about you." I *had* told him about Riley, but for obvious reasons I'd left out a few details that could only be experienced in person.

"Sorry the job didn't work out," Riley said.

As I watched Peter tilt his head to the side and a deep furrow form in between his eyebrows, I froze still. I was in so much trouble. Before Peter had a chance to catch me in another fib, though, I blurted, "Riley's house is a showplace, Peter." It was a left-fielder, I realize that, but I was desperate. Any minute now I was going to be exposed and the lovely new man in my life would think I was out of my mind.

They both turned around, confused.

"Wait till you see it!" I said smiling, but my heart was blasting.

I heard the faint voice of John, somewhere around my knee, say, "See what? What showplace?"

Thrusting the phone back up to my ear I said, "I wasn't talking to you, John. Sorry."

I think he answered, "I love showplaces," but by then the thumping of pulse inside my ears had drowned out every sound in the room.

"Can I call you back in five?" I asked John in a rush. "It's crazy around here."

"Sure but before I let you go, just tell me what kind of dishwasher you own."

I was distracted from trying to lip-read every word between Peter and Riley as they had drifted away from earshot. "Huh?"

"Dishwasher. What kind do you have?"

"I have a . . . I have a—" My neck craned over in their direction as I watched them move toward the kitchen.

"By the way, Peter, has Leelee talked to you about your food stowage needs?" I'm pretty sure I heard Riley say as Peter held open the swing-ing door.

"No, she hasn't," Peter responded. That, I was sure of.

With the phone still in my hand, I frantically waved my arms high above my head to distract Peter but he never looked my way. I watched in horror as the two of them disappeared, alone, into the kitchen.

"I have to go, John. Sorry but I have to go. We have a Hobart here at the restaurant but at home I have a Maytag, I think. Talk to you soon."

I heard him say, "Maytags suck," as I was hanging up. "You should think about switch—"

I tore into the kitchen just as Riley was saying, "I can. Hook. You. Up." His briefcase was set up on the side of the drying board next to the sink and I watched as he popped open the locks and reached in-side, handing Peter a catalog.

With no comment Peter took it and stared at the cover. As he flipped through the pages, Riley pointed over his shoulder, touting the benefits of Tupperware. My heart continued to blast through my ears as I, still paralyzed by the thought of being outed at any moment, racked my brain for a way out. "Tuppa'ware pwoducts help people weduce waste, save money, and pwotect the enviwonment, Peter," Riley said.

Peter never uttered a word. I, on the other hand, was so flustered that I put my foot in my mouth. "Don't you have any samples, Wiley? *I mean Riley*, sorry!" My nerves were shot and I didn't mean to do that. "I'm sure Peter would like to see them."

Peter looked over at me like I had lost my mind, but that was the lesser of two evils as far as I was concerned. I had to get him alone to tell him something, anything, before Riley mentioned the sous chef position.

"Of course I do. They're in my car. And you're wight, Leelee. Seeing is believing." He pointed toward the back door. "Can I use that exit?"

I nodded.

"I'll be wight back." As Riley flew out of the kitchen in a big hurry, I heard him say, "Hi, Kissie. Hi, Sawah. Hi, Issie. Be wight back." Normally I would have been overjoyed to see my family but not then.

I was going to have to own up to Peter about my little white lie right in front of the one who told me to nip it in the bud while I had the chance.

After hugging me first, Sarah and Issie ran to Peter and hugged him around his waist. He picked them up, one in each arm, and leaned down to smooch Kissie's cheek. Kissie was taken with Peter to say the least. She even blushed in front of him. Despite her butterscotch skin, as she liked to call it, I could see the color rush to her face.

"How was school?" he asked.

"I played on the playground for two hours." Issie smiled and held up two fingers.

"Two hours," Peter said. "I wish I'd gone to your school."

Sarah shook her head. "Issie did not play that long. She just thinks it was that long. Mommy, may we please go upstairs?" I had a special room for the girls set up with toys and a TV.

"Sure, lovey, I'll be up in a few minutes." They squirmed down out of Peter's arms and bolted up the back kitchen steps.

Before I had a chance to breathe much less figure out how to give Peter a heads-up without tipping off Kissie, Riley bounded back in the kitchen loaded down with cases—one marked AMWAY under his right arm and a PAMPERED CHEF case in his right hand. Under his left arm he carried a Tupperware box and held a suitcase bearing the Cutco logo in his left hand. After putting his wears down in the middle of the floor, he straightened his I SELL TUPPERWARE button and fiddled with the zipper on his jacket. Kissie's head shifted with every movement he made. Meanwhile my stomach was tied up as tight as one of Issie's tangles. Kissie took one long look at him and said, "Why, Riley, you sure are busy." That was her nice way of saying, "What in the world do you think you're doing, Riley?"

"I sure am busy. That's my job." He turned back around to Peter with a shortness of breath. "Phew. As I was saying, our pwoducts are built to last a lifetime and eliminate the need for disposable containers that add to landfills. We also pwovide stowage and cooking solutions to keep food fwesh longer and increase energy efficiency." Riley took out a nesting of three bowls from the Tupperware box and handed it to Peter.

"According to the EPA, that's the U.S. Enviwonmental Pwotection Agency"—he looked at us for affirmation—"aluminum foil and closures accounted for four hundwed thousand tons of our nation's municipal solid waste stream. Only ten percent of that was wecovered or wecycled, leaving thwee hundwed sixty thousand tons of waste in the landfills. Add to that, two million tons of plastic wap and over one-point-five tons of plastic bags each year."

Peter grinned as he turned over the bowls.

"Tuppa'ware's duwable, versatile stowage pwoducts last virtually fowever and offer a sustainable, weusable option for pweserving food and the planet. They give consumers the powa' to immediately weduce economic and enviwonmental waste."

"Wow, that's quite a spiel," Peter quipped, and handed the bowls back to Riley.

"Thanks. I memowized evewy single word stwaight from the Tuppa'ware Web site."

"I can tell," was Peter's answer to that. I watched him force his lips together, trying to suppress a smile. Riley started to go into more detail when Peter interrupted. "Is Tupperware your full-time job?"

"Funny you should ask, Peter," Riley said, and tore off his Tupperware jacket. One sleeve turned inside out so he hurriedly reached inside to correct the problem and hung it on the back of my desk chair. From one of the cases, he pulled out his chef hat, fluffed it, and placed it on his head, pausing to make sure RILEY was displayed in front. Changing his mind, he took it back off, placed it on top of his jacket, and dug his crisp white Pampered Chef apron out of the same case. He ducked his head under the top loop, wrapped the sash around his middle, and tied a bow in front. Finally he plopped his hat back on his head and stood up straight, stepping into place like a soldier. All he lacked was a salute and a pair of black chef clogs. "In addition to my work at Tuppa'ware, I'm a Pampa'ed Chef Consultant. It's given me all kinds of expewience in the kitchen." He touched the lettering on his apron. "I've discovered the chef in me by hosting sevewal cooking demonstwations, and consequently I've turned into a gweat chef!"

This is it. It's all over.

I watched Peter raise an eyebrow, cross his arms in front, and widen his stance, something he does whenever he's curious. I held on for dear life as the next comment oozed from Riley's lips. "I was telling Leelee that we could make the Peach Blossom Inn the first all-PC westauwant in Tennessee. This illustwious logo"—he pointed at his apron—"could be pwinted on all your menus. We could even have it placed on the window at the fwont of the westauwant." He put his hand beside his mouth and in a lower tone added, "It would incwease your foot twaffic by at least seventy-five percent. Twust me, Pampa'ed Chef is numewo uno." Needless to say, he then held up one finger.

By now my numero uno chef was bemused. I could tell by the way he stared at the floor with his hands in his pockets instead of looking at Riley. Kissie King simply glared at the poor thing. The poison arrows behind her eyes were ready to shoot at any moment. She was beyond bemusement and well on her way to a full-blown stupor. As for me, I had resigned myself to the beating. In fact, I just wanted it over with.

Like a seasoned sales professional, Riley continued. "So *Peter*, are you intewested in helping incwease your foot twaffic at the Peach Blossom Inn, thus incweasing your sales?"

Peter finally looked at him dead on. "Naturally that's the goal of all chefs but I'm not sure—"

"I have a feeling I know what you are going to say, *Peter*. 'You're not sure that you can afford our pwoducts'?"

"Actually that's not—"

"But you're wong, *Peter*! We will (I loved the 'we') have pamphlets at the fwont door and evewy person that signs up because of you and Leelee will be cwedited to your host account. You'll get fwee pwoducts, half-pwice items, ten to twenty-five percent off, *and* fwee shipping."

Kissie's lips were pursed so hard, I thought they'd bleed. But just as she opened her mouth to spew, Peter beat her to it. "Look, man, a co-op deal with Pampered Chef isn't going to work for us. I'm afraid the answer is no." *That's my Yankee Doodle,* I thought. *Straightforward and to the point.*

"Okay, no pwoblem, *Peter.*" Completely shocked at how easy it was to dissuade Riley, I thought I might be home free when the following slipped from his tongue. "Say, Leelee, did you happen to tell Peter that I applied for the sous chef position?"

There it was. My undoing.

Peter tilted his head to the side and I could practically see his brain searching back over our conversations. He answered for me. "Nope, she has not."

"It's too bad it didn't work out. I could have been a gweat asset to your team."

Peter never missed a beat. "Sorry, man."

Thank you, God—oh *thank you,* God. I silently swore right then and there that I would never tell another little white lie again.

Then Riley said, "Surely she told you that I'm an independent sales wep for Cutco." He removed his chef's hat, tore off his apron, and reached down into another box, grabbing a ball cap. It was then that we noticed the front of his white T-shirt, CSP in big letters with CUTCO SALES PROFESSIONAL written out to the side. His hat had the exact same design. "I can't help but notice you use cookware in your business, not to mention knives. Did you know that Cutco has the world's finest cutlewy, *Peter? And* we have an entire line of fine cookware?"

Peter shook his head no and glanced over at me. Under normal circumstances I could have said something to get us out of this mess but I was too busy exhaling a giant sigh of relief. Besides I had sworn off little white lies forever.

"At Cutco," Riley continued, "we stand behind our pwoducts with a fowever satisfaction guarantee. We want evewy Cutco customer to be a satisfied Cutco customer. If at any time you are not completely satisfied with the performance of your Cutco pwoduct, we will cowwect the pwoblem or weplace the pwoduct. Simply send the pwoduct to our main office with an explanatowy note." Without missing a beat he went straight into, "Have you heard about our fowever sharpness guarantee, *Peter*?"

My chef slowly shook his head.

"Our knives have a Double-D edge and will wemain sharp for many years, but after extended use they may need sharpening. Same thing. Just send them to our office for a handling fee of just six dollars for one to thwee knives or nine dollars for four or more. And lastly—" He looked around, making eye contact with each of us. "—we have a fowever we-placement service agweement. Should you damage your Cutco knife thwough misuse or abuse we will weplace that item for one half of the cuwwent wetail pwice." As an afterthought, he added, "Plus tax."

I saw Peter glance at the clock. He looked down at his feet, over at me, then to Kissie, and with a growing agitation said, "Is that from the Cutco Web site, too?"

"How'd you know?"

"Lucky guess."

"I have a gweat memory."

"Wow," Peter said, rubbing his palms together. "You're a one-stop shop."

"I certainly am. I could get you started with your own part-time business if you like. I set my own hours, my office is in my home, and the wewards I have earned are incalculable." I saw him eyeing the pots and pans hanging over the line and he moved over to take a more thorough glance. "This kitchen is something else," he said, turning back around to face us. "Did I mention that I'm an Amway Business Owner?"

I dared not glance anywhere near Kissie's direction.

"Can't say you did," Peter said, shoving his hands back in his pockets. When Riley started back to the boxes to change out of his Cutco getup, Peter, in an abrupt tone of voice, said, "No, no. Don't worry about changing again. You're good."

Instead, Riley reached for his Amway catalogs and handed one to each of us, including Kissie. "Go ahead and flip thwough. We have incwedible pwoducts. You name it; I can order it," he said. "I've been thinking about ways to improve this old house. We could hook a world-class

Amway atmosphere air puwifier in here and attach an Amway eSpring water puwifier to the water pipes."

Peter opened his mouth to speak but Riley interjected, "*And . . .* here's my guarantee, if I don't carry something, I'll find it for you. *I'll* be your gwocery store. Amway carries ketchup and mustard, even Splenda, and peanut butter." He circled his index finger around each finger on his other hand as he listed the items. "Mayo, pawmesan cheese, butter, and so much more."

Peter raked his fingers through his hair and briefly shut his eyes. Something told me he was about to blow. "This is a lot to take in," he finally said. Any trace of congeniality had vanished.

"Do you have a certain place you want me to make my pwesentation?"

"Isn't that what you've been doing?" Peter snapped.

"That was actually my intwoduction."

All of a sudden a loud "Hm hm hm, hm hm hm, hm hm hm" sounded from behind.

"How long is your presentation?" my chef asked, tapping his foot in exasperation.

I closed my eyes, scared to look.

"Let's see. Cutco is fowty-five minutes to an hour, Tuppa'ware can be done in under thirty, but Pampa'd Chef, by the time I do a food demonswation, usually takes an hour. I'll just set up on one of the tables in the dining woom." He bent down and gathered his loot.

As Riley disappeared through the door to the front of the restaurant, Kissie turned to me. Not Peter—me. "What I cain't understand is why that man thinks he don't have to ask permission to do the things he do. Hm hm hm. I never once heard him ask if any of this was convenient."

"I'm with Kissie," Peter said, sighing loudly. "I do not have time to watch 'Riley'—" He used finger quotes when he emphasized his name. "—give us an all-day sales pitch. Holy shit. The guy never lets up."

"Shhh," I pleaded, "He might hear you."

Peter glanced at Kissie. "I don't care if he—"

Riley popped his head through the kitchen door with a singsong in his voice. "I'm weady."

Peter looked at him, straight-faced. "Look, I want to help you out, man, but what you're thinking of doing will take several hours by my estimation and I don't have that kind of time."

"Hmmm, I could cut the time in half," Riley said. "Make one pwe-sentation today and come back tomowwow for the west."

Kissie couldn't take anymore. "Come here, Riley." She motioned to him with her index finger. He shut the door behind him and walked toward her, childlike. She wrapped her arm around his shoulder, directing him off to the side. "I'mo tell you something, and it's only to help you." Somehow she managed to put a semi-nice tone to her voice. "When folks are busy and working real hard, it's best to make an appointment and not show up thinkin' people have all kinds of time to stop what they're doin' and watch your show. Cain't you see these people are busy?"

Riley nodded.

"Why don't you call and make an appointment then?"

"I suppose I could do that," Riley said, glancing back at us.

"That would work much better," Peter told him with a wink.

"I'mo help you pack up your things," Kissie said, moving him toward the swinging door.

"Bye, Riley," I said as he headed out of the kitchen with Kissie.

Once the door shut behind them Peter thrust his arms in the air, fists clenched. "Holy, mother of—I'm worn out, Leelee. I feel like I've just run the New York Marathon."

"He's actually very dear; he just gets a little ahead of himself," I said in a hushed tone.

"That would be putting it mildly."

"Please keep your voice down," I begged. "He gets his feelings hurt easily."

Peter lowered his voice but only a tad. "A guy selling women's stuff? Cutco yes. Amway maybe, but *Tupperware*? And *Pampered Chef*? *Sheesh*." He grasped the top of his head with both hands. "And he's your next-door neighbor?" Then he moved over to the stove and silently stirred his chicken stock while I nervously knotted my hair behind my head.

"Sweet Jesus!" Kissie exclaimed once she made it back to the kitchen. "Riley done emasculated hisself, sure 'nuff."

"You've got that right," Peter called from his stockpot.

I flew to the back window, pressing my nose to the pane, to make sure his car was gone. If he'd overheard either of them I'd have died on the spot.

Kissie marched up to me. "Now you see what I mean about nipping something in the bud? I tries my best to be patient but sometimes my nerves cain't take it another red second. I swear before the good Lawd, that man gone send me to Bolivar. *For real!*" She moved over to the large sink to check for dirty pots. When she found it clean she turned around and popped her hands on her hips. "Peter, it's a good thing you made it to town. That man's had his eye on Leelee since the day we moved in over there."

I shook my head, even rolled my eyes. "No, he has not."

"Oh yes he has," Kissie retorted. Her head was shaky. "I keep telling her she's got to stop being so nice to him. It don't do nothing but encourage that man." She pursed her lips and swiped her hand through the air as if she were brushing away her frustration. "All right now, we've wasted a plenty time already. What needs to be done around here?"

"I tried your recipe for rolls," Peter said, hugging me from behind and pointing over to the cutting board. "Three times. Somehow I missed your secret." He kissed the back of my neck before he moved over to the workstation, removed the damp cloth on top of the dough, and pinched. It stretched only a few centimeters before breaking off into a dry clump.

Kissie burst out laughing, a welcome change from the irritated mood Riley had left her in. "I don't really have a secret, baby. I told you I'd be happy to be your baker."

The sound of tiny feet padding down the back stairs distracted me. Sarah jumped off the bottom step, followed by her sister, and rushed over to me with pleas for after-school snacks. After whispering that they needed to wait just a minute and not interrupt, I gathered Sarah's long brunet hair into a ponytail and rejoined the conversation.

Peter said, "I've waved the white flag and I'm taking you up on it. I don't know that I've had anything that tastes as good as your home-made yeast rolls."

"Thank you, baby. But I wouldn't exactly call my rolls gourmet. And this restaurant is *gourmet*. Why don't you tell Ole Kissie what kind of bread you want to serve and I'll work on it."

When we all appeared to be in deep thought about Kissie's sugges-tion, Sarah seized the lull in the conversation. "I thought this was sup-posed to be a French restaurant," she said. "Why don't you serve French bread?"

As usual Kissie fell over in hysterics. She bent over with hands on both knees, laughing at Sarah sounding so grown-up. She laughed till tears streamed down her face. Watching her, of course, got the rest of us going. Even Sarah and Issie.

"Sarah, how would you like a job running this joint?" Peter said. "Looks like you're the one with brains around here."

Sarah cocked her head to the side. "It's not that hard."

Anguish washed over Issie's little face, and her bottom lip poked out. She snapped her hands on her hips, spewing loudly, "I have brains." Then she burst out crying, turning into my leg. I shot Peter a slight roll of my eyes.

He bent down so his eyes were at her level. "No, Issie, I didn't mean that literally, it's just an expression. You have a great brain. I can tell." When she didn't turn around, he tapped lightly on the top of her head. "Just what I thought, a nice, big brain. Much bigger and smarter than my brain."

Finally she turned to face him with a coy grin. "Miss Nichols, she's my teacher, told me that I have a smart brain because I can read fifty words."

"Wow, that's a lot of words," Peter said sweetly. "Especially for a five-year-old."

"I can read five hundred words," Sarah added, just to be ornery.

"Me, too," said Issie.

"No, you can't," Sarah said.

"Okay, now. We ain't gone start," Kissie said. "You girls gone help Kissie make the French bread. We gone do it at home and we'll make our first batch tomorrow." At that, both jumped in the air clapping their hands, forgetting all about their cross words. "That is if somebody don't put me in the grave first," Kissie muttered under her breath, and gathered the children to leave.

Chapter Six

When Baker and I took over the reins in Vermont we opened the doors to a turnkey operation. Every plate, spoon, salt and pepper shaker, all the pots and pans, even the employees were built in and ready to go. Albeit, everything was old, worn-out, and frumpy but it was still move-in ready. In addition to old tattered furniture and hideous decor, cheap little knickknacks cluttered every inch of the place under Helga Schloygin's regime. And worse, the inn stunk to high heaven. It smelled like a mélange of musty upholstered furniture, garlic, and propane gas on top of a profusion of German body odor. All this was before I took over and went about my business de-stinking and Southernizing the place.

Starting from scratch in Memphis with a newly remodeled kitchen, a fresh paint job, and all my furnishings seemed like the difference between homemade spaghetti sauce and a can of Chef Boyardee. And this time I was determined to make sure my employees, my food, and everything else about the Peach Blossom Inn was high quality, odor free, headcheese free, and most of all free of any trace of Helga Schloygin.

With only one week to go before the party, Peter assured me that the new staff was in place and prepared to do a final run-through before we opened. We had interviewed several people for our waitstaff positions and had settled on two women and two men, each having come from local restaurants. So far a substitution for Pierre's role as maître d' had not been found but we were hopeful the right guy would appear in the near future. A trained sous chef applied for that position and it was just as Peter had said: The man graduated from culinary school but wanted the experience of working with an experienced chef before going out on his own. Gary seemed eager to learn and, most important, ready to respect Peter as head chef. The only person we had left to hire was a dishwasher. Not to worry, Peter told me, he'd take care of it.

The week before Halloween, with only two days left before our grand opening party, I was out on the front porch cleaning the ceiling fan when I noticed a car racing past the inn. The only reason I paid any attention to it at all, besides the fact that I was hoping the driver would get a speeding ticket—after all, there were children on this street— was because of the color of the vehicle. Pale pink. She's long since swept it under the rug, but for a brief time in her life Mary Jule was a Mary Kay saleslady—just for the heck of it—and the opportunity to earn a pale pink Cadillac, which, incidentally, she thought would be a complete riot to drive around town. This, of course, was long before Mary Jule fancied Lancôme or Trish McEvoy. She was newly married, fresh out of college, and after buying two thousand dollars' worth of pink inventory, she finally came to her senses and realized it was just a fad. In the end she gave it away to anyone who would take it. No one dares to bring it up around her husband, Al, because of all the money she wasted. I'll chalk it up to one of her phases. That and needle-point. She did that for a while, too, and spent hundreds of dollars on yarn. Now that yarn is in a big plastic tub in her attic right next to one marked CANNING SUPPLIES. She defends every whim by explain-ing, "Once my children are grown I'll get back to it."

I forgot all about the pink car until a few minutes later when it came barreling down *my* driveway. The gravel kicked up underneath the tires and I watched from my perch on top of the ladder as the car screeched to a stop in a cloud of driveway dust. With its darkened windows, I couldn't tell who was behind the wheel, so I climbed down the ladder, and peeked between two large boxwoods. Seconds later, the front passenger door flew open and from where I was standing I could see an unmistakable rubber boot step onto the gravel. Another foot followed and I noticed the bottom of a plaid skirt skimming the top of the ugly but very familiar Sorel snow boots. A shock of orange hair appeared just above the window, and when she shut the door and turned around, I finally got a glimpse of her face. There in my Memphis, Tennessee, driveway stood my dog's namesake, Roberta Abbott.

About that time the driver's door flung open. A large, and I mean *large,* burly man with a bushy beard and an extra-long, thick handlebar mustache stepped out wearing his red plaid woodchuck cap with earflaps. He took a long stretch before shutting his door. I nearly tripped running down the stairs. "Roberta! Jeb! What on earth are y'all doing here?" On cue, Jeb puckered his lips and whistled "Rocky Top" exactly the way he did in Vermont whenever I walked into the room.

"Did you think we'd let you open another restaurant without us?" Roberta said with a large cheery smile and arms opened wide. I melted into her large squatty frame and hugged her as if it were my last opportunity. Over her shoulder I could see the lettering on the car door, which was filthy with road grime. MARY KAY and the phone number were a bit off balance from the large self-stick letters on the door panel. Having seen the car a hundred times before, I knew the lettering on the other side—JEB'S COMPUTER WORLD. Jeb Duggar shared the car with his mother, Doris, the only Mary Kay saleslady in Willingham, Vermont, population 350.

"I hear you've gut a brand-new Hobart. I couldn't let just anyone break her in," Jeb said, referring to my commercial dishwashing appliance. No one on earth took more pride in its operation, and he knew the one in Vermont inside and out. Jeb was not only my dishwasher when I lived there, but also my handyman, chimney-sweeper, snowplow driveway person, roof-raker, and performer of any other odd job one could possibly imagine. He claimed all this to be his "side work." His "main job," as he liked to call it, was "proprietor of Jeb's Computer World."

"How did you know we needed a dishwasher?" I turned to Jeb and hugged him almost as tightly as I had Roberta.

"That guy reet there called and said it wouldn't be the same without us. We're your early Thanksgiving presents."

I looked back at the porch to find Peter walking slowly in our direction. He hugged Roberta first then vigorously shook Jeb's hand. "Welcome to Memphis, you guys. It sure is nice to have a couple more damn Yankees down here."

I looked them both square in the face. "Are y'all moving here?" I highly doubted it but figured I might as well ask.

"Nuup. Can't move," Roberta said. "Moe's waiting on me back home. Stick season's over in six weeks and I'll have to get back to work up at Sugartree when the ski lifts start cranking again."

In Vermont, leaf season is followed by stick season. It's the period just past October when the sky takes on a monochromatic color and all the leaves have fallen off the trees. The entire state looks like a black-and-white postcard if you ask me. The worst part of stick season is that no one has work, causing a mad dash to the unemployment line.

"But when Peter called for help getting the place up and running, I couldn't turn him down," Roberta said.

"Thank you." I hugged her again.

"You're welcome," she said with a bow. "This is quite an adventure. We've never traveled past New Hampshire." When she smiled I couldn't tell if she was looking at Peter or me. Her right eye wanders way off to the side.

"Speak for yourself, *Roberta*," Jeb said. "*I've* been down-country. Drove all the way to Windsor, Connecticut, to buy my truck. But it was worth it considering the deal I got. I talked that guy down five hundred dollars." He puffed out his chest and twirled his mustache, two of the many Jeb Duggar trademarks. Considering what a penny-pincher Jeb is, no wonder he's still gloating over that deal.

"How was your drive down? Any problems?" Peter asked.

"Aside from some weather in Pennsylvania, it was pretty darn good," Jeb told us. When he caught sight of Roberta he rolled his eyes. "Hold on, I take that back. There was a problem." He cleared his throat. "We spent the night in Virginia last night and Mrs. Freight Train over there was so noisy, she could have woke the living dead. I couldn't sleep a wink. Finally, at three A.M., I had to go out for earplugs."

"What are you talking about?" Roberta snapped, leaning forward with hands on her hips and wide eyes. "You're the one who snored. It took me over an hour to get to sleep in the first place."

I promptly changed the subject, remembering how those two could go at it without warning. "What do y'all think about the outside of the place? Isn't it gorgeous?" I pointed at the gingerbread outlining the eave of the roof.

"I'll say," Roberta said. "And that Peach Blossom Inn sign sure looks nice near the road. Thank goodness you saved it from the trash pile. Helga was ready to burn it."

Helga's ghastly image sprang to mind. Gray hair slicked back off her protruding forehead, pulled into a tight bun—so tight, her temples must have stayed sore. Six foot tall, large framed, and big boned, with a perpetual un-flicked Pall Mall dangling from the side of her lips. Navy blue spectator pumps on size 12 feet underneath navy slacks and a white button-down—her uniform, seven days a week. "Gross," I said with a sigh, puckering my mouth like I'd been sucking a lemon. "I haven't thought of that woman in weeks."

"Apparently not many other folks have either," Jeb said. "Karma. That's what's happening to her. Not much business over at the Peach Blossom Inn these days. I hear she's thinking of changing it back to the Vermont Haus Inn."

"Well, good for her. The Peach Blossom Inn is my baby anyway," I said.

"You tell 'em, boss!" Peter elbowed my shoulder and shot me a deliberate wink. One of his slow, ultra-sexy winks.

"I hope she does," I said. "Those hippos would be much happier." Helga had an obsession over her ceramic hippo collection, her children really, which is something I'll never get over. I once tried packing them away when I first took over, but she had a fit and placed them back in "their home" on the mantel in the main dining room. The night I fired her—and yes, I actually fired her—I told her to take her hippos and never step a toe anywhere near my property again. Well, actually that's a bit of an exaggeration but I did fire her all the same.

"Yuup, they're reet back on the mantel. Exactly where they always were," Roberta said.

"She called me to paint the place back the way it was before Alice and them helped you pick out that nice peach color on the inside," Jeb said. "I hated to rip down that wallpaper the girls brought up from Memphis. It took me three days just to get it off the walls." Alice, Mary Jule, and Virginia had come to save me from Helga's wrath and surprised me with my favorite wallpaper from home to Southernize the place. Jeb slaved for hours over the installation, and considering his proclivity for laziness, I bet all that extra work for Helga nearly killed him. "Speaking of them girls, Alice told me she'd hire me to be her houseboy if I ever made it down this way. I'll be looking for extra work while I'm here." Alice did tell him that, but of course she was fooling. I doubt she'd have ever considered it becoming an actuality. I had to laugh imagining Alice's shrill scream if Jeb rung the doorbell to her Southern Colonial.

Rather than go there I switched the subject again. "So are *you* moving to Tennessee? What about JCW?" Jeb, like all the Northerners I knew, shortened everything. JCW was his aka for Jeb's Computer World.

"You'll find this hard to believe but JCW is struggling a bit. Haven't sold many computers lately." The reason for that is a toss-up between the low inventory and the quality of his showroom. Jeb has one lone computer that he uses for a display and it takes two to three weeks to order in another. Jeb's Computer *World* is housed inside a tiny lean-to in his mama's backyard. When the girls came up to visit he gave us a tour of the place—all one hundred square feet of it. Alice took pictures and gets them out on occasion just to prove that it actually exists. Jeb shoved his hands deep into the front pockets of his jeans. "So I'm keepin' my options open while I'm down here."

"That's smart," I said, wondering how in the world he would find enough work in Memphis. "Keeping your options open is good."

"I'm hoping to do some chimney-sweepin' while I'm here."

"That might be a possibility," I said.

"I'm no longer the handyman at the inn, so my cash flow is down."

"Why aren't you the handyman anymore?" With the three o'clock sun in my eyes I had to squint to see his face.

"I told you. Karma. No one wants to work for Helga after what she done to you. Deliberately splitting up you and Baker was wrong. Word's out."

"I have no doubt about that. Nothing's private in Willingham, Vermont. Hey, let's get out of this cold," I said, shivering. The whole time we'd been talking I'd been hugging myself and rubbing my arms in an effort to keep warm. "I can't wait to show you the inside."

"Cold? This ain't cold. Feels like spring to me," Roberta said. "It can't be any less than fifty-five degrees."

"See what a lightweight she is?" Peter said.

"Gee, girl, how did you ever make it up in Vermont?" Jeb asked.

"Phooey on all of you." I hooked my arms through both of theirs, one on each side, and led them up the front porch steps.

"Hang on a minute," Peter called from behind. The three of us turned around abruptly. "Aren't we missing someone?"

"Oh my stars, I forgot all about him." Roberta let go of my arm and scooted herself back down the stairs, talking over her shoulder. "He finally fell asleep an hour or so ago and we didn't have the heart to wake him." She ran over to Jeb's pink Chevette and opened the back door. I watched Roberta's body disappear as she leaned into the backseat.

Moments later she reappeared along with the head of one of my favorite people in the whole world. His black hair stuck out every which-a-way, but his familiar face brought a big smile to mine. Flying off the steps, I bounded over to the car, nearly banging into Peter on my way.

As Pierre stepped out into the fresh air, I hugged him like Issie would her most beloved stuffed animal.

"*Bonjour, Leelee,*" he said, frantically combing his fingers through his hair. "*Bonjour.*"

"Como talle vous?" I answered, happy to have all four of my Vermont comrades standing in my Tennessee front yard.

"*Très bien.*" The afternoon sun illuminated his hair. It was a bright, shiny shade of black with a magenta hue, thanks to Lady Clairol. Pierre did it himself. Between his shiny dark shock, his widow's peak, and the tux he wore each night in the restaurant, he looked a little like Count Dracula, bless his heart. But many an older woman found him very handsome and when I studied his facial features—soft dark eyes, full lips, and a long thin nose—I could understand why.

"Are *you* still working for Helga?"

Like I said, Pierre didn't speak much English, much less Southern English. He understood that question well enough, though, because he responded, "No Helga," and frantically crisscrossed his hands in front of him. I turned to Jeb and Roberta, knowing a conversation with him would be futile. "What happened? Did he get fired?"

"Nuup," Jeb said. "He decided right after leaf season to quit. He's done with Helga. He said it wasn't the same after you left."

"Awww, that's so sweet." I looked over at Pierre and blew him a kiss, at which he took my hand and kissed the top.

"*Les petites filles?*" Pierre asked, referring to Sarah and Issie. That I knew.

"They're at home. I'll go get them in a minute." I drew an air drawing of the outside of a house with a roof and a door and windows, even a chimney, and pointed down the street. All our conversations eventually turned into a game of charades.

When we all headed back up the stairs, Jeb reached out and turned the bell all the way around, releasing a full-on, headache-inducing shrill. *I might just have to put tape over that thing,* I thought. After stepping inside and into the foyer, I noticed tears in the corners of Roberta's gray eyes.

"Why are you crying?" I asked, taking her hand.

"I'm happy for yous, that's all." She glanced around from one side of the house to the other. "This place is a beauty, just the way I pictured it. I knew you could do it, missy."

Roberta is so kind. I was honest when I said she was my closest friend in Vermont. I wrapped my arm around her shoulder and squeezed. "Aww, thank you. You're so sweet, Roberta. I can't wait to show you the rest of the house."

After a complete tour of the upstairs, and the downstairs, we made it to the kitchen: the place we always gathered back in Vermont. When I eyed the three of them it was hard to believe they were actually standing next to me. I thought I'd have to travel to New England to ever see them again. Jeb headed straight over to the Hobart, lifted the door, and removed the dish rack. A long, slow whistle escaped his lips, denoting his approval. "Can I give her a whirl?"

Roberta said, "Can't you see there aren't any dirty dishes in the sink?"

"Oh, go ahead," Peter told him. "After driving all this way, if it makes you happy, have at it."

Jeb slid the dish rack back into the cabinet of the Hobart, lowered the door, and pressed down the large arm on the side, firing up the machine. "Woo-hoo! That's quite an improvement," he said once it started. "Seems like this girl's twice as fast. How long does she take to cycle?" He glanced in my direction.

I wanted to say, Jeb, honey, do you honestly think I've timed the dishwashing cycle? But, knowing how much he loved a Hobart, I just said, "I'm not sure."

"She's a beaut!"

"I'm gald you like it," I said. "But all I'm thinking about right now is our grand opening party, day after tomorrow."

"It looks like we've gut a lot to do around here before it starts," Roberta said, glancing back to the dining room. "Need to get all the tables set, for starters." The swinging door between the kitchen and the front dining room was open and she walked through, knocking the top of one of the tables. I watched as she tugged at her panties. She started wearing thong underwear for her husband, Moe, despite the fact that her rear end is a little on the heavy side. Roberta was never shy when it came to personal details—her lingerie choices had been the very tamest of some of the information I learned when with Roberta.

"No no no," Pierre said, pointing to himself. Pierre took great pride in the way he set the tables. And the way he folded his linen napkins—now, that was an art form. One day it might be roses and the next day I'd find pyramids atop our dinnerware. His fleurs-de-lis nestled inside our water goblets were magnificent and his birds of paradise should have won him an award.

"Calm down, mister, just trying to help," Roberta told him. "Say, when does the restaurant open officially?"

"Tuesday night," Peter said. "And you're right, there's plenty to do around here. Come on, you guys," he said, moving toward the front door. "I'll help you get your things out of the car." He put his hand on the door-knob and turned around. "Jeb, you and Pierre can bunk up together and Roberta can have the other bedroom to herself."

"I'll call Kissie and ask her to drive over with the girls," I said. "They'll be so surprised to see y'all." I wondered if Peter had already told Kissie. If he had, she was even better about keeping secrets than I thought.

Chapter Seven

My insides felt like they were speeding around a NASCAR racetrack as I drove the three miles from my house to the inn. The more I thought about our grand opening party, the more my stomach jangled and flipped from one end to the other. From the way my heart pummeled against my chest it felt like it had taken on a life of its own and might jump out and drive the car for me. I willed myself to practice my deep breathing, an anti-anxiety technique suggested by my therapist. Frances Folk had just about saved my life over the last few months and tonight I was eager to put all of her advice into action. I was determined to show her that I had grown. After hours of encouraging me to open another Peach Blossom Inn she would be thrilled to hear all about the party, which would be commencing in only three hours.

When I walked in the back door of the restaurant I had my brand-new grand opening party dress in one hand, my brand-new gold strappy sandals entwined through my fingers in the other, and my blue-and-white Vera Bradley weekender holding my makeup, blow-dryer, perfume, and various other must-haves slung over my shoulder. My entire staff was flying around the kitchen like worker bees on a mission. Only this hive had a king on the throne, and he stood majestically in front of the commercial stove with his face over a large honey pot of chowder, sniffing the sweet corn aroma.

"How's it going, everybody?" I asked with an excited nervousness detectable in my voice.

Roberta, who had her hands in the sink, looked up and grinned. "It's goin' great here, missy. How are you? Nervous?"

"You know me, Roberta. I'm plenty nervous. I so want the night to go smoothly."

Peter, who had moved over to his cutting board and was now slicing fillets from tenderloin, never turned around but said, "Hey, boss. You said you were going to trust me. Practice your deep breathing, why don't you?"

"I have been. The whole way here."

All four members of my new waitstaff were dressed in black pants with white shirts and black neckties. Pierre was busy instructing them on the proper ways to open, pour, and serve wine. He had the grand distinction of Master Sommelier, proudly displaying the MS beside his name on his tux jacket, and donned the tastevin from a chain around his neck. Originally the small silver cups were designed to be used by the winemakers when judging the maturity and taste of a wine when in dim light. These days a few sommeliers still use them as a nod to the tradition. Peter and I often laughed about it and felt that on anyone else it would seem presumptuous but on Pierre, endearing.

"Hello, everybody," I said, poking my head into the circle they had formed around our head waiter. "Don't stop what you're doing, I just wanted to say hi." Each greeted me with a cheery hello but went right back to Pierre's impromptu wine stewardship lesson.

"Did you remember to pick up my coat?" Peter called from the stove.

I had picked up his chef's coat from the cleaners but had accidentally left it in the backseat. "It's in the car. Let me put the rest of my stuff upstairs and I'll get it in a minute."

"By the way," he said. "You have a surprise on the table in the foyer."

"A surprise?" I asked.

"A big surprise!" Roberta exclaimed with water trickling down her outstretched arms.

"Really? I can't wait." Sliding my purse off my shoulder, I plopped it onto the desk, laid my dress and the weekender on top of it, and hustled toward the front of the restaurant. As I rounded the corner the sweet fragrance of gardenia hit my nostrils. Right on top of the round table in the middle of the foyer sat a large vase with the biggest, most beautiful flower arrangement I think I'd ever seen. *That Peter is the sweetest thing,* I thought as I sniffed my way over. The first thing I noticed was that my favorite flower, gardenia (they were in my bridal bouquet), spread among an arrangement of every other white flower imaginable. I circled the table counting each variety: daylilies, roses, calla lilies, French tulips, iris, daisies, and hydrangeas.

The card, poking out of the center of the bouquet, had *Leelee* written in cursive. Before opening it I basked for a moment in the joy that my boyfriend had not only taken the time to send me my favorite flowers but had also had them sent from Rachel's, my favorite florist. Finally I ripped open the envelope and read the inscription inside:

> *Leelee,*
> *I am so proud of you.*
> *Good luck tonight!*
> *All My Love*

I closed my eyes and felt the elation ripple through me. *It doesn't get much better than this,* I thought, eager to wrap my arms around Peter and show him my appreciation. When I placed the card back inside the envelope, I wondered why he'd left off his name. *Oh well, the florist must have made a mistake,* I thought, tucking it inside the back pocket of my jeans. I headed to the kitchen, eager to have him sign the card in his own handwriting.

Roberta winked at me from the front of the sink when I pushed back through the swinging door. She was peeling an extra-large potato. "Them are some beautiful flowers you've gut there, missy."

"I know," I said, beaming at Peter, whose back was to me as he continued slicing at his cutting board. I snuck up behind him and wrapped my arms tightly around his waist. "*You* are the sweetest thing in this whole world." I kissed his back, breathing in the faint odor of Tide on his T-shirt. "They are the most beautiful flowers I've ever seen. I love them." I squeezed his stomach before adding, "You forgot to sign the card, silly."

Without turning around or stopping what he was doing for even a second he said, "I wish I could take the credit but they aren't from me. I've been so busy trying to throw this party together."

Quite puzzled but determined to hide my disappointment, I gently squeezed him again. "No worries, I understand," I said. "They must be from my girlfriends. And speaking of, they should be here any minute now."

"This ought to be good. What've you got them doing?"

Without moving my arms from his waist, I twisted around one side of him and caught him grinning. "Oh, anything that pops up. Mostly they'll be goodwill ambassadors, flitting around promoting the restaurant." As an afterthought I added, "And putting out fires."

"What makes you think we'll have a fire?"

"My unwanted party guest? *Shirley Greene?*"

"Old Shirley. How could I forget her?" He swiveled around and pecked my lips.

"A brain freeze I suppose." I patted his arm. "I guess I better head upstairs. I need to look my absolute best. Wouldn't want to add any more fuel to that bonfire," I said.

As my hand slipped from his waist he asked, "What did the card say?"

"What card?"

"The one on your flowers."

"Oh, that card. I don't remember every word but something about being proud of me and good luck tonight."

He paused. "You've got thoughtful friends."

Hearing his words made me smile. "I sure do."

"I can't wait to see them again," Jeb hollered from the big sink, obviously listening to our every word. "I wonder when Alice will want me to start over at her house."

I opened my mouth to say something reassuring, but remembered my new promise when it came to little white lies. Alice could just as easily get herself out of the mess she'd created.

Before going upstairs, I snuck another look at the flowers and re-read the card. I realized it must have come from one person only because of the wording. "*I am so proud of you.*" There was a possibility that it could have come from one of my best friends but it seemed more likely that they would have all gone in together. That's how we did everything else. I dialed Alice's number in a hurry, starting right in when she answered, "Did y'all send me these gorgeous flowers?"

"Thank God they made it on time. We only did it this morning."

"I'm looking at them right now and they are *gorgeous.*" I bent down and inhaled one of the gardenia blooms.

"Le Fleur always does a great job. Mama says they're the only florist in town."

I remembered Alice's mother persuading me to use Le Fleur for my wedding but Daddy insisting we use Rachel's. He had ordered all Mama's and Grandmama's flowers and corsages from Rachel's as far back as I could remember. Besides, Mama always said they had "the most stunning roses in town."

"Hmm," I said curiously. "I love Le Fleur, too, but these are from Rachel's."

"Really?" Alice said. "Virginia took care of it. Maybe she used Rachel's."

"Wherever they're from, thank you so much. They are stunning." I started to tell her that I had to go but added, "Virginia forgot to sign your names."

"Huh. That's weird." Alice paused for a moment. "Oh well. Let me go. I've got to get takeout for the kids before the babysitter arrives."

"What time are y'all coming?" I leaned over and breathed in another whiff of gardenia.

"When do you need us?"

"Now." I giggled. "Just kidding—well, kind of kidding. Keep it like we planned. An hour or so before to help with last-minute details."

"It starts at seven, right?"

"Right."

"See you at six. I'll call Jule and Virginia and make sure they'll be ready. Mary Jule's driving."

"Isn't Richard coming?"

"He wouldn't miss it. But he's coming straight from the office, like the rest of our guys."

"Oh, Alice, I almost forgot. Jeb can't wait to see you. He's ready to be your houseboy."

"My what?" By the tone in her voice, I could tell she hadn't remembered a thing.

"Remember when you were in Vermont and you told him he could be your houseboy if he ever came down to Memphis?"

"Uh. Sort of."

"Well, he's taking you up on it. You better come up with a good excuse to not hire him."

"Thanks for warning me. Can't you just see Richard now when I tell him *Jayeb* is gonna be our new houseboy." My friends started calling Jeb "Jayeb" soon after meeting him, to overemphasize their Southern accents and all.

"To tell you the truth I wish I could. Gotta go. See you soon."

When another flower delivery truck from Le Fleur showed up minutes later with an equally beautiful bouquet of flowers, I was flabbergasted. Jeb answered the door and marched into the kitchen holding a bouquet that was as big as him. I heard his whistling, a bad version of "Tiptoe Through the Tulips," I think it was, and I had to suppress a laugh. Pierre—who, if truth be told, gets terribly irritated by Jeb's whistling—shook his head and rolled his eyes. Roberta looked up from her workstation and said, "This place is startin' to look like a flower shop," while Gary, our quiet new sous chef, simply smiled.

Peter glanced over his shoulder from where he stood in front of his cutting board. "Wow, boss, I'm starting to look bad."

"You are not," I retorted.

"Hold on a minute," Peter said, marching toward me. "I have something for you, too. I was going to wait till you were dressed but I've changed my mind. Put the flowers down over there, Tiny Tim," he said to Jeb, pointing to my desk. He flew up the back stairs, returning in less than a minute. I was about to reach for the card on my new bouquet when he took me by the hand and led me into the front dining room, stopping right in front of the fire that Jeb had already lit. He pulled out a square velvet box from underneath his T-shirt and handed it to me. *Had he actually bought me jewelry?* I thought, as I stared gleefully at the treasure in my hand. A wave of excitement fluttered through me as I slowly opened the box. Looped around an ivory satin lining was a lovely pearl necklace.

"It's so so beautiful," I said, meeting his eyes. I felt my face flush. I fingered the necklace with its clusters of baroque, peach-colored freshwater pearls separated by an interwoven copper wire. "Much more so than those old flowers. Thank you."

"A beautiful necklace for a beautiful girl."

I dropped my head, shaking away his compliment.

He lifted my chin so I could read the sincerity in his eyes. "Why don't you like for me to call you beautiful?"

"I'm not sure," I said, thinking about Mama, about Baker—all the reasons I didn't believe I was beautiful.

"Not only do I think every inch of your outside is pretty," he tapped lightly on my heart, "*that* makes you even more lovely and irresistible." He lifted the necklace out of the lining and placed the box on top of the mantel. Turning me around, he said, "Hold up your hair, beautiful girl." At first he struggled with the clasp but after several attempts he fastened it. I reached up to touch it, curious about its position on my neck. Peter asked me to turn around and smiled as he studied the necklace hanging just below my clavicle. "Go to the mirror and take a peek."

I moved swiftly toward the bathroom but paused instead in front of the large gold leaf mantel mirror hanging in the opposite dining room. Once I realized it was taller than me, I changed directions and headed on inside the powder room. When I first eyed the necklace, a troupe of butterflies waltzed happily inside my stomach and I smiled at myself in the mirror. Peter slipped in behind me, kissing my neck just atop the necklace. With his foot, he closed the door behind him, his arms slipping around my waist. "You are so precious to me, Leelee Satterfield."

I drifted back to the day I first saw him standing in front of the fireplace at my inn in Vermont. I'd been so nervous in his presence, even from the beginning. Everything he said that day made me swoon but I hadn't realized it at the time. Seven long months later we finally had our first kiss underneath the falling snow on the very day I was headed out of town for good. And then there was the day I thought I was going to interview one of Mary Jule's husband's roommates from the University of Georgia but instead it turned out to be Peter. I never thought I'd see him again until he showed up unannounced, and now here he was kissing my neck and whispering that I was precious.

Looking at the reflection of my own eyes in the mirror, I saw that no one else could ever understand how I felt. I was the most content I'd ever been. For so many years, I had loved Baker and thought that our relationship was ideal. But looking back I realize he was always concerned about his own feelings, his own wants and desires, and my happiness always took the backseat. Now standing here with Peter it was clear what being someone else's priority was really like.

He leaned against the bathroom door and I fell into him. When he kissed me I could feel the cares of the world melting, his gentle tongue wiping away all the stress I had felt leading up to this day, his lips a barrier from the firestorm I had imagined. I reached up and ran my hands through his silky hair, pulling him in closer. At that moment, I couldn't have cared less if the launch party went on or not. I only wanted him. And I wanted him desperately.

Loud footsteps startled us. We paused together, faces still close. They grew louder as the person approached the bathroom door. Then there was quiet again. I pulled away.

"Yeah," Peter uttered sharply after a few seconds.

"Leelee's gut another bouquet of flowers," Jeb said, knocking on the door. "And this one's nicer than the others."

I whispered in his ear. "And to think I had forgotten about the lack of privacy in the restaurant business. It's only the beginning." I fell into his chest.

"Just put them with the others," Peter called through the door.

"Is she in there with you?"

"Why do you ask?" We laughed while turning into each other's necks to muffle the sound.

"I just thought she'd want to know."

"I'll let her know."

I whispered again. "What have we gotten ourselves into?"

"I don't know but I better get back to the kitchen if we want this party to run smoothly," he whispered back, patting my butt. "We'll continue this later."

"I'm counting on it," I said as he opened the door. We both glanced at the new bouquet of flowers on the round center table. "Wow," was all Peter said before telling Jeb, "Back to work," and the two of them headed toward the kitchen.

When I opened the new card, it was from Kissie and my two little girls. As happy as that made me, I thought, *Kissie does not have that kind of money.* Their card read: *We love you and are so proud of you.* And it was signed, *Kissie, Sarah, and Isabella.*

So the arrangement in the kitchen must be from my girlfriends, I thought. Stealing back to the kitchen, I grabbed the bouquet, as well as my wardrobe, and headed to the front of the house before anyone had a chance to notice. After setting the new arrangement down in the middle of the large food table in the dining room, I peeked at that card.

> *You'll be the Belle of the ball!*
> *Congratulations and good luck tonight.*
> *We love you,*
>
> > *Virginia, Mary Jule, and Alice*

I slowly folded the card and placed it back in the envelope. Confusion rippled through every part of me. *Who in the world sent me that first bouquet?*

Chapter Eight

"Where's Jayeb?" Virgina yelled, her shrill voice wafting up from the foyer. "I want to see *Jayeb!*"

As soon as I heard her voice I scurried out of the bathroom to the stairwell, leaning over the railing with a finger to my lips. "Shhh. He's in the kitchen. But don't go in there without me. I want to witness y'all's reunion."

"Then hurry up." She looked at her watch. "This party starts in an hour and fifteen minutes."

"I know. Just let me put my shoes on," I said while scurrying back toward the bathroom. I was almost ready, save my lipstick, so I grabbed that on my way out and slipped into my strappy, gold sandals. Sneaking one last peek in the mirror behind the door, I knew I was thrilled with my brand-new dress. I'd been tempted to wear one of Mama's vintage gowns, but opted for a "darling number," as Mama often said, that Mary Jule found in the Nordstrom catalog. It was a fitted sage green sleeveless silk, scoop-necked with a tiny border of ecru lace stitched into the neckline. The lace crisscrossed under the bust, and the dress hit just above my knees. I even wore a smoky green eye shadow to match, something I rarely make time for, and two gold hoop earrings to go with my luscious gold sandals. The outfit was a splurge—oh my, was it a splurge—but opening night of the Peach Blossom Inn Memphis was certainly worth every penny. I chalked it up to a business expense and entered my account number on the Nordstrom Web site as fast as my fingers could type.

As I descended the staircase, coloring my lips on the way down, the bell on the front door rang two long rings. "Will you let Riley in, please?" I said to Virgy, who looked darling herself in a short black cocktail dress. Virginia's shapely legs are one of her best assets.

"How do you know it's him?" Her blond, highlighted hair looked fabulous, too, pulled straight back with a fancy black barrette.

"Trust me. It's him," I said, using extra caution while descending the steps in my four-inch heels.

She turned around and flung open the door. "What's happening, Riley? Don't you look nice."

Bless his heart, he had on black pants and a white shirt, just as I had requested—but his extra-large I SELL TUPPERWARE button screamed from the front of his shirt pocket. On his head sat his Pampered Chef chef's hat. If I didn't know better, I'd swear he had ironed it. I took a deep breath and paused during my descent as I pondered how in the world I would tell him to take both off that instant. "You remember Virginia, don't you, Riley?"

"Of course I wemember Virginia. We danced together in your fwont yard to 'Twist and Shout.'"

"I'd forgotten all about that," I said, shaking my head at my crazy best friend.

Virgina broke into the Twist right then and there. It never mattered if there was music or not when Virgy got the urge. "Riley and I are gonna cut a rug later after the party." Virginia is the clown in our group. Wild, outrageous comments often ooze from her lips.

"You bet!" Riley exclaimed as he awkwardly tried to copy Virginia, shimmying down to the floor along with her. But the poor thing lost his balance and toppled over on his rear end, splaying his feet out in front of him. His face flushed a deep crimson red.

Not wanting to embarrass him any more than he already was, I said, "Your bar is right over there," and pointed to the eight-foot table set up catty-corner in the left dining room. Pierre had set the wine and champagne glasses on one end and ice buckets filled with champagne and chardonnay on the other. In the middle were two corkscrews, red wine bottles, and cocktail napkins. "Do you know how to open a wine bottle?" I asked. "If not, I can have my maître d' do it."

He pulled himself back up and put his hand beside his mouth. "This is no pwoblem, no pwoblem at all. I know all about wine. When I host my Pampa'ed Chef pawties, the ladies like to indulge. I always volunteer to be the bawtender."

"How about this daiquiri maker?" I walked behind the table to show Riley the machine I'd rented from the restaurant supply company, and pointed to the cooler filled with ice and our secret heirloom peach recipe. Serving our house specialty, peach daiquiris, was an absolute must for our grand opening.

"I've got it all under contwol," he said.

"I'd like each daiquiri garnished with a mint sprig," I told him, pointing to a glass filled with mint.

"No pwoblem." When Riley rearranged the glasses and wine bottles, I started to object. I caught myself though, opting to save myself the hassle. If that made him feel useful, then that was fine by me. The only reason I had asked Riley to bartend in the first place is because he must have come over at least five times asking how he could help. There wasn't a little white lie out there that could have gotten me out of it, so I went ahead and gave him the temporary bartender job. As hard as I tried, I couldn't come up with anything else for him to do and Peter flat refused to have him anywhere near the kitchen. It was either that or valet parking. In the end I decided to hire a professional valet company. It wasn't that expensive and the thought of Riley behind some of those fancy foreign cars scared me to death. I'd rather let someone else assume the liability.

Virginia poured a chardonnay from an uncorked bottle in the bucket. "Here, you need this," she said, handing me the glass.

"Maybe you're right." I took several sips before setting it back down on the table.

Virginia poured herself one, too, and looked over at me for a hint as to whether or not she should pour one for Riley. I knew what she was asking even though a single word never left her lips. I slyly shook my head no.

Then, completely out of the blue Riley asked, "Who's the wuby?"

Virginia and I turned our heads simultaneously. "The wuby?" we both said at the same time.

"No, the wuby, with an *arrr*. Who owns the Mawy Kay car?"

"Oh, the ruby," I said, vaguely remembering Mary Jule talking about Mary Kay salesladies earning the names of precious stones as they rose the corporate ladder. "The car belongs to Jeb, my handyman from Vermont. It's not really *his* Mary Kay car, though. Actually it is his but he shares it with his mother, who works for Mary Kay."

Riley looked confused.

"Never mind," I said as the front door swung open. "It's terribly confusing." Alice and Mary Jule appeared in the foyer, decked out in beautiful dresses and fancy heels. Mary Jule's dress was brand-new. I could tell immediately.

"Hey," Virginia and I both said, moving over to join them.

"Did you buy that for my party?" I asked Mary Jule, grabbing her hand and admiring her adorable new blue halter dress with the A-line swing skirt. "You look just like Marilyn Monroe." Mary Jule, hands down, is the best dressed of us all. Fortunately for her, she has a husband who not only can afford her habit, but encourages it. He wants his wife to look like a fashion statement every time she leaves the house.

"Happiest moment of my week was when you told me we were having a grand opening party. I went right out and found it." She swung around in a circle and the dress danced with her. The best part of that last comment from Mary Jule was the "we." I loved the fact that my friends took ownership in the Peach Blossom Inn.

"Where did you get it?" Virginia wanted to know.

"The Pink Door," Mary Jule told her.

"It's unbelievable," I said, taking a step back to look at it once more.

"How about mine?" Alice asked, pivoting around for us to see the back of her black silk sheath. Tiny covered buttons dotted the first half of the dress, hiding the zipper. Her straight blond, shoulder-length hair provided a lovely contrast to the ebony material.

"Fabulous," I said. "Is yours new?"

"New to me. I robbed Mary Jule's closet. She only wore it once."

"If I had known that, I'd have shopped there, too," I said with a laugh.

"Richard put me on a budget," Alice said. "No more new clothes. At least until Christmas." The first thing Alice did was stroll around checking out all the flowers. She reached for the card on Kissie's bouquet, asking, "Which one is from us?"

"That one," I said, pointing to their bouquet in the center of the food table.

She moved over to get a closer look and took a big whiff of the pink lilies. Turning the vase around in a different direction, she took a step back. "Much better."

"Who is that one from?" Mary Jule asked, eyeballing the bouquet on the table in the foyer. "It's *stunning*."

"That's the one I was telling Alice about. It doesn't have a signature."

She walked over to get a better look. "Maybe they're from Liam White," she said, raising an eyebrow. Mary Jule was referring to the rock star who had invited me to spend a weekend in New York City, five months prior, during my brief tenure at the local radio station.

"You have got to be kidding me," I said. "After I left him staring into his hundred-dollar glass of wine? I doubt it."

"You're right. He's much too arrogant," Mary Jule agreed.

Virginia pointed into her palm in the direction of Riley, raising her own eyebrows.

I shook my head rapidly from side to side. "Ab-so-lute-ly not."

"Maybe it's Ben Sanderson," Mary Jule said with her eyes ablaze, referring to the first boy I ever kissed.

I rolled my eyes. "Very funny."

"Well, whoever it is thinks you hung the moon," Alice quipped. "These are very expensive, much more so than ours. Or Kissie's."

"If I call Rachel's, will they tell me who they're from?" I asked.

"Not if the person asked to remain anonymous," Mary Jule said. "This is so exciting, Leelee. Who would send you an anonymous bouquet of flowers?"

"The real question is: Who would *want* to remain anonymous?" I asked, growing more and more perplexed.

"Okay, enough of this, I'm headed to see Jayeb," Virginia said, and blasted into the kitchen with the rest of us trailing behind. As soon as she spotted him with his apron wrapped around his big middle, she screamed "JAYEB" at the top of her lungs, causing everyone in the kitchen to stop and stare at her. The girls had become quite friendly with Jeb while they were in Vermont. So friendly that they escorted him to the Moosehead, the local pub, in his Mary Kay car, and the four of them stayed out till one in the morning while I stayed home with my daughters.

When Jeb saw them, he suddenly became shy. The poor thing had never had a girlfriend in all his thirty-six years, and to have Virginia acting thrilled to see him must have scared him to death. "Hi, girls," he said sheepishly. "Good to see yous."

Virgy slapped him teasingly on the back. "It's about time you made it down to Tennessee, you damn Yankee! I'm living for another spin in your JCW car. When are you picking me up?" That Virginia. There was no stopping her.

"Why, sure," he said, a slight smile forming on his lips. When Alice and Mary Jule swooned over him and told him they were glad to see him, too, he came blasting out of his shell. "What do you say we all go out tonight after the party? Peter told me about a place called the Bobcat Bar and Grill not five miles from here. Sounds like a good time to me."

"Hold on there, Bobcat," Peter called from behind the line. "Let's get through tonight first. There will be plenty of time for going out later."

Loud boot steps clambered down the back kitchen stairs. When Roberta stepped off the bottom and saw my friends, she hollered, "Cat's granny!" and held out her arms. All three left Jeb and waltzed toward her with a warm Tennessee welcome.

Jeb grumbled under his breath, something about doing what he pleased, and dug into the deep chrome sink to wash one of the big pots stacked up on the side.

"Cat's granny?" Virginia said. "What in the world does that mean?"

"It means I'm surprised to see yous," she said.

Pierre suddenly swung through the dining room door and had the same reaction when he saw the girls, especially Mary Jule. They had bonded in Vermont. Mary Jule speaks fluent French. In fact, she was the one who overheard Helga bragging to Pierre in French that she had introduced Baker to his soon-to-be mistress. Otherwise, we would never have known how they met. I could tell how happy he was to see her, and most likely relieved to be able to speak in his native tongue and be understood.

After they had exchanged hellos, he bent down on one knee, giving each a hand-kiss. Naturally he gazed at Alice, the beauty of our group. Her long blond hair has never needed coloring, and she's tall with a perfect figure. Her beauty never goes unnoticed by any man, particularly Pierre. He's a thirty-something trapped in the body of a sixty-something. I have a feeling his French genes fuel his love of blondes, especially blondes in little black cocktail dresses. "You look so nice, Pierre," Alice replied once he had swooned over all of them. His black tux had just come out of a cleaner's bag and the collar on his white starched shirt looked like it might cut his neck. "*Merci,*" he said, and gave Alice a kiss on each cheek.

"Forty-five minutes and counting," Peter announced. "Time to get focused. We need the food to be set and ready on the tables ten minutes before the guests arrive. Leelee, you take care of the last-minute front-of-house details and I've got everything back here."

"Got it, boss," I said with a wink, and gathered my friends to head back to the dining room.

When the piano player that I had hired finally arrived, fifteen minutes late, I breathed a sigh of relief. I had thought it would be a classy touch to entertain my guests with Broadway show tunes with a few classics thrown in between. But when I learned he was also a jazz pianist, I changed my mind. I decided to throw out the classics and turn the Peach Blossom Inn into a classy jazz piano bar for the night, remindful of the Carlyle in New York City.

Right before the party started, Peter walked out to the front of the house, perusing the room for any last-minute details that may have been overlooked. I had just come down the stairs after applying one final coat of lipstick and checking my hair in the mirror. He didn't notice me but I stood at the bottom of the stairs watching, and drooling—at him—as he admired the food table. His fillet bites, temperature-cooked to medium, were on one end with béarnaise and au poivre sauces in dipping bowls next to the platter. His shrimp dijonnaise was set on the other end next to bite-size pieces of pork drizzled with apricot sauce. A grilled vegetable crudité meticulously displayed with asparagus and haricots verts; julienned beets, carrots, and parsnips; red, yellow, and orange peppers and baby artichokes all fanned in colorful rows. An assortment of Greek olives beside heirloom cherry tomatoes formed the border, and a yellow curry dipping sauce inside a red cabbage bowl dotted the center. A large platter of lamb chops dribbled with Peter's rosemary port wine sauce rested next to a chaffing dish of his buttery pommes frites. Finally, smoked salmon apps with garnishes of dill, lemon, and capers were beautifully displayed on one of Mama's silver platters. Our waiters would be passing Pâté de Henry atop small pieces of Kissie's homemade French bread and Crabmeat Justine on tiny toast points along with mini cups of Cajun corn chowder. With two hundred guests expected, and a restaurant with a seating capacity of sixty, a formal seated dinner would have been impossible. Instead this sampling of our menu with luscious morsels, cocktail party–style, was the most cost-effective way to throw a grand, grand opening party.

I watched Peter swoon; I could tell how pleased he was by the look on his face—the one I had grown to love so much. He gave the table one last glance before turning to inspect the bar. When he spotted Riley wearing his Pampered Chef hat and the I SELL TUPPERWARE button, his face paled with terror and then strained against an instinct to laugh. "Sorry, pal," he told him, "gotta lose the hat." He touched the side of Riley's lapel. "And the advertisement. This is Leelee's party. Not yours."

"Oh, well, hmm, I didn't think about that," he said. With his eyes locked on Peter's, Riley slowly unpinned his I SELL TUPPERWARE button and laid it faceup on the table in front of the barware, daring him to object.

As if he had taken a page out of Kissie's book, Peter glared at him, then slowly shook his head.

Undaunted, Riley said, "I can't help noticing that you aren't wearing a chef's hat tonight, Peter," then removed his hat and placed it on Peter's head. "By all means, be my guest."

Instead of confronting him, Peter simply pivoted around on his heels and walked straight back into the kitchen wearing Riley's billowy white PC hat. I had to smile. Could the South be rubbing off on my Yankee transplant already?

Chapter Nine

Peter Owen looked like a movie star. Apparently I wasn't the only one who thought so. Not only was the food the hot topic of conversation, but talk of my steamy chef dripped from many a female lip. I was getting tired of hearing about it, to tell you the truth. Losing Baker to another woman had worked a jealousy number on me that might take longer than normal to undo. Each time I'd see a female who hadn't met Peter, married or not, she'd comment on his adorable face or piercing blue eyes—even his body. "Wow," Terry Hall commented when she had me alone. "What's it like to be naked with that Greek god?" I was dying to say: *None of your dang business!* In reality, I had no idea what it was like to be naked with my handsome chef but since it was absolutely none of her concern and considering my allergy to confrontation I simply went with a demure wink and polite grin. *Is it considered a white lie if you don't actually say anything?* I wondered.

Meeting all our guests in his freshly starched, white cotton chef's coat with hand-rolled buttons and French cuffs, he smiled as he greeted each with a firm handshake. Peter's not one to resort to ostentation, but even the simplicity of the uniform couldn't hide his true charm. The only thing shinier than his cleaned and buffed chef clogs was his dazzling smile. And perhaps, my heart.

Most everyone had arrived on time and Peter and I stood in the doorway, elbow to elbow, greeting our guests. I'd catch him gazing at me in between well wishes. Obviously, it wasn't the place, but it made me want to touch him all the more. Even while saying hello to people I hadn't seen in months I'd find myself fantasizing about what might happen later after the party.

Kissie looked gorgeous, all dressed up in her beautiful new red Sunday suit. "Baby, this gone be the suit I'm buried in. I love it so," she told me when she'd first laid eyes on it. I said, "Do not even think about saying that to me. Willard Scott is going to be wishing you a happy hundredth birthday on *The Today Show*. Eighty is the new sixty," I told her, which tickled her to no end.

Sarah and Issie—dressed in beautiful smocked dresses from the Women's Exchange, a fine children's boutique established long ago in Memphis—helped Kissie with the coats. I had rented hanging racks for the occasion and used the downstairs bedroom as a large coat closet. Even though I begged her to enjoy herself and stay up front with me after the coats were gathered, Kissie spent most of the time in the kitchen with a white apron wrapped around her middle. From time to time she'd venture out to the front of the house with Roberta, and the two of them would gather the dirty glasses and plates. No matter how hard I try to get Kissie to join a party, she always ends up back in the kitchen, the place she feels most at home. Roberta's the exact same way.

I could tell the party was a grand success by the high volume of conversation in the house. The piano music could hardly be heard over the voices and cackles. Peter milled about the crowd, talking with as many people as possible, accepting accolades for his fine cuisine. Tootie Shotwell and her husband, Trey, were there in all their decked-out glory and she was nicer to me than she's ever been in her entire life.

I had forgotten all about her, when I saw the unmistakable reflection of my unwanted guest in the gold leaf mantel mirror. Shirley Greene *and* Sondra were stuffing shrimp dijonnaise in their meddlesome yappers. Mr. Greene was noticeably absent. I suppose it was Shirley's way of making sure *Son*dra was able to attend. It looked like Shirley had just stepped out of the beauty parlor because her temples trumpeted the red stains from her amber dye job.

Mary Jule caught my gaze in the mirror and squinted her right eye ever so slightly. I knew exactly what she was saying. That girl and I started talking with our faces way back in eighth grade. We sat across the room from each other in Geography class and carried on entire conversations week after week. She moved over to where I was standing.

"Can you believe Shirley invited Sondra instead of her husband?" I whispered under my breath.

"*Son*dra?" she whispered back, trying not to move her lips.

"That's what she's calling herself now."

Mary Jule rolled her eyes. "Oh for the love of . . ."

"Mama would roll over."

"Have you spoken with them yet?"

"No. I'm dreading it like the plague."

"I'll go with you so you don't have to do it alone."

"I suppose I might as well get it over with." I followed behind as Mary Jule, with her gorgeous head of brown wavy hair swinging from her shoulders, stopped in front of the Greenes. Sondra was busy talking with Cindy Ryals, who, I could tell by the way she patted Sondra's stomach, was gushing over her couture maternity frock.

"Hi, Mrs. Greene, I mean Shirley," I said. "You remember Mary Jule."

Shirley turned to face us with a pretend smile. "Why, of course. Hello, dah'lin."

"Hi, Shirley," Mary Jule said, and they exchanged brief cheeky air kisses.

"Don't you look nice," Shirley said to me. "That dress is *to die for.*"

"Thanks," I said, looking down at the front of my dress. "That's nice of you to say." I turned to her daughter, who had turned to us from Cindy Ryals. "How are you, Sandy?"

She reached out to me with a scant side hug. It wasn't me initiating the embrace; somehow that made it feel a little less plastic. "I'm going by *Son*dra now. But I'm great." She patted her stomach. "Only three months to go."

"Congratulations," Mary Jule and I both said at the same time.

"It's official!" Shirley exclaimed, raising her drink, her diamond tennis bracelet nearly blinding me. "*At Home Memphis and Mid South* chose the nurs'ry as their cov'a photo. We're thrilled!"

"I'm sure you are." I had forgotten all about the media attention over the birth of Sondra's firstborn son. The same photographer from *At Home Memphis & Mid South* had already arrived to cover my party and I was sure Shirley and Sondra had grabbed quite a few photo ops.

"Has *Southern Living* phoned?" Mary Jule asked with a face as straight as Sondra's perfectly coiffed, flat-ironed hair.

"*Not yet,*" Shirley answered with a song in her voice.

Just at that moment, Virginia, who had been listening to every word of our conversation from a few safe feet away, tugged on my arm. That girl was so good. "*Bon Appétit* is here, Leelee. They're asking for you," she said in a fake whisper that was pointedly loud enough for anyone to hear.

"*Bon Appétit?*" Shirley exclaimed, glancing around the room.

Virginia looked at her, dead serious, not even a hint of bluff. "There's talk we're going to make the cover."

"Excuse me," I said to the group, and floated off with Virgy, leaving poor Mary Jule alone with the Greenes. As she dragged me through the crowd, I pinched the fire out of her elbow. It was all both of us could do to keep from a laughing attack.

Once Virgy and I were a safe distance away, in the opposite dining room, I sneaked a peek back at Shirley Greene. The way she shoveled food onto her small glass party plate looked as though she feared we might run out before she got her fair share. I watched her make her way around the entire table, helping herself to gobs of tenderloin and pork, lamb chops, veggies, and shrimp. Just as I was about to turn my eyes away, I caught her ogling Pierre. She wasn't the first woman in her early sixties to think him handsome. Many a Vermont dinner guest had swooned at the sight of my French maître d'. I watched her gaze, studying him like they were long-lost classmates. Then her face turned beet red when he caught her eye by accident, and Shirley abruptly turned away. *That was weird,* I thought, *but then again, she's weird.* Dismissing it as nothing but her normal menacing, meddling behavior, I walked off to join my more genuine Southern party guests.

One hour into the night, Alice pulled me off to the side with plans of a toast in my honor. I started to object but she convinced me that she would not say anything embarrassing and that it was protocol for this kind of party. She wanted me to find Peter and meet her in the foyer in five minutes. Right as I was about to touch him on the sleeve, Pierre pulled me away and pointed at Shirley Greene, who was right behind us, engaged in conversation with the lady from *RSVP* magazine. *"Madame est très sournoise."*

"Huh?" I said with obvious confusion.

"Sournoise. Eh eh," Pierre became flustered because he couldn't think of the English translation for *sournoise.* *"Elle est commune,"* and he pointed again at Shirley.

It sounded like he was trying to tell me Shirley Greene was common. "Oh, she's common, all right," I whispered inside his ear. "If you only knew."

I stepped away—but turned back to the French man, confused. "Common"—how in the world had Pierre known about that Southern idiom? His English was minimal at best, but somehow he was picking up on the nuances. I'd heard my mother and grandmother use "common" to describe people of a certain "ilk," as Daddy would say. Mama used it to refer to those who parked cars in their front lawns. If either were here, I'm sure they would agree with Pierre's assessment and throw in a few other choice adjectives while they were at it.

"You are vedy smart, Pierre," I said back in my French accent, knocking the top of his head.

He acted as if he wanted to provide me with more French wisdom about Shirley Greene but Riley interrupted, grabbing my arm. "Leelee, we're out of daiquiri puwee."

"What?" I turned around and rushed off to solve the problem, forgetting all about Pierre.

All it took was a trip to the walk-in to get another bottle of our pre-bottled blend. As I plopped it down on the table in front of him, I spied Peter standing on the other side of the room talking with John, Virginia's husband. I rushed toward him, tugging on his sleeve, and whispered that we needed to meet Alice at the base of the stairs. After excusing himself, he took ahold of my hand and we made our way through the clusters of guests, many of whom were smiling politely and tipping their glasses as my charming chef and I weaved through to the foyer.

Alice had already stopped the music when we arrived. "Stay right here," she instructed, and made a short ascent up the stairs, stopping on the fourth step. She held her peach daiquiri glass in one hand, a spoon in the other, and clinked the two together. "Hi, everyone, may I please have your attention?" When no one responded she repeated, a little louder, "May I have your attention, please." Once the rumble of conversation finally died down she proceeded. "Hey, everyone, I'm Alice Garrott, one of Leelee's best friends. I just wanted to take a moment to say that this is a very special evening, one that's been in the making for several months. Well, truthfully, for several years." Alice looked so cute standing up there above everyone, and I could truly feel the pride she felt. "First, we want to welcome Chef Peter Owen here tonight and to Memphis." She extended her hand in his direction and Peter took a slight bow. "He is responsible for the out-of-this-world food that you've all been enjoying tonight." She clapped her hands in the air and initiated a big round of applause. "And Leelee Williams Satterfield. We are so proud of all she has done and the showplace she has created. I don't know if any of you remember this old house but suffice it to say, it needed a major face-lift!" That comment garnered several laughs from the crowd. "Please join me in giving three cheers for a fantastic lady." She tipped her glass in my direction and waved me up to join her.

While my guests cheered and clapped, I could feel the heat rising to my cheeks as I stepped up next to her. Alice was about to say something else when Riley, bless his heart, hollered out, "Hip hip hooway! Hip hip hooway, hip hip hooway!" tipping his own full wineglass in my direction. *So much for the wine ban on Riley,* I thought. He had slipped from behind his post and was now mingling with the rest of the partygoers.

"Speech," John Murphey yelled, and a few others echoed.

Very shyly, I waited for the noise to die down, mustering all my courage to speak in public. My pulse quickened. I felt the urge to knot my hair but resisted. Finally, I forced myself to say, "I want to thank you all so much for coming tonight. It's been my dream to open a restaurant in my hometown for several months now, and I feel very fortunate to have Peter Owen joining me." I extended my hand to Peter and he joined Alice and me on the steps. "And I know all y'all are loving his exquisite cuisine." I slid my arm around his waist. "So have another peach daiquiri or a glass of wine, try some more food, and please, please tell all your friends." As an afterthought I added, "Oh and one more thing. Next spring we'll be serving dinner out on the porch."

Alice initiated another round of applause, which was interrupted by Al, Mary Jule's husband. "Let's hear from Peter," he called from the doorway.

Much more adept at public speaking, Peter nodded and in his gentle manner said, "Thanks, you guys. I can't tell you what a privilege it is to be working at this fine restaurant. When Leelee and I worked together in Vermont, I had no idea I'd ever make it this far down South.

Memphis is all I heard about for months, by the way." My guests enjoyed a big guffaw on that one. "You guys are famous." He cleared his throat. "And it's not because of the barbecue . . . which I've learned is *not* a party in the backyard." More laughs followed and Peter used it as an opportunity to let loose. "I must say it's been quite an experience living down South. I've noticed that instead of a bar on every corner, like where I come from in New Jersey, there's a church." My guests exploded in laugher, which only fueled Peter's routine. "The other day when Leelee told me she was going to carry her girls home, I told her it would be a heck of a lot easier to drive them." Several chuckles escaped from the crowd. "I have to say I'm intrigued by some of the food down here. When Leelee told me she wanted to take me to a meat and three, I asked her what that was. She said, 'A home-cooking restaurant—one meat and two vegetables.' Okay, I thought. Fair enough. But when I looked at the menu, one of the meats was chicken-fried steak." Another large roar came from the crowd.

One of my guests hollered out, "At least we don't eat our bread out of a can!"

Peter smiled. "You'd be surprised but that's actually pretty good. *Weird,* but good. Hey, thanks again, you guys, seriously," he said with such sincerity in his voice, adding, "I did want to mention that we'll be catering here at the Peach Blossom Inn. If you have a party or a special event and would like us to be involved, please let us know. We have menus that you can pick up on your way out the door tonight."

I reached up and whispered in his ear.

"I've been told Miss Sarah and Miss Isabella will be at the front door handing them out as you leave."

After all the guests had left, we all kicked back at one of the round tables in the dining room to recap the night. Kissie and the girls had left as soon as the party was over, and Peter made sure that Riley followed her out of the driveway. If it had been me telling her to let Riley follow her home, she would have given me the eye and said, "Oh no he won't," but with Peter giving her the instruction, Kissie was all smiles.

The only people left were my three Tennessee girlfriends, who had sent their husbands home to relieve the babysitters, and my four Vermont comrades, who were quite tuckered out and barely able to hold their eyes open—even Jeb, who seemed to have lost his desire to party after the party.

Roberta pulled out a chair and plopped down into a seat. "I feel like I've been drug through a knothole," she said. "Woo, I won't last long." Mary Jule plopped down next to her, kicked her heels off, and put her bare feet on my lap. "Me either," she said. "But it sure was fun."

"I thought it was perfect," I said. "Thanks to everyone here." I looked over at Pierre, whose chin was bouncing off his chest.

"I agree," Virgy said, sipping on still another glass of wine.

"Who's driving?" I asked.

Virgy swept her hand toward Mary Jule.

"Me, and we're out of here in ten minutes," Mary Jule warned. "You know how Al gets if I stay out too late."

"Okay," Virginia said in a somewhat irritated tone. "Al needs to get over himself." She settled back in her seat, obviously nowhere near ready to leave. "What was the strangest thing you thought about the evening, Yankee Doodle?" she asked Peter.

"Let's see," he said, glancing off in deep thought. "The strangest thing about the evening. It was probably the fact that half of the people I met tonight asked me where I was going to church. When I said, 'the nearest cathedral, I suppose,' they looked at me like I was half-crazy. Do you guys not have Catholics down here?"

"Yes, but we have way more Protestants," Alice told him matter-of-factly. "Especially Baptists."

"People are mostly Catholic where I come from," he said with a shrug.

"What else is weird for you down here?" Virginia asked.

"You guys wave at people walking down the street whether you know them or not."

"At least we're friendly," Alice said, tipping her glass.

"I was asked to slow down when I was on the phone the other day."
He laughed. "I love that." He leaned back in his chair. "And can I just
ask, why do you guys say 'sure don't'?"

"That *is* odd," Mary Jule said, shaking her head. "I'm with you on
that one."

"You did an amazing job tonight," Virgy said, turning to me.

"*You* were hysterical," I replied, leaning across the table toward her.
"Telling Sondra and Shirley that *Bon Appétit* was in the house."

Virginia screwed up her face in disgust. "She was bugging the fire
out of me. Who does she think she is anyway?"

"She thinks she's slicker than snot on a doorknob," Jeb said. Bless
his heart. He had no idea who we were talking about. He just so wanted
to be a part of the group.

"Eww," Mary Jule said, wrinkling her nose. "That is *so* nasty, Jayeb."

"Sorry," he said. "That's what we say in Vermont."

I glanced over at Roberta. Her eyelids were heavy but she was holding on. Pierre, on the other hand, was sound asleep in his chair.

"I have to ask you girls something," Peter said, scratching the back
of his head. "Why do you make this stuff up?"

We all looked at one another before Alice finally stepped in, taking
charge. "What do you mean, shoog?"

"Just now. You guys are so happy about Virginia making up a big
story to tell Shirley Greene about *Bon Appétit*. What are you going to
do when a review never happens? Won't you be concerned that she
thinks you two were lying?"

Alice leaned in toward him, her chin protruding. "Considering
she's the biggest liar in town, I don't think so. I realize that you might
think this is weird, but we're just having a little fun. Besides, Shirley
Greene deserves it. And so does that annoying daughter of hers."

"I'll tell you this, Yankee boy, Southern girls are fun. Always fun.
Put that in your Northern pipe and smoke it," Virginia declared.

Peter shook his head but kept a smile on his face. "You guys are
nice and polite even when you can't stand someone."

"It's better than starting a catfight!" Virginia teased. "That's what a Northern girl would do."

"I can't begin to understand you guys." He folded his arms in front of him and leaned back in his seat.

Virginia nearly flew across the table. She put on a sharp Yankee accent and retorted right back. "If *you guys* were really smart, you damn Yankee, you'd figure out how to get back at Shirley Greene yourself." She leaned over and yanked on Jeb's handlebar as if to emphasize her thought. "The same goes for you!"

"Hey!" he hollered. "Watch it." Then in an abrupt change of subject said, "Hey, Alice, I'm ready to start work. Just give me the go-ahead and I'll be there any day this week."

A long drawn-out pause followed. If it had been Mary Jule, she wouldn't have missed a beat, but it was Alice and I could see her searching for a way out. "To tell you the truth, shoog," she finally said, stalling with another sip of her daiquiri, "I just hired somebody. If I'd known you were coming to town, darnit, I'd have kept the position open."

"Who'd you hire?"

I could see the panic in her eyes as she hedged. "A guy that helps out at Richard's office," she said shyly.

"What's his name?" Jeb wanted to know.

Peter winked at me from across the table.

"I don't remember details like that. He hasn't even started yet." Alice told the little white lie to protect Jeb. The last thing she'd ever want to do is hurt his feelings.

Virgy slid in for the rescue. "I know what you can do, Jayeb," she said, pushing her chair back from the table. "You can help us poon Shirley Greene's house."

"When?" Jeb asked, wide-eyed, perking up from his slouched position. "Now?"

Virginia stood up, glancing around at all of us. "Why not?"

"No way," Mary Jule said, rising from her seat. "Al will kill me. Plus

I have a League meeting in the morning at eight thirty. I need to get going right now."

"Tomorrow then, or the next night. I'll even buy the supplies," Jeb said eagerly.

Virginia shook her head. "You just drive your Mary Kay getaway car, I've got plenty of supplies."

"Pooning" is the act of ornamenting a glass surface with a surprise tampon. Instructions: Unwrap a super Tampax and dip in water. Once the tampon is bloated, hold by the string and twirl, midair, in lasso rope fashion. Rear arm back and hurl at target. Optimum targets are large glass front doors or picture windows, car windows, or any other window belonging to heinous individuals who deserve a pooning. Element of surprise is crucial.

Although pooning was an activity Virgy and I dreamed up in college, where our targets were usually Waffle Houses or Krystal restaurants at two in the morning when packed full of unsuspecting late-night diners, there is always an exception to the age-appropriate rule. Sometimes life deems pooning necessary in later years. As is the case where a nosy, gossipy woman has been making the lives of others miserable for decades. In that instance one is never too old for pooning.

Once the girls had left and Roberta and Pierre had said goodnight, Jeb hung around the table. He'd been tired before my friends mentioned pooning but now he was wide awake. I thought he'd never leave.

Every time I tried to meet Peter's eyes I'd notice him fidgeting. He'd move around in his chair, drumming his fingers on the table, quickly cutting Jeb off in the middle of his sentences. When he raised an eyebrow at me, slowly winking from across the table, I understood. Behind Jeb's back, he slowly rolled his tongue from one side of his lips to the other. Daringly, I rolled mine right back at him. "I think I'm going to call it a night," he finally said, hoping Jeb would take the hint.

"Me, too," I said with an artificial yawn, pushing my chair back.

"Me three," Jeb said finally, thank God.

Peter jumped up from the table. "I'll make sure we're all-off in the kitchen. Thanks for your help, man."

"Ain't no problem," Jeb said.

I hurried up the stairs to grab my bag, imagining the minutes that would follow once I had Peter to myself. After all the months of yearning for him, fantasizing about the two of us tangled up together on a deserted beach with no one else for miles, I felt an uncontrollable ache whirling inside. I couldn't keep myself from him a minute longer. When I heard Jeb's bedroom door shut, I fluffed my hair in the bathroom mirror, taking care that it hung just right around my shoulders, and crept back out to the upstairs landing. Peter stood at the bottom near the newel post, soft music playing somewhere in the background. Our eyes locked, and I held his gaze as my hand slid down the banister. When I reached the last step, he rested his hand on the small of my back. The electricity in his fingertips ignited my body on fire. He leaned into my lips and the smell of sweet port wine on his breath caused me to gasp, sucking in the fragrance of him. Suddenly, he grabbed me and the two of us kissed our way across the room, pausing briefly in front of the dimly lit fireplace. The embers from the lingering logs cast shadows both inside the hearth and on Peter's face. The way he smiled in the firelight intoxicated the very essence of me. Between the wine, the faint virile odor of his perspiration, and the seductive way we floated around the room, moving to the music, I was entranced in the love of him. We frantically kissed our way over to the wall, using it for support before sliding down to the floor. The fitted skirt of my dress was not conducive to wrapping my legs around his waist but I'd have nearly smothered him had I been dressed in something more casual. Instead I moved around on his lap while we explored one another, fully clothed. I moved my hand slowly up the lapel of his shirt, fingering each button until I reached the few hairs near his collarbone. Softly tracing his jawline with the tips of my fingers, I heard him sigh, and when I outlined his mouth he gasped.

"I really, really want to ask you upstairs," he whispered, stroking my cheek and the underside of my chin. He drew me in closer until our lips barely touched, sweeping against one another's. "I make love to you every night before I drift off."

Hearing his words, confirmation that he longed for me the way I craved him, caused an explosion of tingles inside of me followed by an immense ache, and I hungered for him to carry me to his bed that very moment. I started to scream, Take me you fool! when the face—well, *glare*—of a certain big-wooden-spoon-wielding woman popped into my head, killing—well, obliterating—our moment. My shoulders shrank and I lightly shook my head.

Mary Jule and I were in our basement with the lights out at one o'clock in the morning. I don't know how we ever thought we'd fool Kissie, who was spending the weekend while Mama and Daddy were out of town. She knew we were down there; she just didn't know Jay Stockley and David Hickman, our eleventh-grade boyfriends, were, too. She had fallen asleep on the sofa while watching The Tonight Show *and we had snuck the boys through the back door. I kept a lookout for Kissie while Mary Jule rushed them downstairs.*

She and Jay were spread out on the couch, David and I were blissfully engaged on a pallet under the pool table—when the overhead lights suddenly ripped through the darkness.

My friends scampered up to a sitting position just as Kissie reached the bottom step. She took one look at them and raised a big wooden spoon high above her head, hollering, "Leelee, where you at?" I was well over spanking age but that never stopped Kissie from threatening me with the one weapon she knew would turn my noes into yeses every time. I could see her from underneath the pool table but she had yet to spot me. David and I deftly rolled out the other side and were creeping toward the bathroom when she caught us red-handed. "Leelee Satterfield, don't you hide in that bathroom!" she yelled. "Come over here and set down. Both a y'all."

David and I slunk over to the couch.

She knew David, even knew his parents and grandparents from parties she had catered in the past. "David Hickman, I know your mama ain't got no idea you're out this late. You want me to call her and tell her to come pick you boys up?"

"No, ma'am," David muttered, frozen in fear. He had a Kissie, too, and she wasn't much different.

"Then you better git on home 'fore I take this spoon to you. You boys don't have no business hanging around here at this hour."

Mary Jule and I sat like statues while the boys offered a shy wave and scampered up the stairs.

Kissie wasn't done. "Leelee, I don't know how many times I'mo have to tell you, or Mary Jule. When you spend time with boys in compromising positions, especially in the pitch-black dark, you put yourself in danger of losing your principles. Lawd have mercy alive. Nice girls don't suppose to be sneaking boys into their houses. It ain't decent! Hm hm hm."

I sat there, forcing myself from meeting eyes with Mary Jule. I knew I'd giggle, which was the last thing I needed to do at that moment. Plus, something deep inside me knew Kissie was right. "We weren't doing anything but kissing," I finally said. It was a tiny little white lie. Second base, especially on top of the shirt, wasn't that much more than kissing.

"Hmm," Kissie grunted.

"I swear."

"Hmm," she snorted again, much louder this time.

"Please don't tell Daddy," I pleaded.

She put both hands on her hips, with the long handle of the spoon jetting out between her fingers. Her voice was a little softer when she spoke next. "One day you'll know when the time is right. And if I have anything to do with it, it'll be after you have a ring on your finger! Now ain't that time, young lady."

And neither was this.

I looked up at Peter and he was already smiling, a hint of understanding in his eyes. And his voice. "You have two little girls at home fast asleep but I'm guessing there's someone else at your house who's not."

I shook my head.

"As much as I'd love you to stay, I wouldn't want that certain someone mad at me."

That certain someone was indeed wide awake, or at least had one eye open anyway, trusting me to make the right choice. No, this was not the right time. As unsure as I was of so much these days, of that I was completely certain.

Chapter Ten

While I was living in Vermont, Helga insisted that we close the restaurant on Mondays only. Now that I was boss, both Sundays and Mondays would have CLOSED signs on the front door no matter what. Besides, Kissie had given me a long lecture. "Why do you think they passed the blue laws?" she had said. "Sunday is the Lawd's day and He meant it to be a day of rest. If He wanted us to work on Sundays, the Bible would have said so, hm hm hm." She also told me that He would bless my business if I honored His Fourth Commandment and to tell you the truth, that suited me just fine.

The Tuesday after the grand opening party, I arrived at the restaurant by 9 A.M. When I opened the back door, the kitchen smelled of freshly brewed coffee. All the lights were on but no one was milling about. I headed straight over to the desk and when I put down my purse I noticed the red light blinking on the answering machine. Hoping that it might be full of requests for reservations, I pushed play. The first few were indeed dinner requests and I happily copied the names down in my reservation book as quickly as I could print. When I got to the end of the list, the machine alerted me that there were six more saved messages. The very first one was from Tootie Shotwell. It said to please call her at my earliest convenience and it had been left first thing Monday morning. *I knew I shouldn't have invited that woman,* I thought. *What could she possibly want now?*

There were a few more reservations, which I jotted down hurriedly, and *two more* from Tootie Shotwell, the last one revealing the reason for her call. She wanted *Peter* to cater her tailgate party at Ole Miss for the Egg Bowl, the annual game against Mississippi State. It's the biggest rivalry of the year and without a doubt the showiest tailgate party of them all.

If you ask anyone, the Grand Poobah of all social events surrounding the South's football season is tailgating at the Grove. The Grove is the nickname for the quadrangle in the middle of the Ole Miss campus. It's surrounded by all the old buildings, most of which were built way back in 1848. The game-day parties held at the Grove are wild and unprecedented, giving new definition to fun. While they were certainly entertaining when Virginia and I were back in school, they were nothing compared to the parties that go on today. Some of them resemble engagement parties. If you have the money and the clout, you can rent space and set up a tent for your personal viewing party. I've heard there are some who spend thousands of dollars on their parties by the time they cater in the food, rent tents, bring in big-screen TVs, grand chandeliers, elaborate centerpieces, and the family silver. Tent after tent, it's the who's who of Memphis, Atlanta, Birmingham, Jackson, Columbus, Hattiesburg, Oxford, and Mississippi Delta society.

Everyone around Memphis knew about Tootie Shotwell's illustrious "Memphis Tent." The rumor around town was that she made it her personal mission to top everyone else's tents, and an invitation to "stop by" would be considered the ultimate coup to the grandest of social climbers. I had never received an invite, and that was perfectly fine with me. In truth, I'd rather sip a large glass of warm dog drool than be one of Tootie Shotwell's sycophants. I wanted to call her back right that instant and say no. After all, the game was Thanksgiving weekend and judging by the grand reception we received at the opening party on Friday night, we were sure to be slammed—a term restaurant people use for crazy busy.

When I heard the creaks on the old steps in the kitchen, I pinched my cheeks and fluffed my hair, knowing my sexy boyfriend was about to enter the room. When he saw me sitting at the desk next to the phone, he headed straight over and planted my lips with a great big smooch. "Good morning, boss. I've got great news."

"Yeah? What is it?" Naturally I was elated. The dazzling smile on his face told me something wonderful had happened.

"We've got our first catering gig!" Clearly Peter had checked the voice mail. While his face beamed radiantly, the light in mine blacked out.

"I heard," I said, trying my level best to seem chipper. "I just listened to Tootie Shotwell's message." How would I ever explain to him that I had no desire to cater anything for Tootie Shotwell—that she was unpleasant to be around, gossipy, belittling, and that I felt inferior around her? If that were the case, he would wonder why she received a grand opening party invitation in the first place. If he knew the truth, he would consider it more Southern subterfuge. I had to keep mum.

"Did you *talk* to Tootie Shotwell?" I asked hesitantly, fearful of the answer.

"No, I just listened to her messages. Here's the deal. The game is on a Saturday and naturally I can't be away from the restaurant. But I'll prepare the food and send you and your girlfriends down. I thought you'd love that, since you and Virginia went to school there."

Besides Tootie's unpleasant demeanor, my catering a party for Tri Delt Tootie simply would not do. I'm a Chi Omega. My mother was a Chi Omega and so was my grandmother. He would never understand the rivalry. My mind spun as I pondered several excuses, none seeming to surface fast enough. "Hmm," was all I could think to say.

"Take Riley with you. He can wear his chef hat."

I gaped at him in disbelief.

"I'm joking." He snickered as he backed into the workstation across from the desk, hoisting himself onto the counter.

The door dividing the kitchen and the restaurant swung open and Roberta appeared, heading straight over to the coffeepot. "Good morning," she said cheerily, with a wave. Peter and I greeted her but went straight back to our conversation.

We had already discussed catering in detail. I knew that I'd have to handle the jobs until we were up and running and could hire someone else to manage it; I just never considered that the first catering job out of the gate would be for Tootie Shotwell. When I gave it more thought, I had to be honest with myself and admit that it had less to do with us belonging to different sororities, and everything to do with pride. By the elated look on Peter's face though, I knew there was no possible way out. To say that I dreaded it would be a magnanimous understatement.

When I called Tootie Shotwell back, the first thing out of her mouth was a request for Peter to be sure and wear his chef attire. She wanted to know specifically if he owned a billowy white chef's hat—she hadn't seen him wearing one at the party—because if not, she wanted to be sure and buy him one to wear for the occasion. She thought it much more professional. I hated to break the news to her that not only would he not be wearing a chef's hat, but he wouldn't be there at all.

"Why not?" she asked. I could hear the irritation in her voice.

"Because Saturdays are our busiest nights here at the restaurant and he's the chef."

"Hmm," she uttered after a long pause.

"But Peter will prepare all of the food and it will be just as delicious." Peter, who was still sitting across from me, knitted his brow as he tried to decipher her end of the conversation.

"I'm sure it will be, Leelee," Tootie said, "but I have this vision of a real gourmet chef standing behind an elegant food table while my guests pass through the line. I want it to be spectacular in every way. I'm sure you can understand. It's *the Egg Bowl*. You know what a big deal that is."

I knew full well what a big deal it was. Everyone with the slightest tie to Mississippi attends that game. It's always the last Saturday in November—Thanksgiving weekend. Football season at Ole Miss, or any SEC school for that matter, is half the reason we attend those large universities. Some say football is another religion in the South and if so, Ole Miss—in my opinion anyway—is its most majestic cathedral and bourbon is the holy water. As alums, we do everything we can to take advantage of those seven coveted home game weekends.

After another long pause and an extra loud *tsk,* Tootie said, "Well, that's a shame. If Peter changes his mind, do let me know." I started to say something but she added, "I'll pay him well."

"I'm sure you would, Tootie, and I appreciate that, but I'm also sure you can understand that we have to put the restaurant first."

"I do understand, I just hate that you can't figure out a way to do both. Like I said, let me know if you change your mind. The game is still three and a half weeks away. If I don't hear from you soon though, I'll have to move on to someone else. I want to hire a real gourmet chef."

"Sure will," I said, "and thank you so much for calling." I blinked back the urge to roll my eyes as Tootie and I exchanged good-byes.

"No go, huh?" Peter asked as soon as I hung up the phone. He slid off the counter, put one foot across the other, and folded his arms in front of him.

I shook my head. "She wants you to be there. Won't settle for just your food, you have to be attached."

"That's weird," he said, heading back to the stove.

Roberta walked over with a coffee cup in her hand. "I saw that woman the other night when I was out front collecting the dirty wineglasses." She lowered her voice. "You would have to be a bat not to see she couldn't take her eyes off Peter. You'd think she didn't have a husband by the way she stared a hole reet through him."

"I've been dealing with that woman my whole life. First in high school, then at Ole Miss. For some reason she is determined to stay in my life no matter how hard I try to avoid her," I said with both fury and resignation.

"Why did you invite her to the party?" Roberta asked. A normal question, I realize that.

"It's a long story but Virginia felt like I needed to. She told me it would be worse to leave her off the guest list since we run in the same circles."

"Oh well. Let's fuhgetabout it," Peter said, accentuating those words on purpose. "The longer we're open, the more requests we'll have to cater. We'll get the next one. You wait and see." I heard the door click on the walk-in before he disappeared inside.

Later that morning the doorbell rang and since I was on the phone taking a reservation I ignored it, knowing someone else would answer it. Ever since Shirley Greene showed up unannounced I had insisted that the front door be kept locked. Jeb, just as I figured, stopped what he was doing and headed toward the front door. When he came right back into the kitchen and stood next to me I suspected someone must be waiting. "Who is it?" I asked as soon as I hung up the phone.

"The postman. He has a letter for you to sign."

"That's weird. I wonder who it's from?" I said, rising from the chair.

"I have no ideer. But the guy's waitin'. You better come on."

"I'm coming," I said, somewhat irritated. In defiance, I strolled leisurely through the swinging door and made my way over to the foyer with Jeb at my heels. Sure enough an older gentleman with a full head of silver hair stood on the porch wearing one of those little blue postman outfits. "You could have asked him in," I said over my shoulder, and opened the screen door. "Hi, sir, how are you this morning?"

The man smiled. "I'm fine, thanks. Are you Leelee Satterfield?"

"I sure am."

"I have a registered letter that needs your signature."

"That's odd, I'm not expecting anything."

The postman shrugged. "If you'll sign right here next to the X," he said, handing me a pen. Once I had signed my name, he ripped the green card off the envelope and stuck it in his pouch. "Have a nice day." He handed me the letter and turned around to leave.

Having no idea why someone would have sent me a registered letter, I studied the envelope as I walked back toward the kitchen.

Mrs. Leelee Satterfield
462 Old Poplar Pike
Memphis, TN 38108

The return address was from an

Elliott B. Hightower, Esquire
Hightower & Associates, LLP
121 Day Street
Montpelier, VT 05602

"What in the world could this be?" I murmured softly as I pushed through the swinging door. Looking around for a kitchen knife to use as a letter opener, I noticed my hands were shaking. I wished Peter were there. He had driven over to the farmer's market at the Agricenter to pick up fresh butternut squash for his soup du jour. I turned the letter over and over in my hands, staring at the return address.

"Aren't you going to open it?" Jeb asked with knitted brow.

"Yes, but I'm a little worried about it, to tell you the truth. It's not every day you receive a letter from an attorney in Vermont. I suppose it has something to do with my divorce." I held it up to the light, trying to discern the length of the letter. "I just can't imagine what Baker wants now. If he thinks he's going to lower my child support, he has another thing coming!" I put the letter down on the sink and reached around to knot my hair. When I had finished twisting, my bun pulled so tight, my eyes hurt.

Roberta put her hand on my back. "You're more nervous than a long-tailed cat in a room full of rocking chairs. Relax, missy."

Completely ignoring her advice, I lightly shook my head, peering off into the distance. "His decision to live in Vermont with another woman has nothing to do with me."

"Of course not," she said.

The thought of Baker even trying to lower my child support angered me so, that I tore open the envelope, ripping a corner off the paper inside. After unfolding the one-page letter, it took only a moment to read the first three sentences. I couldn't help the guttural moan that followed.

Barely able to move, I patted around behind me for a place to sit so I wouldn't faint. Roberta took my arm and held on to me as we moved over to the desk and I dropped down into the chair. "What in the world?" she asked with a genuine look of concern.

"She can't do this!" I wailed, bursting into tears. Terrible, terrible tears, the kind you can't control.

Pierre, who had been filling the wine coolers, heard the commotion and sprang over to my side, dropping to his knees. "What es matter, Leelee?" He fanned me with a *Bon Appétit* magazine that he'd spied on the desk. I wished he'd stop but I didn't want to hurt his feelings, naturally, so I just watched the loose strands of hair ripple around my face and latch on to my tearstained cheeks. "*S'il vous plaît, Leeelee, est Baker en tenant les petites filles?*"

"It sounds like you're asking if Baker is trying to take Sarah and Issie back to Vermont?" I eked through my tears, and pointed northward.

"*Oui.*"

"No. That's the only thing that could be worse right now."

"Here, read it to everyone, please." I handed the letter to Roberta, who had barely started to read aloud when Jeb snuck up from behind and snatched it out of her hands.

"Hey, that's not nice," she said. "I was reading that." He wouldn't give it back to her until he'd read the last word. Finally he passed it to her and looked me straight in the eye. "Looks like you need your own lawyer."

Pierre stood back up and threw his arms in the air. *"S'il vous plaît, s'il vous plaît,* what *est* matter *avec Leelee?"*

"Helga!" I wailed. It was a universal noun by now.

He reared back.

I put a finger gun to my head, pulled the trigger, and shot.

His eyes popped. *"Helga est morte?"* He pulled his own finger trigger on his head.

"No, but I wish she was!" My fury suddenly exploded. I stood up and flew around the kitchen, faking like I had a rifle in my hand, cocking and shooting at everything in sight: the pots hanging over the cooking line, the coffeepot, the plates, the Hobart, the walk-in, and finally the desk phone. Jeb ducked when I accidentally pointed my air gun at him.

"Helga went on a shooting spree?" Roberta said.

"No!" I yelled. "She is trying to kill and destroy the restaurant. *This* restaurant . . . here in Memphis. The letter says we have to close!" I slapped the back of my right hand several times with the palm of my left. "Hand it back to me, Roberta. I'll read it to you and Pierre." After a long pause I began to read while the tears streamed down my face.

Dear Ms. Satterfield,

This firm represents Ms. Helga F. Schloygin, a resident of Willingham, Vermont, who is the legal owner of the name, The Peach Blosom Inn.

I stopped reading and looked at my friends. "Some attorney. The idiot doesn't even know how to spell 'Blossom.'"

Ms. Schloygin has registered the mark for use in commerce at the United States Patent and Trademark Office in the category for provision of goods and services in the hospitality industry and we hereby demand you, Leelee Satterfield, to cease and desist all operations of the Peach Blosom Inn in Memphis, Tennessee. Furthermore, we request that you provide evidence that you have done so or be assured

Ms. Schloygin will avail herself of all remedies afforded her by law, including the immediate initiation of a lawsuit against you and all responsible agents. Failure to comply with this urgent matter may result in your having to give up profits and pay all damages, fines, and attorney's fees connected with this matter.

Please direct all correspondence and indication of your immediate cease and desist to this firm as authorized agent of Ms. Schloygin. I remain

Very truly yours,

Elliott B. Hightower, Esq.
Hightower & Associates, LLP

"'I remain very truly yours'? That's the biggest bunch of crap I've ever heard. He's never met me and he's surely not mine," I bemoaned to the group, crumpling up the letter and throwing it across the room.

Poor Pierre. The dazed look on his face showed his confusion. He just sat there but I could tell by the way he pressed his lips together and flitted his eyes he knew Helga was up to her old tricks.

"Very odd," Roberta replied.

"I wonder what's happened to Rolf?" I said. "Has she kicked her brother to the curb? He was an owner, too." Rolf was the chef of the restaurant before Peter came on board. Although he wasn't as bad as his sister, I didn't trust him one bit.

"I could call and ask George if you want," Jeb said, scratching his head.

"No, I don't want you to ask George! I prefer to keep this private. Well, as private as possible anyway." Roberta had slipped into the restroom and returned with a roll of toilet paper. I pulled a large wad off the roll and blew, as hard as I could. "Thank you, Roberta."

"You're welcome," she said before bending down to pick the letter up off the floor. She smoothed it back out with her palm. "Does this letter mean you have to change the name right now . . . today?"

"It seems like it to me!" I writhed in my seat, clutching my fists. "What other name will I use? If we change it, all of our menus have to be changed. Our sign has to be changed and all of our advertising."

"I couldn't tell you," she said. "You're in a tough spot." Roberta handed me back the crinkled letter.

"Everything I've worked so hard to achieve is all going up in smoke, Roberta. All the money I've spent, all the time I've invested. All gone. And for what? So that German beast can use the name *I came up with*? I thought she was going to change it back to the Vermont Haus Inn?"

He shrugged. "Who knows? I'm not her keeper."

"The way I see it, her lack of business is her own fault. The word got around what a wicked witch she is," I said. "No one wants to eat at her old stenchy restaurant anyway."

At that very moment Peter walked in the back door carrying a box full of butternut squash, whistling and smiling like he had just stepped out of a brand-new shiny red Corvette. "Yo, Roberta, will you help me peel the squash? I'll need you, too, Jeb. Once Roberta peels, you can chop them up in cubes. These suckers might be hard to work with, but the end result is mighty fine." He slung the box on the workstation and it landed with a loud thud. "Where's Gary?" he asked, reaching for his apron. Sous Chef Gary hadn't made it in yet. He had called to say he was running late. It took Peter a moment to notice the doom and gloom in the room. "What is it with all you sad sacks? It's our official opening night and we have fifty reservations. I'd say that's pretty darn great for a Tuesday."

My head had been down but when I peered up at him and he saw the tears covering my face and the wrinkled paper in my hand, he slowly put his apron back down on the counter. "What's in that letter?" he asked.

I handed it to him and watched his eyes flick back and forth across the page until he reached the end, never uttering a sound. After folding it back the way it was mailed, he flung the letter onto the counter. "That damn bitch. How did she even know Leelee opened another restaurant?"

"I have no ideer," Roberta said. "But you know how word spreads. George Clark may have heard the news. Personally, I made sure I didn't tell him where I was going before I left." She turned to Jeb. "Did you tell him?"

"Well, I may have said a little something."

"What you do that for?" Roberta said. "Don't you know the word will get around as quick as a beetle bug in a garden?"

"For corn' sake, *R*oberta." He always said her name with a "Row" instead of a "Ruh" when he was mad at her. "There's no need to get your bowels in an uproar. George asked me what I thought I was going to do about JCW while I was gone. I had to tell him something."

"Ay, ay, ay," Pierre murmured, making the sign of the cross on his chest.

"All right, all right, you two," Peter said. "Leelee doesn't need this right now. Let's put our heads together to figure out what we're going to do here." He gently pulled me out of the chair and sat down in my place, lowering me onto his lap. I felt his arms wrap around my waist. It felt like two giant Band-Aids covering the pain. When I turned to look at him, the tenderness in his eyes comforted me, too, and I lay my head on his shoulder.

"The first thing you need to do is call a lawyer of your own, sweetheart," he said, wiping the loose hair from my face. "I bet you know plenty of them, too, right here in Memphis. You should probably call one right away."

"That's what I told her," Jeb said, puffing out his chest.

"I do know lots of lawyers, but I'm not sure who handles this kind of thing." My voice was barely a whisper. "Wait, what am I thinking?" I popped back up and looked him square in the eye. "Richard, Alice's husband. He's an attorney with Glankler Brown. They're the best firm in the city."

"There you go," Jeb said as he fiddled nervously with his handlebar. "Sounds like a plan."

"We'll fight this, Leelee. And we *will* keep doing business. We aren't going to let her cheat us out of what we would earn tonight and this weekend. I'll be damned if I'm going to roll over and let her win."

I breathed a small sigh of relief.

Pierre paced around the kitchen before removing a stack of napkins and started to fold one after another into linen pyramids. Roberta grabbed a butternut squash from the box, found the large potato peeler in the utility drawer, and started peeling over the big trash can next to the sink. Jeb moseyed over to the Hobart, opened the side door, and pulled out the empty plate rack. With no dishes to wash, he kept sliding it in and out, in and out. Peter continued to hold me, never moving a muscle.

When Gary showed up, over an hour late, the morale in the kitchen was as low as the Mighty Mississippi after a three-month drought. Peter never even mentioned his tardiness. What would be the point in scolding him? Chances were he wouldn't even have a job after today.

Chapter Eleven

I called Alice and read her the letter, stopping at every paragraph to wipe the tears spilling down my cheeks. She told me to hang tight and she'd have Richard call me back right away. Even though he was a real estate attorney, he'd have someone in his office handle the case and give me the best representation possible.

Within fifteen minutes Richard had dialed my cell phone number and I blew my nose again before answering. I had moved out into the front dining room and set up a makeshift desk at one of the tables for a little privacy. When I picked up the phone, Richard told me that he had already handpicked an attorney and assured me that we'd get it taken care of. As a matter of fact, he said, he had the lawyer sitting next to him in his office. His name was William Frasier.

Richard asked if he could put me on speakerphone. I agreed, regained my composure, and after introductory pleasantries read the entire letter over the phone. The news William Frasier delivered wasn't exactly what I wanted to hear. "We are going to win this case in the end, but in the meantime," Mr. Frasier told me, "you're going to have to do what they ask. You'll have to cease and desist all operations right away."

Now I knew what "my blood ran cold" meant. My body felt stiff and lifeless as if I were already a corpse. "But what about our reservations for tonight and the rest of the week?" I asked, my voice rising in fear. Peter slowly descended the front steps and pulled up a chair next to mine. I gestured for him to share the receiver with me.

"You could risk it but if this thing goes to court, we want to be able to say we complied with their request. Otherwise, the court could find you liable and you'd have to give up the profits you made while using her trademark as well as pay her other reparations such as punitive damages, fines, and her attorney's fees."

Peter placed his arm around my shoulder. "This is a nightmare. A total nightmare!" I said. "I woke up this morning on top of the moon, now I'm closing the doors of my beautiful restaurant before we even get started?" My voice cracked and I wrapped another wad of toilet paper around my fingers.

William Frasier continued. "The first thing I'll do is send this Elliott Hightower fella a letter back refuting the argument. There is no geographic proximity to the restaurant in Vermont and what you are trying to accomplish here in Tennessee. We'll show that there is no likelihood of confusion by using the two locations because of the long distance between the two states. If we have to, we'll go in front of the trademark examiner. I have no doubt that they will eventually rule in our favor."

"That's a relief . . . I guess. But what am I supposed to do in the meantime?"

"Sadly, you'll have to wait. Shut down for a few weeks. Unfortunately, this kind of thing happens all the time. It's meant to be more of a scare tactic. I believe this person—what's the plaintiff's name again?"

"Helga. Helga Schloygin."

"Right. I believe Helga Schloygin has been told that she won't win but it's meant to scare you into ceasing under the current operation or changing the name of your restaurant in Memphis. That's actually a viable solution, by the way."

"But I don't want to change the name of my restaurant. Everything is in place. My menus, my sign, my advertising, my business license, my liquor license—all of that would take a while to change anyway, wouldn't it?"

"Yeah, it could. I bet we can bring this to a close in about the same time it would take to reapply for other licenses under a different name. I have my doubts that she'll actually bring a lawsuit against you."

"You don't know Helga. Nothing she did would surprise me. She deliberately introduced my husband to another woman so she could ultimately take back the restaurant."

I heard him snicker. "Geez! What did you do to her?" I could hear Richard in the background snickering along with him.

"Nothing! I never did a thing to that woman. She just plain hated me from the minute I arrived in Vermont. She's six feet tall, wears her hair slicked back in a tight bun, and walks around all day with a Pall Mall dangling out of the side of her mouth. The ashes are always dropping on things wherever she goes. She reminds me of Cruella de Vil, minus the cigarette holder."

Both men roared with big bursts of laughter.

"And for some reason, she has declared herself my irrevocable nemesis."

"Most of these cease and desist cases are all about revenge," William Frasier said. "Someone deliberately trying to knock someone else out of business. Happens all the time. I bet the U.S. post office delivers a thousand cease and desist letters a week."

"I could have stopped her from buying the inn nine months ago but I wanted out of that place."

William laughed again before saying, "Listen, Leelee, can you come in here sometime today or tomorrow and sign an agreement?"

I looked over at Peter for affirmation. He nodded. "Sure."

"My rate is three hundred dollars per hour. And because I'm so sure we can clear this up without going to court, you can just give me a two-thousand-dollar retainer. Can you do that?"

Spending another two thousand dollars on an attorney made me nauseated. I sighed loudly before saying, "I guess so."

"Great. If I'm not here, I'll leave the agreement with the receptionist. You can leave your check and a signed copy with her. Oh, and don't forget that letter from the Vermont attorney."

"I won't, although it's not in the best shape. I crumpled it up in a ball after I read it."

"I can't say I blame you," William said.

"Thanks, William. I really appreciate your help. How long do you think we'll be closed?"

"It's hard to say but I'd plan on six weeks, give or take a week. Do you have another way of earning income while the restaurant is down?"

I looked at Peter, raising my eyebrows. "We planned on doing some additional catering. Will that be all right?"

"Of course. Just make sure you operate under another name."

"But we've already printed brochures that say Peach Blossom Inn Catering."

"Print some more under another name for the time being. Call it the Peachy Beachy Catering Club—I don't know, anything. You can go back to the Peach Blossom Inn once this mess is cleared up."

I took in a deep breath and exhaled loudly. "I suppose I have no choice." I closed my eyes and tried to think of another name on the spur of the moment but nothing came to mind. "Thanks so much for your time. I sure appreciate you working me in so quickly."

"Hey, no problem," William said. "We'll get this mess straightened out. I'll be in touch as soon as I hear back from Mr. Hightower."

We exchanged adieus and I hung up the phone, gazing at Peter with "I am miserable" written all over my face. I didn't realize I'd been biting my lip until sweet Peter reached over and covered it with his finger. His hand swept over my cheek and he cradled my face in his palm. "Let's go for a walk. The exercise and fresh air will do you some good."

"Okay," I said softly.

"We'll get this figured out." Peter took ahold of my hand and pulled me up out of the chair. "Hold down the fort, man," he said to Jeb, who had snuck in during our conversation. "We'll be back shortly."

"What should I tell the folks in the kitchen?" Jeb asked.

"I'm not sure yet. Just hang tight."

As we walked out the front door and down the walkway lined with boxwoods, Peter held my hand. The reality of what had happened that morning caused a distress and an ache that wouldn't stop knocking at my mind's door. I couldn't blink it away if I tried. It was always there, permeating my every brain cell. Certainly there was a fear of financial ruin floating around; who wouldn't have that? But the underlying fear, the one that had me the most unnerved, had everything to do with Peter. How on earth would I pay him, and if I couldn't, how long would he stay? Here he had moved down to Memphis with a guaranteed job at the Peach Blossom Inn, and the whole thing had just exploded. It was the reason he hadn't come to Tennessee sooner, and that reality frightened me with an intensity I had felt only one other time. The day Baker left.

Alice and Virginia sat in the rocking chairs on my front porch and told every single person that showed up to the restaurant that we had an unexpected delay and wouldn't be opening for a few more weeks. Mary Jule spent the evening inside, right next to the telephone, fielding phone calls with the same explanation.

I couldn't do it. Neither could Peter. Both of us were so sad and mentally exhausted from explaining to our staff that they wouldn't have jobs, canceling our coveted reservations, and taking a melancholy trip downtown to pay a retainer for an attorney to represent us in a potential lawsuit that we could do little more than stare at one another. Here we'd been higher than Heaven Friday night, and four days later we were in the bowels of Hell.

Roberta and Pierre were collecting unemployment until stick season was over back in Vermont and told me that they still wanted to stay, at least through Thanksgiving. Jeb seemed antsy to get back but when my girlfriends all promised that he could sweep their chimneys, he changed his mind.

"Hey, there is one bright spot," Peter said with a slight shrug of his shoulders. "Now we can cater Tootie Shotwell's party."

"Right," I told him, not daring to let my face nor my voice reveal my displeasure. "It's always good to look for the positive." Inside I felt sick to my stomach. The thought of actually working for Tootie Shotwell, even for a day, was enough to make me want to shoot myself.

Chapter Twelve

*"Are you ready? Hell yeah! Damn right! Hotty Toddy, Gosh almighty, who
the hell are we, Hey! Flim Flam, Bim Bam OLE MISS BY DAMN!"*

The greeting, the cheer, the allegiant anthem of my beloved alma
mater, bellowed fervently across the immense ten-acre, treed, green
space, affectionately called the Grove, brightening my spirits the second we opened the doors of our rental van. The sea of red, white, and
blue tents could be seen the minute we pulled onto campus from West
Jackson Avenue and turned down Rebel Drive. When we passed the
Chi O house, a flood of memories decorated my thoughts and I could
practically see Virginia and me on the front porch decked out in our
red and blue sundresses, laughing and cooing with others in our pledge
class.

I drove the hour-and-a-half journey down with Peter sitting next to
me in the passenger seat. Pierre and Roberta were wedged into seats in
the back amid the food and catering supplies, while my best friends
and Jeb followed behind in Alice's Volvo station wagon. Quite honestly
there was no need for all of us to be there, but the thought of serving
food for highfalutin Tootie without my girlfriends nearby struck me as

a fate aligned with becoming her housekeeper. Even though it was *my* highfalutin catering business, I couldn't imagine standing behind the tables in her tent ladling food onto the china plates of her guests, no matter how magnificent our cuisine. I'd have rather run down the street naked covered in skunk spray than be Tootie Shotwell's maid for the day, but I did not have a choice. With the Peach Blossom Inn on hold, catering would be the only source of our income and I was determined to humble myself, relinquish my pride, and suck it up no matter what. Besides, Peter assured me that he, Roberta, and Pierre would be the ones serving and Jeb would be in charge of setup and teardown. He said I could "manage" and "assist" if needed in between accompanying Virginia, Mary Jule, and Alice as we bopped around from tent to tent socializing. He knew how hard the last few weeks had been and wanted me to have fun and throw my stress in the trash can. At least while I was at Ole Miss, anyway.

Mother Nature cooperated by serving up a gorgeous seventy-degree day, hardly a climate for sundresses, but still warm enough for all the fashionistas to show off the dresses in their latest fall wardrobes. Ole Miss girls, Greek or not, wouldn't be caught dead tailgating in anything less than cocktail attire. Fans from Mississippi State, or "State" as Mississippians refer to the "other university," seem to be content wearing State sweatshirts and fatigues, one of the glaring differences between the rivals. Not so much for the Greeks at State, but for the independents, as they prefer a more casual look. There is a certain Grove dress code for Old Miss fans, and for the women, high heels—no matter how soggy the ground—is an important part of the look. A pair of flip-flops can be stowed away in the girl's purse for later, but starting the day in heels is a definite must. The dress code for men is a little more casual, with nice polo shirts and trousers (you'll find quite a bit of madras on warmer days), loafers and button-downs, with the occasional coat and tie. All fraternity pledges, however, must attend the games wearing navy blazers and ties.

In Oxford the word "grove" has become both a noun and a verb. Fans "grove" next to the same "grovers" year after year, and a common question on Fridays is "Are y'all goin' groving tomorrow?" The stadium holds sixty thousand but close to a hundred thousand people usually turn out for the pre-party in the Grove. Many of the tents have a lounge area and chairs for a ringside, big-screen TV seat. Admission to the Grove is free, so anyone without a ticket is just as content to watch from the confines of the well-equipped tents.

When Virginia and I were in school, people tailgated in the traditional sense, from the backs of their cars. But after years of tearing up the turf, the university decided to ban motor vehicles, and for the last twenty years tent popularity has grown. Lafayette County operates under an antiquated law that forbids beer. Not wine or liquor, just beer, so anyone partying in the Grove must be discreet if ale or lager is their preference. Locks have to be placed on the coolers.

Now some party givers pay dearly, two hundred dollars per game, to have someone babysit the tent when they go into the stadium, eliminating the chance of thievery. And speaking of money, groving is not cheap, at least not for the party host. Aside from the cost of the tent rental, a college boy is hired to stake the spot and erect the tent. No one is allowed onto the Grove until 2 A.M., but the boys stand in line ready to claim the best spots. For that he's paid handsomely, no less than six hundred dollars per game. By the time the tent is game ready, it's adorned with magnificent floral centerpieces, tablecloths, silver services, chandeliers, candelabras and other decorative lighting, big-screen TVs, and a satellite dish. Not everyone goes to that extreme, but anyone who claims to be someone certainly does.

After forty minutes of inching down Rebel Lane and Student Union Drive to get to Tootie's tent we finally parked our van behind several others on the street to unload. Tootie's triple-size tent was erected right next to the Walk of Champions, a coveted spot amongst grovers, and I could see her standing at the edge when we pulled up, using her hand as a visor to block the sun.

"Hi, Leelee," she said when I shut my door. "I've been waiting on y'all." Tootie didn't let her big brown eyes light on me long, choosing instead to focus over the top of the van at Peter. "Glad y'all could make it." The first thing she did was slap a HOTTY TODDY WITH TOOTIE sticker on my chest. "This one is for you, and this one is for—" She waited for Peter while he opened the back of the van, then scooted over to him. "—you. There," she said, patting his chest.

"Hotty Toddy" has no real meaning per se, but it means everything in Oxford. For teachers, students, fans, and alumni, it is a greeting, cheer, and secret handshake all rolled into one. Hotty Toddy is the spirit of Ole Miss.

Tootie dripped in jewels completely inappropriate for an afternoon event: on her wrist, her fingers, around her neck, and in her ears. And I'm convinced her outfit came straight out of a boutique in New York. It was definitely couture. She wore stylish gabardine pants underneath a tweed fitted jacket with large jade buttons encased in silver, a starched white blouse, and a gorgeous wide leather belt with a shiny sterling silver buckle.

After greeting Peter with a toothy smile and a long-drawn-out hi, she took a cursory glance at her watch. "The party starts in two hours, you'll be ready, won't you?"

"We will," Peter said, grabbing a large stainless steel food pan containing four marinated tenderloins covered in Saran Wrap out of the back of the van.

She looked down at the meat. "Oh, you won't be needing that pan; I have my own silver serving pieces."

"Relax, darling." There was a wee bit of cockiness in his voice. "This is simply for storage. How are you today?" He shot her his best smile. I could tell she was weak in the knees. If I had been on the other side of that smile, I'd have melted myself.

Tootie glanced again at the meat and swept her hand through the air. "Of course that's for storage. Silly me. And I'm greaaaat, thanks. A little nervous that all goes well, but I'm great."

"What are you nervous about?" Peter asked. "It can't be the food, and the kickoff is at two o'clock, right?" Tootie wanted her party to start at noon, two hours before the game started.

"Yes, I know it's still two hours away but I want everything to be perfect."

Peter glanced around at the tent, which looked more like the inside of her living room than a parcel of green space. "By the looks of this place, I'd say it's perfect already."

Tootie's tent was one of the largest in the Grove and when we arrived, the floral arrangements had already been placed amid the tables atop freshly starched white linen tablecloths with red, white, and blue linen toppers. Four arrangements to be exact and they must have each been five feet tall. Sunflowers, red dahlias, and every fall fruit imaginable were interwoven among fall flowers in large Mississippi McCarty pots. Pomegranate and orange halves, artichokes, white, green, and orange miniature pumpkins and lemons were beautifully arranged amid ribbons of cast-iron plant. A long floral arrangement snaked around the middle of each serving table with enough room for Tootie's teak serving trays mixed with sterling silver and McCarty pottery. The poles on the tent were decorated with the same large cast-iron plant foliage and more fresh fruit. A large iron chandelier hung from the middle, high above the Oriental rug. I had to admit, it was spectacular.

"We've got a few things to unload here," Peter told her. "You said you've got a generator, right?"

"Yes, I do. It's over there." When she pointed to the back of the tent, I caught sight of her nails. Pale, pink, perfect. I glanced at mine. Short, split, slipshod.

"Okeydoke. We'll be ready before noon." Peter winked at me before planting a reassuring kiss on my cheek. He knew I was the nervous one.

Roberta and Pierre stepped into the tent carrying more food pans. "Hi," Roberta said to Tootie with her usual cheery smile. "I'm Roberta and that there's Pierre." Pierre laid his pan on a table, bowed, and kissed the back of Tootie's hand. Tootie is very beautiful, I'll give her that, and I'm sure Pierre noticed.

"*Well*, aren't you charming," she said. "I think I saw you the other night at the party but I don't think I've had the pleasure."

Pierre put on his happy face, the one where he smiles widely and bobs his head excitedly. "*Bonjour! Madame est* vedy beautiful."

Tootie feigned modesty. "Oh, well, I'm not sure about that, but thank you very much." She finally turned her gaze toward Roberta. "You're not from around here, are you?" Even though she tried to hide it, I could see the stealthy way she scanned Roberta from head to toe. Roberta's tight black polyester pants showed every hump, lump, and bump from her waist down, a total contrast to our perfectly polished, perfectly toned hostess.

"Nuup. We're from Vermont. Came down to help Leelee and Peter get this business off the ground. Good to meet you." The glaring differences between these two women were humbling. The beautiful one had everything money could buy, and the other less attractive one had all the joy money couldn't buy.

"Thank youuuu, nice to meet you, too," Tootie said. "I'd like you to be the cake cutter today. It's Roberta, right?"

"Yuup, I'm Roberta and I'd be honored," Roberta responded with a bow. "That's one of my main jobs in the restaurant, slicing up the desserts. I'd be happy to cut your cake."

"Great! Then you can serve *all* the desserts. Okay, I'd like to have a short meeting when y'all are done unloading," she told Peter, strutting toward him with the tiny heels on her four-inch Louboutins sinking into the earth. "I want to make sure we're all on the same page."

"Right," he said, semi-ignoring her as he waved Pierre over to the van. We had rented a mobile insulated food cart to keep everything warm and it took the two of them to unload it.

Tootie had a list in her hand and followed behind. "You've got the homemade yeast rolls, the lamb kebabs, the shrimp, the smoked salmon—".

"Whoa, hold on a second," Peter said, smiling at her as he and Pierre toted the warmer into the tent. "Give us just a little while to unload and we'll sit down and go over all the food and anything else you want to discuss. Trust me. I've got everything you requested. No need to worry." Without waiting for her response, he put the warmer down and walked over to check out the generator.

When he turned back around and saw Roberta schlepping more gear back and forth from the van to the tent, he said to me, away from

Tootie's earshot, "Where's Jeb? He's here to work, you know. I had a feeling we shouldn't have let him ride with the girls. There's no telling when he'll show up."

"I'm sure he'll be here any minute," I said, anxious. "They may have had to park a ways away."

Towering stacks of white Styrofoam cups inscribed with HOTTY TODDY WITH TOOTIE in red script caught my eye atop a bar set up in the far corner. (A simple twist of a vowel and a consonant, and they'd have read "Hoity Toity Tootie." Irony? Coincidence? Mmmhmm.) I assumed Tootie's husband was a host, too, but I never once saw a "Hotty Toddy with Trey" cup. Bless his heart, it was easy to see who wore the red and blue madras trousers in that family. I still hadn't seen him around but figured he'd be along at some point.

Thirty minutes later, once everything was unloaded, Peter gathered all of us around the food tables. He laced into us, though I knew his anger was misdirected. "Where the heck is Jeb?" The only time Peter ever gets heated is when someone on his staff is not pulling his weight.

"I know reet where he is," Roberta said. "He's off with the girls, having himself a big ole time." If I were Roberta, I'd have been envious, but she never ever felt that way. She always managed to be content, no matter the circumstance.

"That's what I was afraid of," Peter said, shaking his head in frustration.

Pierre said, *"Jeb est avec toutes les belles femmes."* He turned to look outside the tent and blew all the anonymous Mississippi women an air kiss.

"He needs to get his butt back here before I tackle him. He's on our payroll today, not Ole Miss's." Tootie was busy fiddling with one of the flower arrangements when Peter called her over to the huddle. "Okay, Miss Tootie, you can have that meeting now."

She stopped what she was doing, picked up her iPad, and headed straight over. "All right. First let's run over the food checklist. I've put place cards in front of the serving pieces for the particular food items so y'all will know where to put each one."

"I've seen them," Peter said with a wink.

"Great. So we have tenderloin and Kissie's yeast rolls with home-made horseradish cream sauce?" She looked up, waiting for Peter to affirm, so he nodded his head slightly. "Lamb kebabs with home-made rosemary garlic sauce, shrimp dijonnaise, garlic cheese grits, homemade spicy polenta cakes, and smoked salmon with all the con-diments?" Peter nodded again.

She never once looked at me. As she continued down her screen, her pink-nailed fingers scrolling by each item, Tootie made particular mention of "homemade." I couldn't tell if it was for the benefit of any onlookers or just to reassure herself we hadn't made a stop at the nearby Winn-Dixie on the way down.

"A large assortment of crudités with three homemade dipping sauces . . . hummus, blue cheese, and curry? Cream spinach, stuffed mushrooms, and twice-baked new potatoes with cheese, chives, bacon, and sour cream? Oh, and I almost forgot the mini homemade Gouda mac-and-cheese bites."

"You got it," Peter told her.

"Thank God there won't be an Abner's chicken strip anywhere near my table," Tootie said with a wave of her hand. "I take that back, they'll be all over the Grove." Then under her breath she muttered, "They're so dreadfully common."

"Tootie, your cake is gorgeous," I told her. It was truly nothing short of a masterpiece: red, white, and blue, four-tiered with Bully, the Mis-sissippi State bulldog mascot laid flat out in between the layers and a big Ole Miss doghouse on top of him. His head poked out the front with Band-Aids made of icing on his nose and his tail, which pro-truded from the sides of the cake. An icing insignia read, IF YOU CAN'T RUN WITH THE BIG BEARS, STAY ON THE PORCH. The top layer was decorated with red icing pompoms and a large icing dog bone that read, ALL BARK AND NO BITE. Cake is my hands-down favorite des-sert; I was salivating just looking at it.

"Thank yooouuu," she said.

There were many more desserts displayed on freshly polished, elaborate silver trays covered in Saran Wrap. Tootie hadn't asked us to prepare any desserts and I found out later that her cook made most of them: brownie bites, football and Colonel Rebel–shaped sugar cookies with HOTTY TODDY WITH TOOTIE in red icing, lemon squares, and individual pecan pies. When I considered all these desserts and the large abundance of food we had provided, it looked to me that she was expecting two hundred guests instead of the one hundred for which she had planned.

"And your flowers are exquisite," I told her. It wasn't a stretch; they really were out of this world.

"Oxford Floral! They've never once let me down. I wish they were in Memphis. If you ask me, they are way better than Rachel's."

After belaboring all the details of the day—like what she wanted to happen before, during, and after the game—and a strict admonishment about not "partaking" during the party, she said, "And there's one more thing." She walked over to the side of the tent and came back with a small duffel bag. "I have a little surprise for y'all." She dug into the bag and pulled out a stack of red Ole Miss baseball caps and waved them in the air. She handed one to Roberta and one to Pierre, holding on to the others. "Aren't they cute? I don't want any hair in the food," she explained with a nervous giggle. "This one is for the other fellow when he shows up. Is his name Jeb?"

I nodded.

Then she handed one to me. I was not even thinking about messing up my hair with a ball cap. It took every bit of everything I had not to plop it down on her perfect hairdo, so I just forced a smile. Tootie then reached back into her bag and pulled out a billowy white chef's hat with the Ole Miss logo embroidered on the front and handed it to Peter. "Isn't this just the cutest thing?"

I thought I had made it perfectly clear on the phone that Peter did not like chef hats, so I eagerly awaited Peter's Yankee response.

"Tootie. I appreciate you going to so much trouble, but I don't dig a chef hat." Then he winked at her.

"Why, surely you can wear it just this one little time. I feel like it just makes the outfit. You know, with your cute little coat and all." She reached over and tapped one of his knotted buttons.

He shook his head. "Sorry."

"Will you do it for me?" she said, batting her eyelashes. Seriously, she really was batting her eyelashes. I held my breath as the next comment escaped his lips.

"I don't think so," he said like a true Yankee.

She popped her eyebrows up and reared her head back, shocked someone had the nerve to defy her wishes. "Okay," she said, and bobbled her head. "I'll put it right here in front of where you'll be serving." Tootie had to have the last word. Always had.

Peter pulled on my sleeve, distracting me from my thoughts. "Seriously, where is Jeb? He better get back here, otherwise you'll have to take his place and I don't think you want to get that pretty little skirt dirty." He pinched a corner of the fabric and smiled. I don't know that I'd ever seen a man look more stunning in a white jacket. His hair shone with a luster of satin in the noon sunlight, and the light brown scruff on his face gave him a provocative edge. The short hair above his top lip actually made it look even fuller, and those blue eyes of his would cause anyone to get a crick in their neck.

"You're right, we're paying him to be here. I'll call Alice on her cell and find out where they are."

When Alice didn't answer, I called Virginia and got the same result. Mary Jule, however, dutifully picked up on the third ring. "I'm sure you're wondering where we are," she said right away. "We're over at Cary Coors's tent drinking a Bloody Mary."

"With Jeb?"

"With Jayeb."

"Peter is ready to kill him. You've got to send him over here right now."

"I'm telling you he'll get lost. I don't even know where I am. They're expecting a hundred thousand people today and half of them are here already. We told Jeb to stay put until you came to get him. We figured you'd welcome the chance to get away from Tootie." She whispered when she said Tootie's name.

"You have no idea. Okay, I'll come to y'all. Just wait right there."

"Do you know where it is?"

"No, but I'll ask Tootie."

Tootie knew right where Cary's tent was and after letting my crew know I'd be right back, I hauled off through the crowd.

In honor of our school colors, I had worn a royal blue pencil skirt and a darling ivory cashmere cardigan with three-quarter sleeves. Mama's pearls just *made* the sweater, in my opinion, and so did her triple-strand pearl bracelet. My red peep-toe pumps slowed me down a bit on the journey across the Grove, but after years of living in heels, I wouldn't say more than five minutes. Cary's tent was on the other end of the Walk of Champions, but from what Tootie told me, she had a primo spot, too. The oaks, magnolias, and elms, some over two hundred years old, intensified my Southern pride as I gazed up at the remaining canopies of red, yellow, and green leaves. I zigzagged my way through hundreds of beautiful college co-eds running around the Grove in short, fancy dresses. Some wore boots, others sandals or pumps, but all held toddies in their hands.

You'd never know Ole Miss had changed its mascot to the black bear by looking around the Grove. Even though Colonel Reb is no longer the mascot, the diehards don't care. You'll see plantation hats all over the place.

I knew I was almost to Cary's when I saw the inscription on top of her tent. In bright red letters atop a blue background it read, GIVE ME MEMPHIS, TENNESSEE. I raced inside, wishing I could spend the entire afternoon with her. When I saw Jeb with a Bloody in one hand and an Ole Miss pom-pom in the other I laughed out loud. He was decked out in a head-to-toe Colonel Reb suit: red pants, red jacket, and a big plantation hat. Cary is a hoot. She keeps the costume in her tent and chooses someone new to wear it each game.

When Jeb saw me, he turned to Virginia, who had on a Colonel Reb hat herself, raised his glass in her direction, and hollered, "*Are you ready?"* Virginia, Cary, Mary Jule, and Alice joined right in with him but it was Jeb's voice that rang the loudest. *"Hell yeah! Damn right! Hotty Toddy, Gosh almighty, who the hell are we, Hey! Flim Flam, Bim Bam OLE MISS BY DAMN!"* Jeb stomped his right foot to each word and raised his glass at the end of the refrain.

Bless his heart.

Virginia, in her this-is-such-a-riot voice, said, "Jayeb Duggar has switched sides! He says he'll never be a Yankee again. We've totally converted him."

"Yuup! I've crossed over," Jeb said with such surety in his voice, and began whistlin' "Dixie." His arms were wrapped around both Virginia's and Alice's shoulders and he stood smack-dab in the middle between them. Alice and Mary Jule didn't even go to Ole Miss, but you can't help but turn into a Rebel once anywhere near the vicinity of Oxford. "You girls have made a Reb out of me." Alice took a disparaging glance at Jeb's Bloody, which rested on her shoulder. The fun may have been all over if he spilt even a drop of tomato juice on her gorgeous game-day outfit.

"I'm happy to hear it, but if you want to support yourself while you're here to stay, you better get on back to Peter," I said, half feeling terrible about putting a pin in his newfound collegiate bubble of joy. "He's been asking for you. I hate to tell you, but there's a lot of work to do and Tootie's party is starting soon."

Jeb put down his drink, looked at his pants, and ran his hands along the front of the jacket, which was three sizes too small. With countenance drooping, he turned to Cary. "You want me to leave this here?"

"Nah," she said. "It's yours for the day. Wear it with pride, you damn Yankee! Just make sure you leave it when you come back later to *par-tay*."

"How long will you guys be par-taying?" he asked, the light returning in his eyes.

"All night long," she said. "You know what we say down here, don't ya, Yankee boy? 'We may lose the game but we never lose the party!'"

"Hotty Toddy!" Jeb exclaimed, raising both fists.

I told the girls to come on over to Tootie's soon to say hi. "Yeah right," Virgy said. "Be there in five. *Not.*" None of them had any desire at all to come over to Tootie's.

"I don't know what I was thinking," I told her. "I'll be back over here when I can. Come on, Jeb."

As we exited the tent, he turned around again and yelled, "Hotty Toddyyyyyyyyy!" To which the girls echoed, "Hotty Toddyyyyyyyyy!" When Jeb and I passed the Hotty Toddy Potty and the Hotty Toddy Potty II, he did it again. In fact, the whole way across the Grove from Cary's to Tootie's, he Hotty Toddied almost every person he saw.

We had just about made it back to Tootie's when the Ole Miss football players hustled down the Walk of Champions en route to the venerable Vaught–Hemingway Stadium. When Jeb saw the thousands of fans lined up on either side of the redbrick walkway, he busted his way through the bumper-to-bumper crowd, raised his right hand, and high-fived each player that would look in his direction. "Hotty Toddy!" he screamed over and over, feverishly stomping his foot and beaming with Rebel pride.

When a pretty co-ed from Mississippi State came up to Jeb and in a lazy, Mississippi drawl said, "May I git your autograph, Colonel?" he puffed out his chest and felt around in his pockets for a pen. The equally cute girl with her handed him a Sharpie along with her white Styrofoam cup.

Jeb scrawled *Jeb* confidently across the top. But as he started to write the *D* for Duggar, he hesitated a moment and drew a line through the *J*, adding an *R*. "Think nothin' of it," he said, stealing a sip of her toddy, and went right back to cheering for the home team.

Jeb had never even been to a college football game before that day, much less a tailgate party, and here he ended up at the mother of them all. *Sports Illustrated* calls it "the number one tailgating site in the country," and *Sporting News* says it's "the holy grail of tailgating sites." *The New York Times* claims it's "the mother and mistress of outdoor ritual mayhem," and by the appearance of my tailgating-party-challenged, Yankee-turned-Rebel handyman, Ole Miss had a brand-new talisman.

Chapter Thirteen

When we finally made it back to Tootie's around eleven thirty, Peter was peeved. He, Roberta, and Pierre were in their places behind the tables, and all the food was set up and ready to go. The tent was crowded and it seemed many of Tootie's friends had arrived ahead of schedule. He took one look at Jeb and rolled his eyes. "I don't even want to know where you got that getup."

"Cary gave it to me," Jeb said, like they were old friends. When Jeb Hotty Toddied Peter, he completely ignored him, but when he started doing it to every person he saw in the tent, Tootie pulled me over to the side.

"I'm glad your worker is excited to be here, Leelee, but quite frankly he's getting on my nerves. You'd think he'd never been to a football game by the way he's acting."

"He hasn't."

"You're joking, right?"

"No," I said with a quick shake of my head. "I'm not. He's just excited. But I'll ask him to stop."

"I would appreciate that," Tootie said. "Oh and one more thing. He told me that he was the proprietor of a computer business back in Vermont called Jeb's Computer World? Sounds like quite a business."

"Enterprise is more like it," I told her, picturing the tiny lean-to with the fat orange extension cord running out the door to the power outlet on the front porch of the main house.

"He asked me what kind of computer I owned. When I told him a Mac, he shook his head and said, 'Bad move.' I don't know what to say about that other than he probably shouldn't say that to this crowd. It makes him look . . . *unintelligent*." Tootie screwed up her face and shrugged her shoulders.

"I understand," I told her. "I'll talk to him."

She turned her head back around toward Jeb. "Look, he's over there handing out his business cards."

Peter overheard Tootie, left his post, and strode over to Jeb, tapping him on his shiny red sleeve. "Enough," I heard Peter say before relegating him to the catering area.

It wasn't as bad as I thought once the party got going. I wished I could get back all the time I'd spent worrying about it. Several times during the party, I'd catch Peter bragging on me. He'd go into detail about what a great job I had done and how smart I was to start a restaurant from scratch, basically giving all the credit for our business to me. When asked if I was a chef by one of the men, he got the cutest smile on his face and said, "She's learning."

Several of Tootie's guests complimented our food and the staff. I didn't know what to say when asked about the closing of the restaurant, though. How was I supposed to explain Helga Schloygin and the vendetta she had toward me in five minutes or less? When asked, I just told the truth, minus the history with Helga. I explained that when I sold the restaurant in Vermont I'd never thought about the legalities of using the same name in Tennessee. I could tell some people felt bad for me, but for the most part our setback had no effect on them at all. They went right back to the party and Ole Miss football. The other party host, Trey Shotwell, was quite pleasant. He seemed ecstatic with everything about our catering company and took every opportunity to let me know.

Just before 2 P.M., as Tootie's guests were leaving for the game, folks filled their HOTTY TODDY WITH TOOTIE cups with toddies and grabbed a red pom-pom from one of two cute high school girls standing at the edge of the tent. I hadn't been able to talk to Roberta at all during the party, what with all the socializing I'd been doing. Granted, Alice and them had never graced us with their appearance, but I was perfectly content chatting with several lovely Tri Deltas I knew at Tootie's party. When I glanced in Roberta's direction she was serving one final piece of cake to a man with little Colonel Rebs sprinkled all over his red cotton trousers. We caught eyes and as soon as the man left, she beckoned to me from her spot behind the dessert table.

"I'll have a piece, please," I said, swiping a small glob of icing off the edge of the platter and discreetly licking it off my finger. "And make it a big fat one."

Roberta served up a large piece on one of Tootie's bone china dessert plates and handed it to me along with a sterling silver dessert fork. "I've been wanting to tell you something for an hour or so, but I haven't had a minute to breathe," she said.

"Really? What is it?" I asked, ravenously shoveling a huge hunk of the deliciousness in my mouth.

"I think I saw Baker a little earlier."

I choked on the extra large bite still in my mouth. After a long coughing fit, I managed to say, *"You what?"*

"I think I saw Baker."

My eyes brimming with choking tears, I put the cake plate down, grabbed both her shoulders, and looked her square in the eye. "You think you saw him, or you saw him saw him?"

"I saw him saw him," she said with keen affirmation. "I looked reet at him. He was standing outside this very tent. I think he saw me, too, but he didn't say nothin'."

Although he called the girls once a week, we hadn't laid eyes on my ex-husband since leaving Vermont, nine months earlier. "Roberta. This is very serious. Are you sure it was him?" I relaxed my arms. "He called the girls Thanksgiving night but never said he was in town."

"I'd almost swear it was him."

I had to know and could think of only one way to be sure. "What did he have on?"

"Let's see. Khaki pants and a golfer's shirt. Orange I think it was."

I sucked in a loud gasp of air. "Oh my gosh. You did see him. That's exactly what Baker would wear. A Big Orange, University of Tennessee golf shirt and khakis. He wears that everywhere he goes, I don't care what campus he's visiting. Was he wearing suede bucks?"

"I couldn't say. I didn't look at his feet."

"Was *she* with him?" I asked in a panic. Running into her would be far worse, believe it or not, than becoming Tootie's maid.

"I didn't notice if she was."

"Hmm. Did Pierre or Jeb see him?"

"I don't know."

"Did Peter see him?"

"I don't know that either." God bless her. She seemed unfazed by my deluge of questions.

"Actually those two have never met. I don't think Peter would recognize him even if he had seen him." Hundreds of thoughts and scenarios were racing through my mind. Most important, I couldn't help picturing Sarah and Issie and how this would affect them. "Let's not mention this to my girls. They will be so sad if they learn their dad was here and never came by." I didn't want her to mention it to Peter either but I was afraid to out-and-out say that. Suddenly I remembered my conviction to avoid little white lies. "I don't mean that I want you to lie or anything. I just mean that I don't think we need to mention it to anyone right now. Not till we know for sure it was him."

"Got it."

I wasn't sure why I didn't want her to mention it to Peter. Probably it had more to do with my own insecurities about Baker than anything else. But why I thought Peter would care if Baker Satterfield was within one hundred miles of Memphis was beyond me.

Once Tootie and Trey left their tent for the game, we covered the left-over food, making sure to put the meat, shrimp, and other spoilable items back in the warming drawer and cooler. Most of it had been eaten already but Tootie had wanted to keep the dining open for a little while longer after the game. So Peter made sure to comply with her wishes, always aware that a recommendation from Tootie was well worth the extra hassle.

There were a few stragglers left in the tent without game tickets, mostly men who were well on their way to midday inebriation. The few women without tickets had wandered off, leaving four guys in Tootie's lounge area in front of the extra-large big-screen Sony TV. One of the men, having just left the bar, invited all of us from Peach Blossom Catering (we decided to simply leave out the "Inn" when we reprinted the brochures and William Fraiser had given us the thumbs-up) to join him in the lounge area for kickoff. Welcoming the chance to take a break, all five of us took seats on one side of the lounge while the men were seated on the other. Looking around, it dawned on me that Roberta and I were the only two females left in the tent.

Around the middle of the first quarter, State took the lead, and the Ole Miss fans used the break as an opportunity to head back to the bar. Shortly thereafter, Chuck, a lawyer in a high-powered firm in Jackson, returned to the lounge with a plateful of food and a cardboard carrier containing four cups of beer. Roberta, Pierre, and Peter each had cups in their hands, but my hand was empty. When Chuck offered a beer to me, I politely declined. He went back to his seat, kicking his feet up on a coffee table that Tootie had imported from home. He must have thought it curious that I didn't have a drink in my hand because he leaned over in my direction and said, "Are you a teetotaler or something?"

"No," I told him with a laugh. "I'm just not drinking right now."

"Why not?" he asked, glancing at the other three Ole Miss guys in astonishment.

"We're working and Tootie prefers us not to drink while on the job," I answered.

He dramatically sat up in his chair and simulated a spit. "What? You're kidding me?"

I shrugged.

"To hell with Tootie, she's not even here. Look, Trey Shotwell is a buddy of mine. He won't care. You need a *drank*."

"Really I'm fine," I told the guy. "But thanks anyway."

He kept going. "Can you believe that? She's not drinking," he said, looking at his buddies for support. None of them, thankfully, paid much attention to him. And apparently no one on my side did either. Peter appeared to be quite interested in the game, something that both surprised and delighted me. Pierre sat watching too, oblivious of our conversation. He had a HOTTY TODDY WITH TOOTIE cup in his hand and the content was deep red. Somehow he had covertly slipped over to Tootie's bar, satiating his fond affection for merlot. Jeb continued to keep his eyes glued to the TV set. Roberta kept watching, too, though I knew she hadn't much interest.

Ole Miss ran the football thirty yards for a first down. First and goal on the Mississippi State ten-yard line, and State called a time-out. Unfortunately, Chuck seized the commercial break as another chance for small talk. With his eyes locked on me, he said, "Who are y'all for anyway? State?" A drunken explosion of laughter followed, which was echoed by one of the other guys.

At first I ignored his stupid comment, but then he asked again. "Who are y'all for? Are you State dogs?"

Finally I looked him dead in the eye and said, "Of course not. I went to Ole Miss. We're all Rebels here. Well, sort of," I said with a laugh, glancing at my bunch.

"*Yeah,*" Jeb said emphatically, punching his fist. "Hotty Toddy."

"So, you went to school here?" he said.

I nodded my head, forcing another half smile.

"What sorority were you in, little darlin'?"

"Chi O," I said with a half eye-roll, wishing he would be quiet and just let me watch the dang game.

He bolted up out of his chair. "You were a Chi O at Ole Miss and you're sitting here stone-cold sober at the Egg Bowl?" I looked at Peter, hoping he might step in, but he kept his eyes focused on the TV. The guy was mashing on my last raw nerve, as Kissie would say. I wished he'd shut up.

Ole Miss made a touchdown and all the Ole Miss men, including Jeb, jumped up screaming, "Hotty Toddy! Go Rebs! And hey'ell no, you State dogs!"

During the second quarter, Chuck finally ceased his foolishness but continued his stares. I could see him out of the corner of my eye. At that point, he was too inebriated to say much. When I got up to get a Coke and was headed back to my seat, he patted his lap and with slurring words said, "I've got a nice warm seat for you, Little Miss Chi O. Why don't you get on top. I bet you like that." I totally ignored him, thinking, *You are such a good ole boy, redneck.* When I sat back down in my own seat and looked over at Peter, raising my eyebrows as if to say, Help! he only raised his eyebrows back with a funny look on his face. Surely he knew this guy was out of line. *Why isn't he doing anything?* I thought.

For several minutes, Chuck left me alone and immersed himself in the plays of the game but when Peter got up to find the Hotty Toddy Potty, Chuck took his seat. "You are one hot little mama," he whispered under his liquor-scented breath.

At first I brushed it off, still trying to be polite and maintain my composure. But when he said, "Why don't you ditch chefy-poo and come home with me. I'll show you a real good time," I just wanted out of there.

"No thanks," I said, irritation lacing my voice. "I would appreciate you not talking like that." I got up from my seat in the lounge and walked over to the cake table. Roberta followed right behind. Peter walked back in at that second but instead of reclaiming his seat waved at Jeb and

Pierre, motioning to them for help in the catering area. I watched as the three of them gathered the empty food pans in preparation to load up when the party was over. I'd try catching Peter's eye but he never looked my way. Still fueled by my anger at Chucky-poo, I finally sauntered over to him with hands on my hips. "Did you hear that guy?"

He had just bent over to pick up a large dirty pan and was heading to the van. He stopped right in front of me. "I heard him."

"I thought you would have said something."

"Why didn't *you* say something? You just sat there and took it. He's been staring at your chest all day."

"You noticed that, too?"

"Yeah, I noticed."

"Then why didn't you tell him to stop?"

"It's your chest. *You* should have told him to stop." He turned away and kept walking to the van.

My heart plummeted. All the men I know would have taken up for their woman in a minute. Baker would have never let a guy talk to me like that. Why was Peter allowing it?

I followed behind him. "I did tell him to stop. You were in the bathroom."

"Good. I'm proud of you," he said after placing the pan in the back of the van. "But you should have done it before then."

I thought about what he said and the biggest part of me knew he was right, but he was expecting me to conquer the very thing that was hardest for me. "I . . . wish I could be more like that. It's just difficult for me." I was beginning to think my lack of confrontational skills might be more of a personal weakness than a Southern thing. But I was not alone when it came to that, and Dixie customs are what they are. Not only did I have girlfriends who would have a hard time standing up to a drunken fool, there were plenty of Southern men who would never have stood by and allowed their women to be harassed the way Peter had let that man harass me. Even Frances Folk would have to agree; we had a conundrum.

He inhaled and exhaled before speaking, and then a softening washed over his face, replacing the sour look. I could tell he was choosing his words carefully. "Leelee, you are lovely. I mean that. But you are going to have to learn how to stand up to people. Otherwise you will be eaten alive."

I sighed.

I watched his eyes light on mine, the hint of a smile playing around his lips. "Come here." He held out his arms and I tucked inside. I felt him kissing the top of my head. I knew we needed to have more discussion about it but it was neither the time nor the place. "I'm going to start loading up some stuff in the van. If you want to go over to see your friends, you should probably go now."

"Great idea," I said, feeling immediate relief, and looked around for Roberta. Once I spotted her, I slipped away from his embrace and moved over in her direction. She and Jeb were bent over, stacking dirty plates back in the boxes they were delivered in. "Why don't you walk with me over to see Virginia and them?" I said. "I'd love to show you a little bit more of the campus."

Roberta stood straight up and rubbed her hand along the small of her back. "I think I'd like that, missy."

Jeb started to protest but Peter told him to stay put.

As Roberta and I meandered over to Cary's tent, admiring the stately buildings towering over either side of the Grove, I shared with her several memories of my days at Ole Miss. Never having attended even one day of college, Roberta listened intently and laughed as though she was living vicariously through my experiences as a co-ed. I thought it might have saddened her that she missed out on college life, but she never once acted as if she had any regrets.

It was a much different scene than it was when I trekked across the campus earlier. Sixty thousand people had moved to the stadium. While forty thousand or so still mingled around, it was no longer elbow-to-elbow. We passed an Elvis impersonator in a Colonel Reb costume who gave us a, "Hotty Toddy, little sisters." Roberta's gleaming gray eyes grew double their size—as did her well-lipsticked mouth. Clearly, she loved the attention and I loved watching her.

The setting sun had turned the sky a brilliant orange with streaks of crimson and pink marking the horizon. I thought back to all the fall football games when Virginia and I were in college and how we'd vie for a seat in the sunny section for warmth. With today's setting sun, cooler temperatures had set in and I snuggled closer to Roberta on the way across campus. "Are you cold?" I asked her.

"Nuup. I've told you before. I've gut plenty of extra padding." She patted her tummy.

It dawned on me that I hadn't seen her tug on her panties since that first day she arrived in Memphis, so I asked her, "Are you not wearing those thong panties anymore?"

"Not while I'm here. I only do it for Moe, you know, and with him not around to see me, I'm wearing my granny panties again." She raised her blouse and showed me the top of the thin white cotton panties reaching her belly button. "See? Much more comfortable." I smiled as we moved among the tents—enjoying just how much my Northern and Southern friends completed me.

Ten minutes later, I could finally see Cary's tent in the distance, brimming with people. I hooked my arm through Roberta's, picking up the pace, anxious to finally be amongst my friends. With only a few tents left to pass, I happened to take a cursory glance to our left when—*boom*—my heart fell down to the floor like a runaway elevator. A guy wearing an orange golf shirt looked like a lone orange crayon in a big box of reds and blues. His back was to us, revealing a thick mop of careless dark brown hair, a slender frame, and freshly pressed khakis. I didn't need to see his face to know his identity. I knew it precisely.

Adrenaline rushed through every pore of my body, and I started to pant. I thought we'd make it by without being noticed but just as we started to pass, he happened to turn around. Our eyes locked. I felt that familiar quickening in my heart, the feeling of vivacity, and although I tried to dismiss it, I couldn't deny that it was there. Whether it came from excitement or anger I wasn't sure, but not knowing how to proceed, Baker as usual made the decision for me. I got one foot farther before he called, "Leelee."

I turned my head toward him, as did Roberta. He stepped out of the tent and paced over to us, his classic suede bucks with the red bottoms making a pathway through the manicured lawn. "Roberta Abbott, what are you doing here?" he called, swirling what I knew to be bourbon inside his UT orange cup. "Are you a Rebel now?" He had a winning grin on his face. Baker exuded charisma. That had not changed.

"Nuup, I'm only visiting," she said, tipping her ball cap. "Jeb thinks *he's* a Rebel, though."

He went to hug Roberta and as sweet as she is, she hugged him back. He stepped forward to hug me, but I stepped backwards. It was an instinctual movement, awkward in my high heels, and I teetered for a moment. "You look nice, where are you headed?" he asked, carrying on as if nothing were unusual.

"To Cary Coors's tent," I mustered in a voice that sounded surprisingly calm. I offered nothing else. There was no reason for small talk.

"Ah. I'm sure a lot of your buddies are over there."

"Yup," I said, sounding more like a Northerner than a Southerner. "And they're waiting on me. Come on, Roberta." I pushed her elbow forward.

As we started to walk off, he said, "Wait, Leelee, I was gonna call you. I'm staying at my parents' house and I wanna come by and get the girls. I want them to spend the night."

"Okaaaay," I said, hesitating. They had spent the night with their grandparents since we'd been back in Memphis, but only a few times. Baker's parents weren't the sit-on-the-floor-with-your-grandchildren type. "Can we talk about this later? I'm in a bit of a hurry."

"Sure," he said, just as chipper and nice as he could be. "I'll call you tomorrow."

"Fine," I said, leading Roberta away.

"Bye, Baker," Roberta called over her shoulder as I pressed ahead.

"Oh my God." My heart would not stop racing. In fact, it felt like I was on the Autobahn.

"That was weird," she said once we were out of earshot.

My feet were moving toward Cary's but my head was reeling in every direction but forward. I could hardly think. "Weird?" I finally said. "How about mind-blowing? When I woke up this morning, Baker Satterfield was the furthest thing from my mind. Now he's back in Memphis, wanting to spend time with the girls. We haven't laid eyes on him in *nine months*."

"That's a long time to be away from your kids."

"No kidding. Let's hurry. I have to find Alice and Mary Jule."

"Won't Virginia be there?" Roberta asked.

"She and John have tickets to the game."

Alice was talking with a man I didn't know when Roberta and I made it inside Cary's tent. Since I was exploding with anxiety, I grabbed her arm and yanked her away from her conversation. "Sorry," I said to the guy, "but this is a 911." I pulled her over to the corner. "Baker's here," I said, sounding like I was out of breath.

"Really." It was more of a declaration than a question.

"She's not making it up," Roberta said.

"That's the last thing I expected to come out of your mouth. You sure don't need this right now," Alice said, shaking her head wildly from side to side.

Mary Jule must have seen Alice's head shaking, because she flew over to our side of the tent. "It's about time you got here. What's wrong?"

"She's just seen Baker," Alice told her, and took a long gulp of her drink.

Mary Jule, bug-eyed, looked at me for affirmation.

I shook my head yes.

"Did y'all talk to each other?" Mary Jule wanted to know.

"Oh yes," I said, my heart still thumping. "He was very talkative."

"About what?" Mary Jule asked.

"He wants to see the girls," Roberta said.

Alice bobbled her head, and with a sarcastic tone to her voice uttered, "It's about time."

"I thought he had a job at a *ski resort*," Mary Jule said mockingly. "Fifteen hundred miles away. What's he's doing in Memphis?"

"Oh, I've got that one figured out," I said. "It's stick season up in Vermont. He's got a two-month break."

"Yeah, but he had a two-month break last spring during mud season, and he never came home then," Alice said.

"Huh, what could be different now?" Mary Jule added, drumming her fingers on the side of her cheek.

"Who knows? I'm just ready to get this day over with." A chill ran through my body and I couldn't tell if it was from the temperature outside or plain old high anxiety.

"How's it goin' with Tootie?" Alice asked.

"Actually pretty well now that it's almost over. It started out rough but I can't be too critical. She is helping to put food on my table."

"You've got a point," Mary Jule said. "I just wish it was someone else helping your table."

Feeling a flash of strength all of a sudden, I looked over at the bar. "We have time for one toddy," I said. "I haven't had a thing to drink and I sure could use one. How about you, Roberta?"

Later that night when Tootie paid the check, she had high praise for the job we'd done and said she'd spread the word about Peach Blossom Catering. As I turned the check over in my hand, I thought about how much she had helped us out. How was I supposed to not like Tootie Shotwell anymore after she jump-started our catering business? She was actually helping to sustain us during our legal crisis. It had been three weeks since I received the cease and desist letter, and I'd only heard from William Frasier once. He had exchanged correspondences with Helga's attorney but they were holding firm. Tootie's catering job had saved us. The way she acted in college and when I'd see her around town had left a terrible taste in my mouth, but I had to admit we'd be in a lot deeper hole if it weren't for her. As snooty and gossipy as Tootie is, she actually got me out of a big bind. It caused me to take a long, hard look at myself. Was there something inside of me that was jealous of Tootie Shotwell?

The minute I hit the back door, I snuck into the girls' bedroom and lightly brushed my lips on each of their foreheads. Part of me wanted to wake them but I knew I'd pay for it the next day. I hated being away from them for this many hours at a time and when I saw Kissie standing in the doorway watching us, I silently thanked God for her. The girls had lost their grandparents on my side, but Kissie was a better surrogate than they could possibly hope for. She loved us all so much. Yet there was a great deal about her that I didn't know, like the story about *her* parents or her childhood in Mississippi. I knew all about Frank, her no-count husband who spent her hard-earned money at the dog track in West Memphis, but that was about it. How about her first love or perhaps a love she had had since then? She knew everything there was to know about me. I thought about how selfish I'd been to never ask about things like how hard *her* divorce had been or the death of her child, Josie. Here she'd been investing in me every day since I was born. I decided I'd start asking tomorrow. I was too tired tonight.

When I drug myself out into the den to tell Kissie that I was off to bed early, she had just put down her Bible. I thought about mine, the one collecting dust on my bookshelf. Kissie's was full of underlining. Mine had no underlining at all. Daddy's mother had given it to me when I graduated from high school, taking the time to have my name embossed in gold on the cover.

I plopped down next to her on the sofa. "Hi." There was no zeal in my tone.

"What's the matter, baby? Something bothering you?" She knew me so well.

I exhaled loudly. "Whooo, what a night."

"How was it?"

I turned toward her. "It was much better than I expected, actually."

"That's good."

"Don't get me wrong, Tootie's still a snob, but how can I continue to begrudge her when she hired me? And paid us well."

"That's right," Kissie said. "Mmhmm." Kissie took a sip of the Coke next to her on the end table, a white paper napkin classically wrapped around the glass.

"Peter and I had another hiccup, though."

She gulped in a hurry. "You don't mean it."

"Yes, I'm sorry to say, but I do." I propped a throw pillow behind my head and stretched out on the other end of the sofa with my feet in her lap.

"What happened this time?"

I explained the whole thing about Chuck and how Peter had not done one thing to come to my rescue. I told her how he had just sat there staring at the TV, and when I asked him why, he turned it around on me, as if it was my fault. "I don't understand, Kissie. He thought I should have spit in his eye or something. He thought that by my not telling him to lay off, I was inviting his advances."

"This don't have a thing to do with him not wanting to help you or defend you, I've seen him do it in other ways. He's a big help to you at the restaurant. He goes out of his way to make sure he don't waste no food, he gets the best prices, you don't even pay him all that much to be your chef. But this kind of stuff has to do with the way you two were raised. I've told you before. They ain't like us down here. You want a sip, baby?"

I raised my hand. "No thank you. I'm at a loss as to what to do, though. What do you think?"

"I'm not sure I know either, but I do know that your hearts are very similar. You're both smart and you're both kind people but when it comes to culture, that's another story." She straightened in her seat. "Look at the way he dresses. You don't see him wearing no khaki pants and a starched button-down shirt. No loafers neither. He wears jeans and flannel shirts and work boots. He told me the other day that everywhere he goes, people be asking him where he goes to church. He say, 'Kissie, where I come from we don't ask: Which Catholic church do you go to? We don't even ask that question at all.'" Kissie laughed and slapped her thigh. "He say, 'I'd heard of the blue laws but until I got here I didn't know how blue they can make you.'" She thought that was the funniest thing she'd heard in weeks. I could tell by the way she giggled and laughed, the very antidote I needed.

"I understand what—"

"When I told him that the town I come from in Mississippi still don't allow no alcohol, he fell out." Kissie laughed even harder. "Ooohwee. Yes, sir, said he'd never heard of such."

The sight of her momentarily took my mind off our issues, but when she stopped laughing it came right back. "I understand what you're saying but I just don't know what to do about it," I said sadly. The thought of losing him stung like frostbite nipping my heart. "It's starting to hurt our relationship."

"Baby, it's not hurting your relationship; you're just *allowing* it to hurt your *feelings*. Peter moved down here only eight weeks ago. Y'all still have so much getting acquainted to do. I think y'all make a beautiful couple but you just have to get to know one another a little better, that's all."

"That's not the only thing that happened today. I've been saving the most unbelievable for last." I sat up and looked her dead in the eye.

Kissie gazed at me, waiting.

"I saw Baker."

Not a word escaped Kissie's lips. She just sat there as frozen as a Popsicle.

"He was at the game. A hundred thousand people and our paths cross."

Her nostrils flared as she took a deep breath. "What did he have to say for hisself? Not even calling his girls over a holiday."

"We didn't talk long but he said he wants them to spend the night with him at his parents' house." I reached for the copy of *Garden & Gun* on my coffee table and nervously flipped through the pages. "I don't want them to do that. They have finally stopped crying about us getting a divorce."

"No, baby, he's their daddy. You cain't keep them from him. They need both a y'all."

I knew she was right but didn't want to admit it. I was still furious at him. After pausing to take a quick glance at an ad for an Atlanta interior design firm, I said, "Here's the crazy part. He was so nice. Like nothing was wrong and we were friends, as if the past eighteen months had never happened."

"Maybe that's what he wants."

"I can't be his friend," I said, abruptly closing the magazine.

"You don't know that. Time will take care of the past. Was his girl-friend with him?"

"Not that I noticed. But of course I never asked about her either." I tossed the G & G back on the coffee table and threw my head back onto the sofa.

"I wouldn't be worrying about her or Baker if I were you. You've got a plenty else to occupy your mind. You need to call that lawyer and see about getting your business straight over there so you can get that restaurant you spent all your money on back in business."

She was right about that. We were closing in on a month with no operation, and William Frasier had told me that he thought he could get us up and running in six weeks. Second order of business was to have a long talk with Peter. Somehow we were going to have to call a truce to our North–South culture clash. I would not let something as silly as that come between us. He had become my lifeline and I was determined to fight another Civil War if I had to, as long as he was the result of the peace treaty.

Chapter Fourteen

"Can we go to church with you this morning?" I asked as Kissie stood at the stove frying bacon and stirring a large pot of Cream of Wheat. Most Sundays—well, some Sundays—the girls and I tried to make it to our own Episcopal church; the one my family attended for generations and the place where we were all christened. But it was way down past the University of Memphis. Funny, in all the years I'd heard her talk about her church or the Mother Board, or "Pastor," I'd never gone with her. The reason came down to one rather sorrowful fact: It just wasn't done. The thought had occurred to me, on numerous occasions, that more whites and blacks should attend church together and that that might bridge some of the racial divide in Memphis. I decided right then and there to do my part.

Kissie moved her long wooden spoon through the milky mixture before answering. Without a trace of surprise or doubt, she simply turned around and said, "You better hurry, then. Church gone start at ten o'clock. I'mo fix you and the little girls some breakfast while you git everybody ready."

"You have enough Cream of Wheat there to feed the whole neighborhood."

"That's right. And you could use most of it, too. You ain't any bigger than a stalk a' wheat." In Kissie's mind, thin is not "in."

At that moment Issie ran into the kitchen, naked as a jaybird, her little head a big mess of strawberry curls. "Where are my Snow White panties?" she demanded with hands on her hips. "I want to wear them today."

"Oooh-wee, chil'," Kissie said, "you better git on back to your room. You not suppose to be runnin' around here buck neckid in the winter. You'll catch your death."

"They're in the dirty clothes, lovey," I said. "You can wear them tomorrow."

Issie stomped her foot and crossed her arms in front of her. "Nooo, I want to wear them today."

Kissie tapped her spoon on the side of the pot and waved it toward Issie like she was going to spank her. "I mean it. Get on back there, you hear?" Issie squealed and giggled while Kissie stepped forward with the spoon, sweeping it toward her. When she tore off running back down the hall, Kissie shook her head and smiled. "That's a sweet baby, right there," she said, and then went straight back to stirring her pot.

I hugged her from behind and kissed her cheek, still greasy from the Vaseline she wore to bed every night. As far as Kissie was concerned, Vaseline was the best and only product ever invented. She used it as a facial moisturizer, and a balm for the soles of her feet, her elbows, her cuticles, and even her eyelashes—swearing hers were longer and fuller because of it. I remember her showing me how to avoid diaper rash by slathering Vaseline on my baby's bottoms every time I changed their diapers. That alone made a believer out of me. Never one time did either of my girls have a red, painful behind.

———

On the way out of the driveway, Riley, as usual, was sweeping the fall leaves in his front yard while Luke Skywalker, his "part Lab, part something else" mutt from the pound kept a watchful eye on our cove. When my engine startled him, he waved, motioning for me to roll down my window before I made it to the mailbox.

"Hi, evewyone," he said, bending down so he could scan the inside of my car. He was wearing his PTH sweatshirt—PROFESSIONAL TUPPERWARE HUNTER. "Don't y'all look nice. Where are you headed?"

"Church," Sarah said from the backseat. Kissie had on the red suit that I bought her for the grand opening and a pretty cream-colored hat on her head. She had me dress the girls in the same smocked dresses they had worn for the party and I had on a brown wool skirt and a pink blouse with a striped bolero jacket. It was a gorgeous, warm morning for December 1. None of us even needed an overcoat.

"That's a nice thing to do on Sunday," he told us.

"What are you doing, Riley?" I asked.

"Luke has a playdate with another dog at the pawk," he said. "We're headed over there now. Then I'll come home and get weady for my PC demonstwation tonight at Mawy Fwanks's house. Business is booming!"

When I heard a peeved "hm hm hm" from the passenger side, I said, "Well, good luck tonight, Riley, we better get going so we aren't late." I rolled up the window and waved through the glass. Issie and Sarah blew enthusiastic air kisses, and Kissie managed a half wave herself.

Thirty minutes later we pulled up to the New Hope Missionary Baptist Church on East Trigg Avenue. The second I parked the car and Kissie stepped into the parking lot, toting a coconut cake she had made the night before, the arriving church members started waving and greeting her with hugs. "Good morning, Mother Kristine," said one older man, svelte and polished in his three-piece light-tan suit, tipping his hat.

"All right, Brother Wallace," she answered. He smiled at the girls and me before opening the car door for another woman on his way to the front door.

"Mother Kristine!" a middle-aged lady hollered. "You sure are look-ing sharp this morning! You want me to take that cake to the fellow-ship hall for you? I'm headed that way now."

"That would be right nice, Sister," Kissie told her, and then intro-duced us as "her white family."

With Sarah holding Kissie's hand and Issie's in mine, we walked past other Sunday-morning worshippers and into the front door of the modest, spotlessly clean church. No stained glass windows decorated this place of worship, which was constructed of white clapboard with a redbrick foundation and a small steeple. Compared to the brick mega-churches found on every corner in my neck of the woods, this one looked more like a chapel. Kissie told me that the members of the con-gregation had built it by hand, board by board, fifty years ago. She was among the oldest members, thereby earning her a position on the Mother Board, a group of older ladies who mentor young females, pray for the pastor and other members, and gather together to host a variety of church activities. On the second Sunday of every month, Kissie told me, and other occasions, such as funerals and christenings, the ladies of the Mother Board wear white as a symbol of holiness and uniformity.

After taking a bulletin from one of the female greeters in the vesti-bule, the four of us took a seat in a pew near the front. I counted fifteen rows on either side of the main aisle, carpeted in red. Kissie seemed elated that we were there; I could tell by the sweet "hm hm hms" she chanted while she sat quietly reading her bulletin, waiting for the ser-vice to begin. It was late getting started but no one seemed to mind. Kissie took the extra time to introduce us to those seated nearby. Ev-eryone was kind and welcoming and a few ladies told me they felt like they knew me from all the nice things Kissie had said about me over the years. Isabella was a little timid at first but soon moved onto the lap of a kind lady on the other side of Sarah until the service began.

"Good morning!" a gentleman, presumably the pastor and the only man dressed in a formal robe, bellowed from the altar.

"Good morning!" the congregation responded happily.

"This is the day the Lawd has made. Let us rejoice and be glad in it!"

Instantly, the distinctive tone of a Hammond B3 organ reverberated from the altar and the congregation leaped to their feet. The rhythm section, composed of all males spanning several generations, electrified the room with the sound of sweet Southern gospel with their drums, guitar, and bass. Later, a small choir, six men and six women, took the music to another level and I was astounded by the quality of their voices. Song after song, some I recognized, others I didn't; the music filled every person in the room with exhilaration. Before long, people were dancing in their seats. Kissie—my eighty-three-and-a-half-year-old Kissie—had been transformed into someone I'd never met. She was crooning out the words to the songs without the aid of a lyric sheet, clapping and swaying in her seat. By the smiles on my daughters' faces I could tell that Kissie's dancing had them highly amused and they swayed right along with her. There was a very young, soft-spoken man on the B3 who looked no older than sixteen years old, but as soon as he opened the hymn's chorus, it was sheer bedlam—unadulterated reverence from believers happy to lead with song. The music lasted almost an hour.

Once the music ended, the pastor and others thanked God for everything from the food on the table to the car in the driveway, steady jobs, and rain for healthy crops to provision for clothing and a roof overhead. With a song in their hearts they thanked God for things I never would have thought to be grateful for, like five fingers, the ability to tie a shoe, ears to hear, cash to put in the offering plate, and a few extra dollars to go to the movies. One lady called out thanks for her son's safe return from Iraq and another gave thanks for the money to pay her light bill. Pastor Percy, a fifty-something nice-looking gentleman, thanked God for laughter, tears, and passion; while still another praised Him for his son's musical talent and his daughter's good grades. As for me, I just sat there in the pew, awestruck and overwhelmed.

With everything that had been going on, it had been a very long time since I'd thanked anyone other than Tootie Shotwell or Peter for anything. I'd been utterly confused by problems that were actually a privilege—and I'd forgotten to say thanks along the way. I started to have the distinct feeling that for all the propriety and gentility I found in my Southern culture, I may have lost some of my genuineness.

When I cleared my head, Pastor Percy had concluded his sermon and a lady moved over to the mic, inviting the visitors to stand, state their home church, and tell what brought them to New Hope Missionary Baptist. A handful of people stood in the back and while each spoke of the reason for their visit, my heart beat uncontrollably.

Finally, when it looked like no one else would stand, I took my turn. "Hi, everyone, I'm Leelee Satterfield," I said, "and these are my daughters, Sarah and Isabella." I motioned for them to stand up next to me. "Our home church is St. John's Episcopal and Kissie—uh, Mother Kristine—is the reason we are here today. Thank you for the warm welcome and the kindness you have shown us. Kissie has been a mother to me, too, and we are delighted and proud to congregate with y'all today."

"That's right!" someone hollered out.

"I can tell that all y'all love her as much as I do," I said.

Pastor Percy, whose sense of humor had peeked through the sermon, said, "Oh yes. We dearly love Mother Kristine. And she's a character, too." From the sound of the response, it seemed as though the entire congregation thought that was hilarious.

"I'm not the only one who's noticed that, huh?" I said. That made the church members laugh even harder.

"Oh no, chil'. You're not the only one. Believe me." Pastor Percy laughed even harder this time. "Mother Kristine has made a *lasting* impact on many, many members of this church. She is very well loved here."

"Tell me about your mother," I asked Kissie as we drove out of the church parking lot. The girls were in the backseat singing to the radio.

"What you want to know?" she asked.

When I turned off the radio so Kissie and I could hear one another better, the girls complained. "No, Mommy!" Issie wailed.

"That's one of my favorite songs," Sarah whined. "Please turn it back on."

"Okay," I said, switching the volume to the rear. I glanced at Kissie. "Did I act like that when I was their age?"

"Shoot. What you talking about? You were exactly like Sarah Satterfield. You may have looked like Issie, but you were every bit as sassy as your oldest chil'." Issie has my curly red hair and Sarah takes after Baker with long, thick brunet locks that cascade past her shoulders.

Her answer made me smile. I was tempted to ask more questions about my childhood but instead, I switched the subject back to her. "I want to know about your mother. What was she like?"

A smile played on Kissie's face and she closed her eyes, like she was basking in remembrance. "My mama was a wonderful woman. The most wonderful woman I ever knew. She was kind to everybody."

"You're kind to . . . most everybody." We both started laughing.

"I ain't nice like she was. Everybody loved my mama. And she could *cooook*. Oooh-wee, that lady could cook."

"I bet she was something else."

"*Mmm-hmm,* sure was." She reached over and touched my sleeve, as if she had something extra important to tell me. "I come from a long line of cooks, baby. Stretchin' all the way back to the Civil War. My great-great-grandmother was a slave."

Hearing that word come out of Kissie jolted my heart. "*A slave?* I never thought about you being only a few generations removed from slavery." I could tell Kissie was warm by the perspiration beads on her forehead, so I turned on the air and moved the vents in her direction.

"Even though the Emancipation Proclamation ended slavery, most of the women kept workin' in houses. They were called house servants. My great-grandmother did that and so did her daughter, then her daughter, and so on."

"Did you know your grandmother?" I asked, stealing glances at her while driving.

"Sure did. But only for a little while; she died when I was real young."

"How old were you when your mother died?"

"She passed about fifteen years ago. I was sixty-seven, I believe."

I urgently grabbed her arm, trying to keep focused on the road. "That was right around the time Mama died."

"Sure was. They died three months apart."

"Why didn't you tell me?" The pain I felt spilled into my words. I had no idea she had been through that kind of grief; I was off at college and too busy dealing with my own mother's death.

"I don't rightly know." Kissie didn't appear to be upset or bothered, but *I* was beside myself. "I was busy taking care of you and your daddy, I know that."

"Oh my gosh, Kissie. I feel horrible." The pain in my voice was no comparison to the ache I felt for the lady who had sacrificed her own family for mine. She shouldn't have been taking care of us; she should have been taking care of herself.

It all made sense now.

I walked in the back door, laden with two large bags of dirty laundry. The drive from Oxford to Memphis didn't take long but I was tired from having taken an Algebra test only hours before. The smell of homemade rolls perked me up though, and I looked around for the pan, which was on top of the stove. Kissie was in front of our Formica countertop, preparing a chicken for roasting. Her hands were covered in oil, and she hastily finished seasoning "the bird" when she heard the screen door slam. "Hold on a minute, baby, and I'll help you with that," she said over her shoulder.

I was already in the laundry room. "I've got it," I called. "Don't worry about it." Once I dumped the laundry on the floor, I came right up to her and hugged her from behind.

She turned her cheek in my direction, and we exchanged kisses. "Lemme wash my hands and I'll be with you in a minute."

"Just finish what you're doing," I said. "I don't need anything. Where's Daddy, still at work?"

"Is the sun gone come out tomorrow?" Normally, she would have busted out laughing at herself for saying something like that, but her voice was emotionless and unmoved. I chalked it up to a bad mood.

"Roasted chicken sounds good. What else are you making?" I pinched off a warm roll and popped it in my mouth. They never needed extra butter: there was plenty on top. Normally Kissie would have made an attempt to shoo me away, but she said nothing. I had to ask her again. "What else are you making?"

"Scalloped potatoes, turnip greens—"

I turned up my nose.

"They're your daddy's favorite. Mine, too." This time there was a touch more emotion in her voice.

"I'm not eating with y'all, anyway," I said. "I'm going out to dinner with some friends tonight. One of my sorority sisters from Sumner is staying with us. She'll be here in a few hours. Normally Kissie would have wanted to know all about her, where in Sumner she lived and who her people were. Instead, she never asked a thing.

A little later, as I readied myself for a large night out with other girls from my pledge class, I smelled something burning. I ignored it at first, but when the fire alarm sounded I hurried down the stairs. The kitchen was full of smoke, and Kissie was fanning it out the back door with newspaper. The Pyrex dish that held her scalloped potatoes was black on the top and the spillage had caused smoke to billow out of the stove. I'd never seen Kissie burn anything before, but there was a stretch of weeks that fall when we were picking black soot off several of our dinners, and it wasn't like Daddy ever left his office on Cotton Row to even notice.

Now I realize that in my own grief, I hadn't seen how Kissie's grief left her, and our food, scorched in remembrance.

"You don't need to feel horrible. My mama's buried out there with Josie, right next to where I'll be one day."

"I don't even want to think about that day," I said, feeling my spirit deflate in anticipation.

A big smile took over Kissie's face. "I think about it all the time."

I quickly glanced in her direction, surprised by her comment. "You do? Why?" Death scared me just about more than anything.

"I'll finally be with Josie, my mama, and all the rest of my people."
She talked as if she had a party waiting for her.

"It sounds like you're looking forward to it. Aren't you afraid?"

She laughed. Even bent over and slapped her knee. "Of course not.
It'll be my homegoin', baby. I'll finally get to see the face of my precious
Lawd."

Chapter Fifteen

Roberta sprinted out of the house when we got home. He wasn't used to being locked up for that long and I watched from the sliding glass patio door as he lifted his leg and watered the ladder on the rickety slide. He sniffed all over the yard and when he paused, smelling a certain blade of grass for over five seconds, I knew what was coming. First he pressed his ear down on whatever the vile odor was that had attracted him in the first place, then he tucked his head and rolled onto his back, squirming around happily while the scent coated his fur. "Roberta," I scolded, and he popped up instantly, looking straight at me. "Don't rub yourself in that nastiness. Get in here." He obediently charged back up the steps and into the den, plopping himself on the couch, bad smell and all.

The ringing of our home phone startled me away, and when I turned to answer, Sarah had already beat me to it. "Hi, Daddy!" I heard her say, a wide grin enveloping her little face. "Tonight? Let me ask Mommy." She didn't bother covering the receiver when she turned to me. "Daddy's home! He wants me and Issie to spend the night with Mimi and Poppy. Is that okay?" Sarah stood on her tiptoes, dancing in place.

A multitude of thoughts raced through my mind. I knew I couldn't keep them from him, but we had yet to discuss this. It didn't seem right that he decided to show up in Memphis without warning and expected them to pick right back up where they'd left off. Certainly, I hadn't seen him since we left Vermont, but more important, the girls hadn't either. And what would happen when he left? Would we have to start the grief process all over again? Plus there was school tomorrow and . . .

"What time?" I heard myself saying.

"What time?" Sarah asked. I watched her nod and then cradle the receiver in her neck. "He wants us to come now. He's been trying to call us all day." The smile on her lips took over her whole face.

"May I please talk to Daddy?" I said, reaching out for the phone.

"Mommy wants to talk to you," she said, the elation leaving her voice. She jerked the cordless phone toward me.

"Hi," I muttered, trying my best to push the negative feelings I had away, and put Sarah's feelings first.

"Hey," Baker said eagerly.

I started to walk out of the kitchen but turned around to Sarah, covering the receiver. "Why don't you let me talk to Daddy while you take Roberta outside?"

"He just went outside."

"I know but you could take him down the slide. He loves that."

"Okay," she said, annoyed, before stomping off to the back of the house.

"Baker, don't get me wrong, I'm thrilled that you want to spend time with the girls. But you can't just come and go in and out of their lives. They haven't even seen you in nine months."

"I get it. And I'm sorry. I want that to change."

"How long are you staying?"

"I'm not exactly sure."

There was a long pause. I thought about grilling him about the nip and tuck cougar but decided to leave that one alone. "Okaaay. When do you want to come by?"

"As soon as possible. My parents are dying to see the girls, too. They've turned my old room into a girl's room."

"I've seen it. They've spent the night there four or five times already."

"I know," he said defensively. "My parents really love our girls."

"Of course they do. Look, I'll have them ready in an hour. Say, two thirty?"

"Yes. See you then."

When I told the girls that Baker would be there in an hour, I could see a sparkle returning to their eyes. Sarah dashed around her room, looking for things to show her daddy, and packed them in her overnight case. Issie leafed through her doll collection, picked out two American Girls, and promptly changed their clothes. She packed her doll suitcase with pajamas and another outfit for the next day while I packed for her. This was the first time in six weeks I'd had to spend a night away from my girls, and as I neatly packed their little clothes for school, a growing feeling of unsettlement gnawed deep inside. I was the one who had spent the last two years, since the day he left us *stranded* at the inn, caring for them. Now, out of nowhere, he wanted to slide back in and win them over. Tears pooled in my eyes but I couldn't tell if it was from anger or fear—fear of the unknown or unresolved fury from what he had done to us in the past. I had every right to be worked up. The guy had thought only about himself, not Issie and Sarah, or me—his chief concern was always Baker. I'd been so good about keeping things vague when it came to him, always mindful of our daughters' feelings. They were well aware that their parents had gotten a divorce—lots of kids in their classes had the same situation, but when it came to ours, I made sure to keep my resentment to myself. Kissie walked by the room and our eyes met. I rolled mine, purely out of frustration. She never commented but I knew exactly what was on her mind.

The closer the time got for them to leave, the more nervous about this whole thing I became. My girls hadn't laid eyes on their father since we left Vermont last February. Aside from spending the night with his parents every other month, and their bimonthly phone call from Baker, they had pretty much designated that side of the family as an every-now-and-then relationship. What would happen now? Would they come home wrecked and forlorn from missing their father and have to go through withdrawals again after he returned to Vermont? And as much as I hated to admit it, there was a part of me that wondered the same thing about myself. Truthfully, when it came down to it, *I* was a nervous wreck about seeing him. After all this time, I had finally let him go—moved on—but seeing him at the game had hit a nerve that I had long since deadened.

Thirty minutes later Roberta was barking from doorbell chimes. Issie and Sarah raced one another to the door and I watched from the kitchen as their smiles fell to droops. "Hi, Riley," Sarah said.

"Is your mother home?" I couldn't see his face, but I could hear him loud and clear from the stoop outside.

I walked up behind the girls and poked my head around the door. Luke was right next to him, wearing one of Riley's CUTCO SALES PROFESSIONAL T-shirts. Roberta and he were turning circles with their snouts in stinky places.

"Hi, Riley. What's going on?" I said. I couldn't help staring at *his* T-shirt—ASK ME ABOUT MY AMWAY VISA.

"I was wondewing if I could take a shower at your house?"

My eyes bulged. Not an ordinary request. Even for Riley. "What?"

"My hot water's out."

Out of nowhere, Kissie appeared next to me. "No, Riley. Now is not a good time. You gone have to ask someone else, I'm afraid."

Baker's green Ford Explorer pulled slowly down the cove and sprang as it hit the end of our driveway, the undercarriage scraping as he pulled to a stop. Sarah and Issie pushed past Riley and flew down the steps.

"Who's that?" he asked.

"Never mind," Kissie said, downright irritated at the intrusion. "Please head on back to your house. Sarah and Isabella ain't seen their daddy in nine months."

Riley whipped his head around. "That's their father? I thought he lived in Vermont."

"Yes, and you don't need to be in the middle of their reunion neither. Go on home now, you hear?"

I watched as Riley waved at Baker and the girls, half waiting to see
if there would be an introduction. When nothing happened he strode
over to his yard and watched the reunion from under his tulip poplar
tree.

Halfway down the driveway, the girls seemed a little uncertain and
crept the rest of the way to Baker's car. After all, it had been nine months.
All that changed, though, as soon as Baker stepped out of the Explorer
and squatted down with his arms outstretched. Issie and Sarah ran
straight into him. I couldn't hear what was going on, but by the girls'
body language, I could tell they were elated. Kissie and I watched as
they clutched Baker. Issie rested her head on his shoulder and Sarah
hung on to his neck. Finally Baker stood and took each by the hand,
walking toward Kissie and me.

"Just remember, baby, he's their daddy," Kissie whispered as Issie
and Sarah skipped back up to the front door with Baker jogging in between.

"Hey," Baker and I said at the same time. Then turning to Kissie,
Baker said, "Kissie! You look wonderful. How is it that you don't age?"

Kissie smiled at him and explained, "Oh I'm aging, all right. You
should see my insides." She wrapped her big arms around him and
squeezed him into her large bosom. I hoped it was an act of habit, or a
sign of comfort to the girls, but I'd be lying if I didn't admit a twinge of
jealousy.

Roberta sniffed up and down Baker's legs and on top of his shoes,
prompting Baker to bend down and pat his head. "Who's this?"

"Roberta," Issie and Sarah said at the same time.

Baker cocked his head and bent down to look our dog over. "Roberta's got a penis," he said, and Issie giggled.

"Mama named him after Roberta," Sarah said. "I told her it was a
girl's name but she said it was andoginous."

"Androgynous," I corrected.

"Androgynous," Sarah repeated with a bounce of her head.

"Come see our room, Daddy," Issie said, pulling him into the entry hall.

"I'd love to see your room." He glanced at me for permission, at which I slightly nodded my head. As Baker and the girls took off down the hall, I could have kicked myself for not shutting the door to my bedroom, which was right across from theirs. Last night's outfit was strewn around the carpet, and the bed was still unmade. I heard Issie ask him to play *Hi Ho! Cherry-O,* a board game she remembered playing together when she was younger.

Ten minutes later, as Kissie and I sat right next to each other on the couch in the den, whispering about what was going on back there, I heard Baker say from the hall, "Come on, girls, we have to go. Mimi and Poppy are waiting on us."

"Can we take *Hi Ho! Cherry-O?*" Issie wanted to know.

"That's up to Mommy, but Mimi has games and she's cooked a nice Sunday supper."

A part of me was jealous that Baker still had his parents and that they would all sit down for a nice family meal. I loved the Satterfields, they had always been kind to me, but I hadn't seen much of them since we moved home. I had to admit I missed them, but they were no longer my in-laws. They were my children's grandparents, though, and one overnight every other month was hardly enough time for the girls to foster a devoted relationship.

I handed Baker their small overnight bag. "Did you pack their school clothes?" he asked once they had gathered in the foyer.

I hesitated, stifling a snide remark about who'd been their acting parent for the past year and a half, but simply said, "Yes, they're in the suitcase. I put a note in there with directions to their school and what time they have to be there. All that kind of stuff."

"Thanks." Roberta pawed on Baker's legs for another scratch. He squatted down to pet him, and when he did, it was like we were back in our house in Chickasaw Gardens and Roberta was our old dog, Princess Grace. I blinked away the memory.

"Sarah can show you where to drop her off. Issie, too, but if you have any questions, you can call me." Truthfully, it was *I* who had the questions. There were a hundred unanswered stories and questions begging for validation, clarification, confirmation. But now was not the time.

"Okay, see y'all," he said, darting his eyes from Kissie back to me.

"Give Kissie some sugar," she said, stretching out her arms to both girls. After hugging Kissie, they loved on Roberta and finally turned to hug me. Kissie and I watched as they skipped down the driveway wearing their Hello Kitty backpacks. My heart stung as Baker opened the back door to let them slip inside.

"Wait!" I yelled. "Issie needs her car seat." I tore back through the house to the carport, pulled her booster seat out of my car, and ran back down the driveway. While I was securing it in Baker's backseat I happened to glance in the way-back. It was brimming with fishing gear and golf clubs, even a pair of waders, and his stowed-away shotgun. Duck season in Tennessee always started around Thanksgiving weekend and the inventory now made it all clear. No wonder he didn't call the girls before now: he'd spent his Thanksgiving in a duck blind. I felt a momentary glimpse of . . . was it pity? I was relieved he had been in the great outdoors, and unable to call our girls—a better excuse than indifference, but a holiday shooting duck seemed terribly lonely.

Once I had Issie securely fastened in her seat, I kissed her little lips. "Bye, Mommy," she said. "I'll miss you so much." She hugged my neck and kissed me again.

"I'll miss you, too, baby." I stretched across to Sarah and told her the same thing. Then, in a soft tone I added, "Girls, remember what I told you to do whenever you see a gun?" They each nodded. "Then say it with me." All three of us recited the motto simultaneously, "If you see a gun, don't touch it, leave it alone, call an adult."

"Good job. I'll pick y'all up from school tomorrow, okay?"

"Don't be late," Sarah said.

"I won't."

"You promise?" asked Issie.

"I promise. I love you both very much." I shut the door and turned to Baker. "I'm assuming your shotgun isn't loaded." I felt fear catch in the back of my throat as I pressed my lips together, genuinely fearful of a loaded gun.

"Your assumption is correct." Baker crossed his arms in front of him.

"Good. Say hi to your parents for me." Better to end on a note of congeniality.

"I almost forgot. They told me to tell you the same thing." He glanced away briefly. "They have always loved you, Leelee. They know what a great mom you are—" He paused. "—and the same goes for me."

"Thanks," I said, waving and blowing kisses to the girls. "See you later."

I turned from his SUV and began the long walk to our front porch, turning to look back when I got to the top step. My girls—the entirety of my blood family—stared back at me. Baker stood near his driver's-side door, the very same man I'd given my heart to a decade ago. In the towering sunlight, only the few glistening gray hairs from his temples hinted at the time, and pain, that had since passed between us. Otherwise his dark brown hair looked full and shiny and for a second I was back in high school, staring into those two gorgeous sapphires for the first time.

Baker Satterfield led the team to state championship our senior year. Everyone knew who he was. He'd been quarterback since the tenth grade, a rarity among high school sophomores. "Never has a boy passed through these halls with that much raw talent," Coach Jim Freedman had said of Baker.

Baker Satterfield hardly knew I was alive. For two years I watched him date Lisa Earp and he never once noticed me. "Maybe I'm Amazed" by Paul McCartney was "their song" and I hated it from that day forward.

The evening everything changed the air outside was hot and thick, making it hard to breathe. I hated my hair in the humidity—it doubled in size—but since I didn't plan on seeing anyone I'd want to impress, I never bothered to tame it. Virginia and I were spending the night with Mimi

Hall, who was having a small pool party. She lived way out in Raleigh, thirty minutes away, and most people didn't like driving that far out so when he walked into the party, my heart stopped. He hadn't been expected to show, and his presence shifted the party's energy.

I was a late bloomer, Mama used to say. My bosoms finally blossomed after our junior year in high school and I looked much different in a bikini that summer than I ever had before. When Baker jackknifed off the diving board that day, the other guys hooted and hollered and praised his magnificent splash. As the water sprayed all over the group of us spectating from the edge of the pool, Baker swam up underneath the water, grabbing my calves, dangling freshly shaven in the water. He popped up from the surface and whipped his head with a jerk, his long hair wrapping around to the side, just between my legs. The water made small triangles out of his long thick eyelashes and that smile of his took my breath away. By nightfall, we were inseparable. We made-out for two full hours that evening in Mimi's basement while listening to U2's Rattle and Hum *over and over. A few weeks later we declared "Desire" as our song.*

I fell in love with Baker Satterfield that day. From the moment his eyes rose from Mimi Hall's chlorinated water and locked with mine, an intense and heart-stopping gaze remained unbroken until the day he left me stranded in our snowy mountaintop nest at the Vermont Haus Inn. Sixteen years is a long time with one person, especially when I consider it's nearly half my life.

Chapter Sixteen

Monday morning I arrived at the restaurant by eight thirty. I had washed and straightened my hair, shaved my legs, and doused myself in Jo Malone pear body lotion. Dressed in jeans, boots, and a lightweight cardigan sweater, even I had to admit I looked nice, something of utmost importance considering the talk I planned to have with Peter. I knew we had to discuss what happened on Saturday with obnoxious Chuck and find a way to accept, and ultimately laugh, about our cultural differences. Frances called not talking about something "brushing it under the rug" and I wanted to make sure we were dust free.

When I pulled into the driveway, Roberta and Jeb were carrying their suitcases down the back steps. I rammed the gearshift into park and rushed over to Jeb's Mary Kay car. "What are y'all doing?" I demanded. "Don't tell me you're leaving." I hadn't been given any warning and it was the last thing I expected. Somehow, I had to change their minds.

"Yuup, got to get on the *road*." By the way Jeb drug out the word "road," I could tell he was peeved.

"Already? You haven't been here long enough," I said, genuinely distressed over their sudden departure.

"I'm afraid so," Roberta replied. "Moe called last night and said it just ain't the same without me. I better get on back home, missy. We've been here over four weeks already and stick season's over in two."

"Were you going to leave without telling me?"

"Of course not," Roberta said. "I was just getting ready to call you when I saw your car."

Jeb said, "*I'm* her only ride." Now I knew the real reason he was mad.

"She could take a plane," I said to Jeb before turning around to Roberta. "You'd fly right into Albany plus you'd be home in a couple of hours instead of three days. That way you could stay longer."

"Nuuuuuup. I ain't taking no plane. Jeb's gonna have to drive me, missy." She tapped on Jeb's trunk for him to open the latch.

"If I'd known, Kissie and I would have fixed a big dinner for you last night. We could have had a little going-away party at my house." Thinking about how wrapped up I'd been about Baker, and the realization that I'd missed their last day in town frustrated me immensely.

"Pooh. That wasn't necessary," she said.

"Tell Alice I'm sorry I won't get to be her houseboy," Jeb muttered, fumbling for his key.

"All right," I said, still pondering a way to convince them to stay.

"And tell Cary I had a good time *partaying* in her tent." He lifted the trunk, hoisting their suitcases inside. Once shut, he slapped it with his right hand. "And tell her I'll be back next year."

"I'll tell her," I choked out, sadness audible in my voice.

"We never got to poon Shirley Greene's house," Jeb said, giving Roberta the evil eye.

She ignored his comment but I said, "Trust me, she probably has cameras around her house. She probably wasn't the best target."

Peter walked out the back door carrying a small cooler. He descended the steps and paced toward us. "There's plenty for you guys to eat and drink in here," he said. "It should last till you get home." He walked over to the car and slid the cooler into the backseat. "You should have no reason to stop, except for gas and sleep."

"Did you know they were leaving?" I asked him.

He shook his head before planting a kiss on my lips. "Roberta sprang it on me this morning at the coffeepot. I tried talking her out of it but I think she misses Moe's hot bod." He turned around and winked at her. Roberta blushed.

"She sprang it on *me* last night, right after she got off the phone with him. I'm thinking of driving straight through," Jeb said.

"Oh no you won't," Roberta retorted. "You ain't goin' to fall asleep at the wheel with me in the car."

"I don't want to have to listen to you snore while I'm trying to go to bed in some flyby motel. The way I see it is, if you do it while I'm driving, it will at least keep me awake."

"Where's Pierre?" I asked, changing the subject. I crossed my arms in front of me and rubbed, determined to stay warm despite the chilly air.

"He took my truck up to the drugstore," Peter said. "He's decided to stay. I've asked him to help us with the catering until we get up and running again."

"That's a relief," I said.

"Leelee's Peach Blossom Inn is his home, whether it's in Vermont or Tennessee," Jeb said. "I think he loves it down here anyway."

Roberta put her hand beside her mouth and whispered, "It's the pretty women he loves."

"We are going to have to find him a cute Southern honey," I said. "Age appropriate."

I looked over at Jeb and could see the ungentlemanly thoughts written all over his face. If I didn't know better, I'd think he was reconsidering his decision to leave.

"Keep us posted," Roberta said. "About the lawsuit and all."

"You keep us posted," Peter told her. "If you hear anything about that witch, no matter how small, please call and let us know."

"And you know we'll hear about it," Roberta assured him. "I have a feeling George will have an earful for me when I get home. No telling what he's uncovered at the gas station." She opened the passenger door and finished our conversation with one Sorel snow boot up on the doorframe.

"Keep your police scanner on," I told her. "Maybe she'll get arrested for meanness and they'll broadcast it all over the state."

"Don't yous worry. It's not been off a day since Moe bought it twenty years ago."

"Call us the second you hear anything, promise?" I said.

"I promise."

"Roberta," I moaned, lamenting her departure. "I wasn't prepared for this. I'm not ready to tell you good-bye again."

"This isn't good-bye, missy. I'll be back down. Now that I've ridden this far once, I know I can do it again. I'll bring Moe with me next time."

I hugged her tightly and reassured her that she always had a job in Tennessee if she ever needed one. I told Jeb the same thing but his confidence about his employment was already secure. "I had three job offers when I was at the game," he reassured me. "Cary said I could set up the party tent for her in Oxford every home game. Then another lady, I forgot her name though, said I could sweep her chimneys. So did another lady. Of course Alice said things could always work out over at her place sometime in the future. She's not so sure about the houseboy she's got now."

I nodded and smiled. "You'll be the most popular damn Yankee in town, Jeb Duggar."

"Hey," Peter said, "I thought I was."

"You're not a Yankee anymore, silly." I pushed on his chest play-fully.

"Neither am I," Jeb said, moving around to the driver's side. "I'm *a Reb.*" He balled that hand of his into a fist and popped it high above his head.

Peter placed his arm around my shoulder, snuggling me into his side. I instinctively leaned in closer, burying my nose into his laundered flannel shirt. "Be safe, Colonel!" he yelled.

Tears immediately pooled in my eyelids and that old familiar lump grew in my throat. I blew kisses as my two friends disappeared into the car and waved as Jeb floored it down the driveway. Having Roberta in my life again had been pure pleasure, even if it was short lived. I started to feel the deep ache of her leaving when seconds later I heard the sound of an engine in reverse and tires skimming over pea gravel. The pink car reappeared again with the driver's window rolled all the way down. *"HOTTY TODDYYYYYY!"* Jeb screamed before gunning it once again through the tiny pebbles.

Peter tugged on my shoulder, guiding me back toward the house. Slowly the two of us walked across the driveway smiling, arm and arm, and we ascended the steps. He squeezed me closer. "I know you're sad, sweetheart."

"I'm *so* sad."

"But you sure look nice today." His casual glance at my outfit was followed by a wink.

"Thank you, so do you." I smiled shyly and knotted my hair as he held open the back door.

Peter squinted, shooting me his curious glance as we walked inside. "What's bothering you?"

"How can you tell something's bothering me?" I hung my coat on the hook Jeb had installed in the small mudroom at the back door.

"You just twisted your hair in a bun. I've known that about you since we met."

I glanced up at him, surprised. "You've never said you knew that about me."

"There's a lot I've never said."

His words lay heavy for a moment and I, somewhat shyly, asked, "Really? Like what?"

He took my hand and the two of us moved into the deserted kitchen, drab and dismal from the absence of flesh. The lifeblood of the restaurant had vanished. Not only was the absence of Jeb and Roberta a dark and sore reality check but also, too, the departure of the rest of our employees. As I looked around at all the money I'd spent on the place, fear gripped me, like it would smother me whole. The more I thought about it, the more suffocated I became. I had spent every red cent I had on the Peach Blossom Inn. The Hobart dishwasher alone cost me six thousand dollars, and it was used. Suddenly the fear that had been bubbling up inside turned to nausea and I felt sick to my stomach.

"Like I love you."

The words left his lips and floated down onto the floor, pooling in a heap at my feet. I heard what he said but it didn't have the effect it would have under normal circumstances. It was the biggest moment in our relationship and for some reason I couldn't say it back. I felt him entwine his fingers with mine, twirling me around to face him. "*I said, I love you, Leelee.*" The tenderness in his eyes began melting away most of my despair, and though I still felt queasy I closed my eyes and finally drank in his three little words.

"You do?"

He nodded. "Yes. I do." I rested my head on his heart and in the stillness could hear each beat. His face smelled like Irish Spring when I reached up to kiss him and as I put my hand on the nape of his neck I could feel the dampness of his freshly washed hair. We kissed for a couple of minutes before he pulled away, staring at me for an extralong moment. "Do you love me? Because normally when you tell someone you love them, particularly the first time, that person usually answers right back. If indeed they feel the same way. At least, that's the way we Yankees do it." A shy smile formed on his lips.

"Of course I love you." No doubt about it. I loved him. Deeply.

"Are you sure you mean it and aren't being a sweet, nonconfrontational Southern belle?" He questioned me teasingly, but with a perceptive trace of sincere insecurity.

"No. Of course not. I love you. I honestly do." I looked straight into his tender blue eyes when I said it.

He scratched at his earlobe. It's Peter's gesture when he's not sure of something.

"Don't you believe me?" I sighed a little louder than I intended. "I've hurt your feelings." I covered my face with my hands, genuinely melancholy over wounding him.

He tugged my hands apart and peeked into my eyes. "I'm not sure that I'd call it 'hurting my feelings,' but it certainly wasn't the reaction I was expecting. What's wrong? I mean besides the restaurant collapsing. I can tell something else is going on."

Truth was, there was so much going on. Aside from the fact that my restaurant, the one I had worked so hard to reestablish, had been ripped out from underneath me, I felt the weight of Peter's job crumbling before us. His hesitancy to move in the first place was the fact that there wasn't a job for him in Memphis and now that had changed dramatically. Where I would get the money for a full-blown lawsuit was beyond me, as was how we would secure more catering jobs to provide those funds. Roberta and Jeb leaving was unsettling and . . . how would we pay Pierre? Heck, how was I going to pay Peter, never mind myself? Then there were our "disagreements." The differences between us were surfacing and I knew all of this would need to be addressed. And lastly, Baker. His sudden appearance yesterday had me completely unnerved. "I have so much on my mind," I finally said, staring down at the floor. "And I honestly have no idea how to deal with any of it."

"Let's go for a walk. What do you say we go up to the market for a coffee and a bite to eat?" Peter said tenderly.

"I'd love that."

Early December can be chilly in Memphis; it's hit or miss. But on this particular day it was almost pleasant. Even so I put on a light jacket, wrapped a scarf around my neck, and slipped on a pair of cotton gloves. There was no wind to speak of, and the remnants of yellow leaves on the trees burst through the early-morning sunlight. The warmth of Peter's hand inside mine cloaked me with a respite from my fears. The day itself had all the makings of perfection, but I had never felt so far from it.

"So are you ready to talk?" Peter asked as we walked along, crunching leaves under foot. The relaxed tone in his voice gave the impression that he, for the most part, was content.

I breathed in, hesitating for a moment. "I guess." His three little words had taken away the urgency I felt yesterday to talk about the challenges in our relationship. Even though he said I hadn't hurt his feelings with my delayed response, I could tell it had bothered him. There was no way I could chance him misinterpreting my feelings one more time today. There would be a better time, way down the road, when we could sort out our cultural differences and so forth. A time when I wasn't so emotional, when the restaurant was back up and running. I'd do it when Roberta's leaving wasn't so fresh. When Baker was out of my life once again. Out of my life? He wasn't even in my life. Or was he? One thing was certain. I had to find a way to tell Peter how afraid I was about the possibility of him leaving. For some reason, it was killing me to even bring it up. "I'm gonna be okay," I said, still evading the issue. "It's just all this junk with Helga on top of having to hire a lawyer and now Roberta leaving, it's a lot to think about."

He nodded, listening intently. "What else?"

Pausing, "I . . ." Closing my eyes, I lightly shook my head.

"What? Tell me what it is that's bothering you?" Now his voice was stern.

I had no way out. I might as well say it. "What's bothering me, what's terrifying me is that you came to Tennessee only when there was a job for you. Now you don't have a job."

"What are you talking about? I've got a job," Peter said, seemingly unaffected by the very thing that had me ready to jump off a cliff. "Listen to me. Helga is not going to keep us down for long. Didn't you hear what that lawyer said? It'll only be six weeks max. That's a little less than two weeks away. We'll be up and running again soon."

"But what about your salary?"

"I told you. We'll get more catering jobs. There are two messages right now on the voice mail from people wanting bids on Christmas parties."

"Christmas," I moaned. "That's supposed to be our busiest time of year. How are we—?"

He halted abruptly and turned to face me, holding my reddened cheeks with his ungloved hands. His eyes pierced mine. "I am not worried about this. Leelee, you don't need to be worried about this. Got it?"

"Got it." I hesitated, dying to say the three words that he had said to me thirty minutes earlier. He looked at me as though he thought I would say them, too. "Thank you, Peter," were the only three that left my lips. I felt the other three. I wanted to say them. I was dying to say them. But something wouldn't let me.

Chapter Seventeen

Every time I walked into Frances Folk's office, even after six months of visiting, I could feel a mixture of both anxiety and anticipation mounting. I'd been seeing her every three weeks or so and I never knew what to expect or what new epiphany was bubbling under the surface waiting to burst through, at times awakening me with revelation and other times ready to inflict my life with havoc. The longer I was "in counseling," as Peter called it, the more I wished I'd started as a teenager. That may have saved me all kinds of stress and anxiety; at the very least I'd probably know how to recognize the symptoms as they arose. Frances says I have many tendencies that are common in adult children of alcoholics. She says constantly seeking the approval of others is number one on the list and, naturally, I didn't have to look far to spot that. Being Southern, she says, is a double whammy.

Her little waiting room always had music on in the background and plenty of magazines on the coffee table. *Psychology Today, Grief Digest,* and *Guideposts* were stacked and arranged with the titles showing when I arrived. I had just picked up the November issue of *Guideposts* when she opened the door to her office.

"Well, hello there," Frances said. That woman was always in a pleasant mood.

I gave her a hug—we'd started doing that only a week in—and followed behind her dainty steps. I took my same spot on the sofa and she sat across from me in her overstuffed wing chair. Frances is very maternal, which is one of the reasons I like her. She's old enough to be my mother, probably sixty I'm guessing, and her soothing voice is a balm in and of itself. Oftentimes Frances sits with her tiny feet tucked underneath her, but today she kept them planted on the floor. "So," she said, "good few weeks?"

I shook my head. "Anything but."

"Uh-oh." She leaned in toward me. "The last time you were here, you were as happy as I'd ever seen you, just before your grand opening party. Am I right?"

I nodded. Determined as I had been not to cry, it was the first thing that happened. I surprised myself by just how hard and fast the tears fell. I think hearing her kind, compassionate voice opened the floodgates, and before I knew it she had walked over to hand me the box of Kleenex. I filled her in on everything. We talked about Helga and the possible lawsuit. I told her about having to close the restaurant and my fears about Peter leaving town from lack of work. She listened intently before reassuring me.

"He's all in," she said. "From everything you've told me about Peter, he doesn't seem like the type to leave you holding the ball. He knows the cease and desist is out of your control."

"That's what he said. But I'm not so sure."

"Hmmm. It sounds like there might be something else." Even Frances could see I was holding back, pressing onward that there was more about Peter causing me worry than just his paycheck.

"Things have started to come up," I said, fiddling with my hair, which I had styled to hang loose around my shoulders. "I mean . . . he's having a hard time understanding me and the way we do things down here."

Frances seemed to know exactly what I meant. "When you were up in Vermont it wasn't as evident, because you were in his world. Now that he's moved here, things are bound to surface."

"We weren't in a relationship then either."

"That's right and now that he's here, your worlds are colliding. He's direct and tells it like it is. But I don't have to tell you that. You know all about *Yankees*." She whispered when she used the term.

I laughed and it felt good.

"Now he has to adjust to not only *living* in the South but a relationship with a Southern woman. And one who does everything she can to avoid confrontation and please everyone around her. It's hard for you to understand a person, much less a boyfriend, who isn't equally as concerned with perception as you are. A lot of this comes from living in an alcoholic home. Make sense?"

I nodded. We'd touched on my people-pleasing personality before, but only recently had I begun to understand the full effect it had had on me. When Mama was drunk, I had to tiptoe around her, avoiding conflict at all costs. I would say yes when I wanted to say no. Anything to keep the peace.

I explained the entire Ole Miss incident in great detail and how Peter had stayed silent. "I felt so misunderstood," I told her. "He just sat there and let that guy talk to me like that and what's worse—he felt like I was inviting his advances because I didn't shut the guy down. Maybe it's me, but I'm used to men stepping in and taking up for their women. My father would have decked the guy and I'm not kidding."

Frances laughed out loud. "Most fathers would do that. But Peter is not your father." She scooted around in her chair, drawing her feet up underneath her. "There are plenty of Northern gals who don't even like men to open their doors for them. They are insulted when someone calls them 'ma'am,' and some prefer to pick up their own tabs. It's not entirely Peter's fault. Again, it's the differences in culture."

I shook my head. "I'm much better off down here. I could never get used to that."

"Things are changing, though, especially with the teens and twenty-somethings. With the influx of Northern and Western transplants down South, and with the way the economy is today, Southern women are becoming more independent. They're much more career driven and they know it takes two incomes to raise a family."

"Maybe so, but I think Southern girls will always want to be treated like a lady. I don't see our gentility ever going away completely. Do you?"

"Heavens no. That's one Southern vestige that's sure to stand the test of time."

"I don't want that vestige to destroy our relationship, though."

"Well, Leelee, you can't have it both ways."

We talked about the restaurant saga until what was left of my time had evaporated. It never failed to shock me when I realized an entire hour had passed. I paid Frances the ninety dollars for our session and left her office with a new determination to put faith and trust in my new relationship, and become the woman I was meant to be—strong yet teachable, kind and compassionate, always with a keen and discerning eye. Above all I would be secure and independent, not relying on a man for my sufficiency. It might take rolling up my sleeves and digging into some murky trenches, but my vision was 100 percent clear.

Chapter Eighteen

When Baker called on Thursday to see the girls again, I was surprised. Number one, he hadn't been definite on how long he would be in town. And number two, I couldn't imagine his girlfriend ever letting him stay away from her that long. Naturally I had quizzed the girls—covertly, mind you—to find out if she had been at Mimi and Poppy's house. "Did Mimi and Poppy have any company?" I had asked when they returned. Neither said a thing about another woman in the house but if I knew his girlfriend, which thankfully I don't, it stood to reason that any "other woman" would fall over backwards to impress the parents and the children. So I felt safe in my assumption that she had not made the trip down South.

"Hey!" he said enthusiastically when I picked up the phone, as if we were good friends.

"Oh, hi," I answered, like we weren't.

"I need to talk to you. Is there a convenient time in the next day or so?"

Big pause. "I guess."

"Okay thanks—should I come to your house? Or meet you somewhere?" His voice sounded happy and upbeat. I could picture him snapping his fingers gleefully, a gesture he had been doing since I first met him.

Meet me somewhere? And take the chance of running into a Tootie Shotwell or a Shirley Greene, who would spread it all over town? I think not. "My house. It'll have to be early, though, I get to work by nine A.M. and I drop off the girls by eight A.M., so between eight and nine o'clock would be the only time." My tone bordered on icy.

"Okay, how about tomorrow morning? Does that work?" His, conversely, was still buoyant.

"Sure." I shrugged my shoulders and sneered, even though he couldn't see me. "You didn't tell me you were staying past Monday. What changed?"

"That's what I want to talk to you about."

I hung up baffled. What in the world could Baker want to tell me, and why in the world was he still in town? I shuddered at the thought. Another reason I told him to meet at my house is because I wanted Kissie there to umpire any colossal brouhaha that might present itself. When I told her about it, she figured Baker wanted more time with the girls and that he probably wanted them in Vermont for Christmas. My guess was that it had something to do with lowering the child support or alimony, both of which weren't enough to put in a canary bird's eye, as Daddy would have said.

The doorbell rang once at eight o' clock sharp, Baker-time. Unlike me, he was *always* prompt. Roberta slid across the parquet floor into the door and barked up a storm until I finally made it to the foyer. I swore then that if I lived in this house much longer, I would ask my landlord to install a peephole, as there were no sidelights on either side of the door. Kissie was busy in the kitchen. She still had on her bathrobe, the pink flannel one with a sash around the middle. I could hear her old fuzzy slippers sliding across the floor. She had just taken pork chops out of the freezer for dinner and I heard the refrigerator open and close as she removed the telltale ingredients for a pound cake.

When I opened the door, Baker had his hands in the pockets of his khakis. A brand-new ski jacket made him look very Vermontish, but the baby blue button-down peeking out from underneath labeled him a good ole Southern boy. He smiled when he saw me. I invited him in and escorted him to the den, where he settled familiarly into one of the club chairs flanking the fireplace. I sat on the far end of the couch, as far away from him as I could possibly get. Roberta sniffed Baker's legs while he rubbed the top of his head, once more commenting on his name. "A dog named Roberta. Sounds like a country song or something."

I shrugged my shoulders, trying to appear indifferent.

"I bet Roberta is flattered." Baker snickered a little but I could tell no malice was intended.

"I think it makes her happy. But I didn't do it to please her. I did it because I miss her. She's very dear to me."

When Roberta nudged Baker's hand, he bent down and scratched between his ears until the dog started to pant. Baker reared back abruptly, fanning his hand in front of his face. "Get this dog a Tic Tac, will ya?"

I rolled my eyes but had to laugh. Baker always did have a silly sense of humor. Kissie never came out of the kitchen but I could hear her rambling around in there just the same. After a few minutes of small talk, I glanced at my watch. "I have to be at work in less than an hour. What's goin' on?"

He exhaled loudly, an indication of impending drama, then crossed his legs. He gripped both armrests. "I'm moving back to Tennessee."

I reared back, gaping at him like a bulging-eyed cartoon character.

"I know it's surprising, but I'm going back to work for my dad."

Surprising? Are you kidding? What happened to not being able to stand the insurance business another second? Isn't that why we moved to Vermont? I continued my silence, seething inside, but let him continue.

"I miss the girls. They are my everything." There it was, his justification.

"What about your job at the ski resort? And your . . . girlfriend?" The last word came out with an attitude. I couldn't stop myself.

"We aren't together anymore," he said, tightening his lips. Hesitantly he muttered, "It didn't work out." I noticed him looking off to the side as though he were searching for even more of an explanation. Finally he returned his gaze to me. "Look. She represented something I thought I wanted at the time. A different life, a different career path; I don't know, an answer to something I'd been missing. It's awkward trying to explain this to you."

That infuriated me. "Really? *Huh.* Don't you think it's about time *you did* explain it to me?" I could feel the heat rising in my face, and I bit the corner of my bottom lip to try and control myself.

He hunched in his chair, elbows on knees, and rubbed his temples with the palms of his hands before looking back up. "She was exciting, Leelee. Wild and carefree. She made me feel like a million bucks. And the job she offered me made me feel like a *trillion* bucks."

Anger exploded inside but I said nothing, waiting for the explanation he couldn't give me a year and a half ago. I felt a lump inside my throat but I would be damned if I was going to cry.

"I was no longer a sous chef at an inn in Vermont that my wife *hated* and spent every day longing for home. I wasn't sitting behind a desk either, in an insurance company taking phone calls from people who had just wrecked their car or from someone with busted water pipes. I was the operations manager for a successful *ski resort.*"

"AND *WHY* AM I SUPPOSED TO BE OKAY WITH THAT?" I asked—well, shouted.

"You're not. That's why I'm here. But you have to understand, people respected—" I started to interrupt but he said, "Please let me finish. Then you can say whatever you want."

As fury filled my body, I leaned back in my seat, folded my arms, and tapped my fingers agitatedly against my skin. Feeling out of control, like I might explode, I literally forced myself to hold my tongue.

"People respected me there. I increased the revenue last season by twenty percent. I made the decision to construct an alpine slide for the summer, and I added a concert series—it stayed in the black *and* made a three-hundred-thousand-dollar profit. In its first season!"

That was it. I couldn't hold back another second. "Then why on earth are you leaving? And furthermore, why are you returning to the very business you despised?" The pounding heartbeats inside my ears were deafening.

"Because I don't love Barb. I never loved her the way I love you."

A bang thundered from the kitchen. It sounded like a pot top hit the tile floor, rolled several feet, and spun to a stop.

I looked down at my feet and then over at my ex. That was the last thing I ever expected to slip from the lips of Baker Satterfield. "I'm not sure what you want me to say," I said, aware of my heavy breathing and trying to compose myself.

"You don't have to say anything right now. I just wanted to let you know." Baker's voice softened. "I want us to be a family again, Leelee. I know what I did was wrong and I'm here to ask for your forgiveness."

His words left me utterly speechless. This time I peered at him with no expression whatsoever.

"I miss our life. I miss our daughters and most of all I miss you." If I didn't know better, I'd swear I saw a tear in his eye. In fact, I know I saw a tear in his eye. "You don't have to give me an answer right now. I'm just asking you to think about it."

Without hesitating for even a moment I answered. "Baker. I have a new life now. I started a new restaurant on my own with no help from you, Daddy, or anybody else for that matter. And I have a—"

"I know that and I think it's awesome. I'm so proud of you." Baker shifted in his seat. "I don't expect you to make a decision overnight."

I crossed my arms in front of me and shut my eyes.

Neither of us said anything for a minute or two. Finally it was Baker who broke the silence. "Speaking of the restaurant, I heard about what Helga did to you."

My eyes blasted open. "How did you hear about that?" I snapped.

He shook his head. "It's not important how I heard. I'm just sorry it happened to you."

I sat up straight. "What do you mean it's not important? It's huge!" I leaned toward him even though he was twenty feet away. "Helga Schloygin is trying to ruin me. I'd like to know how you heard about it."

Baker knitted his brow. I could tell he was conflicted.

"Did it come directly from Helga? Do you talk to that beast?"

"Hell no. I don't talk to her."

"She's the one who introduced you to your girlfriend, I mean ex-girlfriend—*whatever*. Did *she* tell you about what Helga's doing to me?"

"No, Barb did not." Now he leaned in toward me and held up his hand, palm out. "Okay, I'll tell you. Mom told me."

That was a bombshell. Here I thought Baker had already surprised me for the last time. "How did your *mother* hear about it?"

"From Shirley Greene."

And that was an earthquake. "Oh for gosh' sakes!" I stood up and threw my fists in the air. Roberta jumped down and followed at my heels. "That woman—" I pursed my lips together. "That woman . . . is going to be THE DEATH OF ME!" I yelled, circling behind the couch, around the TV, and pacing to the front door and back. I didn't know with whom I was more inflamed, Baker or Shirley Greene. "How did *she* hear about it?" I said on my second circle around the couch.

"Calm down."

"*Calm down?*" I stopped in my tracks and turned to face him, arms in the air. "How do you expect me to calm down? Shirley Greene is spreading *my personal business* all over Memphis."

"The restaurant closed before it ever started. People are bound to be talking about it." Baker lightly shrugged his shoulders, as if his pronouncement made all the sense in the world.

"I realize that, Baker, but *excuse me* if I don't want her to be the one telling everybody. Oh how she loves to be the bearer of bad news." I put my hands on either side of my head and squeezed. "What have I ever done to her? And why would your mother want to play bridge with her? Will you tell me that?"

"I don't know." Now Baker stood up and paced around his side of the room.

I stood in the middle with hands on my hips, my eyes darting with every step he took. "Look at it this way: She's spreading gossip about your mother's grandchildren. Well, it's sort of about them."

"I hear you. I'll talk to Mom. She means you no harm. I swear."

"I didn't say she did!" I imagined Kissie right in front of the fridge with an ear pinned to the door.

Baker stopped pacing. "Look, I didn't come over here to argue." He moved in closer until we were only a few feet apart. "I came over to tell you that I want you back . . . and that I love you."

Silence filled the room. And remained for several extra-long seconds. Then out of nowhere, the smoke alarm went off, ripping through his three little words and our predicament like a civil defense warning. Baker and I both jumped. He ran one way and I the other. Just as I put my hand on the kitchen door, Kissie burst through, almost knocking me down. Smoke clouded behind her and she waved it away, shouting, "Everything okay, everything okay! I got so distracted, I done burnt my bacon."

"Kissie, you scared me to death!" Baker said, dramatically holding his hand to his heart.

Her eyes narrowed and she popped her hands on her big hips. "Well, you can just git yourself *un*-scared then, hm hm hm. Ain't nothing but burnt bacon!" She turned around and huffed back to the kitchen, slamming the door behind her.

When Baker held up his hands in a what-did-I-do gesture, I shook my head and shot him a don't-even-go there look right back. He gained his composure and took a step toward me, resting his hands on my shoulders. "I. Love. You. Leelee," he said, this time histrionically, pausing between each word.

Why are you saying this? I wanted to scream. I had every right to flail my arms, throw myself on top of him, and yell until my voice was gone. Instead I pushed away from him, marched over to the sofa, and said nothing. I don't know why. I just sat there saying nothing. Roberta jumped in my lap. I scratched down his back feverishly, and when I did his little nose rose high above his head and his back foot thumped my thigh.

So, on top of everything else, I now had Baker telling me he still loved me. What else could possibly happen? I closed my eyes, pulling my legs underneath. By doing so it caused Roberta to slip off my lap. Baker stared at us from his position in front of the fireplace.

"Why are you telling me this?" I said in a voice barely loud enough for him to hear.

"Because I can't hold it in any longer."

I took a long, slow, deep breath and exhaled loudly. "I'm tired, Baker. So very weary and tired. I was just starting to be happy again when a postman rang my doorbell and delivered a registered letter from an attorney in Montpelier."

"Will you think about it? That's all I'm asking."

For a moment I was back at our home in Chickasaw Gardens. The one I had spent over a year decorating, the one with my very favorite wallpaper in the whole world in the dining room and the one in the very neighborhood where Virginia and John live. I saw myself in the rocking chair in the girls' room, stroking Issie's little red head and singing lullabies until she fell asleep. I envisioned Sarah, with her shiny long dark hair, getting ready for her fifth birthday party, peeking through the box at her cake in the kitchen, Princess Grace Kelly dashing out into the backyard with high hopes of catching a squirrel, my small garden out back with beautiful perennials and the loaded gardenia bush. Then I saw the swing set that we dismantled to take to Vermont back in its place and the window treatments back on the windows in the living room, my special room, the one I didn't let the girls anywhere near. I saw Baker's Explorer pulling in the driveway right after work and my daughters and Gracie meeting him at the back door.

Baker was the father of my children. We had a history together stretching back to high school. My girls loved their daddy very much, and if everything I read and all the advice Kissie gives is correct, they need him every bit as much as they need me. If I didn't consider reconciliation, would I be depriving them of the happiness they deserved? A life free of brokenness?

"I don't know," I said.

"Okay. Does that mean you're thinking about it?"

"I. Don't. Know," I repeated, mimicking his earlier theatrics.

"Well, that's not a no. It's not as good as a yes. But it's not a no."

"I have to go, Baker. I've got to get to work." I stood up from the couch, furious at him all over again for playing yo-yo with my heart.

"No problem. Take all the time you need to think about it." He started to move closer but I raised my hands. "No. I don't want you to touch me."

"Fine. I don't want to do anything that makes you uncomfortable."

"Thanks." I walked toward the door, expecting him to get the hint.

He followed behind me. Once he reached the foyer he said, "Now that I'm back, the girls can start spending the night with me. I'll be at Mom and Dad's till I find my own place."

"Whoa, Baker. This is all so sudden." I wanted to say no, but Sarah's and Issie's faces sprang to mind. "The girls can stay with you. *Some*."

"Some? But—," he started to object but stopped himself. "Fine. I'll call you about next weekend. Let's start there."

"Baker, our former marriage aside, we have to be consistent and stable with our girls. You must be certain you're really staying for good—regardless of me—and only then can we tell them *together* that you're back in town to stay."

"I won't say anything."

"I'd appreciate that. It's not fair to them."

He moved closer to the door. "See ya, Kissie!" he hollered.

She appeared in the doorway leading from the kitchen to the dining room with a dishrag in one hand and the other on her hip. The remnant of smoke still hung in the air. Her tone was, well it was . . . pure Kissie. "Good-bye, Baker."

"Try to talk some sense into Leelee, will ya?"

"She don't need no sense talked into her. She's got a plenty sense already, hm hm hm."

"You're right about that," he said merrily, never picking up on Kissie's irritated hm hm hms.

I opened the front door and Baker lightly touched my arm on his way out. "I'll talk to you soon, I hope."

I started to close the door behind him when he turned back around. "How'd you like your flowers?"

Yet again, he could have mopped me up off the floor. "*You* sent those to me?"

"Of course I did." Well, now—my mysterious flower flirter had finally been revealed. It was Baker who sent the secret delivery from Rachel's. No wonder it had all my favorite flowers.

Under my breath, I recited the words I had memorized on his card, "I am so proud of you. Good luck tonight. All My Love." It was all starting to make sense. "Why on earth didn't you sign the card?" I asked.

He shrugged. "I'm not exactly sure."

"Well," I said, pushing the loose hair off my forehead, "I have to admit, they were stunning." A shy smile forming on my lips surprised even me and I felt heat rising to my cheeks.

"I'm glad you liked them," he said through his own smile. "See ya."

After shutting the door behind him I put a finger to my lips and motioned for Kissie to get on one side of the dining room window while I hid behind the other. We watched him walk to the Explorer. Once inside, he adjusted his rearview mirror and stared at himself. When he had backed down the driveway and was headed down the street, Kissie shut the curtains, the very thing she does every single day to avoid an unwanted encounter with Riley. "I declare," Kissie said. "I need to *sit down*." She ambled into the den and took her normal seat on the kitchen side of the sofa.

I followed behind and plopped down right next to her. "I'm sure you heard every word."

"Every *single* word."

"You could tip me over with a feather right now. That's the last thing I ever thought I'd hear out of Baker Satterfield's mouth. The *last* thing."

That tickled Kissie to no end. "Oooh-wee, chil'. He sure is acting like a new man."

"I'm not so sure," I said, thinking back over our conversation.

"What makes you say that?" When Kissie crossed her legs, I noticed the long dark hairs. I'm not sure she's ever shaved her legs. Well, if she did, I never noticed.

I moved forward in my seat and turned to face her. "I don't trust him."

"I'm glad you said it first, 'cause I don't neither." She tightened her lips and narrowed her charcoal eyes.

"But he *is* the father of my children."

"Yes. He sure is. But he has to *prove* himself first. He cain't do what he done to you then turn around and expect you to run right back in his arms. Only time will tell if he's truly changed."

I looked at my watch. "Well be that as it may, there is another man in my life and I have to figure out a way to make sure he gets a paycheck. I'm headed over to the restaurant right now."

"Are you gone tell him?"

I sat there silently, drinking in what she had just asked. There it was. It seemed I was faced more and more with opportunities to either spit out the truth or hide it away to avoid conflict. But even I couldn't deny that it was one thing to hide a visit, a temporary appearance from Baker—but another to conceal his efforts at reconciliation. "What would you do?" I already knew the answer when the sentence left my lips.

"I'd go on and tell him. He's likely to find out now that Baker's home anyway. You might as well get it over with."

I exhaled loudly. "It's not going to be easy. I'm not sure how he'll react, to tell you the truth."

"As long as you're telling the truth, you have nothing to lose. There ain't nothing to be afraid of."

I patted her on the leg and stood up. "What are you doing today, Kissie? I'll pick up the girls from school so you can go back to your house for a few days if you want. I can manage."

"Okay, baby. My social security check comin' tomorrow anyway. It'll be the fourth day of the month, you know."

"Where does the time go?" I leaned down, kissing Kissie on the cheek. "I don't know what I'd do without you."

"And I don't know what I'd do without you."

When I started to walk off, Roberta sprang up from his lying position and peered up at me with his head cocked to the side. "Okay, you can come." The tone in my voice must have reassured him. While I made my way through the kitchen, his hind feet slipped happily atop the tile as he sprinted toward the back door.

Chapter Nineteen

When Roberta and I crept in the back door—well, Roberta didn't creep, he ran, hopeful a delicious treat lay in wait under the stove— Peter was sitting at the desk singing along with Kim Carnes. "I feel a gypsy honeymoon comin' around again." The morning newspaper was spread out in front of him; a half-filled coffee cup rested beside it, and his laptop was open. New stacks of printed brochures were piled next to the phone. He had thought endorsements from past catering jobs would be a good way to advertise, and since the only person who could provide that was Tootie Shotwell, her name had managed to make an indelible print on our business. He had advertised Peach Blossom Catering all over town and online, making sure to leave off the "Inn." He updated our Web site and Facebook page and had even started a Twitter account, posting recipes twice weekly, featuring one new local ingredient per post. We had only one Christmas party on the books for December and that was because of Alice. A lawyer in Richard's office had hired us. I felt the word on the streets about the restaurant closing had put a damper on our early momentum—but Peter remained hopeful. To me, it looked as though my soufflé of a dream was officially deflating.

Pierre, who had little to do these days, sipped from his coffee cup while removing the few dirty dishes from the Hobart. Peter looked up from the desk as soon as I walked into the kitchen through the mudroom. As usual, a large smile enveloped his entire face. "Hi, boss," he said with a finger-flutter wave.

"Hi."

"*Bonjour, Leelee.*" Pierre, God bless him, was always pleasant. "Roberta, Roberta," he called bending over and clapping his hands. My pup gladly pounced over and rested by his side, knowing full well that Pierre's treat jar was located in the walk-in fridge.

"Bonjour," I responded flatly. All the oomph had evaporated from my voice. I hardly recognized myself anymore. "What are y'all doing this morning?"

"Working," Peter said. "I got a call not fifteen minutes ago from a friend of Tootie Shotwell's wanting us to give her a bid for a New Year's Eve party. I told you it would all work out."

I wish I could say his confidence was infectious but it wasn't. "That's nice," I murmured.

He stood up from the desk and wrapped his arm around my shoulder. Holding me close, he kissed the top of my head. "Your hair smells good," he said, running his fingers through my curls before a big tangle stopped him from moving past my shoulders. "You look like you could use a hot cup of joe." With his arm still wrapped around me, he moved us over to the coffee station. After reaching underneath for a cup, he filled it with coffee and tipped the open cream carton, turning the liquid from black to a light tan. I watched as he dumped three teaspoons of sugar into the mug and handed it to me. "Cream and sugar with coffee, specially mixed for Leelee with love."

I smiled shyly and took it from him. "Thanks."

He picked up his coffee mug and with his arm still wrapped around my shoulder guided me over to the swinging door. With his other hand he pointed at the phone. "Catch the phone for us, will ya, Pierre? Leelee looks like she could use a pep talk."

"*Oui,*" he responded, and settled down in front of Peter's computer, placing his hands on the keyboard. Roberta stretched out underneath him.

Peter and I made our way over to one of the tables in the front dining room and he pulled out a chair, motioning for me to take a seat. "Southern gentility will never escape me, ma'am."

"Will you please make sure that front door is locked?" I said, settling into the seat.

"Certainly." He moved over to the door and twisted the dead bolt. "Shirley Greene safe," he said with a laugh before taking the seat next to mine. He sipped his coffee and placed it gingerly back down on the table. "Okay, spit it out. What's wrong?"

I had to tell him about Baker. How much, I wasn't exactly sure but I knew I had to tell him something. The whole way over in the car I'd been thinking about our conversation and the I-still-love-you bombshell Baker dropped in my living room. The biggest problem with that bolt from the blue, and quite frankly the biggest shock, was how confused it had left me. Wouldn't it be better for my daughters to have their family intact? Both parents to kiss them goodnight? But, I was finally over Baker. Wasn't I?

And I thought our last conversation was confrontational, I thought, taking a long sip of my coffee. I noticed that my hand was shaking when I set down the cup. My heart pounded in my ears as I mustered all my courage. "Aside from everything that was wrong before the lawsuit, I have another biggie." Our eyes met and I forced a smile.

He leaned back, cradling the back of his head in his hands. The front legs on his chair lifted six inches off the ground. "There are lots of biggies in your life. Let's have it."

"Baker came over." It spilled right out.

"That's great. Were the girls happy to see him?"

"Does that hurt your feelings?" My voice sounded shaky. I wondered if he could tell.

He stared at me like I was crazy, mouth twisted out of shape and head cocked to the side.

"Okay, of course it doesn't. That was stupid," I said.

"I'm happy for the girls to see their dad."

"Of course you are. Because that's who you are. Happy for others." I took another sip. With the cup still in my hand, I said, "He's moving back home."

"Really," he said, distinctively less happy. He moved forward again, the chair legs landing with a thump.

"Really." I went into the whole thing about how he missed the girls and how he was living with his parents until he got his own place and how he wanted to start having them over to spend the night. I told him about Baker's breakup with Barb and how he was going back to work for his dad. I went on and on about everything but stopped short of telling him that Baker wanted me back.

"Wow. That's a shocker. I thought he was super pumped about his new career as a ski resort manager."

"Me, too. But he claims he misses the girls and that they are his whole life. Can you believe he's just now figuring that out?"

"Not really." He hesitated for a second before continuing, "No more than I'm surprised he hasn't figured out that you were his whole life."

. I twisted my hair around in a super tight bun and inadvertently started fidgeting. My right foot danced underneath the table and I straightened my blouse. I crossed my legs. Then I uncrossed my legs. Finally I looked at him with a phony look of surprise.

I watched his head cock slightly and the scant movement of his shoulders. "He did tell you that, didn't he?"

"Tell me what?"

"*Leelee.*"

"Well, he may have said a little something like that."

"What did he say exactly?"

I didn't answer him.

"I'd appreciate you letting me know." Peter pushed his hair straight back off his forehead, a gesture I'd seen him do when he was mad.

"He said that he always knew I was a good mother."

Peter tilted his head to the side, raising his eyebrows, as if to say, Go on.

"And that he was proud of me for opening another restaurant."

"As I am, and others who truly care about you. What else?"

"That's it, that's all he said."

"Why don't I believe you?"

I released my bun, letting my hair spill all over my shoulders, but twirled a long strand on my right side tightly around my finger.

"Why aren't you telling me everything he said?"

I closed my eyes, held my breath, and dived in. "He told me that he misses me and that he loves me and that he made a big mistake. Then he asked for my forgiveness." There it was. I told the truth, the whole truth, and nothing but the truth.

"*Wow!*" He sat back and crossed his arms in front of him. "I must say I never thought I'd be hearing that. What did you say?"

"Nothing. I said nothing."

"Does he want you back?"

I nodded, but only slightly.

"Do you want him back?"

I didn't have a truth to give him. And for once, I didn't have a little white lie either.

He got up from the table, opened the front door, and walked out onto the porch, leaving me alone in the stillness. I watched the minute hand on my watch tick away sixty seconds, my heart blasting with every stroke, and then sprang out the door. Peter was sitting in a rocking chair with his feet up on the porch railing. I pulled up the other rocker and sat right next to him, keeping my feet planted on the floor. His next words sent a shiver down my newly hardened Southern spine. "I tell you what," he said, looking me square in the face. "I'm going home to Jersey for a while so you can figure this out. I don't want to stand in the way of you getting back with your ex-husband if that's what you want." I started to object but he said, "Let me finish. Sarah and Issie need their dad. Maybe it would be better if you and Baker worked it out. Do I think it will? *No.* Do I think he's all of a sudden morphed into a Cliff Huxtable, *Hell no.*" He pushed his feet to make the chair rock once and then stopped abruptly, looking my way. "I think I've been pretty good about holding my tongue in this relationship when it comes to Baker but I'm finding that impossible to do right now."

Anger, maybe it was misplaced, but it bubbled up from the deep and spewed all over him. "This is not a cut-and-dried decision, Peter," I said, raising my voice much louder than I intended. "Granted, I didn't tell him no, but I didn't say yes either. This is not about me!" I stood up and turned to face him with my back to the porch railing. "I'm trying to put my children first. Can't you see that?" After a five-second staring contest I put my head in my hands and said, "Oh God. I just need time to think."

Another uncomfortable lull passed before he said, "And I'm giving you the space to do that. I'll take Pierre with me. He needs work and I might as well take him back to New England."

The possibility of him leaving for good started to sink in and I felt a wave of panic. Not only would the final nail be hammered into the front door of my restaurant, but I would also lose the kindest, most caring man I'd ever met. I sat back down in the chair, facing him. "When are you coming back?" I asked with an edge of hesitancy and fear in my voice.

"I'll be back for the catering job in two weeks. If you decide once and for all that Baker is not for you, then I'll stay. But I don't want to be sitting around here while you try to figure that out."

"I wouldn't expect you to," I murmured, casting my eyes away from his and onto the wooden porch floor.

"When I told you I love you, I meant it. I don't say those words to just anyone. I take their meaning very, very seriously." He rose from his chair and took one step toward the door.

I jumped out of the rocking chair so rapidly, it took on a life of its own. "Wait, this is all happening so fast. I . . . I don't know anything anymore. I'm just scared." I clasped his hand, twisting my fingers around his. "Scared of Helga and her lawsuit, scared of losing this business and everything I've worked so hard for, but mostly *I'm terrified* of losing you." My voice cracked and an explosion of tears poured down my cheeks like a salty geyser.

The way he furrowed his brow frightened me almost as much as the conviction I heard in his reply. "You can't have us both."

Chapter Twenty

The damn Christmas cookie swap. It happened to be the very next night, and Alice insisted we all attend. It was the last thing I wanted to do, given my predicament, but Alice, Mary Jule, and Virginia did their best to convince me it would be the perfect remedy. "Can you imagine anything more hilarious?" Alice had said, when I called to recount my word-for-word conversations with both Baker and Peter over a four-way conference call. "It's exactly what you need." All three of my friends were sympathetic and outraged by the men in my life but still insisted I seize the riotous opportunity.

"Not attend a Pampered Chef Christmas Cookie Swap, with Consultant Wiley Bradshaw? Have you lost your mind?" Virginia said, during the call.

"What do you even do at a cookie swap?" I asked. "Besides the obvious?"

"Drink." Virginia declared. She, like the rest of us, had never been to one. Riley swore it was "all the wage," and promised a good time. I suspected Virginia had as much faith in Riley's definition of "good" as I did. But raised on a steady diet of cotillions and garden parties, Virgy subscribed to the same philosophy Mama did: alcohol could make any social gathering tolerable. I hoped Riley wasn't the exception to the rule.

"Drink what, virgin eggnog?" The mere thought of that thick, syrupy sweet, nutmeg-infused, raw-egg mixture turned my already churned-up stomach sideways. "Y'all know I hate eggnog."

"I've already thought about that," Alice said. "I'll bring a large pitcher of Cosmos just in case the party's dry. Even if we have to hide it in the bushes and fake like we need fresh air, I'll make sure we have plenty of good booze."

Mary Jule spoke up in her ever-present, kindhearted way. "Between Baker and Peter, bless your heart, you need to tie on a big one," she assured me. "Come on, Leelee, I don't want you to be alone tonight."

Weaseling out didn't appear to be in the cards.

I let out a sigh. "I suppose I could use a night of fun."

"Oh, it'll be fun," Alice said. "Trust me."

"I'll be the DD," Mary Jule offered. "I'm still hung over from Al's office Christmas party last night. The thought of a Cosmo right now makes me want to vomit."

"Speak for yourself," Virginia said. "Can't you picture us now with Riley out on the dance floor? It'll be a riot."

"There won't be a dance floor," I told her. "It's a dang Christmas cookie swap—at some random lady's house."

"Then we'll make one." Honestly, we didn't need to attend a cookie swap or any other party to have a riot. Virginia Murphey was the riot.

Right around lunchtime the next day, Kissie asked, "What in the world are you doin', Leelee?"

I was staring forlornly into the refrigerator, wearing one of those blue gel eye masks pushed up around my forehead. After crying all night my eyes looked more like two babies' bottoms turned to the side.

"Trying to figure out what to make the girls for lunch," I said, pulling out the grape jelly and the milk and setting both on the counter. I could hardly see her sitting over there at the breakfast room table for the mask. The elastic strap hadn't much pull left and kept slipping back down on my nose. "I swear, I don't know how I'm going to make it to that swap tonight," I said, dreading it all over again. "I look awful."

As I was headed into the pantry for the peanut butter and paper plates, she perked up from reading the newspaper. "The *what?*"

"The Christmas cookie swap. You got an invite." She had received an invitation, but I'd found it torn in three big pieces in the trash.

Kissie slowly turned a page on the paper and smoothed it down with her hand. "I ain't going to that," she said, keeping her eyes on the print.

"Why not? I'll get another sitter for the girls." I plopped the loaf of bread down on the counter and removed two glasses from the cabinet.

"And watch that man make a grand fool out of hisself? No thank you."

I grinned. "Oh, come on. You've never met a cookie you didn't like."

Without moving her head even an inch, she simply peered up at me over her reading glasses. "Well, I met a man I don't like."

I giggled, hard. But she didn't. So I went about my business of making the girls' lunches, cutting the crust off the bread and slicing apples. When I walked over to the table with their sandwiches Kissie stopped reading, folding her arms in front of her. "What kind of cookies you bringing?"

I dropped the plates in midair and watched the apple slices and sandwich halves tumble onto the table.

"The swap due to start at six."

I looked at my watch. "Crap. That's in five and a half hours." I grabbed my coat off the back of the chair and slipped the handle of my purse over my shoulder.

"Where you going now?"

"To Kay's Bakery. I can only pray they have some cute ones left." I tossed my eye mask back into the freezer.

"*Say what?* Kay gone charge you three dollars and change per cookie. By the time you buy six dozen and pay the sales tax that's well over two hundred dollars. You got that kind of money?"

I whipped my head around. "I'm only buying a dozen."

"Then you better stay home. The invitation that man sent say you need to bring *six* dozen."

I glanced at the front of the fridge where Riley's cookie-shaped invite was held in place by a magnet, and stared at it through the slits in my eyes. Kissie was right. It occurred to me that if we were swapping evenly, six dozen cookies meant Riley was inviting six dozen women. I shuddered to think how it was that Riley had managed to cast such a wide net in this town. Six dozen women willing to attend a cookie swap with host Riley Bradshaw? From our standpoint it was worth our attendance for the hoot factor alone, but how many of the other women were actually taking it seriously?

Kissie folded back up her newspaper and stood up from the table, pointing. "Go git an apron out of the drawer and find my rolling pin. Hm hm hm." She pushed in her chair and paced over to the sink, mumbling, "Over two hundred dollars on cookies for a Pampered Chef cookie swap. What's this world coming to?"

Five hours later, Kissie, Sara, Issie, the kitchen, and I were coated in flour. But we had eight dozen sugar cookies, six for the swap and two for us, in the shapes of Santas and snowmen, drizzled in red and white powdered sugar glaze. When I noticed the clock over the sink, I panicked. Alice would be here any minute. The party was way out at a home in Collierville but only a few miles past my house, so the girls had offered to pick me up. I threw off the apron and ran back to my room to toss on something suitable.

I heard Alice honk twice. Actually, she laid on the horn twice. I waved out the front door and rushed back to my bedroom to smudge blush on my cheeks and throw my hair back in a ponytail. I was half way down the hall when I turned back around for a squirt of perfume. I hadn't had a chance to bathe all day.

When I made it out to the car with my cookies, all six dozen wrapped in Heavy Duty Reynolds Wrap on top of white paper plates inside non-Christmasy Kroger sacks, Alice motioned for me to sit up front. I took one look at my friends and burst out laughing. All three were dressed in tacky Christmas sweaters. "Didn't get the memo," I said, shutting the door.

"It was on the invitation," Alice said.

"I hardly looked at it," I told her.

Virginia hurled an extra from the backseat. It landed on my head, covering my face. "I found yours this morning at a thrift shop over on Summer. I knew you'd forget."

"Thanks Virg," I said, removing the sweater I had on and slipping the tacky one over my head. "Honestly, I'm lucky to have cookies. We just finished baking them ten minutes ago. They're probably still warm."

"I haven't eaten a thing," Mary Jule said. "Wonder if they'll have real food, or if we'll just OD on sweets for dinner."

"I have no idea," I told her. "But I'm starving, too. I've been too sad to eat."

"You poor, little thing," Mary Jule said, reaching up from the back-seat to pat my shoulder.

"The party will do you good," Alice reassured me. "I know what I'm talking about."

"I thought you were the designated driver, Mary Jule," I said, turning around.

"I am. Al's car's in the shop and he needed my van. I'll drive Alice's car home." Mary Jule and Al have three children. All under the age of six.

The weather was actually nice that evening. Chilly, but with a pleasant tone to it—normally a night I'd enjoy, but tonight it felt like it was mocking my melancholy mood. We pulled up to the large home in a brand-new Collierville neighborhood and Alice parked on the street behind several other cars. "Looks like there's quite a party goin' on. Where does Riley meet these people?" she asked, looking over at me.

I shook my head. "Beats me. He's an enigma."

Virginia was applying a last-minute coat of lipstick. She twisted it back down into the case and plopped it into her purse. "He's a nerd-do-well."

We all laughed and stepped out of the car with a collective twenty-four dozen Christmas cookies between us. I could feel the puffiness in my eyes as we traipsed up the driveway. There had been no point in wearing mascara. My eyelashes were hidden anyway. Alice hid the pitcher of cosmos in her coat with one hand while carrying her large red bag of Christmas cookies in the other. When we reached the walkway, she pushed back a bush and nestled the pitcher safely inside. Mary Jule rung the bell and we could hear Christmas music the minute our hostess opened the door.

"Welcome," she said cheerily. She was a tall lady, close to six feet, I'm guessing, probably about forty, and had a cropped blond hair-do that came to a point in the back just above the nape of her neck. She, too, had on a tacky Christmas sweater with a nametag that read, Tannenbaum. "I'm Hege, your hostess. But call me Tannenbaum!"

"Hi Tannenbaum," I said awkwardly, and my friends did the same. *Weird, I thought, but oh well. I'm here and I'm going to make the most of it.*

After stepping inside I noticed a large basket filled with multicolored round ornaments resting on a plant stand. Hege hooked one on each of our sweaters as we introduced ourselves. "It's great meeting you ladies," she said. "Please pick out a nametag." She motioned to a table next to her with several Christmas-themed stick-ons arranged in rows. "It's your party name." Virginia quickly snatched up Grinch and plastered it to her left bosom. Alice grabbed Scrooge, Mary Jule chose Snowflake, and I picked Rudolph. "Now, you must pay close attention to all the other nametags my guests are wearing because you must use that name when you address that person," Hege explained. "If you goof, and call someone by their real name, then they get to steal your ornament. Got it?"

Trying to be nice and polite I said, "How cute." But it was really a little white lie and I knew it. I didn't have the energy to resume my honesty resolution.

"The person with the most ornaments pinned to them at the end of the party wins a prize," Tannenbaum said, with a smile.

All four of us oohed and aahed. After all, we are nice and polite . . .

and Southern. Hege returned the sound effects and it was hard to tell who was doing the better job of faking sincerity. Opting for a quick change in topic, she glanced at our outfits.

"Cute ugly Christmas sweaters," she said with a jingle in her voice.

"So is yours," Alice replied in a similar tone. "It was on the invitation, after all."

"There's a fantastic prize for the ugliest!" Tannenbaum said excitedly.

"What is it?" the four of us asked in unison.

"A Pampered Chef baking product of course."

I felt a foot mashing on my big toe. Out of the corner of my eye I could see that face Virginia gets when she's about to lose it.

"How do you know Riley?" I asked, changing the subject to preempt one of Virginia's moments. This painfully long interlude on Hege's tiled foyer was seconds away from turning into a full-blown laughing attack.

"Through Amway," she said. "But when he showed me the Pampered Chef line of bakeware and cookie products I couldn't resist hostessing a PC swap. He's such a doll."

"He *is* quite dear," I told her. And meant it.

When two more women showed up at the door, the four of us moved along. "Put your cookies on the table in the dining room, ladies," Hege called. "We'll be starting our first game soon."

Virginia pinched an inconspicuous chunk out of my arm. "Love it," she whispered.

The dining room table was covered in a holiday tablecloth with a large Santa and his sleigh decorating the center. It was full of mouthwatering holiday goodies, each kind on separate trays, labeled with cards indicating the baker's name and the type of cookie. Extra cards were provided and there was a place to display the recipe, which none of us had thought to bring. As hungry as I was, I wanted to plaster my face in the middle of the first tray—pecan chocolate fudge—my crème de la crème. There was a large pewter tray on one end with a card that read: Place your extra dozen here for tasting. I headed that way.

We unwrapped our cookies, placing them in the appropriate spots on the table, and circled around admiring and sampling the other delicious confections. Alice had baked her coconut-frosted chocolate snowballs, a recipe she'd been perfecting since she was in high school. Mary Jule had tried, and quite frankly flopped, with an extremely difficult Martha Stewart recipe—salted caramel shortbread bars. The shortbread had no taste and the salt overpowered the dark chocolate. Virginia simply brought Pillsbury slice and bake. Oatmeal raisin.

A separate large table was set up in the corner with one sign that read: "Packaging Workstation" and another that read: "Fill your six swap boxes here." It was stocked with many white cardboard baker's boxes, tags and sticky labels, ribbons and twine, sturdy paper plates, baggies, scissors, hole punches, tissue paper, and colored cellophane. It seemed Hege had thought of everything or Martha Stewart had stopped by.

But lots of little un-Martha-like decorations were scattered throughout the tables: Music boxes and tiny candle-holders, nutcrackers and a collection of Santa pyramids with little wooden propellers. A large cuckoo clock hung on the wall. It all looked very, I don't know, Austrian.

Once we had had our fill of samples we moseyed on into the next room in search of alcohol. An extremely tall, skinny, middle-aged woman, Mistletoe, spotted us and hurried over to wrap a necklace of candy canes around each of our necks. "You can't say C.O.O.K.I.E," she said, spelling out the word. "If you do, you lose your necklace to the person you said it to."

Alice and I exchanged looks. "How cute," I said again, as Mistletoe draped my neck. *Well, I guess I'm back to the little white lies again,* I thought. *Everyone needs a night off eventually.*

"The person with the most necklaces at the end of the party wins a prize." Mistletoe seemed angry almost, or at the very least unenthusiastic about our chances of winning.

"I'll probably win," Virginia told her, sensing a challenge. "I'm real good at stuff like this."

"Then you'll have to spar with me," Mistletoe retorted. "I've won the last three years in a row."

"You're not from around here, are you?" Virgy asked.

"Not originally. I'm from Delaware."

"I thought I detected an accent," Virgy told her. When Mistletoe left to drape another lady's neck, she whispered, "Yankee."

Tannenbaum reappeared holding a tray full of frosty julep cups. "Ladies, please help yourself to an eggnog." My friends instinctively looked right at me.

Alice reached in for the rescue. "Sorry, Leelee, none for you." She turned back to our hostess before taking a sip. "She's gluten-free."

In a flash, one of the other cookie swappers we'd not yet met, Yule Log, whooshed up to Alice and snatched the ornament right off her sweater. "You forgot to call her Rudolph!" she crooned, and hooked Alice's silver ornament next to the three balls on her own tacky Christmas sweater. It happened so fast; no one knew what to say. But by the look on Alice's face, I could tell she wanted to rip it right back off of her.

"You're in luck, *Rudolph*," Tannenbaum said, sliding the tray toward me. "Eggnog is *naturally* gluten-free."

I swiped my hand through the air. "I knew that," I said, picking up a julep cup and faking a sip. One whiff and I nearly gagged.

"It's my grandmother's recipe. Been in my family for generations."

"How lovely," I said, forcing a smile that was about as pleasant as the noxious eggy aroma wafting up from the goblet.

When Tannenbaum moved over to serve another group of ladies I glared at Alice. "What were you thinking? Now I can't eat cookies." Alice looked at me blankly. "Gluten." I said. "You just told Tannen-pants over there I can't eat wheat!"

"Details, details. Of course you can. Just sneak." It was a wonder Alice ever made it through our all-girls disciplinary schooling; she had a knack for bending the rules just so.

I shrugged. "Okay Einstein. Now help me figure out a way to get rid of this." I tipped my cup in her direction.

I saw Virginia eyeing the vast collection of beer steins in Hege's living room. Before I could say "don't you dare," she reached over and grabbed one off the bookshelf. "Pour it in here. Hurry," she said.

Against my better judgment, I looked around to see who might be watching. When I hesitated, she snatched the cup of eggnog out of my hand, poured it inside, and flipped the top shut with her thumb. In one stealth motion, she placed the stein back on the shelf.

"You are going to get us kicked out of this party," I told her. "Lord."

"By the time she discovers it, it will be dried up and gone," Virginia said, glancing around. "There's got to be some booze in this house." With that she walked off to find out.

When she came back with the report that the party was totally dry except for the eggnog, she had four red plastic glasses in her hand. "We're in luck, though. Our Cosmos will never be noticed in these."

Mary Jule took a cup. "I suppose I can have just one."

"Absolutely," Alice said, moving toward the back patio door. "And if I don't get one right now I'll never make it through this swap. Who's coming with me?"

"Me," I said, and the two of us slipped outside, running around to our stash out front.

When we made it back with four full cups, Virgy and Mary Jule were waiting at the patio door. Riley, well Frosty, spotted us and flew over to where we were standing.

"Hello ladies!" He was wearing his PC hat and apron, along with an extra-wide Rudolph tie. "Don't y'all look cute in your ugly Chwistmas sweaters? Did Hege tell you I've donated a pwize for the ugliest?"

Alice ripped off his ornament so fast he didn't know what hit him.

Riley looked down at the front of his apron, disappointed. "I said Hege, didn't I?"

"Yep!" she said proudly, and pinned a brand-new gold ornament to her sweater. "Oh well, come take a look at my demo table," he said, returning to his normal enthusiastic self. "You'll be glad you did."

The four of us strolled over, happily sipping our cosmos.

Riley stood proudly at the side of his well-appointed table and pointed as he spoke. "This is the Pampa'ed Chef cookie pwess." The way he held the thing would make one imagine he was handling a rare diamond.

Virginia reached over and lifted Riley's candy cane necklace from around his neck. "You said C.O.O.K.I.E. Sorry, Riley."

The poor thing looked pitiful but soon recovered when he saw Mary Jule intently studying his wares. After demonstrating the way the press pushed the dough from its barrel, he handed it to her. "And look at the PC baking sheets." He knocked on one. "See how durable it is?"

Mary Jule's wide eyes confirmed he had hooked a big fish.

"But the best pwoduct I have for the holiday season is the Pampa'ed Chef Easy Accent Decowator for only $24.00."

Mary Jule picked it up and set it back down immediately. "I'll take one of each."

Riley reared his head back, shocked, straightening his spine. He looked around at the rest of us but we weren't buying. "Everything on this table is bakewy fwesh without the baker pwice," he said loudly. "And this is my personal favorite, Mawy Jule! The PC pie gate."

"What's that?" she asked with all the enthusiasm of a woman learning a good shortcut for losing weight.

"I'll show you, Mawy Jule." He moved his PC pie plate in front of her and picked up a triangular-shaped object. "You put this in the pie, after you cut your first piece. It keeps the pie filling where it belongs. Inside the cwust!" Then Riley stretched it out from its original position. "You can adjust it from the first piece to the last. Believe you me, this little dandy is a steal. Only $6.50."

Mary Jule went wild. Not only did she add the pie gate to her order, she bought something called a mega lifter, a tool for hoisting heavy cakes from the oven, and the mini tart shaper—a handy wooden tool that Riley explained, "pats pastry, dough and wonton skins into wells of the Deluxe Mini-Muffin Pan." In addition to all that, she purchased two cake pan sets, four loaf pans, two sets of cookie cutters, five cookie sheets, and six mini tart pans. By the time Riley finished his sales pitch Mary Jule had spent $292.00.

"When did you become a baker?" Virginia asked once Mary Jule had completed the order form.

"Today," she said, signing her name to her check. "I've been dying to bake and this just got me inspired." I suspected the cosmos might have played a small role.

The clanging of a spoon on a drinking glass saved Al from an even bigger tab. "Okay, everyone," Tannenbaum shouted over the chatter. "It's time for our first game. You've all heard of Pin the Tail on the Donkey, but I bet you haven't played Pin the Nose on the Rudolph!" Virginia pinched an even bigger chunk out of my elbow, and mashed my big toe so hard I let out a moan.

Our hostess slowly closed the double door dividing the dining room from the great room to reveal a large poster of Rudolph the un-nosed reindeer. "And ladies, ladies. May I have your attention, please? I am thrilled to announce—" She waved to Mistletoe, who scurried over with something black in her hand. "Riley has donated this as the prize!" Mistletoe held up a stackable cooling rack. "To the person who gets Rudolph's nose the closest."

Squeals and claps were heard from the other cookie swappers.

Riley hollered, "You can use each Pampa'ed Chef wack flat or extend the legs and stack them for space-saving cooling. The nonstick gwid surface keeps the cookies, muffins, or cakes from falling thwough."

The first lady to line up, Mrs. Claus, moved in excitedly to have Tannenbaum apply her blindfold, which was a long red sash of material. The four of us moved to the end of the line. While we were waiting our turn, I snuck back outside with Virginia to refill our glasses.

When it was finally my turn to pin on Rudolph's nose, our hostess brought it to everyone's attention. "And here's Rudolph," Tannenbaum announced. "Let's see how close he gets to his own nose." After she had spun me around three complete turns, I could feel the effect of the vodka. Very woozy, I moved ahead, arms outstretched, certain I was making a straight beeline to Rudolph's face. When I heard Virginia's unmistakable cackle, I removed the blindfold only to learn his nose was pinned to his butthole.

A pitcher of cosmos later, and a nip into Tannen-pants' not-so-hidden liquor cabinet, the most outrageous moment of the evening came when Yule Log opened her prize for the most ornaments. Tannenbaum proudly presented her with a huge basket of cookies, which was tied up neatly in red cellophane, concealing the contents. "My cousin donated these cookies to the party," Tannenbaum announced proudly. "She received them at another swap last night and said they are outrageous."

Yule Log bowed, proudly accepting her award. "Thank you," she said to all, with a total of fifteen Christmas balls amassed on her sweater. "It's my fifth year in a row." She untied the cellophane and let it fall around the basket so we could all take a peek. One loud scream by Yule Log came next. Dozens of penis-shaped cookies, half with white icing and the other half chocolate were folded inside.

Tannenbaum yanked the basket away. "Oh shit," she yelled, which seemed to embarrass her even more. I could tell by the way she covered her mouth. She tore off to the back of her house and returned with an armful of PC products. "Please forgive me, Yule Log," she said, handing her the bakeware. "My cousin is shameful. I should have known better than to give that lascivious basket away without checking it first."

Without missing a beat, Virgy turned to Alice and said, "Well, shoot, Alice. And here I thought your fuzzy snowballs were risqué. Huh."

The best cookie prize, *Good Housekeeping's The Great Cookie Swap Cookbook,* went to Candy Cane. Hers were hands-down the best of the night: melt-in-your-mouth, iced lemon tea cookies with a swirled icing Christmas tree on top. Alice actually came in second with her coconut-frosted, chocolate snowballs and third place went to Sugar Plum, who brought eggnog thumbprints. Needless to say, I didn't swap for those.

Virginia Murphey actually ended up with the most necklaces. Mistletoe, I could tell, was not happy about it at all. She ended up with nine but Virginia edged her out with a total of ten. Every time any of us would catch Mistletoe's eye, she'd frown. *Oh for gosh sakes,* I thought. *It's a cookie swap. Not the freaking lottery.*

At straight up seven, I knew the party was over. I saw Hege helping some of the ladies with their coats, which was fine with me considering I was plenty tipsy and starving for some real food, with gluten. We had already packed up our assorted cookie swap boxes to give as gifts. The girls and I got in line behind the other ladies to thank Hege for the party.

As we were leaving, just trying to be jovial and polite, I said, "Hege sure is a unique name. Is it from your family?"

She nodded. "I'm named after my German grandmother."

"You're *German?*" I asked. *So that's why she has all those little European knickknacks around the house. And the huge collection of beer steins. The Beast did the same thing. They were all over the place when we bought the inn in Vermont.*

"German and proud of it," she said. "Hege is actually short for Helga."

I dropped every one of my damn cookie boxes and watched them crash at her feet.

While my friends hurried to pick up the mess, Hege kept talking. "Helga is terribly outdated, though. I was on the Internet the other day and found out only thirty-two Helgas have been born in the U.S. in the last thirty years."

I forced myself to stay silent.

"But the good news is Helga means holy and sacred. And in Scandinavia it means prosperous. As much as I've hated that name growing up I realize now it's very special."

"So special," I said. Sometimes a bold-faced lie is just the kindest thing.

Right before bed, I tried calling Peter. There's no telling what I would have said, had he picked up; the alcohol would have done all the talking. If I'm honest, it didn't surprise me that he ignored the call. Who could blame him? Even still, I missed him so much I ached. It's all I could think about. My mind would not turn off the thoughts no matter how I tried. I wanted to hop on a plane. I seriously considered leaving that instant and taking a red-eye to New Jersey. I could leave Kissie a note and she'd understand. But then I remembered Sarah's Christmas program at school. Correction. I remembered Sarah's Holiday Program. The one I had volunteered to chaperone, and make sure all the refreshments were ready to be served once the program ended.

Thinking about it reminded me that Sarah had asked Baker to be there, and also his parents. *Of course she asked them,* I thought. *They are her family every bit as much as I am.* Family. It was all so confusing. My girlfriends thought I was crazy to consider reconciliation with Baker but none of them were divorced. Not a one of them could possibly know how it feels to have your family ripped into separate parts. I never ever wanted my daughters to grow up in a broken home, miles away from their father. I didn't know how to solve this problem, to put us all back together. Kissie had made it perfectly clear, though, that she didn't trust Baker. She made no bones about it. But she did help me understand that Baker should be involved in the girls' lives—she said it a million times—but she hardly thought he'd changed enough for me to take him back.

It just seemed that it was taking so very long to figure out how to rebuild everything that had been broken since our disastrous move to Vermont. Everything seemed to be changing again, just when it finally looked like life was getting back to normal. I thought about Kissie's faith and wondered how she does it; how do you really "know" things will turn out OK? I didn't know how much longer I could keep on balancing so many unresolved issues: Peter, Baker, my growing girls, our rental house, and now the restaurant. I suspected the eggnog I'd hidden on Tannenbaum's bookshelf would petrify first.

Chapter Twenty-one

"When you come to the end of your rope, tie a knot and hang on," I recited as I whipped into the small parking lot. The FDR quote Frances had given me last summer meant much more to me now than ever before.

Her one o' clock appointment was just leaving when I opened the waiting room door at two o' clock sharp. I glanced at the tear-soaked woman as she passed; our mutual forced smiles an affirmation of one another's pain. Seeing Frances in person, standing in the doorway to her office, had an immediate calming effect on me though, and after an extra-long embrace I settled onto her overstuffed sofa.

"He did the only thing he could do," she said after I had filled her in. "He had to give you space to make this decision on your own." Frances peered at me over her reading glasses. "Because that's what's in front of you now. You can't have them both."

"That's exactly what he said." I fiddled nervously with the ring on my right hand, Mama's engagement ring. The sun had been streaming in through the window and the diamond caught the radiance, casting a colorful prism upon the ceiling. "I don't want them both. I just want what's best for my children." Peter had been gone ninety-six hours already and each minute of all ninety-six had been torture, with the exception of the PC cookie swap. Alice was right. It had been the perfect remedy. Naturally, I'd been second-guessing myself, wondering if I did the right thing, but each time Peter's image floated into my mind, pictures of Sarah and Issie followed. To make matters more complicated, Baker had called the girls every day, drawing them back in to the comfortable relationship they once had.

Frances stroked her neck, gazing out the large window overlooking the grove in the back of her building. It took her a moment to respond. "You need to think long and hard about something, Leelee. Before you let Baker back in, I'd give that some serious consideration."

I heard what she said, and she was making a good case but I still wrestled with the facts. "He is the *father* of my children though. Don't I owe it to them to try?" I leaned in toward her, resting my elbows on my knees. "Wouldn't I be letting Sarah and Issie down if I didn't at least give him a chance? I'm trying to be the best mother I can be."

Frances's response required no thought. "Leelee, you are a very good mother. But being a good mother is not predicated on taking back a man that *abandoned* her after moving fifteen hundred miles from home to chase his own desires."

Hearing that word was chilling. I repeated it out loud. "Abandoned. That's a sobering word, is it not?" I sank back into the sofa.

"It certainly is," Frances said, vigorously nodding.

I chewed on it for a minute and washed the word around my mouth as if it were mouthwash. Finally I spit out the poison. "Frances, how could I have been so blind? So utterly stupid?"

"You aren't stupid," Frances said, her emphatic tone making me feel a little better.

"For the last week I've been acting like his abandonment never happened. I suppose I've tried so hard to forgive him that I've put what he did out of my mind altogether."

"And it's wonderful that you've forgiven him. Without that, you would remain bitter and you'd never be able to trust or love again. Yes,

Leelee, by all means, you must forgive Baker. But running back to him is not the answer."

"I see that now."

"I doubt he's changed that quickly. I don't know Baker but from what you've told me he can be very persuasive. And charming."

"You have no idea."

"Your girls will be fine." After several minutes of reassuring me about the girls' well-being, she guided our conversation onto something more current. Obviously she considered the case with Baker closed. "What's going on with the restaurant? Have you heard back from the attorney?"

"No, but I plan on calling him when I leave here. That's my second order of business for today."

"Why don't you just change the name?"

"The attorney mentioned that. But we decided that the time it would take to apply for new licenses and redo all the advertising, the printing, et cetera, is the same amount of time it would take to get this mess cleared up. He doesn't think she will win, it's just a large inconvenience."

She nodded.

"Besides, I was the one who came up with the name in the first place." I waved my hands this way and that, using verbose gestures to emphasize my point. "The Peach Blossom Inn is my baby." I patted my chest. "I created it. If I changed the name, I'd have to order a new sign and a new—" All of a sudden, today's epiphany was as bright and colorful as the iridescence from Mama's diamond. I'd been digging in my heels, holding on to the Peach Blossom Inn name, but that had allowed Helga to dig into me. "So what?" I yelled, jumping up from my seat. "Who cares? She can have the name. I can come up with something similar, or much better for that matter."

"Of course you can." Frances jumped up, beaming across from me. "Keep 'peach' in the title if you want to, but let her have the name."

I thought about other possibilities and after a few short moments the perfect solution dawned on me. And when it did, I became angry at myself for ever allowing Helga Schloygin to intimidate me. Not once but twice! Amazing how quickly we can revert back to our old ways when challenged. My old demon may have thought he had a place to re-roost but I would be damned if I was going to let him nest. "The Peach Blossom Café! It's not an inn anymore anyway."

"I love it!" Frances said before settling back down in her chair.

"I will not let that woman bully me ever again. If Attila the Hun wants the Peach Blossom Inn, she can have it! I'm going to call my lawyer the minute I leave here."

"Do it!"

As if on cue, her clock chimed eleven times. After writing out my check, I stopped in front of her desk and repeated the words she had told me many times since our first appointment. "I may not be there yet, but I'm closer than I was yesterday. Who did you say made that up?"

"Author unknown," she reminded me.

"Ahh. Well, I'm making it mine."

She smiled. "Good work."

After our departing embrace I headed out the door.

I had ten minutes to make it to the girls' school before I was officially late. When I whipped into the carpool line, I could see Issie in the distance, standing patiently with a handful of other kindergartners. Her teacher opened the back door and strapped Issie into her booster seat. "Miss Isabella had a great day today," she told me. "She's reading very well."

"Thank you, Erica," I replied, turning around to Issie. "My girl is very smart."

"Her name is Miss Nichols," Issie retorted.

"Ahh, excuse me. Thank you, *Miss Nichols*," I said with a wink.

Issie waved at her from the back window as I pulled up in the carpool line where the second-graders were waiting. My cell phone vibrated from its place next to the gearshift. I let it go on to voice mail. I didn't recognize the number. As soon as Sarah had settled into her seat though, I checked the message. "Hi, Leelee, it's William Frasier. I have some news about your case. Please call me at your earliest convenience." Naturally, my stomach hit the floor. It always did when I received a call from an attorney. I tried to decipher the meaning behind his call by analyzing his tone, which was quite businesslike, but that only caused more gut fluttering. I almost called Alice first to see if she knew anything but instead took a deep breath and hit re-dial.

"Why are you on the phone?" Sarah whined.

"It's Mr. Frasier, *my attorney*. I promise to be off soon," I said, catching her eye in the rearview. When the receptionist told me to hold, I continued my deep breathing and put the cell phone on speaker to free my hands, carpool rule.

"You sure are breathing loud," Sarah added. She never failed to pout whenever I talked on the phone.

"I know and I'm sorry. But it's a *very* important phone call. I need you girls to please not say anything while I'm on."

After three or four minutes of waiting, my attorney finally picked up. "William Frasier."

"Hi, William, it's Leelee Satterfield. Sorry I missed your call earlier. I'm in the carpool line."

"Would you prefer to call me back?" His voice, very controlled and void of pleasantries, filled me with dread.

"Oh no, this is fine. As a matter of fact, I was going to call you as soon as I got home."

"That's a coincidence. What can I do for you?" His voice had a little more enthusiasm, but only a touch.

I regurgitated my pent-up emotions from the morning session with Frances directly into the phone. "I've decided to change the name of the inn. The more I think about it, the more I know it's the best decision. I know you tried suggesting that in the beginning, but I felt strongly about keeping it and besides, it was going to take just as long to reapply for more licenses, get a new sign made, change my menus, and all that. Now, I just want it over with." I could see our afternoon crossing guard giving me second glances, having noticed my extensive gestures flailing about the car. "I want to get my business up and running again. I can't believe I've let it go on this long. I'm going to start the reapplication process in the morning and change the name to the Peach Blossom Café. It's not an inn anymore anyway. If I had known from the start what this would do to my life, my relationship—"

"Lee—"

I vaguely heard William try to edge into my ranting but I couldn't hold back. "My *heart*. I would have never dug in my heels the way I did. I am over it! She can have it! I just want that woman out of my life forever. If I—"

"Leelee, may I interrupt you for a moment please," William bellowed, in the politest manner possible—but enough to overpower my harangue.

I was riled up, and had to force myself to let him get a word in edgewise. "Yes. Sure. Sorry."

"The reason I'm calling is to tell you that it's over. You don't have to change the name."

I heard what he said, but it seemed like a hallucination. "Will you repeat that please? I think you said I can keep the name."

He snickered. "I did. The Peach Blossom Inn is all yours."

"Are you serious? Why? What happened?" I paused. "Is Helga dead?"

William Frasier laughed hard. "No, she's not dead. I found a loophole in the case. I wish it hadn't taken this long to confirm, but dealing with the U.S. Trademark Office is worse than dial-up Internet service."

"What kind of a loophole?"

"I didn't catch it at first but the letter that Mr. Hightower sent to you had a misspelling."

"I caught it!" I said, feeling immensely proud. "It was 'blossom.' I just figured it was a typo."

"No typo. His fatal error was when he and Ms. Schloygin made the application. When I saw a copy of the actual trademark application and 'blossom' was spelled with one *s*, it struck me as odd. I immediately turned around and filed another trademark with the correct spelling."

"*Yes!*" I screamed.

"As a professional courtesy I called Mr. Hightower to bring it to his attention. He was indignant at first but had to acquiesce. Ms. Schloygin, he told me, had provided him with the wrong information. She's the one who can't spell. He chalked it up to her being German."

"This is fantastic news. What's next?"

"Start running your restaurant."

"That's it?"

"That's it. You can start tonight if you want. But I do need you to stop by my office to sign the paperwork for the new trademark application. I'm assuming you don't want to turn the case around on her and send *her* a cease and desist."

"Oh no. That bi— Sorry, that *woman* can do whatever she wants. I'm headed your way. I don't want this to go on a minute longer."

"My wife and I will be your first customers. Let me know when you reopen. Richard has told me all about your talented chef."

Hearing mention of my talented chef broke my heart all over again. "Sure will, see you soon."

When I hung up from William Frasier, Sarah chimed in from the backseat. "You almost said a cussword, Mommy."

"Almost saying a cussword and saying a cussword are two different things. How do you know that word anyway, young lady?"

"I'm not a baby, Mom. I've heard it before."

"So now I'm 'Mom,' huh?" I snuck a peek at her in my rearview mirror and caught her smiling.

"Just when you almost cuss."

On the way home from William Frasier's office, I picked up that night's dinner from Central BBQ, one of Memphis's finest barbecue restaurants. Since barbecue is Memphis's calling card, great barbecue restaurants have popped up all over the place. Aside from the fact that it's my favorite comfort food, Kissie loves it and so do my girls. It seems they would eat it every night if I'd let them.

We come by it naturally. If my daddy loved anything, he loved a good old-fashioned—*pulled* not chopped—pork barbecue sandwich. He would order his "white pig strictly lean." Then he'd gob on the sauce and coleslaw before washing it down with an ice-cold Coca-Cola. He referred to it as "one of the finer things in life." I completely agree. It might be the best combination of foods on earth. Something about the mixture of the two flavors, the savory and the sweet, sets my taste buds on fire. And the more carbonated the Coke, the better. If it doesn't burn my nose, it's not a good Coca-Cola.

All through dinner I was distracted, hardly hearing a thing anyone said. Each time Sarah and Issie wanted to tell something about their day at school, I'd have to ask them to repeat it. When Kissie relayed an earlier "disturbing incident with Riley" about him ringing the doorbell six times and asking her to "dogsit" Luke, I hardly commented. All my thoughts were on Peter. I deliberated about phoning him, what would happen the minute he picked up, and whether he'd be happy to hear from me, or hesitant.

With each bite of my sandwich, I'd obsess over my choice of words. After first giving him the fantastic news from William Frasier, I'd tell him that I'd been stupid. I'd tell him that I longed for him the minute he left and that it had only gotten worse as the days passed. I'd beg for his forgiveness for even considering reconciliation with Baker. On second thought I'd tell him the good news after I let him know how deeply I missed him and how much I longed for his touch. Without realizing it I had stopped thinking about the phone call. Instead we were tangled up in bed together, passionately kissing, when I heard Issie say, "Uh-oh. Bad boy, Roberta." When we all turned around, my pooch was on top of the kitchen counter with his head buried in the white Styrofoam container, chomping on pulled pork with tangy red barbecue sauce smeared all over his white mustache.

Cars were parked down High Point Terrace Road when I pulled up around 9:30 P.M. Baker's favorite hangout had always been the High

Point Pub. Only native Memphians know about it. It's a tiny little joint in the middle of the High Point neighborhood just off Walnut Grove Road near Highland. It sits right next door to the High Point Barber Shop, which sits next to the High Point Grocery. Inside the pub there's a shuffleboard table that never sits dormant and they offer numerous brands of ice-cold "brewskis," many advertised by neon and other vintage signs on the walls. There's a dartboard at one end, a big-screen TV over the bar, and another smaller TV in the corner, neither of which operate without a ball game on the screen. *Monday Night Football* always draws a crowd and since it was Monday I knew for one hundred percent positive that my ex would be there in all his UT second-string quarterback glory. The bartender could see him coming from twenty feet away and would have a cold bottle of Bud waiting on him. In Memphis football circles, Baker Satterfield would always be a celebrity.

I had to park a ways away. In the distance, I could see through the big picture window on the front of the pub, jam-packed with football people. Just before crossing the street, I happened to catch sight of a certain green Explorer parked right out front. He must have arrived early.

As soon as I stepped off the curb I could hear the clatter inside the pub. A man standing at the glass front door noticed me approaching and held it open. As soon as I stepped inside, the noise from the TV on the wall caught my attention and I paused to glance at the game. The Titans were actually beating the Steelers ten to three.

The men in the room outnumbered the women three to one and the ages ranged from early twenties to late fifties. The place couldn't hold more than fifty people but it appeared as if it were right at capacity. As soon as I eyed the shuffleboard table I spotted him. Dressed in his usual UT orange—this time a V-neck sweatshirt—Baker's hand was tightly clasped around a Bud bottle as he waited his turn. His back was to me and a girl, dangerously close, stood by his side. I hung back, about ten feet away, surveying the situation. She leaned in to him and I watched the two of them engage, laughing. I saw her beam at him and him beam back at her. Then he laid his hand on her shoulder, as if it were a gesture, part of the conversation.

I knew better.

Several people blocked my path but I excused my way through the small crowd, stopping behind him. With my right index finger I knocked—well, hammered—on the top of his right shoulder blade. Baker whipped his gorgeous head of hair around—so did she—and by the look on his face, I thought he'd pass out.

"Hey. What are you doing here?" was all that A-hole could think to say. The girl had no idea who I was and I could tell by the indignant look on her face she felt I had moved into her personal territory.

"Coming to talk to you," I said calmly.

"Now? Here?" He glanced around and I thought I saw him roll his eyes to his little friend.

"Yes. I need to talk to you now, please."

He didn't bother apologizing to her. Nor did he tell her he'd be back. He just strolled off behind when I turned around to leave. I excused my way back through the crowd and pushed through the front door with Baker at my heels—well, actually at my tennis shoes. I sat down on the iron bench in front of the barbershop window. For some reason I changed my mind and stood right back up, slamming my hands in my coat pockets. I bunched my jacket tightly around to the front, as if that would keep me warmer. Baker stood in front of me clutching his beer bottle, the other hand in his pocket.

"I don't even want to know if you are on a date with that girl," I said, ire lacing my voice. He started to explain but I closed my eyes, raising my palm. "It doesn't matter because I don't care." I shifted my weight from one foot to the other and leaned into him. "I don't want you back, Baker. I don't want you back now or any other day in the future. You got that?" My heart pounded.

"Why?" he asked.

"You abandoned me!" I pointed my finger in his direction. "One thousand four hundred and seventy-three miles away from home, in a foreign *frigid* corner of America, you left not only me but both of our daughters. And Princess Grace Kelly," I slipped in as an afterthought.

His face was expressionless and I watched him bend his head down, staring at the ground.

"What's to say that you won't do it again?"

He looked back up, lightly shaking his head. "I wouldn't do that."

"That's not good enough."

"Why?"

"Because I don't trust you. Why should I?" My voice escalated. My heart thumped.

"Shhh, you don't need to make a scene."

"Fine, I'll lower my voice." I looked around to see if anyone was watching. With no one hanging around outside I went on, much lower. "Even tonight, I walk in this place and there you are happily occupied with a girl—very cute, I might add—with no thoughts of us." *Frances was exactly right.*

"You don't know my thoughts." His voice was controlled.

"I know *you*, Baker! You care about *yourself* first, sports second, and everyone else last. I don't want to be in a relationship where I'm last any longer."

He wouldn't look me in the eye.

"It's too big of a risk. Don't get me wrong. I'm not looking for a man to put me first. I simply want a partner. Someone who wants me to be all I can be. Someone who rejoices in my accomplishments and grieves over my losses. I need a man who won't abandon me when the going gets rough. When things aren't rosy, and God knows life isn't always rosy, I need someone who hangs in there with me. *You are not that person, Baker.*"

He said nothing. Never even tried to argue my point.

"But I know someone who is." I threw my hands out to the side and made a sweeping motion. "Go on back into the High Point and enjoy your football game." As an afterthought I added, "And your little friend."

He stood a moment before shrugging his shoulders. Then shook his head. "Don't come crying back to me when that doesn't work out for ya. You've got your own issues."

"That's one thing you don't ever have to worry about. And as far as my 'issues' are concerned"—I put finger quotes around the word—"I'm working on them."

I turned to walk off but something made me turn back around. *Why become angry and bitter at this point?* I thought. *What will it accomplish?* Baker and I had to put our differences aside, and put our girls first. When I saw him standing there, left hand slammed in his pocket, right clutching his beer, the UT orange sweater—*still living his college dream*—I felt sorry for him. He had made a huge mistake. He no longer had his wife and little girls to welcome him home from work. His family was no longer a unit and he had lost a woman who once loved him desperately.

I forced aside my anger, literally pictured it floating away like a red helium balloon. Our daughters' little faces, smiling and playful, popped into my mind and I silently decided right then and there that the breakup of our marriage would never sour their feelings toward either of us, no matter who was at fault. They could still be happy and content as long as they had both of us in their lives. Suddenly, Baker's moving home made sense and I felt a burst of elation. Not for me, but for Sarah and Issie. "Let's just concentrate on being the best parents we can be," I said sweetly. "We might not have a marriage anymore but there's no reason our girls have to suffer. They can have us both, can't they?"

A smile slowly crept over Baker's lips.

"We can figure out a way to put them first no matter who we're with. Can't we?"

He put his beer down on the pavement, slowly extending his hand toward me. I stared at it, an olive branch enshrouded by a large, well-played quarterback's hand. A hand that once touched me tenderly, filling me with immense pleasure. I wrapped my small hand around it, feeling the chill from his beer, and let the warmth from mine transfer to his. We stood there for an extra-long moment, before he drew me tightly into his chest. "I'm sorry for all I've put you through," Baker whispered inside my ear. "I mean that sincerely."

I knew he meant it. I could feel the regret and the remorse in the urgent way he cradled my head inside his palm. All the anger I'd been harboring slowly floated away, like an untethered rowboat drifting from a dock. I nodded and reached my arms around his neck, burying my head deeper underneath his chin. "I know you do, Baker. I really do."

Chapter Twenty-two

After dropping off the girls at school early the next morning, I called Kissie to tell her that I would be at the restaurant all day. I had deliberately stayed away since Peter left, the sadness was too great, and now that we had the clearance to operate again, I wanted to rehang my sign. I didn't know when we'd be able to reopen, but Christmas was only sixteen days away and we needed to start taking holiday reservations—if and when they came in. It didn't escape my notice that all of this was contingent upon our head chef's return. He was due back in a week for our catering job. But I was planning on calling him the minute I got to the Peach Blossom Inn, in hopes that he'd come sooner.

On the way over to the restaurant I stopped by a Christmas tree lot. As I wandered around inspecting the Fraser firs, it made me miss him even more. I couldn't help envisioning a grand tree in the back of his truck and the two of us unloading it together, stringing lights, and hanging ornaments. Decorating the old Victorian for Christmas was something I'd been looking forward to since signing the closing papers. There was an air to the architecture that begged for ornament, for wreaths, and garland. The detailed scalloping of shutters and siding invited intricate and over-the-top decoration. This peachy-adorned home was one of the few that could withstand a healthy dose of Southern gold frosting and still maintain its original dignity. As ironic as it seemed, my Dixie home was perfectly built to complement any holiday caricature known to man. But none of it seemed worth it without Peter.

I consulted the man who was helping demonstrate the best way to hang wreaths on windows. He sold me plastic suction cups, claiming the installation would be a snap. I counted out the right number of premade ivory silk bows and envisioned how delectable they'd look on the wreaths—complemented by the peach satin ribbon I still had left over from the opening night's decorating. Another man at the lot tied a large ten-foot tree to the top of my car and I drove away with five feet of tree protruding over the hood of my small BMW.

I parked in the restaurant driveway, unloaded four of the twelve wreaths, and hurriedly plopped them on the porch. The weather had turned ghastly all of a sudden. Besides the dark and dreary sky, it was freezing cold outside, and the streetlamp on the street in front of the entrance was illuminated despite the morning hour, casting light onto the empty ivory pole where our beautiful sign once hung. While trekking back to the house with the last of the wreaths, I looked at the eerie light directed toward a sign that wasn't there to illuminate. I fantasized back to the happy day Peter and I hung it together in Vermont.

The first wreath went up easily and after adding the peach bow with its long, draping ribbon I retracted down the front steps to look back at my handiwork. I noticed the ribbon was a tad crooked so I marched back up to adjust the satin. When I turned around for the next wreath, I heard the restaurant phone ringing—and hoping it might be Peter, I sprinted through the front door. The ringing abruptly stopped, leaving me in front of the staircase, the spot where Peter and I had had our last conversation. My stomach wrinkled in sadness. That old familiar pang of angst, followed by an explosion of remorse, crept inside and there wasn't a thing I could do to make it go away. Peter had stood on this very spot promising that he'd return if I decided that

Baker was not the man for me. I understood perfectly why he left. There wasn't a man alive that would hang around waiting for a confused woman to choose between him and another. But now, I was desperate to apologize, frantic to tell him that I'd been wrong and beg, if I had to, for his return.

Glancing around at the tables, I noticed they were still perfectly set the way Pierre left them: linen birds of paradise atop each plate, salt and pepper shakers, stemware and flatware, all arranged with precision. We could be up and running by the weekend but it all depended on Peter. Yes, we would have to rehire our employees but I'd been in contact with each of them every week since we closed and all had been collecting unemployment, ready to start work at a moment's notice.

I pushed open the swinging door and wandered into the empty kitchen, which was noticeably warm in comparison to the rest of the house. I could have kicked myself for leaving the heat turned up and couldn't help but wonder how much my oversight would cost on the next utility bill. With a cursory glance at the answering machine, I hoped there might be a message or two, but found no blinking light. Keeping my eyes on the telephone, and without another moment of thought, I dialed Peter's cell. By the first ring, I could feel butterflies in my stomach, and by the third I almost hung up. *Will he still want me? Did I push him away completely?* On the fifth ring I heard a kind and surprisingly sanguine, "Hello."

"Hi," I said, my jitters easing slightly.

"How are you?" He sounded genuinely happy to hear from me.

"I'm pretty good. How are you?" The beats in my chest slowed.

"I'm good," he said as though nothing had happened between us.

"I have amazing news," I told him, slowly lowering myself into the desk chair.

"Yeah? Let's hear it."

"I wish you were here so I could tell you in person." I looked over at the stove.

"Where are you?" he asked.

"I'm at the restaurant." I paused before adding with a shaky voice,

"It's cold and lonely here without you. I'm looking at your ghost in front of the stove right now."

"You must be at the desk."

"How'd you know?"

"I just know. Pour yourself a coffee. That should warm you up."

I stood up and moved over to the coffee station. "Not like you warm me up." With the phone cradled inside my neck, I dumped a package of coffee in the filter and hit the brew button.

He cleared his throat. "Do you want me to warm you up?" There it was. My cue to tell him exactly how I felt.

Just hearing him ask the question gave me hope that he was willing to forgive me and come back to Memphis right away. "Of course I do. Today, tomorrow, always."

"I'm happy to hear that," he said. "How are things going there?"

While waiting for the coffee to brew I told him about the tree I'd selected and the wreaths for our windows, deciding to wait a moment before diving in to the details about the lawsuit. Once I'd finally poured my coffee I turned around to take a seat at the desk. A creaking noise in the front dining room startled me. It sounded like someone was in the house. I jumped, gasping into the phone. Coffee trickled down the side of the cup and burned my fingers.

"What's wrong?" he whispered, seemingly panic-stricken. "Is it a ghost?"

I whipped around as the swinging door slowly inched into the room. "*AAAAAHH!*" I screamed at the very top of my lungs. When his blue eyes caught mine I dropped my coffee cup and heard it smash against the white tile floor. Coffee sprayed all over me, all over him, and seeped out across the floor like a cracked window. "You!" I squealed, holding my heart. "You got me." I nearly slipped trying to get my arms around him.

"Careful," he said as I fell into him. "I didn't mean to scare you *this* bad." The smirk on his face, however, told me just how pleased he was with himself.

I reached around trying to slap him on the rear but he quickly moved away with a burst of laughter. "When did you get back?" I asked.

"About two this morning."

"I had no idea you were here." I laid my head on his chest and he walked us backwards out of the coffee mess.

"My truck's out back. Didn't you see it?"

"I never went around back," I said, peering up at him again. "My car's parked next to the porch. I've been unloading Christmas wreaths."

"This place could use some Christmas cheer. It's only sixteen days away, you know?"

"Of course I know." I squeezed him tightly. "Thank God you're back. There's so much I want to tell you."

"There's a lot I want to tell you, too." He peered down into my eyes. "You go first. What's your good news?" he asked, wrinkling his forehead.

I removed my arms from around his waist and took a step back. "Are you ready for this?"

"I don't know. Am I?"

"It's over. The lawsuit, I mean. We can open back up tonight if we want."

His eyes grew large and his mouth gaped. "That's fantastic. What happened?"

"Helga screwed up the trademark application. She misspelled 'Blossom,' and her idiot lawyer never caught it. William Frasier called me yesterday afternoon. We won on a technicality."

"A technicality. Who would have thought?"

"William went ahead and filed for a trademark with the correct spelling while he had the chance. He said we're free to use the name forever."

He crossed his arms in front of him and widened his stance. "Forever, huh?"

An awkward pause stalled our conversation. I knew it was my turn. "Can we go out front and sit down?"

He shrugged. "I should clean this mess up first. It's the least I can do."

"It can wait."

I sensed nervousness when I took his hand, something I'd never seen. I led him out to the front dining room, past the place where we'd had our last conversation. He politely pulled out a chair at one of the tables and motioned for me to sit. His gentility made me smile as I settled down onto the seat. After spinning his chair around to face me, he sat down, raising his eyebrows. "So what's up?"

"I owe you an apology. A huge apology," I finally said. Shifting, I gnawed on my bottom lip and drew in a breath.

He swept my words away with his hand. "No you don't." It was a gesture of forgiveness but I could see the sting in his eyes.

"Oh yes I do. I should have never let you walk out this door."

He didn't speak or move. Yet his gaze pierced my heart.

"When I came over here that day, I had just seen Baker. He appealed to my greatest weakness, which, as you know, is Sarah and Isabella. I know you don't know Baker but he can be incredibly persuasive." I glanced at Peter for affirmation that he understood. When he nodded I continued. "My reason for considering a reconciliation was for them. Not for me."

His eyes darted down to the floor and back up again. "What changed your mind? Or, have you changed your mind?"

"My mind was never made up. I was confused, certainly, but now I am one thousand percent positive that it's not just that I never want to be with Baker again, but more important, I only want you."

A shy smile passed his lips. "I am very happy to hear you say that."

"It's the absolute truth."

"I've thought a lot about your relationship with your ex over the last few days," Peter said. "As much as I want to blast him, I think it's best that I say as little as possible."

"And I appreciate that. But I need you to know that I'm working very hard on not letting him or anyone else for that matter take advantage of me. I'm taking care of my inner Southern belle." I smiled and we both laughed.

"Speaking of her," he said, grasping my shoulder. "I've given her a lot of thought, too. If I'm going to live down here, I have to get with the program. I owe you a big apology, too. I never should have sat by and let that man talk to you the way he did. I'm sorry."

I swept away his apology the way he had mine.

"I mean it. He was drunk and obnoxious."

"And such an idiot," I said, reflecting back.

"I was the other idiot." He rolled his eyes and shook his head.

"All this is about our worlds colliding. I thought about it last night. If that's the worst struggle we have in this relationship, then how lucky are we? I have friends whose problems are far worse, even with South- ern husbands. You are tender and kind and loving." I wanted to say: and masculine and sexy and I cannot stay away from you one more moment. The rolled-up sleeves on his red flannel shirt made me want to rip the thing off so I could see more than just his arms.

"Thanks," he said somewhat bashfully.

"And I don't know what I would do without you." I leaned in closer to look him square in the eye. "And I pray that I never have to spend another week without you again. It's been pure torture."

By the way he studied my face, with an overflow of love and com- passion, I knew I was forgiven. He pulled me out of the chair and onto his lap, peering straight into my eyes. "I don't know that you'll ever know how tough it's been for me. The minute I crossed the Shelby County line I started doubting myself, but I was mad so I kept driving. The entire way from Tennessee to Vermont I tried talking to Pierre about it and you know how far that got me." We laughed. "I was telling him all of my deepest thoughts and feelings and he'd nod and act as though he under- stood every word."

"Pierre is dear like that." I caught his eyes and wouldn't let go. "What made you come back early?"

"Honestly?" he asked, looking into my eyes.

I nodded my head yes.

"I decided to fight for you. Even if I lost, I couldn't fathom not doing everything I could to win you."

No man had ever said anything like that to me before. It seemed like a hallucination not a reality and I couldn't suppress the familiar twinge of doubt creeping back inside. I wasn't sure I believed I was worth fighting for. But this time, I cast out the thought and refused to let skepticism cripple me. "I missed you so much, it was physically painful. My stomach hurt. My head ached. It was awful," I said, raking my fingers through his silky hair.

With our lips only inches apart, both of us could feel the heat and we drew together like magnets. We madly fondled one another's hair and faces. When he leaned into me, I slipped around in his lap and pushed my legs up on either side of him. I pressed in against his chest, reaching out for his hands, resisting the urge to rip the buttons off his shirt. Looking back on it I think I felt the front chair legs tip, but I was so wrapped up in love with the man, I didn't care. When the back legs slipped on the wooden floor and we toppled backwards, crashing with a loud thud, neither of us knew what hit us. We lay in a crumpled heap on top of one another.

"Owww," Peter finally moaned. By the way he grimaced I could tell he was in pain. His body may have cushioned my fall, but my leg was tangled up inside the bottom of the chair. I eased it loose.

"Are you okay?" I said, rolling off him, massaging my calf.

"I'm not sure," he said, struggling with his words.

Despite the ache in my leg, I scampered up, holding out my hand to help him. "Here. Try to get up."

He made an arduous effort, reaching around to rub his back and grimacing as he rose. "Wow. That hurt."

"Can you stand up?"

He nodded. "Yeah, but it'll take a minute." After a deep breath he finally stood up straight, glancing over at me. "What happened?"

"I guess we got carried away," I said with a giggle in my voice.

He popped his finger on top of my nose. "You're lucky we fell when we did. I don't know how much longer I'll be able to resist you, Leelee Satterfield."

I smiled. "You're not the only one." So far we'd managed to avoid the subject. Even though he'd been in Memphis only a short while, we both knew it was inevitable. As much as I wanted him, though, there was a bigger part of me that wanted to wait. *I'm still old-fashioned,* I thought, *despite what everyone else does. It's not quite time.* "How bad is it?" I asked, touching his lower back.

"I think it's probably just a wicked bruise."

"Let me look at it." I yanked his flannel shirt out of his belt and examined his back. The skin was scraped and red with the beginning shades of blue peeking through. "It's ugly," I told him.

"It's fine," he said, straightening his shirt. "I'll be right back." He moved over to the steps, holding on to the same spot on his back with one hand and the banister in the other. I watched him limp up the stairs.

"Are you sure I don't need to take you to the ER?" I called.

He turned around. "I'm sure." After taking three more steps, he turned around again. "I forgot to tell you Pierre's back. He's up here asleep."

"He decided not to stay in Vermont, huh?" I asked.

"I decided for him. Besides, he belongs here with us."

He certainly does, I thought.

A minute later, Peter hobbled back down wearing his jacket.

"Are we going somewhere?" I asked.

He nodded then pointed over to the corner where our sign had been collecting dust for the last six weeks. I smiled as he ambled over and lifted it off the floor.

"You can't carry that," I said. "You can barely walk."

"I'm fine," he retorted indignantly. "You can open the door for me though."

I opened the front door and the two of us walked, slowly, onto the porch, down the steps, and out to the boxwood-lined walkway, following it all the way down to the lone ivory pole near the road. I got on one side, Peter stood on the other, and we hoisted the sign, hooking it in place. We stood a few feet back, admiring the way it hung on the pole, the design and the two peach blossoms for *O*'s.

"It would have been a shame to have to send this back to Helga," Peter said, stifling a laugh.

"No kidding," I replied with little emotion. Having the sign back in its rightful spot should have made me elated—especially after all we'd been through. But for some reason I just stood there, tilting my head to and fro. It wasn't that it hung the wrong way on the pole; it hung the wrong way in my head. I kept staring at it, hoping it would straighten, but for some reason it still looked crooked.

"What is it? You don't look satisfied," Peter said, tilting his own head.

"I'm not."

He tried readjusting the sign. "Do you want me to turn it around the other way?"

"No, I just don't think—" Suddenly the sign came perfectly into focus, the epiphany I had had at Frances Folk's office enlightening me for a second time. "It's the name! I think we should change the name."

Peter looked at me like I was crazy. "To what?"

"The Peach Blossom Café."

"Are you serious? That's not much of a change."

"I know that, but I've changed." I turned to face him. "First of all, it's not an inn anymore, we're really just serving food, not shelter. And 'Café' is a nod to Pierre's French heritage. But more important, this restaurant represents our new life here in Memphis."

A big smile crept upon Peter's lips.

"Maybe, just maybe, the tight grip I had on the old name was about stubbornness and the desire to beat Helga. But mostly it was about the memory of a time and place when I stood on my own two feet for the first time and met beautiful, wonderful you."

He closed his eyes, breathed deeply, and leaned his head back, as if he were inhaling my praise.

"The Peach Blossom Inn name has been hard to give up. But I realize now that the old name doesn't really apply to this new place in Memphis. This restaurant is about both the old and the new. It's the North and the

South. It's me and you, Kissie and my daughters, the girls, Roberta, Pierre and Jeb—even Baker. I really had already decided to change it when William Frasier phoned."

"Whatever you say, boss. I'm behind whatever you want to do and whatever makes you happy." Peter wrapped his arms around me from behind and whispered in my ear. "I'd like to fix you dinner tonight at the Peach Blossom Café. That is . . . if you're free."

"I think I can make that happen," I said, turning around, catching the sweetness in his eyes. "What time is my presence requested?"

Chapter Twenty-three

"You look like a princess, Mommy," Issie said. "Can I go with you?"

"No, baby. I wish you could."

She stared at me intently before sucking in a gasp of air. "You have on makeups. Close your eyes so I can see." I leaned down to her level, fluttering my eyelashes. "Put some on me," she said, lightly touching her tiny fingers to the copper eye shadow on my lids.

"Not tonight, lovey. But we'll do it tomorrow." Issie stormed off in a huff and hid behind the couch.

"Where are you going?" Sarah wanted to know.

"To the restaurant. Mr. Peter is fixing me dinner."

She moaned, expelling a raspberry. "You're always at the restaurant."

That broke my heart. Especially since my original plan was to move into the upstairs of the Peach Blossom Inn so I wouldn't have to spend as much time away from the girls. When Peter moved to town that changed everything. I sat down on the couch and pulled her into my lap. "I know, baby. Pretty soon we're going to move there. We'll live upstairs and I'll be with you every night."

"When?"

"Soon. I'm not quite sure when, but soon. Have you finished your homework?" I tucked her hair behind her ears, peering into her dark sapphire eyes.

"Yes, ma'am. It was easy. Ask me some multiplication." Sarah had been promoted to an accelerated math class. Clearly, that was due to a Baker gene.

"Let's see. What's two times two?"

She looked at me, rolling her eyes. "Please. Ask me a real math problem."

"Okay then. Five times six?" I expected to stump her.

It took a second but she answered, "Thirty." After correctly answering five more math problems, which I considered to be tough for her age, she asked for more. Clearly, she was stalling. She didn't want me to leave either. When I decided to reopen the restaurant, I knew this would be the downside. *I'll talk to Peter about it when I see him and make a new plan,* I thought. *Something has to give.*

"Issie, please come here and give Mommy a kiss. We're getting our Christmas tree tomorrow and we'll be together all day." A nest of red hair poked just above the couch pillows. Then I saw her smile. I held out my arms. "Please come here."

She hurried over and scooted her sister out of my lap. Sarah frowned as she pushed her back.

"Hey. There's room for you both." Wrapping my arms around each, I said, "It smells mighty good in here. Let's go see how we can help Kissie."

The unmistakable aroma of pot roast drew us into the kitchen. I directed the girls over to the silverware drawer to set the table. Kissie was mashing her red potatoes; her grandmother arm jiggled each time she pressed firmly into the bowl. Earlier that day I could have sworn I saw disappointment in her face when I told her that Peter had invited me for dinner. I had a feeling she wanted to cook a big meal for him now that he was back. She didn't say so but I know her so well. Cooking is one of the ways she best expresses love. When I slipped my arm around her waist, she cut her black eyes at me. "Peter gone like that dress," she said. It was a light blue soft cotton V-neck with a small thin ruffle running from the right shoulder down to the hem on the left. Snug in all the right places, it had three-quarter-length sleeves and a shirring of fabric at the waist.

"Thanks. I really want tonight to be special."

"He's a good man. You need to hold on to him." She tilted a carton of cream into her potatoes and emptied it.

"I know that," I said, sensing a bit of frustration in her voice. "I just hope he wants to hold on to me."

"I'mo tell you one thing." She let go of her masher and glared. *Uh-oh, Leelee lecture time.* "You need to be cookin' for *him*. If you let Peter be the one doin' it all, he gone get away from you sure 'nuff." Her chin quivered as she pursed her mouth. "Don't you be lettin' him do it all the time. I don't care if he is a chef." She lowered her voice so the girls couldn't overhear. "The bedroom ain't the only place a man like a woman to be skilled."

"*Kissie!*"

Both hands were on her hips. "I wudn't born under no rock. I know what I'm talkin' about." She shooed me away with both hands. "Now, get on over there. But remember what I tole you. A man likes a woman who can cook."

"I know that. I'm going to cook for him—"

"This Sunday. You and I gone cook him a fine meal. He don't have to know I helped." Picking back up her masher, she went back at it full force.

"Okay. I appreciate that."

"Pierre, too. He can come."

"Great, I'll ask him. What about Riley?" I added for a little comic relief.

"Go on now. *Shoo.*"

I kissed her cheek and did the same to my girls. When I grabbed my keys, Roberta didn't run to the back door like normal. He sat right by Kissie's side, waiting for any delicious people-morsel that might accidentally fall from the counter.

When I pulled onto the gravel driveway, I noticed the glow. White light flickered in each of the front rooms, like hundreds of lightning bugs trapped inside. Peter had told me to come in through the front door. Now I knew why. I parked next to the porch and walked down the walkway to the front steps covering my head with the back of my raincoat. A light mist hung in the air, the hands-down worst climate for curly hair. Through the window I caught sight of the giant, twinkling Christmas tree, at least ten feet tall, in the bend of the staircase. Encircled in white lights, a gold star flickered from the top, but there were no ornaments. Unable to resist, I turned the doorbell once, then a second time just for fun. Pierre opened the door wearing his tux jacket, bowing when I stepped inside. The tastevin dangling from his neck swung as he bent his head down. *"Bonjour, madame,"* he said, his smile large and full of promise.

"Bonjour," I replied, adding a courtesy. Nat King Cole's velvety baritone floated through the air, "O little town of Bethlehem, how still we see thee lie." Logs cracked in both fireplaces, and from my location in the foyer I could see my shadow cast on the stairwell. The entire downstairs was bathed in candlelight. Pivoting around I noticed both mantels were covered with candles of various shapes and sizes. In the center of the left dining room a small table was set for dinner, a nosegay of white roses adorning the center. When I saw the white fleurs-de-lis napkins inside two wine goblets, on top of a white tablecloth it struck me that every single thing in the room was white. Pierre said, *"S'il vous plaît,* Leelee, I'm coming back." He disappeared through the swinging door and returned moments later holding a tray with a glass of white wine in the center. When I gripped the bowl of the glass, Pierre shook his head. "No. I'm show you." He put down his tray on the sideboard and gripped the stem. "You hold this way, okay?"

I did as he suggested and took a sip. I knew it was Rombauer chardonnay the second it touched my tongue. Rombauer would always remind me of Peter. He introduced it to me in Vermont. It was his favorite and now it was mine.

"White wine es cold. Touch glass and wine warms. Not good."

"I didn't know that," I said. "But it makes perfect sense, now that you tell me."

"Dinner almost ready," he said, pulling out my chair.

"*Merci*," I answered while scooting in closer to the table. "Where is my date?"

"Peter es coming in—"

Before he had the words out of his mouth, Peter pushed through the swinging door. The sight of him took me aback. He wasn't wearing his chef pants or his jacket. Instead he wore a pale blue cotton dress shirt with tan slacks, a red star-pattern silk tie, and brown dress shoes. Come to think of it, I'd never seen him dressed up before. His face was freshly shaven for a change and he was carrying his own glass of white wine, gripping the stem. The moment he walked through the door, his eyes fixated on me and he beelined over. When he buried his face in my neck, I could smell the musky scent of his aftershave. He sat down next to me and tipped my glass with his. "You look mighty beautiful." *There's that word again,* I thought. Instead of changing the subject, I let it slide down my throat and coat my insides with confidence.

"Thank you. You look beautiful, too," I told him, touching his tie.

He smiled and leaned in for a peck. "I can clean up when I try."

"I don't know that I've ever seen you cleaned up," I said, smiling. I giggled to myself. "Cleaned up" was definitely a Yankee expression.

"Enjoy it. I don't do it very often." He turned around in his chair. "So, do you like the ambiance?"

At first I had no words. I could merely shut my eyes and shake my head. "I don't know what to say. I've never seen anything like this. You couldn't have stopped all day."

"Pierre helped quite a bit."

"It's magical in here."

"That's what I was hoping you'd think."

I turned to look at our tree. "All the tree needs is vintage ornaments and a popcorn garland. I was thinking it might be fun to decorate it like they did when the house was built."

He nodded. "And we need to get another one for your house," he said. "I'll take you and the girls tomorrow if you want."

"I just told them tonight that we'd get ours tomorrow. Thank you." My mind flashed back to the year before, when Peter took the girls and me into the Vermont forest near our house to cut down a real live Christmas tree. That was the day I knew I was falling in love with him.

Pierre set two bowls of soup down in front of us. I knew what it was right away. She-crab. I could smell the sherry. A garnish of parsley with a dollop of crème fraîche floated on the top. I smiled at Peter as I picked up my spoon. A lump of crabmeat filled my first bite. "This is magnificent," I said.

"It's your favorite, right?"

I nodded. While eating our soup we talked shop. We discussed our reopening, the employees, our victory over Helga, and the catering. Our second catering job was one week away and we talked about how the logistics would work, with Peter back at the restaurant.

Pierre reappeared holding a wine bottle and a carafe filled with red wine. Pouring a tiny taste into his tastevin, he sipped before pouring Peter a sip. "Vedy, vedy good wine. Vedy good year," he proclaimed.

"2005 Silver Oak Cabernet Sauvignon. I've been letting it open up for the last two hours," Peter said, lifting his glass and breathing in the aroma.

"What do you mean?" I asked.

"By letting it breathe inside a carafe, you experience the full flavor of the grape." He took a sip. "Pour away," he said to Pierre, who poured us each a full glass. I watched as Peter swirled the wine. I did it, too. I had no idea why I was doing it but did it just the same.

"Isn't this nice?" he asked after another sip.

"So nice," I said after swallowing mine. Honestly, I had no idea if it was nice, but it tasted good. I knew that.

He put his nose in the glass and breathed deeply. So did I.

"Can I ask you something?" I said while swirling, careful not to spill it on my dress.

"Of course."

"Why are we swirling?"

He lifted his chin and laughed. "When the wine falls down the sides of the glass, it creates vapors, which we perceive as aromas. Smell it again and tell me what it reminds you of."

I did as he suggested, whiffing deeply.

"What does it smell like?" he asked.

"Wine?"

He chuckled and breathed in the wine again. "I smell plums, eucalyptus—"

"*Eucalyptus!*" I exclaimed. "How in the world do you know what eucalyptus smells like?"

"You don't?" he said smiling.

"*No.*"

"What about black cherry? Smell that?"

I tried again. "Maybe," I lied.

Reaching for my white wineglass, he gingerly placed it beside my red one. "Here, smell the white."

Once again, I took a deep whiff.

"Don't you smell figs?"

I shook my head.

"What about peaches? Maybe a hint of vanilla?"

"Sorry but not really."

He shook his head and smiled. "Okay, let's take another approach. Take a sip. Let it sit on your tongue and then tell me what you taste." We both took hearty sips. When he set down his glass he said, "Maybe a little pineapple or apricot?"

I shook my head; connoisseurship was clearly not in my future. "I can see why you'd describe it as buttery but as far as tasting pineapple or apricot—I just taste wine."

"You're hopeless," he said with a wink. "Cute but hopeless."

When Pierre served the entrée, I knew the smell with my eyes closed. Beef Wellington. It was one of Peter's Vermont specials. He prepared his with a nontraditional mushroom pâté, knowing I'm not a fan of goose liver. Tonight he served it with cracked black pepper Boursin scalloped potatoes and haricots verts.

I took a bite of my beef, a perfect medium rare, letting the flavors explode inside my mouth. I glanced at Peter, smacking my lips. "I taste mushrooms, red wine, maybe some onion, a little black pepper."

Peter grinned. "Fine. Be that way." He took another long whiff of his wine.

I swept my hand over my plate. "How do you do this? Honestly, I'm amazed. Every time you get behind the stove, not only do all of your dishes come out perfectly, but you make each look effortless." When it comes to the kitchen, what takes him hours takes me days; my minutes are his seconds.

"It's what I do."

"We should put this on the menu."

"Maybe someday. For now it makes a nice special."

Suddenly an idea came to mind. "We should do a cookbook! A Peach Blossom Café cookbook."

Peter put down his wine and sat back in his chair. "Leelee Satterfield, that's an amazing idea. We could sell them right here."

"Of course we could. Between your recipes and Kissie's, it would sell like crazy."

"I bet Kissie King would love that."

Hearing her name reminded me of our earlier conversation. I changed the subject abruptly. "I want to cook for you, Peter."

He swallowed the green beans he had just put in his mouth. "I'd really like that. Thanks."

"How about Sunday? You and Pierre come over to our house and we'll all eat together as a family." The last word, "family," just slipped out. "Issie and Sarah would love it. They've been having a hard time with me being away so much." I stopped short of telling him that we'd have to rearrange our living situation. I wanted to give it more thought before unplugging his lifestyle.

We took our time, savoring every bite of the meal. His leg next to mine shot titillating vibrations *all over* my body. I rubbed my bare foot against his sock, partly to feel the warmth but mainly because it felt so darn good to touch him. Restraining myself had become nearly impossible.

"Do you mind if I switch away from Christmas music for a while?" Peter asked. Nat King Cole's album had been playing since I first arrived.

I lightly shook my head. "No. I've been hearing it all day on the radio. Go for it."

Peter stood up and meandered over to his iPod, which was in the docking station from the kitchen. He turned back to me. "Do you like Marvin Gaye?"

I nodded.

"Good." He pushed play and came back to sit down. "So—" He picked up his fork and took the final bite of his dinner. "—ready for dessert?"

I smiled. "Always."

Peter turned toward me and reached for my hand. He stroked my hair. His eyes captured the radiance from the candlelight and I couldn't resist caressing his face, lightly sweeping my fingertips over his lips. We'd been kissing intermittently throughout the dinner and when Pierre cleared our dinner plates I became aware of how careful he had been to keep his presence unknown. I was enjoying the most romantic dinner I'd ever had.

Ten minutes later Pierre set dessert down in front of us. White chocolate mousse. Peter had created it as a dish in Vermont in honor of my love for white chocolate and my obsession with spotting a moose. He served his in a wineglass, swirled with a raspberry coulis, garnished with a mint sprig and a plump raspberry on top.

I wasted no time digging in. The sweet creamy mixture melted on my tongue and when I tasted the raspberry, my mouth puckered ever so slightly. It was every bit as good as I remembered. "You know it's going to be hard for me to cook for you, don't you?" I said. "Between you and Kissie, I don't stand a chance."

He leaned back in his chair, correcting when the chair legs tipped. "Cooking is my job, sweetheart. I've been doing it for years. I don't care if you ever cook a gourmet meal. Just having it done for me is nice enough."

"Sunday night. Pierre, too," I said, spooning another bite from the glass and sucking it off the spoon.

The familiar first chords of a Motown song I recognized rang out from the docking station. "I love this song," I said, peering at him. "Is it 'Distant Lover'?"

He nodded. "Would you like to dance?"

I took his hand and he drifted us to the front of the fire. He wrapped the other tightly around my waist, slowly pulling me into him. Intoxicated by the music, the wine, the heat from his body, I closed my eyes, laying my head on his chest. Listening to Marvin Gaye's velvety vocals, nestled into Peter, took me away from Memphis, onto that remote beach I'd been fantasizing about. We turned slowly with the chorus. With every word of the song, I felt more and more in love. This was the man I longed for. This was the man who made me feel safe and secure, worthy of owning every millimeter of my heart. After several turns, I pulled away and looked straight into his eyes, finally uttering the three words I'd been so afraid to say. "I love you."

I felt his hands grip my waist. We peered into one another's eyes, holding gazes through blinks, pushing through bashful smiles, never once darting away from one another. "And I love you," he said slowly. I could feel his love. In his hands, his smile, his eyes—every part of him, really. I knew that he loved me, but even more important, I absolutely knew that I loved him.

We slow-danced through two more songs. When the last played its final chord, he led me back to the table and pulled out my chair. "You haven't finished your dessert," he said once we were seated.

"I don't know that I can after that dance. Or the rich meal." I was so high on love, I felt like I could float through the room.

"Sure you can." He lifted my spoon, dipped it inside the mousse, and fed me a large bite. It was much too big, so I tapped him on the hand.

"Too much," I said, garbling my words.

He handed the spoon back to me. "Sorry about that."

I swallowed and spooned another, much smaller bite into my mouth, setting the spoon back on the plate.

"Can't you finish it?"

I shook my head. "I've had she-crab soup, beef Wellington, scalloped potatoes, green beans, and tons of wine. Do you want me to fit through that door?" I said, pointing toward the foyer. "I can't put another bite in my mouth."

"You don't know when I'll make it again." He spooned the last bite out of his own glass and shoved it into his mouth. "Lightweight," he said with an artful smile, followed by one of his seductive winks.

"I am not."

He shrugged.

I took a large bite of the mousse and shoved it in my mouth. I noticed him watching me intently.

"Are you satisfied?" I asked him.

He shook his head. "No."

"Fine." I took the spoon and dug the last three bites out in one big heap, shoveling it inside my mouth. As the last few dollops dissolved, I felt something. I looked over at him curiously before spitting it into my fingers. When I realized what it was, I dipped it inside my water glass. I left my body for a moment and floated on top of the table, peering down at the redhead seated next to the handsome blond. Peter took the candle from the table and held it next to the ring in my hand. A diamond solitaire with two baguettes on either side. The radiance cast streaks of luminescence as I flicked the center diamond to catch the light.

He plucked it from my fingers. My hand was shaking as he slipped it onto my left ring finger. Awkwardly, he tried pushing it over my knuckle but there was no use. "And I thought your hands were small," he said. "My granny's must have been tiny."

"It's okay," I said, my eyes pooling with tears. "It is so beautiful." I took it off and slipped it on my left pinkie. "We can get it sized in a day. I know right where to take it."

"So does that mean it's a yes?"

I smiled at him.

He shook his head and tipped his forehead. "I'm obviously not very good at this." Taking my hand with both of his, he peered lovingly into my eyes. "Will you marry me? Will you be my Mrs. Owen?"

I breathed in his words. "Yes! I love you. I would love to be your Mrs. Owen."

He reached over and took me into his arms. With his thumb he swept my tears across my cheeks. There were tears of his own pooling in the corners of his eyes. "Remember me telling you I stopped in at Mom's last week?"

I nodded.

"She's been keeping this ring for me. It was her mother's."

"I am so honored to have it," I said, taking another peek at the tiny ring on my finger.

"Who would you prefer I ask for permission to marry you? There may not be any men in your life, but you sure have a host of Southern belles."

"And proud of it," I said, with a smile. "I think we should ask them all. Starting with two little ones and one large one."

"This late? Are you sure?"

"I am absolutely positive."

Chapter Twenty-four

SIX BLISSFUL WEEKS LATER

The call came in around one in the morning. It will forever be referred to as "the call," because it was the one in which my entire life turned on a dime, or on a tire as is more the case. The Angel of Death showed up one night on a snowy highway in rural Vermont, just outside of Willingham.

"Hello," I eked sleepily into my landline, an edge of panic in my voice. Midnight calls scare me to death. I mean, who in the world calls with good news in the middle of the night? From my experience, a late-night call always means trouble.

"Missy? I hate to call you so late, but you told me to call you if I ever had news." Roberta's somber tone sent a zero-to-sixty shiver from my toes to my nose.

I sat straight up in bed. "Are you okay?"

"I'm okay."

"Something's wrong. I can tell. Is it bad?" I reached over to my nightstand and fumbled for the light. When it illuminated my bedroom, I had to squint. My Roberta sleepily picked up his head and yawned.

"That depends whose side you're on."

"Side? Wait. What are you talking about? Is Jeb okay?" My breathing became heavier and more rapid.

"He's fine."

"Then what is it?" The panic in my voice hit the ceiling.

Roberta, on the other hand, was as calm as an ocean breeze. "Well, I'll tell you. About three hours ago—Moe and I had just slipped under the covers—we heard a report on the scanner."

Uh-oh, I thought. *News from the police scanner could only mean one of two things. Trouble or gossip.*

"There was a wreck out on the old toll road. You remember the Inn at Swallow Creek, don't you?"

"Yes!"

"Well, it's darker than a pocket out tonight. No moon at all—"

"Yes!" I hated to be pushy, but I needed the poor thing to spit it out. The suspense was killing me.

"Reet past the inn, a car crashed. It occurred at twenty-three hundred and three hours." Whenever Roberta talked about the reports she heard on the scanner, she always relayed them in military time, the way they were announced by the police.

"IS ANYBODY DEAD?" I shrieked.

"Nuup. No*body's* dead. But it's pret-near a miracle she ain't. She's mighty shook up, though, from what the police reported on the scanner."

"Who? Who's shook up?"

"Helga. She was a hell-a-tee-ding-dong past—"

"Whoa, interpretation please. What's a 'hell-a-tee-ding-dong'?"

"It means she was speeding."

"Tell me something I don't know."

"Well, she was doing it again tonight, down that hill past the inn there when she came upon a bull moose licking salt off the road."

I sucked in a loud, audible gasp. "A bull moose? What are the odds?"

"Very small, I can tell you that. She must not have been paying attention, them things are dark you know, and she hit that monster broadside." (She said "monster," but I was thinking "angel." I couldn't help it.) "The impact broke his legs and he broke through the wind-shield and landed in her car. Reet in the passenger seat next to Helga."

"I've never heard of such."

"It happens more than you think," Roberta reported authoritatively. "You remember that car she drove, don't you? The Subaru Outback?"

"How could I forget it?" My mind conjured up the image of Helga speeding up to our inn, parking along the picket fence. Her car was always, always filthy with road grime. She never bothered to wash it.

"The police reported that had she been in another car, she might not have made it. They said those cars are tougher than boiled owl, one of the best snow cars money can buy. I told Moe we are going to put back every penny we've gut till we can buy one for ourselves. Yes sir, Mr. Dooley, Subaru has made a believer out of me. I figure it will take—"

"*Wait,* Roberta, sorry to interrupt but what happened next?" I stacked both pillows behind me and reclined back, crossing one foot over the other.

"Well, a car finally pulled up behind her, a man and his wife coming home from eating dinner up at Sugartree. Two tourists staying at the Inn at Swallow Creek. They got out to help her and called 911. Three state troopers arrived on the scene, an ambulance followed, and so did a fire engine."

"Wow. That many emergency vehicles, huh?"

"Yuup. This is *big.* Very big news." While she was talking, I glanced at my jagged fingernails and grabbed the nail file on my nightstand. "Soon as I heard all the commotion, I called Jeb and he was already headed straight over to the scene."

"Does he have a scanner now?"

"Aunt Doris does." They aren't kin either, but Roberta still calls Jeb's mother Aunt Doris.

"Have you talked to Jeb since he arrived on the scene?"

"Sure have. He's the one that relayed most of the details to me. He said Helga didn't have a scratch on her."

Well, crap, I thought, but held my tongue.

"Said she was fine physically but they weren't so sure about her mental state so they took her straight to the Brattleboro Retreat. Said she couldn't even talk and had a faraway look in her eye like she had lost her marbles."

A loud guffaw escaped from down deep. I couldn't hold back. Helga Schloygin had been sent to the Vermont Bolivar. "Wow, Roberta. I don't know what to say."

Roberta snickered, too. I bet she couldn't hold back either. "Did you know it used to be called the Vermont Asylum for the Insane?" she asked me. "Way back when it was first started? Sometime in the mid-1800s."

"No, but all those places used to be called insane asylums." The visual was too good. Lady Attila the Hun with her tight gray bun, loose and messy from the trauma, tongue hanging out the side of her mouth, in between two men dressed in black as they lifted her by the elbows—feet dangling—and up the front steps of the Vermont Bolivar. I knew it was terrible for me to be thinking like that and that God might strike me down dead, but it was out of my control. I flat couldn't help myself. "What happened to the moose?" I asked, genuinely concerned. "I assume the poor thing's dead."

"As a doorknob."

"Oh well. At least he didn't die in vain."

"I've got one more piece of news for yous."

"Whatcha got?" I asked, wide awake, now on to filing my toenails.

"The police reported that Helga was on her cell phone when the wreck happened, which was probably the cause—that and her speed. Anyway, as soon as I heard that reported, I called Jeb on his cell phone and told him to investigate. I don't know, it got me curious."

"That's right, Roberta. You're learning. The Gladys Kravitz Agency girls would be so proud."

"Thank you. You won't believe what Jeb uncovered."

I stopped filing. *"What?"*

"Well, when he called me back an hour later he had news that Helga was talking to someone with a Memphis, Tennessee, telephone number."

She may as well have told me that Elvis was not only not dead but out in my living room ready to serenade me. *"WHAT? YOU'RE LYING!"* I screamed. Then, with a sudden fury flooding every part of me, I jumped out of bed, threw my nail file in the air, and flew around my room in a rage. "That slimeball! I can't believe he'd do this to me, just because I told him I didn't want him back." As soon as I said it, I reached up and covered my mouth. The girls were right across the hall.

"No no no, missy, calm down. It wasn't Baker."

I halted abruptly. "Then who was it?"

"Have you ever heard of a Shirley Greene?"

My blood ran ice cold. *"SHIRLEY GREENE!"* I screamed, waking the dead. *"SHIRLEY GREENE!"* Hearing that woman's name in the same conversation about Helga Schloygin was like putting Cruella de Vil and the Wicked Witch of the West together in the same movie. That much wickedness. *"HOW DOES JEB KNOW THAT?"* I shrieked into the telephone. My heart was beating so hard, I could almost picture it knocking a hole through my chest.

"You know Jeb. He hung around the scene to eavesdrop. When the police recovered Helga's cell phone from the car, they searched through the calls to find out if she was on the phone when the wreck happened. Sure enough, the last person she was talking to was a Shirley Greene with a 901 area code. If you want the phone number, I'll give it to you. It was reported on the scanner."

"Yes, I want it!" About that time Kissie opened the door and slid into my bedroom, squinting from the light. Her hair was sticking out every which-a-way and black hairpins poked out from the two balls of hair on top of her head. They're actually buns, but she calls them "balls." She wears her long hair that way when she sleeps.

"Have you got a pen?" Roberta asked.

"Somewhere. Hold on, though, I've woken up Kissie." I put the phone on my shoulder as I searched for a pen on my bedside table. "Helga's in the Vermont Bolivar," I crooned, which naturally tickled Kissie's funny bone. She burst out laughing. A Kroger receipt was the only thing I could find to write on, so I flattened it out with my palm. "Okay, sorry, what's that number?"

"901-555-0000."

"Roberta. Do you realize what you've done?"

"I'm not sure."

"You and Jeb have successfully completed the biggest, the best, and the most important Gladys Kravitz Agency mission imaginable. I'm so proud of y'all."

"Well, thank you."

"In fact, I have no doubt that the girls will all agree. You've just won the GKA Gold Medallion Award and are officially now a full-fledged member. I can't wait to tell Virginia, Mary Jule, and Alice. We'll have to fly you down for an official induction ceremony."

"Nuup, I don't fly."

"Then we'll bring you down in a limo. Thank *you*, Roberta. Thank Jeb for me, too, and tell him he's now an official GKA member himself and I expect him back down in Tennessee for the ceremony with you."

"Sure will."

"Y'all have just discovered the answer we've all been searching for: how Helga knew all the details about the Peach Blossom Inn Memphis in the first place." All of a sudden, I realized something that had escaped me until that very second, something integral to the case. The missing clue. The last puzzle piece. "Wait a minute, Roberta. How do Shirley Greene and Helga Schloygin even know each other?"

"I have no idear."

My mind whirled as I tried to come up with any possible scenario but I couldn't come up with a reason to save my life. "I need your help. I've got your first assignment as an official GKA member."

"I'm ready, boss."

"Somehow, we must find out how Helga and Shirley know each other. Do you think you could do some digging up there? I'll dig around down here but I need a scout up in Vermont."

"Why, sure. My shovel's ready."

"Great. I knew I could count on you. Call George Clark at the gas station. Call Betty Sweeney at the Town Clerk's office. Call Rolf Schloygin, I don't care. Do whatever you have to, but try your best to find out how those two she-devils know each other." I looked up to smile at Kissie and she was still laughing.

"I'll do it. First thing in the morning."

"Thank you. That's perfect. You go on to sleep now. You'll be closing your eyes all day at work tomorrow."

"It was worth it, missy. Glad I could be of service."

"Goodnight, my friend. Great work. I'll talk to you soon."

As soon as I hung up, I filled Kissie in on every last detail. By the time I got to the end of the story, funny tears were streaming down both our faces . . . at one thirty in the morning. Once we stopped laughing, Kissie said, "That's a doozy if I ever heard a one."

"Can you believe it?"

"No, I cain't. That woman finally done herself in. *Oooh-wee!*" she exclaimed with a pop of her head to emphasize. "Shirley Greene gone wish she kept her mouth shut this time. Everybody in town be talkin' about her for a change."

"The real question is, how do Shirley and Helga know each other?"

"I don't know, but I have a feelin' it gone come out."

"Mommy!" I heard from across the hall.

"Uh-oh, you done woke up the baby," Kissie said.

"Mommy," my little one cried again.

"Coming, Issie," I called, and flew into their bedroom.

It took a long time for me to fall back to sleep. I envisioned everything from the wreck to the moment of impact and that moose landing in the car with Helga. Seriously now, what are the odds of it happening and more miraculously what are the odds of her living? *No wonder she lost her marbles,* I thought. *I certainly would have.*

I called Peter the minute I woke up. He chastised me for not waking him in the middle of the night, but I wouldn't have dared. He had been working overboard and overtime since the restaurant reopened, all through the Christmas season, practically falling asleep at the stove.

After I told him every detail of my conversation with Roberta, he wasn't so tight-lipped about his elation over Helga's demise. "The old witch finally got her due," he said. "She had it coming to her." When I asked him what he thought about the connection with Shirley Greene, he told me that he had no idea but would leave the investigating in my very capable Southern hands. "I'm sure you and the girls will figure it out in no time," he said, and told me he'd anxiously be awaiting the outcome.

But it was that outcome that was driving me crazy. How, how, did Helga Schloygin and Shirley Greene meet? Obviously it had to do with me, and their shared disdain, but who introduced them? Was it Baker? The nip-and-tuck cougar? Baker's mother? I had no idea but would stop at nothing to find out.

When I hadn't heard back from Roberta by five o'clock, I called her anyway. She told me that she had driven over to see George Clark after work and had waited in line for fifteen minutes to get gas. Since Clark's Service Station is the only one in town and since the ski resorts were back in full swing, tourists had returned, providing George with all kinds of business. Unfortunately, she said, George didn't know a thing about the likes of a Shirley Greene. "But boy did he know everything about the wreck," she said. "His scanner is cutting edge." I told her that I had no doubt about that and added that it probably would most likely qualify as state of the art.

She also told me news of Helga's wreck had spread all over Southern Vermont and that SAPA, the local news crew, had been reporting from the front of the Peach Blossom Inn. I had to laugh when she said local news crew. When I asked what SAPA stood for, she told me Springfield Area Public Access Television, housed inside the high school. Roberta also went on to say that Betty Sweeney in the Town Clerk's office was as clueless as Jeb. "Nobody's got any info about Shirley Greene," she told me. "But don't worry, Jeb and I are on the case."

Chapter Twenty-five

One week to the day after "the call," I dropped the girls off at school, ran some overdue errands, like driving all the way over to Petco for Roberta's "natural" dog food, and finally pulled into the restaurant at 10 A.M. It was a Wednesday in early February; the weather outside was ridiculous and I ran up the back steps shivering from the few seconds it took me to get from car warmth to house warmth.

In preparation for that night's dinner, the kitchen was a bustle of activity. Sous Chef Gary was dicing carrots on the mandoline; our new prep cook, Andy, stood at the sink deveining shrimp; and Dave Matthews blasted from the docking station. I love Dave Matthews, but early in the morning it's a little hard for me to hear him at that volume, so after telling all hello, I sashayed up to my sexy fiancé and asked if he minded my turning Dave down a decimal or two. "Whatever makes you happy," was his response, and after turning to walk away, he nudged his knee into the back of mine. I whipped my head back around and caught sight of his seductive smile. Not only did my knee want to cave in but so did the deepest part of me. Our wedding was two weeks away, and restraining myself had become torturous. We had made a vow to wait till we were married—heck, we had waited this long and we both thought it would make our wedding night all the more intimate and romantic. Feeling him next to me always weakened my resolve, though, and I craved him more intensely than I ever had anything. When his body came close to mine, I could feel the magnetism, our bodies pulling at one another from a force out of our control. It's a good thing Gary and Andy were in the kitchen, because I may have grabbed the man and jumped on top of him right then and there.

After we were married, the girls and I would be moving into the upstairs, Kissie would be moving back into her house, and Pierre would have to move into a new place. In Vermont, he lived in a little one-room cottage on the property. Finding something comparable in Germantown was turning out to be a bit of a challenge. Yet when I considered the challenges we had all endured since opening this restaurant, I wasn't worried. All the thoughts that I would normally give to worry about Pierre, I was directing to my current dilemma: finding out how Helga Schloygin and Shirley Greene knew one another. An entire week had already gone by since "the call" and it seemed I was no closer to finding out then than I had been when Roberta reported the incident.

Alice had suggested that we fly to Vermont with a picture of Shirley Greene to interview the townspeople of Willingham. Although her tongue was firmly planted in her cheek when she said it, I knew she was half-serious. Mary Jule wanted to leak it to *The Commercial Appeal* or to Sallie Wallace, Channel 5's top investigative journalist, in hopes they would run a story, uncovering each pertinent detail. But it was Virginia who came up with the best game plan yet. She thought "we" should call Shirley's house—number blocked, of course—pretending to be the Vermont Police Department investigating the accident. "We" meant Alice, the best prank phone caller known to man. It was agreed that we meet that afternoon at my house. One o'clock sharp.

I spent the majority of the morning at the restaurant preparing payroll, and after writing more checks to our wine, meat, and fish suppliers, I snuck off about 1 P.M. to join my friends for our urgent GKA commission. Mary Jule had to bring Brooks, her three-year-old, but we set him up in front of the TV to watch *Star Wars*. Mary Jule always keeps an emergency DVD in the car. The rest of our children were at school, and Kissie had a Mother Board meeting at her church. The house was ours.

I turned up the heat the minute I stepped in the door and set munchies out on the table. I learned a long time ago to keep an appetizer on hand. A Brie wedge with fig preserves, water crackers on the side, and a large bowl of red grapes. A GKA meeting always calls for a nice canapé. Once everyone arrived, I set out drinks and we crowded around my breakfast room table. Cokes for Mary Jule and me, a Diet Coke for Alice, and a Tab for Virginia. I can't believe she's actually given up Coke. I never thought I'd see the day.

"I've got to hand it to you, Virgy," I told her after setting the Tab down in front of her. "You've come up with some master schemes over the years, but this one's a doozy."

"I know," she replied confidently, popping the can top.

Alice said, "Actually, if you ask me, her best was coming up with the idea of throwing all Baker's clothes on the ski lift."

Virginia leaned into the middle of the table to dress her water cracker. "That was good," she said with an affirmative nod. "But this one has the potential of being even better. It all depends on Alice though."

Alice reared back and shimmied her shoulders. "I've got this. Worry about something else." She globbed her own cracker with Brie and fig preserves. It dripped on the table on the way to her mouth. "Shoot. Where are the napkins?" she asked, moving over to the sink.

I pointed to the pantry. When she looked confused I said, "Just use a paper towel."

"I'm not worried," Virginia said, "but Shirley Greene is one tough opponent. That woman's a master."

"But Alice is the best of the best," Mary Jule said. "Dial the number."

Alice scurried back to the table. I placed my cordless telephone in front of her and hit the speaker button. With the Kroger receipt in my hand, I punched in the numbers Roberta had given me, making sure to

start with a *67. All four of us huddled over the phone. As the line connected, Alice Garrott closed her eyes. When she opened them again,
she was Sergeant Salo, a surname we had pulled from an old Vermont
phone book, of the Vermont Police Department.

Shirley answered on the second ring. "Hel*lo*," she sang into the
phone, her voice lifting on the "lo."

"Is this Shirley Greene?" Alice asked in her extreme, businesslike
Yankee accent.

"Yes, it is. Who's callin' please?" Shirley responded in her extreme
Mississippi drawl.

"Sergeant Salo from the Vermont Police Department." Alice never
cracked a smile. She was in character.

Shirley's warm tone turned to ice. "How may I help you, Sa'geant
Salo?"

"On January twenty-ninth at twenty two hundred and three hours,
Helga Schloygin, a resident of Willingham, Vermont, was involved in a
serious car crash." When Virginia heard that, she fell off her chair,
holding herself, a gesture that had always indicated she could wet her
pants.

Shirley coolly replied, "I'm sorry to hear that."

"When we recovered her phone, we discovered that you were the
last person she was talking with. Can you please tell me the nature of
your call?"

"I fail to see how Ms. Schloygin's crash has anything to do with me.
We've all been warned about the dangers of cell phones while drivin'.
'Don't talk and drive' is and always will be *my* motto."

"We are simply trying to help the investigation by talking with any
party who may have additional information about the accident. Were
you on the phone with her when the wreck occurred?" Virgy had to
bury her face in her hands.

"She may have dialed my phone number but I was not talking with
her."

We all looked at each other as Alice hesitated, stammering over her
next response. "The log registered a seven-minute conversation be-

tween your phone number and hers just before impact, Ms. Greene," Alice lied. "Are you sure you aren't referring to another conversation?" Virginia had to leave the room. I watched her put her hand between her legs as she slipped down the hall.

"Again, Sa'geant Salo, I fail to see what any of this has to do with me. I'm not comfortable speakin' with you about this right now. My son-in-law is a lawya', howev'a. I'll have him talk with you. It's been a pleasure."

She was just about to hang up when I frantically scribbled a note on the Kroger receipt. *Ask her how she knows Helga,* I wrote, shoving it toward Alice.

"One last question, Ms. Greene. What is the nature of your relationship with Ms. Schloygin?"

A long pause passed before Shirley spoke again. "First of all, it's *Mrs.* Greene. *Mrs. Charles William* Greene. The nature of our relationship is . . . strictly business."

"How did you two meet?" Alice said, slightly falling back into her Southern accent. She made "meet" a two-syllable word. "Rather, make acquaintance with one another?" She tried to recover but the damage was done. Even the best of the best make a mistake from time to time. Virginia tiptoed back into the room, taking her seat at the table.

"Who is this?" Shirley said, icicles dripping from her lips.

"Sergeant Salo, Vermont Police Department."

"I've had enough of this conva'sation. If you need anything else, talk with my lawya'. Have a blessed day." And the line went dead.

Alice pushed the off button and slammed the phone down on the table. "I failed."

"No, you did not," Mary Jule said. "So you lost your accent for a second. So what?"

Alice reared her head back. "I'm usually much better. I just wish I could have scared her into admission."

"She's seasoned," Virginia said.

"How about that 'have a blessed day' crap?" Alice said. "When did she get so religious?"

"Kissie will have a field day with that one," I said.

We may have hit a dead end but we finally had a confirmation. Shirley Greene and Helga Schloygin were friends. But how?

We hung around my house until everyone had to leave for the carpool line. All kinds of theories were thrown out as to how the two had met. Yet none of us could come up with anything concrete. Helga might be a hellcat and Shirley a top-shelf yenta, but the collision of their worlds was pure mystery. Even if the common denominator was me.

The rest of the week dragged by. I could hardly focus on my wedding for obsessing over Shirley Greene. If Mama only knew what her nemesis had done this time, she'd . . . Well, I don't know what she'd do but suffice it to say Shirley would long for the days before messing with the daughter of Sarah and Henry Williams. I bet the whole ordeal would have given my grandmother a heart attack if she were alive.

Roberta called later with an update but it was still the same news. No one in Willingham, Vermont, had ever heard of a Shirley Greene. I seriously considered a drive over to Baker's mother's house, sitting her down and talking with her woman-to-woman. Surely by now she had a hint as to Shirley's evil ways. It would be hard to miss, especially after playing bridge together year after year.

The next morning, Riley stopped by with his Amway delivery. This might come as a surprise, but I caved. The thought of his long face, week after week, with no orders from the Peach Blossom Café was too much to take so I went ahead and placed a small weekly order. There wasn't much that we could use but I did manage to find something. Splenda and sugar packets for the tables, honey and peanut butter. I also ordered paper towels, laundry detergent, and even a gallon of motor oil that Amway had on special. What in the world could it hurt? I figured. When I brought home the Amway peanut butter to give to Kissie, she pressed her lips together so hard, they turned white. "I'mo stick with Peter Pan," is all she had to say about that.

Since we were slammed, as they say in the restaurant business, preparing for the weekend customers, we were too busy to engage with Riley. He finally took the hint and slipped forlorn through the back door. The phone had been ringing nonstop all morning for reservations and when it rang again, Pierre, who was seated at the desk, answered on the first ring. As long as it was a reservation, he could handle the call with ease. He always wrote down the phone number of the party in the reservation book and never failed to ask the caller for the correct spelling of his or her last name. When he hung up the phone he happily announced, "Four more," to everyone in the kitchen.

"How many are we up to?" Peter asked before slipping into the walk-in.

"Seventy-two," Pierre answered enthusiastically. I knew the T-word was zipping through his head, as he mentally calculated his tip potential for the evening.

"What are their names?" I asked, hoping it might be someone I knew.

"Greene for four," he responded, holding up four fingers.

Peter caught Pierre's response as he stepped back out of the walk-in, carrying a vacuum-packed bag of tenderloin. "Old Shirley's coming to the inn," Peter called, slapping the meat on his cutting board. "What do you know."

"No way," I said, flying over to the reservation book. Could it be fate or just a disappointing coincidence? I wondered as I pulled out the Memphis phone book and looked up Shirley's home phone. "Not our Shirley Greene!" I hollered out somewhat disappointedly.

"Too bad," Peter retorted. "I was looking forward to a showdown. You and the girls could have pounced all over her." He made a loud yowling noise followed by a hearty meow.

"Southern belles don't have catfights, my darling. We are too lady-like for that. We'd rather outsmart her." After putting the phone book back in the drawer, I started to walk into the front dining room, when something dynamite dawned on me. Pierre had been trying to tell me something about Shirley Greene at the grand opening party! I'd been so busy that night that I forgot all about it. Now it was all coming back.

He thought she was common. I wondered how he knew that word, considering it was an old Southern expression. It was the busiest night of my life and I'd been unable to give his comment a second thought. Until right now.

I did an about-face. *"Pierre!"* I cried, placing my hands on either side of his shoulders. *"Por favor!* (I know. I get mixed up.) What were you trying to tell me at the party about Shirley Greene?" I shook the poor thing so hard, one side of his glasses slipped off his ear.

Pierre narrowed his eyes and cocked his head. *"S'il vous plaît, Leelee. Qui est Shirley Greene?"* I knew what that meant: Who is Shirley Greene?

"She was at the grand opening party," I said, my voice a little louder than normal. It's something I do inadvertently, not only to Pierre but whenever I'm around any foreigners. "You told me she was 'common.'" I practically screamed the word right into his face while I pretended to be sipping and toasting champagne. "Do you remember her?"

His eyes grew into saucers. Then a scowl shaped his face. "Ay, ay, ay," he muttered, *"Elle est synonyme de problèmes."*

I could tell by the way he shook his head that he knew something that I didn't but it would be hard for him to communicate it to me. Grabbing the French-to-English dictionary that I kept in the desk drawer, I frantically flipped through the pages until I found the word *commune.* It meant "township" or "town." *That can't be it,* I thought, reading on to the second meaning. Sure enough, it meant "common, joint, or mutual." I looked up at Pierre, practically screaming, "Did you mean to say that Shirley Greene has a familiar face?"

Between the deep creases in his forehead and the pained look in his eyes, I knew he was frustrated, trying hard to convey his thoughts. When he said, *"Shirley Greene est un femme très curieux,"* I had the solution. I may have had no idea what he was saying, but I sure knew someone who would.

"Don't go away," I said. "I'm calling Mary Jule." My dear friend had spent her junior year abroad attending the Sorbonne in Paris. When I got her answering machine I left an urgent message. "Mary Jule, you have to call me back immediately. I think Pierre holds the key to figuring out the Shirley Greene mystery and you're our only hope. Hurry, please! My life depends on it."

Pierre pulled out the desk chair and took a seat. He leaned down, pretending to eat soup.

"Shirley Greene likes soup?" I asked.

"Oui!" He kept shoveling soup in his mouth.

"She eats a lot?"

He cradled his chin in his hand and shook his head. Then he sprang from the chair and crossed the kitchen to the pantry, returning with the large can of Vermont maple syrup we always kept on hand.

"Shirley Greene likes maple syrup!"

He nodded.

"How do you know that?" I asked, my face rumpled with curiosity.

"You're wasting your time," Peter said. "Relax. Mary Jule will call you back. When has she ever not called you back?"

In the meantime I busied myself by chopping. Peter gave me three large onions to dice and a bunch of parsley. I could feel my mascara running by the time I got halfway through the first onion.

When Mary Jule finally burst through the back door, about twenty minutes later, my eyes were terribly bloodshot. "I got here as soon as I could," she said. "I didn't know you were so upset."

"It's the onions," I said, "and thank God you're here." I let go of the knife and rushed to her side.

"I wish I could stay longer but I have to pick up Emma from mother's day out."

She walked straight over to Pierre and gave him a hug. They exchanged *bonjour*s and *como talle vous* and other French words until I couldn't take it a second longer. "Enough already. I can't stand it."

"Sorry," Mary Jule said, "I couldn't be rude. I have to at least ask him how he's doing. The poor thing has to be dying to talk to someone who understands him."

"You're right, you're right," I said, lamenting my impatience. "He hasn't had a decent conversation since the grand opening party."

"What should I ask him first?" Mary Jule said.

"Ask him why he thinks Shirley Greene is common. And how he knows she likes maple syrup."

"Got it." Mary Jule met Pierre's eyes and asked him the questions. The French words rolled off her brilliant little tongue. As she was speaking, I thought about Daddy. If he said it once, he said it a thousand times. "Dah'lin', when the day comes, and it will, you'll wish you hadn't taken the easy way out. French is much more eloquent than Spanish."

Mary Jule listened intently to Pierre's long response, nodding her head with every other word. I watched her eyes, the way they danced around, and the way she caught her breath when he'd speak with his hands. When her mouth popped wide open, revealing the gold crown on her back lower molar, I knew we were on to something big. Her hand covered her heart and she reared her head back, sucking in a fresh breath. I distinctly heard the word "Helga." Not once but twice. She said a few more sentences to Pierre in French before finally turning to me. "You're not going to believe this." Her words were purposeful and she seemed horrified.

"It's bad, isn't it?"

Mary Jule nodded, curling her lip. "Pretty darn bad."

"Give it to me straight."

"Pierre says that he tried telling you this at the grand opening party." She sounded annoyed almost, or at the very least frustrated.

"I know that, Mary Jule. That's the whole point. I was super busy that night."

"What he's been trying to tell you is that he waited on Shirley Greene at the Peach Blossom Inn."

"Huh? She's never been here," I replied.

"Not this one. The one in Vermont," she explained.

"When?" Peter and I both said at the exact same time. At this point Peter had left his cutting board to witness the tête-à-tête.

"After you left. When Helga took back over. Shirley Greene was with two other women. They were probably on a girls' trip, or as Pierre called it, a leaf peeper's trip."

"Ask him if she was with Baker's mother."

"He won't know that," Mary Jule replied.

"Can you describe her to him, please?"

Mary Jule turned to Pierre and must have asked him if he remembered the other women, because after he answered she told me, "He said the only reason he remembers Shirley Greene is because she was *fouineur* which means 'nosy.'"

"He's got that right. Ask him if she met Helga."

"Of course she met Helga, sweetheart," Peter said. "That's obvious."

"I know," I said before turning back to Mary Jule. "But ask if he has any more details about how she and Helga got to know one another."

Once again, Mary Jule turned to Pierre and after conversing a minute or so more, she turned back to me. "Helga came out to their table, like she does to all the tables, and when Helga learned Shirley was from Tennessee, they started talking. He said Helga stayed at their table for quite some time. She even sat down with them. Helga told him later, after the women had left, that Shirley Greene was from Memphis and that she knew you and Baker."

"Is there anything else?"

"That's pretty much it but I think we can all assume that Shirley, being the Nasty Nosy Nellie that she is, just had to see the inn that you—well, we—decorated and made so lovely."

"Of course she did. I'm sure Baker's mother had told her all about it," I said.

"Plenty of Southerners go on leaf peeper trips to Vermont. That's not unusual," Peter offered. Even he was into the details.

"No, it's not. And I'm sure Baker's mother has kept her apprised of our situation at the bridge games. Shirley just had to see it for herself," I said. "She couldn't stand not knowing what all the ruckus was about. She said it herself when she barged in here before we opened." I crossed my arms in front of me, lightly shaking my head. "Why in the world they are still friends is killing me though."

"You have to let this one go," Mary Jule said. "You can't do a thing about it. Besides, they deserve one another."

Peter raised an eyebrow. "Don't take this the wrong way, but you belles are . . . I'll just put it politely—complicated. To think someone would travel all the way to Vermont just to poke around in someone else's business. Sheesh."

"Do not put these belles in with that belle, Mr. Yankee Doodle," Mary Jule said. "We are two completely different breeds."

Hearing the word "belle" suddenly made me miss Mama, and it made me miss her terribly. So much so that I had to sit down. It came out of nowhere really, and it quickly turned into an intense longing. I pretended to be checking something at the desk but I simply needed a moment to blink back an eruption of tears. If only I could have picked up the phone and called her, we could have laughed about the Shirley Greene mess together. She would have said, "Leelee, dah'lin', now don't you take it personally. Shirley, bless her h'aht, is not right. She's as crazy as a loon and I don't want you to pay her any mind." Even better, I could have driven straight home to hear her say it in person. Mama would have wrapped her slender arms around me, fiddled with my ponytail, and whispered that I was her heart. Then she would have led me by the hand out to her rose garden and chosen the showiest, most fragrant single red rose of all, clipped it with her pruning shears, and presented it to me as a prize. She may not have been able to say the words "I love you" all that often, but she indeed loved me more than anything or anyone else in the world. It was clearer to me now than ever before. Mama may have had her demons but I was without a doubt her grand prize.

Chapter Twenty-Six

ONE MORE EXTRA-BLISSFUL WEEK LATER

The time for the Big Reveal had finally arrived. After waiting what seemed like an eternity for my brand-new sign, I finally got the long-awaited phone call that it was in and ready to be installed. When we ordered it, I was told it would be a while but had no idea production and delivery would take eight full weeks. So when I got the call, I scheduled the event for 4 P.M. on Wednesday, February 22, exactly four days before our Sunday-afternoon wedding. At last we could officially operate under our new name.

It deserved a ceremony—at least I thought it did—or a proper unveiling at the very least. After all, it was the final step in my moving on—putting Helga Schloygin and the events of the last couple years behind me once and for all. If the woman's name ever came up in conversation again henceforth, I had decided it would be reason for thanks. Thanks for giving me the gift of rebirth. Our new name and new sign would forever be a symbol of my perseverance, strength, and above all my independence. I'd always be a Southern belle though, and proud of it, but I'd never allow another Helga person to bully me again.

Besides Kissie and my daughters, Peter, and Pierre, I invited my girlfriends, of course, and even decided to invite Riley. Jeb and Roberta had sent their regrets due to the busyness of the winter season, and as sad as that made me, I understood perfectly. There's an old saying up there: Moonlight in Vermont or starve.

The afternoon of the unveiling, I took the girls out of school early. Kissie drove with me to pick them up and after a quick lunch at the Booksellers Bistro, a scrumptious place inside our indie bookstore, we drove into midtown for final alterations on our wedding gowns. As the girls twirled in the mirror admiring their white batiste dresses with ivory lace collars and peach satin sashes, I thought about how angelic they would look walking in front of me down the aisle of the church. Issie had been "playing wedding" with her dolls for weeks, and Sarah's teacher told me that Sarah had made a special announcement about being a flower girl in her mother's wedding to the entire second-grade science class during a discussion about the life cycles of plants. Seems she had plans for her own family's life cycle: two more siblings, both baby brothers.

I don't think it hit me that Peter and I were actually going to be husband and wife until I stepped in front of the tri-fold mirror wearing my wedding dress. Both the front and the back were visible from where I stood on the center platform and I swooned at the sight. Second wedding dresses are impossible to find, by the way. I didn't want a long white gown with a train, or a veil for that matter. I wanted something shorter—champagne, pale yellow, or possibly even pink. I scoured the Internet, department stores, and bridal boutiques. None had a single thing that I felt appropriate. I was honestly ready to give up and buy any old thing when I happened upon a vintage shop on Central Avenue called Flashback. I almost passed the place by. The window had been decorated with '60s clothing and retro furniture but something told me to turn around. Just in case. The minute I walked in the door, I spied it on a mannequin and could scarcely take my eyes away: a 1950s *pale peach* strapless sheer silk organza, tea length with an A-line skirt. Both the front of the bodice and the skirt were adorned with embroidered floral appliqués and a satin band wrapped around the waist. Underneath, a layer of crinoline added fullness. There was a tiny pin-size spot on the bodice, the sash had some loose threads, and the tulle of the crinoline needed reattaching. But other than that it was easily repairable and utterly perfect.

When my cell phone rang I saw Peter's name on the screen and asked Sarah to answer.

"Hi, Mr. Peter," she said. "I'm fine . . . trying on my wedding dress." She giggled. "Mommy's is so beautiful. Issie thinks she looks like Cinderella."

"Hardly," I called from the background.

"Okay, hold on please . . . Mr. Peter wants to know what time everyone is coming for the Big Reveal."

"Four o'clock. Why? I thought he knew that."

"Why?" she echoed before turning back to me. "He just wanted to be sure plus he has something to show us."

"Tell him we'll be there in an hour or so. I have a couple more stops to make and with the traffic on Poplar Avenue it will probably be three thirty or later before we get there." It was the last day I'd have off before the wedding and I still had a zillion things to do before Sunday.

Sarah said, "We'll be there about three thirty . . . yes, sir . . . bye."

I glanced over at Kissie. "What's up with him? He knew the reveal is at four."

"I don't know," she replied, her eyes as big around as a 45 rpm record.

"*Kissie*. You do too know."

"I done told you once. I don't know." When she turned her head I could have sworn I detected a thin smile.

The seamstress helped us carry our dresses to the car. Garment bags protected each, and I hung the girls' on the hooks in the back. After transferring books, soccer shoes, and other superfluous junk into the backseat, I put both Kissie's and mine in the trunk.

Just as I thought, the drive out to Germantown was awful and it seemed like we inched through the school zones all the way down Poplar Avenue. The pre-sunset sky brightened the drive though, and every time I stopped for a red light I watched it in my rearview. As far as I'm concerned, there is not another city in the South with a more magnificent sunset than Memphis, Tennessee. The city stretches east to west before dead-ending into the Mississippi. When looking across to Arkansas from the downtown bluff there's not an obstruction in sight, just acres and acres of flat cotton fields gifting the beholder with a panoramic view of the melting fireball as it bleeds into the earth.

We drove past the church where Peter and I would finally become man and wife. The idyllic spot turned out to be a place I had passed almost every day since buying the inn. Exuding character and charm, the Germantown Historic Presbyterian Church dated back to 1851. A white clapboard with green shutters and a simple cross atop a belfry crowned with a patinaed dome, it had survived both the ravages of war and the yellow fever epidemic. The old oak floors buckled in a few places and it still had the original mahogany pews on either side of the center aisle. From the outside it seemed it might be too small but after inquiring I learned it had seating for a little less than 200.

We decided to forgo the expense of a rehearsal dinner and put our money into the reception, which, of course, would be held at the restaurant. Originally we had hoped to keep the guest list at 100 people but it became impossible to pare down. In the end we sent out 130 invitations. And yes, I even included Tootie Shotwell.

When we finally pulled into the driveway, Peter was out by the road getting the mail. He had already draped the new sign on the pole with a large black covering. Alice's Volvo station wagon and Mary Jule's minivan were parked on the street in front, and I could see the back of Virginia's Camry at the end of the driveway. For fun I tooted my horn and rolled down Kissie's window. Peter opened her door and put his foot on the ledge. "Give me a lift," he called, grabbing ahold of the doorjamb.

"You better *git* down from there!" Kissie hollered up at him.

"Step on it!" he yelled with a roar of a laugh, and I flew through the gravel with the girls squealing in the backseat. He leaped off when we rounded the corner, right before I stopped the car.

Kissie glared at me, then leaned her head out the window as soon as her door swung shut. "Peter! Don't you do that again, you hear? You're liable to git yourself killed. I declare."

Peter reopened the door for her. "Oh, Kissie. That's no different than riding my motorcycle. I've been hoping you'd take a spin on it with me next spring."

"Who you foolin'? I ain't gittin' on no motor scooter," she answered, arduously pushing herself out of the seat.

"I'll ride with you, Mr. Peter," Sarah said, scampering around the side of the car.

Kissie yanked on Sarah's coat sleeve, stopping her in her tracks. "Over my dead body you will."

Peter laughed, tousling Sarah's hair. "Maybe when you're older. We don't want to give poor Kissie a heart attack." He walked up the steps and held open the door for all of us. "After you, ladies."

Kissie humphed at him as she walked inside.

Virginia, Mary Jule, and Alice were standing in the kitchen, each holding a filled-to-the-brim flute of champagne. Alice held a full bottle in her other hand and Virgy held an extra glass for me, which Alice filled the minute she saw me. Pierre appeared with a tray of flutes and sparkling apple juice for the girls. When Peter offered Kissie a glass of champagne, she declined, saying, "Thank you but no thank you. I don't drink no liquor."

"Champagne isn't liquor; it's sparkling wine," he said, smiling. When she didn't respond, he leaned into me, kissing my lips. "Happy Reveal Day." The scruff above his lip tickled and I felt a flutter. Just from the smell of him.

Another smell had hit me the minute I walked in the door. "Something sure smells good in here," I said.

"I thought it would be nice for all of us to have dinner together before we leave on our honeymoon. The rest of this week is stacking up to be crazy." Peter walked over to the stove, opening the oven door. Two large pans of lasagna had just started to bubble around the edges. There was a large bowl of salad on the prep table. "We'll be ready to eat right after the reveal."

"Lord, you're starting to cook like Kissie," I said. "Who in the world do you think is going to eat all that food?"

He shut the oven door with his foot. "Lasagna freezes well, sweetheart. It's just as easy to make two pans as it is one." I almost asked him why he didn't wait to cook the second pan but changed my mind. *What do I know about lasagna*, I thought. "We'll need to have everything cleaned off the tables by five thirty. Our first reservation is at six o'clock."

Virginia looked at her watch. "Only fifteen minutes till the Big Reveal. Will we have music?"

"I hadn't thought about that but it's a great idea," I told her.

"You should have hired a marching band," she said waggishly, tipping her glass in my direction.

"Today is a very big day, thank you very much. And by the way, this sign is even nicer than the old one."

"That's because it's made in the South," Alice teased, winking at Peter.

"Honey, I'm home," Riley called from the back door. "Weady for the Big Weveal."

"Glad you could make it, Riley," I called, setting my glass down on the counter. "Come on in."

"What's that I smell?" he asked.

"Peter's yummy lasagna," Mary Jule said.

"Made with Amway Pawmesan cheese I hope," Riley said. "Oh, speaking of, Amway has a bwand-new line of—"

"What did you want to show us?" I asked Peter, switching the subject as fast as I could. Kissie was already bugged at Peter, and I was taking no chances on what she might say to Riley.

"Hang on." Peter moved over to the desk, picked up a book, and waved it in the air. "Guess what we got in the mail?" Our brand-new cookbook, *Servin' Up Dixie*, had finally arrived.

"I knew it!" I said, "Let's see it."

"This is just our final mock-up before the printing. All we have to do is check it over for any last-minute mistakes." He handed it to me and I flipped through the first few pages, stopping to show the pictures to Kissie and the girls. When I came to the recipe titled "Kissie's Clouds," her fluffy, melt-in-your-mouth yeast rolls, I saw the pride in her eyes.

"This isn't your only recipe," I told her. "There are plenty more."

"Let me see it, baby." She took the book and held it out in front of her. "I need my glasses." She glanced at Sarah. "Baby, get my glasses out of my pocketbook, will you please?" Sarah did as she was told and brought them back to Kissie, who was chanting her happy hm hm hms. "Oooh-wee. I believe we'll be able to sell fifty copies or more at church."

"Make it a fund-raiser," Peter said. "The church can have them at cost."

"Leelee, the Big Reveal?" Virgy said. "I wish I could stay longer but I have to get home. John's got the kids at his office."

"Let's get this pomp on the road," Alice announced, marching toward the back door. Our beverages were on the workstation. She held up the bottle of champagne in one hand and the sparkling cider in the other. "Fill up your glasses before you leave."

Moments later we all filed out the kitchen door and down to the road, holding our toasting glasses. It was chilly outside, forty degrees at the most, but for once I didn't care. I was ready to unveil the new me for all the world to see. When we made it down to the road, I asked everyone to form a circle around the pole and I positioned myself right next to it. I reached into my pocket, pulling out the short speech I had prepared the night before. I cleared my throat. "Thank you for being here, everybody," I began. "As each of you know, this has been a very long and arduous journey."

A loud honking noise interrupted my speech and we all turned to see a filthy dirty black truck with a huge snow shovel attached to the front. The passenger window lowered. "Surprise!" Roberta said, waving both her hands excitedly.

"What?" I exclaimed, turning to Peter as Jeb screeched into the driveway and parked next to the mailbox. "I knew something was up." I marched toward the truck.

"Did you think we'd honestly miss your wedding?" Roberta said, stepping out next to me. She held out her arms and pulled me inside her embrace.

"Or the Big Reveal?" Jeb said, prancing over to the circle. He edged in between Virginia and Alice. "Sorry we're late."

"I thought y'all were too busy to come," I said, happily.

"It weren't no problem for me," Jeb replied. "For some reason Vermont's having a light winter. Hardly much snow."

"That's gotta be a first," I said, returning to my position next to the pole. Sarah motioned for Roberta to stand between her and Mary Jule.

"Leelee," Virginia interrupted. "The Reveal?"

"Oh, yes, sorry." I looked back down at my paper to check my notes. "This is a remarkable day. It's full of new beginnings. Each of you, and I mean every single one of you—" I looked around at each person standing in front of me. "—has helped me achieve my goal of running a brand-new, French-influenced restaurant in my beloved Memphis. It marks my independence and especially my desire to set a good example for my daughters." I leaned in toward them. "Girls, don't ever forget this. We can be strong, kind, and gentle Southern ladies, but we should also have the chutzpah of a Yankee broad."

"Don't forget fun," Virgy said, turning to Sarah and Issie. "You two have my permission to be and have as much fun as you want. Always make the South proud."

"Yeah. Hotty Toddy!" Jeb yelled, pushing up his fist.

"Hotty Toddy!" both Virgy and I echoed.

I strolled back over to the sign and picked up the edge of the tarp. "This new sign, along with our restaurant, represents the best of both cultures. I realize now that the Peach Blossom Inn doesn't really apply to this new place in Memphis. This restaurant is about both the old and the new. It's the South and the North. The past and the present. Our new sign will forever be a symbol of the future that Peter and I have together." I tugged on the tarp. As it slowly inched away from my brand-new sign underneath, I beamed radiantly. At long last, the North Dixie Café had been revealed to the world. "The North Dixie Café," I said as the tarp landed on the lawn below. "May it always bring happiness *and fun* to all who enter."

Everyone was shocked; I could tell by the looks on their faces. I had not told anyone about my last-minute name change, except my fiancé, of course. I loved my second choice, Peach Blossom Café; at the time it seemed like the perfect compromise. But the more I thought about it, the more I knew it wasn't right either. I wanted to own and operate a place that was just as much about Peter and my other Yankee friends as it was about the South and me.

I could never let go of the peach, though. It was too important. Besides, so much about my restaurant was peach. The outside was painted that way, peach is my favorite color, and peach daiquiris were our house specialty. I'd never give that up. So I designed our new sign in the shape of a giant, juicy peach, with streaks of yellow added to make it look even more authentic. It was edged with shiny gold paint. The stem was a brown metallic color and two green leaves covered the hook from where it hung. All the letters were etched in gold right into the wood. The first two words, NORTH DIXIE, were on one line, and CAFÉ was centered underneath.

"A toast," Peter said, holding up his glass. "To the North Dixie Café! And to my Dixie peach, the sweetest, most beautiful girl I've ever known." Everyone raised their glasses and downed their champagne— or their sparkling cider. "Let's eat," Peter said from where he was standing, and everyone broke out of the circle.

"Hip hip hooway!" Riley yelled, raising his glass, a little late, bless his heart. "And here's to a gweat future between North Dixie Café and Amway."

"Like I said, let's eat," Peter said again, louder this time, before Kissie could say a word.

We all traipsed back down the boxwood-lined walkway toward the house. Jeb, who seemed to be galloping down the walk in front of everyone else got to the porch first and held open the door for the rest of us. Peter and I were the last to make it through, and when we finally stepped inside, a curious hush fell over the room. The only sound at all came from the heat whirling through the old vents. All eyes seemed to be fixated on me. Jeb moved to the bottom of the stairs with his hands in his pockets, wearing a smile as big as his stomach. Smiling was such a rarity for Jeb that I'd forgotten he knew how. Roberta was beaming, too, but of course that was her norm.

"Why are y'all being so quiet?" I said, curiously looking around at everyone. They all looked at me like my dress was tucked in my underwear or something. I even turned around and checked my backside to make sure. "What is it?"

Still no one moved or said anything until Issie finally interrupted the hush. "What's that?" she said, pointing to the top of the entryway into the right dining room.

I followed the direction of her little finger and when I saw what she was pointing at I gasped. Both my hands involuntarily shot up, covering my mouth, and I took a step back. All I could do was gape, in wonder, at two black eyes staring back at me. "Is *that* who I think it is?"

"Shore is," Jeb answered proudly. Chin up, chest out, shoulders back, like he was standing at attention.

A giant, and I mean massive, moose head—a *bull moose head*—tremendous antlers and all, hung over the entryway to the right dining room, centered perfectly between the crown molding and the top of the doorway. Its rack had a span of—well, it had to have been four feet—and with my index finger I counted fourteen points in all. His beard must have been a half foot long and his large round schnoz gave him a rather kind appearance. His fur was mostly black, with a brown streak running down the middle of his face onto his nose, and he seemed to be beckoning me with his eyes.

"How . . . in the world . . . did you get him?" I asked, slowly turning my head toward Jeb.

"He had to fight for him, I tell you that," Roberta said, and with that wonderful eye of hers, I couldn't tell if she was looking at me or the moose.

Jeb put one hand on his hip and pointed at the moose with his other. "When the warden from Vermont Fish and Game arrived on the scene to haul him off, I asked if I could save him the trouble. He said no, but told me which processing plant the moose would be taken to. So I called the next morning and asked if I could have his head."

"I am flabbergasted," I said, still motionless.

Jeb reverted to his military stance as he explained. "At first the guy wanted to charge me a hundred bucks but after I told him that I wanted it for a wedding present he went ahead and gave him to me free of charge." *Lucky for us*, I thought. *If Jeb had had to pay for him, I don't think I'd be looking at him right now.*

"I have to touch his beard, I just have to," I said, turning to Peter. "Is there any way you would please get me the ladder? It's out back."

Pierre patted his chest. "I'm get ladder." Then he flew out of the room.

"So everyone has known about this but me?" I asked, pivoting around for a look at the rest of my family and friends.

Mary Jule shook her head. So did Alice and Virginia. "We didn't know a thing till we got here," Alice said.

"I didn't know, Mommy," Issie said, hands on her hips.

I glanced at Kissie and she shook her head.

"You knew," I said to Peter.

He winked. "Maybe a little something."

Sarah ran up and hugged Jeb, a first-of-its-kind gesture that took him by surprise. "You sure know how to keep a secret, Jeb," she said. He reached down and awkwardly hugged her back.

"He's your wedding present. From Peter, me, and Roberta. And Helga, too, I suppose." Then he started whistling, "Here Comes the Bride."

Pierre pushed back through the swinging door and walked over to us with the ladder in front of him. He set it down just underneath the moose and held it sturdy while I climbed on top. When I touched the beard, it moved. I jerked my hand back and everyone underneath me laughed.

"Careful. You don't want to damage his bell," Jeb said as if he were a moose aficionado. "Butch, he's the taxidermist, told me that it has to be kept sturdy. It's not a beard, it's a bell."

After examining it more closely I realized "the bell" is actually two flaps of skin covered in fur. I traced my finger down the bridge of his nose and examined his teeth.

"He is wonderful," I squealed, fingering his ears. "I think I'll call him . . . Gabriel."

"Why Gabriel?" Roberta asked.

"Ohh, it may have something to do with a guardian angel." Leaning over, I planted a light kiss on his big bull nose. "Welcome to your new home, Gabriel. The North Dixie Café is right where you belong." I crawled back down the ladder.

"Look at Gabe's face," Jeb said. "Do you notice something you don't normally see on moose head mounts?"

I tilted my head, studying Gabriel intently. "To tell you the truth, I don't know that I've ever seen a moose head mount, darlin'. And I'm not sure anyone else here has either."

Suddenly Kissie burst out laughing and pointed straight at the moose. "I see it. I see it, Jeb. Look at him, baby."

I studied Gabriel's face intently, but nothing seemed *funny* about it. "Is it the brown streak running down his nose?"

"No," Kissie said, nearly hysterical at this point. "Lo-look closer, baby. That moose is smiling."

Every single one of us started laughing at the same time. Kissie was exactly right. Gabriel was wearing a big toothy smile.

Jeb walked over and stepped up the ladder, putting his hand on the moose's mouth. "After I told Butch what Helga did to you, he did this for you special. The bull gives a certain look when he's in heat. He drops his bottom lip, and his nose and top lip will flare, causing him to expose his teeth. It makes him look like he's smiling."

A smile almost as big as Gabe's took over my face, as I wrapped my arms tightly around my husband-to-be. The moose really was smiling at me. And at Peter, my girls and Kissie, at Jeb and Roberta, Pierre and Riley, my three best friends—and everyone else who would ever seek Southern comfort and fine cuisine at the North Dixie Café.

Acknowledgments

When I think about the fact that I've actually written three novels, and been given the grand opportunity to have them all published, I can scarcely believe how richly I've been loved by my Heavenly Father, from whom all blessings flow. The first thanks goes to Him. Not only has He given me the talent to write the books, but also the focus and discipline to finish, which—trust me—is not part of my natural gifting. Miracles abound in my life, most recently in the person of Stuart Southard, who, by the time this book is printed, will be my husband. I can't believe I get to live out the rest of my life with a man as lovely, honoring, loyal, trustworthy, and fun as he is, and who has encouraged me every single day while writing this book. He believes in me in a way I sometimes can't believe in myself. Stuart, you are my gift from Above and I love you with all my heart.

Next I'd like to thank my lovely and talented editor, Katie Gilligan, and all the nice people at Thomas Dunne Books/St. Martin's Press: Sally Richardson, Thomas Dunne, Aleks Mencel, Katie Bassel, Melanie Fried, Peter Wolverton, Meryl Gross, Cheryl Mamaril, Ellen Torres, Dori Weintraub, Lisa Senz, Lauren Hesse, Anna Gorovoy, and

Michael Storrings. I'd also like to give tremendous thanks to Holly Root, my lovely and talented agent, whose tenacity is the reason I ever got a publishing contract. Samantha Howard and Taylor Haggerty at Waxman Literary get big thanks as well.

I must thank my precious sons, Michael and Will, whom I'm so proud of. You'll never know until you have your own children how very much you mean to me. Thank you for always encouraging me to keep on keepin' on, even when you see me ready to yank out my hair. Even I can't come up with enough words to express how much I love you.

And my new kids: Shannon Harris, Sara Beth Cline, Sloane Southard, and Whitney Sorensen. I am honored to be a part of your lives and now your family. Thank you for your encouragement and advice. I can't wait to see what life holds in store. I love you all.

A lofty thanks to my dear friend and next-door-neighbor, Kathy Peabody. A day never goes by that you don't call me with a "how's the writing goin' today, author?" That means almost as much to me as you do. How I'll ever move away from you after fifteen glorious years is beyond me; I love you so much.

My other dear girlfriends who always encourage my writing life mean so much to me and I want to thank them from the bottom of my heart: Becky Barkley, Sarah Berger, Alice Blake, Lisa Blakley, Theresa Brady, Cary Brown, Genie Buchanon, Kim Carnes, Gail Chiaravalle, Lindsey Cleek, Katie Creech, Elise Crockett, Jan Cross, Lyn DiGiorgio, Wilda Hudson, Tammy Jensen, Emily Kay, Jodie McCarthy, Lucie Mouka, Mary Norman, Anne Marie Norton, Vicki Olson, LeAnn Phelan, Penny Preston, Terry Robbins, Mimi Taylor, Margie Thessin, Sallie Wallace, Kathy White, Lisa Wilder, Jennifer Williams, Linda Yoder, and Amy Young.

My Nashville author girlies who constantly encourage me deserve huge thanks too: Paige Crutcher, JT Ellison, Susan Gilmore, River Jordan, and Joy Jordan Lake.

My good friend and Webmaster, Bernie Chiaravalle, molte grazie for all the hard work.

To Julia Black, Devonia Crawford, and Christine King, thank you for loving me into adulthood. You showed me not only what it's like to be a good mother, but the Love of the Father. The color of our skin may have been different, but you treated me like I was your own. I am eternally grateful and I love you all.

Others who helped me with valuable research include: Karen Williams—Ole Miss fan extraordinaire and overall lovely person, Mr. Rob Westfall, Esq., Mr. Butch Bragg—Vermont Taxidermist, and Laurie A. Henderson from the Germantown Historic Presbyterian Church. Thank you, sincerely, for your help.

To all the indie bookstore owners and worker bees that have helped to spread the Dixie news and put my three babies in the hands of readers, I owe you big hugs and sincere thanks. Jarrett Robinson, the former manager of Borders in Franklin and the current manager of BAM in Spring Hill, Tennessee, who played a big role in launching me as an author, I am forever in your debt.

And to all you lovely readers who have stuck with me through the entire Whistlin' Dixie trilogy. I know how precious your time is and I love you for spending all these many hours with me. My greatest desire is that I have made you smile a time or two, and hopefully given you a laugh.

I may have forgotten someone as I was in a rush to complete my thank you page. As a true born-and-bred Southerner, embodied with all the quirks and neuroses that come with the distinction, this is my worst fear. If that someone is you, please accept my sincerest apology ;-).

My Dear Readers,

If you have read all three of my books in the Dixie series, or if this is just your first, I want to extend a sincere, heartfelt show of gratitude. All three novels have been a labor of love from the start, rooted in the desire to show my two artsy sons that creative people can live their dreams, as long as they are willing to put in the overtime and hard work.

I love to laugh. Nothing makes me happier than a good, hard, tears-rolling-down-my-cheeks belly laugh. When I started this journey I thought, if I could provide one laugh-out-loud moment in my books I will have accomplished something big. I hope I have done that for you!

People think that Leelee is me. That's only partly true. Yes, we both have frizzy red hair and hail from Memphis but she embodies everything I wish to be—minus the dysfunction! But aren't we all a little bit dysfunctional? I prefer to think of Leelee as deliciously flawed. She is a little bit Rachel Green from *Friends*, and a lot Lucy Ricardo. Lucille Ball is my greatest inspiration. I bet I have watched each episode of *I Love Lucy* fifty times over the years. I can certainly recite the dialogue; I know that.

While writing Leelee's adventures, or misadventures I should say chock-full full of antics, calamity, and heartbreak—my favorite part was the fun. I would picture myself as Leelee and try to write about the most enjoyable, hilarious situations I could possibly imagine for her, Kissie, Alice, Virginia, Mary Jule, Roberta, Jeb and last but not least, darling Peter, who, incidentally, is not based on a real person. He is my idea of the perfect man. And we all know perfect, a-hem, *people* don't exist!

The question I get asked most is if Kissie is based on a real person. The answer is a resounding yes! I had a Kissie in my life who passed away in 2000 and I miss her every single day. While writing the books, I was able to resurrect her and make believe she was still alive. Burying her once more broke my heart all over again.

Southern as a Second Language may be my last book in the Dixie series but it's certainly not my last novel. I can't wait to start something new and bring my readers more of what I love most—good, clean, fun, humorous Southern stories. With all the tough, trying situations we all have to encounter in life, it's important to "take time to laugh. It's the music of the soul!"

My Love Always,

Lisa

St. Martin's
Griffin

1. As the title suggests, the South seems to have its own language. In fact all regions in the United States have their own cultural differences. Some may seem quirky, others downright weird, but we are always the last to recognize our own idiosyncrasies. What are some of the peculiarities prevalent in your neck of the woods?

2. On the whole, Southerners aren't fond of confrontation. Most will do anything to avoid it. Northerners, on the other hand, seem to be more direct. Which category do you fall into?

Discussion Questions

3. Leelee finds it easier to tell a little white lie than to hurt someone's feelings. Be honest, are you the same way?

4. Do you have a nosey Nellie like Shirley Greene in your life? Someone who drives you stark raving mad? Do you put up with her just for the sake of appearances and avoiding confrontation?

5. Kissie is Leelee's voice of reason. She doesn't hesitate to correct Leelee when she is walking on shaky ground. Do you have a trusted someone in your life, other than a parent, who won't hesitate to let you know when you're making, let's just say, a poor choice?

6. Do you think Northerners have a more rigid stereotype of Southerners or do you think it's the other way around? Could it be possible that finally these stereotypes are melting away?

7. Although Peter is in her life and treats her like a rare gemstone, once Baker tries to convince Leelee that he has changed she strongly considers reuniting with him for the sake of her daughters. Would you do the same thing?

8. Since the setting is a restaurant, *Southern as a Second Language* invokes some serious mouth watering. Did the gourmet cuisine at the Peach Blossom Inn tickle your taste buds? Or could you take it or leave it? Do you consider yourself a "foodie" or, in more impolite terms, a food snob?

9. One of the themes of *Southern as a Second Language* is inner strength. Is there a pivotal moment or event in the book when Leelee realizes the depth of her Southern grit?

10. Leelee and her friends still enjoy their shenanigans together. What is the craziest thing you've ever done with your adult girlfriends? Are you ever too old for pranks?

11. Leelee is downright fascinated by moose. After three heartwarming stories in the Dixie series, a Moosehead mount actually comes to live at the newly named North Dixie Café. What do you think the massive animal symbolizes?

"Funny, heartfelt, and loaded with Southern charm."
—ADRIANA TRIGIANI,
bestselling author of the *Big Stone Gap* series and *Lucia, Lucia*

WHISTLIN' DIXIE
in a
NOR'EASTER

a novel

LISA PATTON

THOMAS DUNNE BOOKS 🦅 St. Martin's Griffin